Tapestry of Power

By Joshua J Marsh

Be-Mased Publications

Be-Mused Publications
POBox 841
Ravensdale, WA 98051-0841
www.be-mused.com

Printed in Canada

ISBN: 0-9704868-2-0

Table of Contents

1: Eat, Drink and Be Merry..............1
2: For Tomorrow We Die..............8
3: The Mountains of Lathinor..............26
4: Times of Trouble..............35
5: The Forest of Raia-Torell..............42
6: The Council of the Three Realms..............52
7: City of Darkness..............67
8: In the Company of Wood Elves..............73
9: The Night of the Feast..............79
10: Escape From Darkness..............86
11: On the Road to Juassax..............92
12: The Dungeon of the Palace..............102
13: The Garden and the Inn..............106
14: Conflicts of Interest..............112
15: Hatred Anger and Despair..............121
16: The Falling Darkness..............131
17: Reunion..............143
18: The Darkness of Leilaora..............152
19: Halfashon..............157
20: Memories..............164
21: Darkness of Heart..............177
22: Darkness of Spirit..............186
23: Defeat..............195
24: Two Battles..............203
25: The Mountains of Scalavori..............222
26: Return..............234
27: The Rising Storm..............246
28: The Battle..............256
29: Farewell..............318
30: Far Distant Suns..............328

Chapter 1
Eat, Drink, and Be Merry

"And I tell thee this, this child shall not die, nor shall he be thrown from the Three Realms and branded as outcast. Nay, he shall be my son, and I shall be his father; it shall be my blood which courseth through his veins. He shall have his chance to grow great in the eyes of man and creature and to seek salvation from the curse which lieth so heavily upon him. Thou shalt not have his blood today." Thus spake Lyght, King of the Realm of Magic.

Twenty-seven years passed after those words were spoken. The Realm of Earth was torn by war. Thousands of years ago, the Realm of Earth had been ruled by the great dragon Norenroth, but he had been cast down, and his place had been taken by the three most powerful wielders of magic in the Realm of Earth. Powers they were called, and, for thousands of years, generation after generation of Powers rose up to rule over Lairannare, as the Realm of Earth was commonly called. Some were good, but most were evil. The Powers who ruled now cared nothing for wisdom, virtue, and justice and instead sought to force the whole of Lairannare into subjection.

War ran rampant throughout the land, but, even in the midst of darkness, the kingdom of Nor was filled with joy, for the feast of Pallath-gaon was upon them. Pallath-gaon was the greatest of all the feasts celebrated in Nor. It was the last celebration before the end of the winter. This year it was met with even greater merrymaking then upon years previous, for the people of Nor knew that it would be one of the last occasions of joy for a long time; with the spring there would come war.

Of all the cities of Nor the high-walled city of Zaren was most filled with celebration, and of all the many places of celebration in Zaren the palace of the king was most joyful. It was aglow with a thousand sparkling candles, and it was alive with the sound of hundreds of different voices lifted up in song and cheerful conversation.

The banquet hall was filled with merry-making. The long wooden tables which lined it were laden with all the fruit, meat, and drink that a Norian could possibly desire, and many a burly soldier could be found standing there, helping himself to plate after plate of food. The air was filled with the most delicious of smells--meats, breads, and the smoke of the candles; one would have been hard pressed to find a person whose mouth did not water at it.

The space not filled with the tables was taken up by couples dancing. It mattered not one's station; the kitchen maids and servant girls danced with knights and lords, and a page or a stable boy, if he were particularly polite, might win a dance with a lady. Even King Ibrahim and Queen Malcah could be seen gliding across the floor.

Everyone within the palace spent the night in merrymaking--all save one. Orion was his name, and, though he stood in the grand banquet hall where the greatest of the celebrating took place, he stood apart and looked thoughtfully, and even rather mournfully, upon those gathered there. Though now a common soldier, he still bore a remnant air of the savage, wandering warrior he once had been. He was of but average height, though it was clear that he was exceedingly strong; the sleeves of his plain, green tunic were short and left bare his muscular arms. There was a certain hardness to him--not the hardness of cruelty but the hardness common to many men who had lived the rough-and-ready life of a roving warrior.

He was rather handsome in his own way. His long, auburn hair flowed freely over his shoulders and down his back. That in itself lent him a somewhat wild aspect, but it was his eyes which truly gave him the look of some inhuman creature. They were piercing eyes, so intense and blue that they defied description. They were like the eyes of some exotic specter looking out from beneath his dark and brooding brows.

Everyone else within that hall was filled with merriment, but Orion did not even smile. He was lost deep in thought; troubling thoughts they appeared to be, for his brow was deeply furrowed and his mouth grimly shut.

"Orion!" a cheerful voice broke into his thoughts. Orion started from his reverie and, turning slightly, found himself looking up at Prince Gideone.

The Prince was several inches Orion's better in height and slightly leaner also. He was a few years Orion's elder, but that meant little considering Orion had yet to reach even the age of thirty. Orion was, no doubt, the better of the two when it came to brute strength, but Gideone was every bit as good a warrior.

It was rumored that the blood of High Elves flowed through Gideone, but, if those rumors were true, the High Elvish quality showed itself through no more than his black hair. His eyes were not even black but instead a very dark brown.

He cut altogether the most dashing of figures, and his closely cut black beard did naught but add to his image. It was not for nothing that all of the women of Nor looked upon him as the most gallant and swashbuckling of heroes.

"Your Highness," said Orion as he bowed before the Prince.

Gideone laughed and said, with the most aristocratic sounding of accents--common to all well-bred Norians--"Orion, this is a night of rejoicing, but you stand here and look as joyful as one being forced to eat his own stomach! Look at all the maidens--young and fair every one of them--and know I that certain ones of them would give all they posses to dance but a single dance with you."

Eat, Drink and Be Merry

"Someone should teach them not to commit such folly, Your Highness," replied Orion, "for 'tis unwise of a young maid to give all she has for a single dance with any man, much less with one who would not even make a good partner at the moment."

"Nonsense! You could dance better than most even with both your legs broken and your hands tied behind your back."

Orion had to smile at the images Gideone's words brought to mind, but he replied seriously, "Nay, nay, I will not dance... unless, of course, you command it, Your Highness."

"What good would commanding you do?" cried Gideone. "You'd still not be enjoying yourself, which is the whole purpose of celebrations."

"Yes, Your Highness."

At Orion's reply, Gideone's hopeful features fell. He looked out over the many people gathered there and then turned back to Orion.

"I see that nothing I can do will make you enjoy this evening," said the Prince suddenly solemn, "so I can but leave you to your melancholy. But remember this, Orion: war comes swiftly upon us. Take what joy you can now, for there will be precious little of it in the months to come."

"I would that I could, Your Highness," replied Orion.

Gideone turned and, leaving Orion to his sad solitude, returned to his merrymaking.

Orion, for a while longer, stayed in the banquet hall and watched those who celebrated the feast of Pallath-gaon, but such mirth, when doom he knew lurked so close, bided not well with him, and he soon slipped silently from the hall.

There was in the gardens of the palace a small, secluded fountain which was frequented by few save Orion who found the quiet of the place somehow comforting. Night had fallen upon Zaren, and the shadowy alcove to which Orion had taken himself seemed to fit well with his thoughts. It was a warm night, for, though it was yet winter, it never snowed in Nor. Orion found it rather peaceful to sit there alone, with the warm breeze caressing his face and the soft sound of music drifting across the garden.

For many minutes he sat alone, wrapped in his thoughts. Presently, he heard the soft sound of someone walking through the garden, and, looking up, he saw a darkly veiled woman approaching. It was Princess Mystia. She was dressed in a long, flowing robe of midnight blue satin, and her face was almost completely covered with a veil of the same color. Her long black hair flowed down around her waist, and so little of her skin could be seen that she seemed to glide through the garden like a shadow.

As she approached, Orion rose and bowed.

"Your Highness," he greeted her.

"Hello, Orion," said she with the same accent her brother bore, as she curtsied. It was a beautiful accent. The "a"s were turned to "au"s and the "er"s to "eh"s such that "chance" was "chaunce" and "never" "neveh". It sounded very noble, and Orion never tired of hearing it.

Mystia sat down upon the edge of the fountain and, motioning with her hand, said, "Please, sit." She was trying so very hard to appear nonchalant, but it was obvious, at least to Orion, that she was deeply troubled.

As he sank down beside her, she began to speak then hesitated and fell silent. Her veil covered all save her black eyes, but it took only her eyes to show how great her struggle was.

"For two years now you have resided among us," said she at last, forcing herself to speak. "Tell me, how go your days?"

It was clear that that was not what she had come to speak to him about, but Orion answered truthfully, "They go well, Your Highness."

"And Nightfall, how does he?"

"Nightfall," repeated Orion slowly as his thoughts turned to his griffin companion. "What Nightfall thinks I know not, Your Highness. He goes where I go and does so without complaint. Several times have I asked him if he truly wishes to stay with me, and I doubt not that, were I to ask him yet again, I would receive exactly the same response as before: a tilt of the head, a blink of the eyes, a rather confused look, and 'Thou speakest of impossibilities.' Then he would begin preening himself as if I were not there."

Mystia gave a laugh, for Orion imitated Nightfall's croaking voice right well. But she became solemn again almost before the laugh had left her lips, and she spoke. "As you have asked Nightfall, so now do I ask you. Do you wish to stay here in the service of my family, or would you rather be free to leave and not face the war which shall soon come?"

Orion tilted his head to one side, blinked his eyes, and said, "You speak of impossibilities, Your Highness."

"I speak not in jest!" cried she as she rose and faced him. "Why do you speak so?"

"I spoke in all seriousness, Your Highness," said Orion as he also rose to his feet, "but perhaps it was a poor choice of words. Please, forgive me."

"Orion, two years ago you came to this place so that you might return a helpless princess to her family. My father would have given you almost anything as a reward, but you wanted only to be a soldier and a servant to the Crown. You have served us well; I wish not to repay you with your death."

Orion stared down at the ground and remained silent.

"War with Delovachia is inevitable," continued Mystia when she saw he would not speak. "Have you not heard all that has been done to the people who have come before us? You cannot say that you fear not. I--we--Nor cannot escape, but you can. Take this chance while you yet possess it."

For a moment he was silent--his head still bowed.

"'Tis still impossibilities of which you speak, Your Highness," said he, when he finally looked up at her.

Mystia sat down upon the edge of the fountain once more and was silent for a long moment. She would not raise her eyes to him or anything else in that beautiful, moonlit garden. Her breast rose and fell with the breathing of one filled with inner turmoil.

"Do you fear?" asked she and, after a slight pause, added, "Answer me truthfully."

"Yes," answered Orion, but it was his eyes telling her how great his fear was.

"Then take this," she said in a halting voice. In her hand she held a golden chain from which hung a ring with the strangest of stones in it. It was a clear jewel but filled with a soft red light. She hesitated for a moment, but, after taking a deep breath, she stood once more and, reaching up, hung it around his neck with one swift motion.

"Keep it always with you," said she with a trembling voice, "but let no man know that you possess it. Unless luck be found in knowing that you hold a ring of the most terrified creature in Lairannare, this will not give it, but perhaps it will remind you that my prayers and hopes go with you into battle."

She bore such a troubled look and gazed so intently upon the ring now hanging from his neck that Orion was forced to say, "Forgive me, Highness, if I speak with ingratitude, but methinks you don't truly wish to part with this ring. If that be true, then reclaim it, for I wish not to possess anything--especially something so precious as this--if it be not freely given."

Mystia looked at him for a moment, then tilted her head, blinked, and said, "You speak of impossibilities."

Orion went down upon one knee before her, "Thank you, Your Highness."

Mystia placed her hand upon his head, and, though she plainly wished to say something more, words seemed to elude her.

"Goodbye, Orion," she said simply then walked away, leaving him once more in solitude.

* * *

The people of Zaren retired long before dawn--for it was not easy to celebrate and drive all dark thoughts of war away--and it was upon a somber and silent city that the first rays of dawn fell.

The sky had barely begun to glow with the morning sun when the guards who stood atop the main gates of the city looked out and saw a lone horseman riding furiously down the road toward Zaren. It was clear the matter that brought him was important indeed, and, though the gates were not supposed to be opened for yet another half hour, the guards quickly called for them to be opened regardless.

The rider galloped through the gate and immediately began to reign his horse in. When he stopped, he looked quickly around, searching for someone in authority.

He was young, perhaps not even twenty years of age. His clothes were covered with dust from his furious journey, and his long, disheveled brown hair, hung down in front of his hazel eyes.

Several soldiers approached him and, as they did so, the rider said, "I bring a message f'r King Ibrahim." Perhaps it would have gone better for him had he not spoken, for the moment he opened his mouth his Delovachian accent became obvious.

"You 'ave a message for our king?" cried a soldier.

"Aye, a dagger in th' 'art," muttered another.

The rider's face clouded as he said, "Accents ar'na things ye can change. I may speak like a Delovachian, but I be as Norian as any o' ye." His words merely succeeded in bringing a loud round of laughter from the men present, and, with several hearty shouts, they started pulling him from his horse. He struggled against them and began crying out who he was and why he came, but it did not keep him from being overcome and tied up.

Word was sent to King Ibrahim that a Delovachian spy and assassin had been captured while trying to gain entrance to the palace. Ibrahim had the murderous dog brought before him, but it seemed rather strange that a man who would soon be dead would show such joy when brought into the presence of he who was to seal his execution.

"Majesty, I bring--" began the Delovachian scoundrel, but his words were cut off as he was thrown roughly to the ground. Because his hands were tied tightly behind his back, he could not stop his fall, and the loud crack of his chin hitting the floor could be heard throughout the whole room. That effectively put an end to his speaking for the moment, as he lay in stunned pain.

"You need not treat our enemies with cruelty," said the king in soft rebuke.

"Your Majesty," interrupted a man, "if I may be allowed to speak?"

Ibrahim turned to face the grave middle-aged man who spoke, "What is it, Stavros?"

"Vayan here is no Delovachian, Your Majesty," said Stavros. "I raised him as if he were my own son, and I'll vouch for his loyalty."

"Joretham save us!" exclaimed the king. "Soldiers, cut him free!"

The Delovachian was immediately cut free, and he rose to his knees.

"Please, forgive us," said Ibrahim. "I had no idea you were a Norian, young man--'Vayan' was it?"

"Aye," spoke Vayan as he rubbed his chin, "'Vayan' it be. Well, I may have gotten here th' long way," here he cast a foul look at those who had dragged him in, "but a' least I got here. I come t' tell ye that Niavi has been conquered, and tha', e'en as we speak, th' Delovachian army marches toward Zaren."

"What?" cried Ibrahim, half rising from his throne in alarm. "But winter is still upon us. How can Kozan send his army now?"

"Quite easily it would seem," murmured Stavros.

The king forced himself to sit back down, and for a moment he was silent.

Finally, softly but with dignity he spoke. "I see." He turned to one of the men who stood by his throne and said, "General, you know what to do. 'Tis best to begin as soon as possible."

"Yes, Your Majesty," replied the General who saluted smartly then left the throne room.

"Vayan, come, sit beside me; I would speak with you," said Ibrahim. "Servants, bring food and wine, for he has come a long way."

Vayan did as he was asked, and the servants quickly went off to do as they were ordered.

King Ibrahim leaned forward and, looking intently at Vayan, said, "Now, tell me all you know about the army that is approaching."

* * *

The whole of the city of Zaren was in a flurry of excitement, as all of the women and children prepared to leave. It was, however, an organized flurry; all of the preparations had been made before hand, and it was not many hours before the long line of carts and the soldiers who were to accompany them where ready to move out.

Orion stood upon the wall of the city and looked down upon the long procession of carts, slowly making its way toward its destination--Nortath's Fury, high in the Mountains of Shem-Joloch. He had not seen Princess Mystia-- she was never seen in public--but he knew that she was among those who fled to the safety of the mountains. He could feel her ring pressing against his chest, and, as he held his hand to it, he murmured softly, "'Tis well that you spoke not to me this day, for I would have done as you desired and not as virtue required."

* * *

It was upon the second day following the evacuation that the army of Delovachia came to Zaren. The sound of their approach could be heard from many miles away. The tramping of their feet mixed with the steady beating of their drums, and the songs of war being played on pipes, filled the air. The enemy spread out and surrounded the city. Where once there had been a vast and open plain there now stretched the huge black mass of the enemy's camp.

The large, red sun hung low in the sky when Orion and his sleek, black griffin companion looked out upon that terrible sight. Nightfall, who stood as large as a horse, rested his forepaws on the edge of the wall as he gazed out over the Delovachian army. His great black wings were slightly opened, and his tail flicked back and forth. He blinked his great white eyes and said, in his croaking voice, "'Twould seem the days of feasting and celebrating have come to an end."

"Aye," said Orion softly, "it would seem so indeed."

Chapter 2
For Tomorrow We Die

These are the words of Magianna, prophetess of Joretham: Twelve staves are there, with twelve stones upon them, for the twelve arch-sorcerers to bear, but there shall come a time when a staffless sorcerer shall arise and carry with him the power to degrade them.

The morning dawned, and a fairer day had not shown itself in Zaren for many a month. Yet the beauty was swallowed up by the sight of the huge camp spread out in all directions upon the large plain surrounding Zaren.

The sun had barely begun to show itself above the horizon when there could be seen a rider slowly approaching the city. An ominous figure made he, in his black armor upon his sable charger before his dark army. The only thing not of black was his head, for, though the rest of his body was fully armed, he wore no helmet. Although his face could be seen, it took not away from his imposing countenance. Indeed, with his proud, ruthless visage and his long, brown hair falling wildly over his broad shoulders, he was even more fearsome than had he worn a helmet.

"Ibrahim!" he cried in a voice heard by all. "Sirrah! Come out if you dare; I would speak with you!" The men of Zaren who stood upon the high walls of their city looked down with anger and contempt upon he who so insulted their king.

Slowly, the gates of Zaren opened so that one solitary rider might pass through them. He was tall and solemn, with gray eyes that spoke of great knowledge and experience. His brown hair was just beginning to show gray. With a slow, steady gait he rode toward the dark man of Delovachia, and, when he reached him, he stopped and spoke solemnly, "Who are you to so churlishly demand that the King of all Nor come and speak with you?"

"And who are you that the cowardly dog Ibrahim sends to speak in his stead?" demanded the black rider, his voice thick with a strange and foreign accent.

"I am Stavros, servant of the great and good King Ibrahim." Stavros answered with a stern voice. "Speak what you will, then scurry back to your master Kozan or return to whatever strange and foreign land you sprang from but trouble us no more."

"Hah!" laughed the black rider. "Does the cat run from the mouse, or the serpent from the rat? So neither will I run from you. Listen to my words if you have ears to hear and courage to uphold you. I am the Dark Sorcerer; I stand at the right hand of Kozan, Power and King of Delovachia. I lead this vast army that now stands ready to destroy you.

"Listen well, cur. You have refused to pay tribute, blasphemed the Powers, and insulted Kozan by refusing him your princess, and now you will be destroyed. My army will sweep through your pitiful city and slaughter all that breathes. When I have finished there will be not even a sad piece of ash which can be laid to rest beneath the earth unless you surrender yourself, pay double tribute, offer yourselves as perpetual servants to the Powers, and give Kozan that which his heart most desires: the Princess of Nor, for it has been said that she is fair beyond all women, and he would fain take her as his wife."

"You speak the words of a knave not those of a sorcerer of power," replied Stavros. "Run back to your master, dog, and tell him this. Were he to assail us with ten times the number he now sends, still would we stand against him. We will die before we submit to the fate Kozan would give us. And as for giving your pig-master that which his heart desires most, tell him to take pleasure in his two wives and countless concubines, but turn not his lustful eyes toward our princess. She is not his, nor will she ever be his, and if he dares lay one finger upon her the vengeance of Nor will be swifter and more torturous than that of a wrath-filled griffin. Now away, insolent cur and return to Delovachia and your dark lord."

"Proud words for a fool," The Dark Sorcerer sneered. "I shall enjoy forcing them down your throat." With a loud yell he spurred his charger and galloped back to his camp.

* * *

Orion and Nightfall stood upon the high walls of the city and looked down upon the exchange. As the Dark Sorcerer returned to his army, Nightfall whispered, "We shall feast upon blood today. May Joretham be with us, for it hath begun!"

* * *

There was, in one of the towers of the palace, a small, dark room--not dark with evil, but unlit and still so that the world might be kept out and the spirit of Joretham allowed to enter. There was no window, for sight was not needed in a battle of magic such as was about to take place.

The room was filled with the tools of magic, and, in the midst of these, King Ibrahim knelt with his staff laid on the floor before him. He wore not the rich garments befitting a king but instead a simple robe of light blue. His golden crown he had laid aside on a nearby table. His head was bent and his hands clasped in supplication as he prayed, saying, "...And let not this, your kingdom, be destroyed. Let not these, your people, be killed and sold into slavery and left to wander Lairannare as outcasts. Grant me strength that I might overcome my enemy."

He rose to his feet, and, taking up his staff, he whispered, "Be with me, Lord." The crystal stone on his staff began to glow as the battle of magic began.

* * *

The ground shook as tens of thousands of Delovachians lifted up their voices in cries of battle. Like water released from a floodgate they rushed forward-- weapons glinting in the sun, eyes blazing, and hearts bent upon blood.

With a shout, the soldiers on the wall began to rain flaming arrows down upon their enemies. Hundreds upon hundreds of arrows sped through the air into the midst of the Delovachians, and small fires began to spring up as men were struck. The cries of war were mixed with the screams of agony as soldiers fell wounded to the ground.

The Delovachians continued to swarm forward. In their midst they bore a huge battering ram, which they set against the gate of the city. The hollow "Boom!" of the ram striking the oaken doors of the gate rang again and again over the cries of battle.

* * *

Far away the Dark Sorcerer sat upon his black horse and seemed to do nothing but look out over the battle. But had one been close enough to see his face, one would have seen that he did far more than merely watch the battle, for he fought an invisible war of magic. Great was his power, but King Ibrahim was a worthy opponent.

* * *

The men of Zaren were strong and proud. Outnumbered they may have been, but that served only to spur them on to greater fury. Already the cries of the dying and the smell of death filled the air. Boiling water was poured down upon those who held the battering ram, and, when others ran forward to take the place of those who had fallen, they were struck down by scores of flaming arrows. But there were always others to take the place of those who fell.

The men of Zaren stood upon their high walls and laughed and sang and taunted their enemy, for they feared not battle or death.

"Ho! Sirrahs!" cried Gideone, leaning over the city wall. "Is all of Delovachia filled with women that Kozan would send milksops such as you to fight us?"

Stavros, who stood beside the Prince, cast a rather amused look at him then, turning back to the battle, took careful aim and shot a flaming arrow into the midst of the Delovachians.

"Run back home to your embroidery and leave the game of war to the men, for we know how to play it!" cried Gideone, ignoring Stavros.

Stavros cast another glance at Gideone and calmly fired another flaming arrow into the army below.

The boom of the battering ram against the gate echoed throughout the whole city.

"Hah!" laughed Gideone when he saw that the gate still held, "Is that the best you can do?"

As if in answer to his cry, there suddenly arose from out of the Delovachian ranks hundreds upon hundreds of dark, winged creatures. Their wings and raiment were of darkest sable, and their skin was purest white. Their faces were those of beautiful women, with their features delicate and alluring. With large, slanting, innocent eyes they looked upon the men of Nor, but they held their clawed hands ready. They were at once the most exotic and the most deadly creatures. With shrieking cries, they sped through the air toward Zaren.

"Is Delovachia filled with women? Run back to your embroidery. Is that the best you can do?" repeated Stavros rather sardonically.

"I think I prefer the men over the women," muttered Gideone as he drew his sword.

* * *

Orion and Nightfall looked in awe upon the dark mass of flying creatures.

"Harpies," said Orion in a hushed voice.

"Demon spawn!" spat Nightfall.

"Fail me not this day, Ronahrrah," spoke Orion as he looked upon his crystal-bladed sword.

Within seconds the harpies descended upon the city of Zaren. Nightfall gave a hissing war cry and leapt up to do battle in the air. Orion turned his sword on all that descended upon him, and the dark red scales of his armor were soon turned black with harpy blood.

He gave a cry as a harpy leapt onto his back and dug her claws into his shoulders. With a snarl of fury he spun around, flinging her from him. She tumbled to the ground, then, with a shriek, caught herself and sped back toward him. His teeth were bared in a growl, as he sent his sword slicing through the air toward her. She saw the blade speeding toward her, but she could not stop her flight. She raised her arm to defend herself and gave a scream of pain as the sword sliced through her arm and deep into her side. She tumbled to the ground and lay there, still alive yet unable to move. Blood splattered everywhere as, with another growl Orion sent his sword slicing through her neck.

To his right, from out of the sky, he saw another harpy speeding towards him. Even as he turned to face her, he heard Nightfall cry out, "Orion, behind thee!" Before he could turn, he was struck from behind with an overwhelming blow that drove him to the ground. He rolled onto his back and tried to regain his breath, but, before he could recover, a harpy sprang down upon him and grabbed him by the throat. She gave a terrifying hiss as she dug her claws deep into his skin. With a snarl of rage, he threw her from him as if she were nothing more than a child, and, giving a fierce almost animal-like cry, he fell upon her and grasped her neck with an iron grip. She slashed at his arms and face.

Orion was like one possessed. He gave another snarling cry and grasped her even tighter. His lips turned up in a look of almost evil pleasure as he slowly tightened his grip. Her eyes bulged, and she looked up in terror upon him, but he continued to squeeze her neck until suddenly there could be heard the sound of her spine popping. She gave a small gurgle then gave up her life.

Orion grabbed his sword from where it had fallen and, giving a cry that was more terrifying than that of the harpies, turned upon those gathered there. They scattered in fear before him.

* * *

Far away, in the place of Nortath's Fury, Mystia suddenly gave a scream of pain or terror and fell to the floor where she lay gasping for breath. Her maid was almost immediately kneeling at her side, asking what was wrong. Mystia could only murmur incoherently with a strangled voice.

"Bring her here and let her lie down," ordered Queen Malcah coldly, as she motioned to a place beside her upon the ground. "This child has always lived in a realm filled with the invisible. Sleep should cure her of her ills."

Mystia, still groaning, was led to the place her mother had indicated and was covered with a thick, warm blanket.

* * *

All through the day Gideone traveled along the walls of the city, fighting and lifting up the spirits of the men. He was covered with blood, and pain filled his body. He was exhausted, but he forced himself to go on, and there was not one group of soldiers which he visited that did not fight all the harder when he left.

The cries of war filled his ears, and the stench of death was strong. Blood flowed everywhere. The Prince gave a cry and held up his arm as a harpy sped over his head. Dead soldiers covered the top of the wall; some had been pushed down to the ground below, but the walkway along the parapet was still covered with them.

Gideone coughed and ran to the edge of the wall. The Delovachian army seemed as large as it had been before. Its soldiers swarmed around the base of the city. He could still hear the hollow boom as the battering ram struck the gate again and again. All day had it done so.

Suddenly, Gideone saw a movement out of the corner of his eye. Turning, he saw a Delovachian charging toward him. The Prince gave a cry of both surprise and anger as he raised his sword to defend himself. The Delovachian rammed into him, sending Gideone reeling back beneath the blow. With a snarl Gideone lunged forward striking at the man. His blow was blocked, but with a cry he sent another blow down upon him, then another, and another. Suddenly, the Delovachian gave a cry and stumbled forward. Gideone leapt back out of the way. The Delovachian dropped his sword and fell to the ground, an arrow sticking up from his back.

Already more Delovachians were battling atop the walls. Gideone looked wildly around for where they were coming from. Suddenly, he saw the top of a ladder, against the north side. Delovachians were swarming up and over the wall. With a cry, Gideone ran forward, but before he could reach it, two Norians ran toward it and managed to push it back away from the wall. Gideone could hear the screams of the Delovachians as the ladder tipped backward and sent them plummeting to the ground.

Gideone stopped and took quick gasping breaths. His lungs cried out for air. He looked up; the sky was nearly dark. The battle had to end soon. When? His body screamed out for rest.

Suddenly, as if on cue, the sound of a horn pierced through the cries and screams of battle. It rang through the air, and at its sound all of the Delovachians stopped their battling and turned to return to their camp.

Gideone breathed a sigh of relief. The battle had ended.

He had little time to rest, however. Scarcely had the fighting ended before he was running back through the streets of the city, into the palace, and up into the tower in which his father was.

All was quiet as he peered into the dark and silent room. It took a moment for his eyes to adjust to the almost complete blackness, but when they did he drew back in horror, for he found his father lying as one dead upon the floor.

"Father!" he cried in alarm as he rushed to Ibrahim and knelt beside him. He rolled his father over onto his back and could then but wait for any sign of life. Slowly the King opened his eyes. Looking up into his son's dark eyes, he said with labored breath, "Fear not, I still live."

"Are you wounded? What can I do for you?" cried Gideone, as he anxiously looked down upon his father.

"Nay, I am not wounded," said Ibrahim as, with a grimace, he sat up. He cast Gideone a wan smile and said, "'Twas a furious battle indeed, and several times I thought certes all would be lost, but Joretham smiled upon me. Help me rise."

"Are you certain you're well, Father?" asked Gideone as he did what Ibrahim asked.

"Yes," answered Ibrahim, with a rather halfhearted smile.

There was a moment's pause before the King spoke again. "This man who leads the Delovachians is not Kozan--one would sooner see Mystia at the front of an army--but, though Power he may not be, a potent Magic he is nonetheless. Tell me," and here a look of fear and anxiety flashed across his face, "does he bear the staff of a sorcerer?"

"I saw no staff," answered Gideone truthfully.

Ibrahim's sharp intake of breath caused Gideone to look in alarm upon his father.

"You saw no staff?" repeated Ibrahim, fear welling up within him. "Yet he calls himself a sorcerer does he not?"

"Aye, he calls himself a sorcerer. And as to his staff, if he has one, he kept it hidden."

"No," groaned Ibrahim as he lifted his face to the heavens. "No."

"And what does it matter if he has a staff or no?" demanded Gideone, fear making his tone grow sharp. "Are you not still an arch-sorcerer? Can you not still defeat him?"

"Have you not heard the prophecies, boy!" cried Ibrahim. "He is the staffless sorcerer, and he comes to destroy me."

"And what are prophecies but the words of fools and madmen or those who seek to profit from the superstitions of others? How many hundreds of prophecies have been spoken, and, of them, how many have been fulfilled? One, two, perhaps three. Why then should you heed the idle words of a long dead daughter of sacrilege?"

"Magianna was a prophetess of Joretham."

"And what means Joretham to me? Is one foolish prophecy reason enough to give up hope? You are the king of Nor. What will the men of Zaren say and do when they learn that their king has no faith that they shall be triumphant?"

"Gideone, even now this sorcerer gathers his strength, and he shall soon have power enough to break the magic which seals the gates of Zaren. I had hoped that I would have strength enough to hold him back, but now I know that with him my death shall come." Gideone opened his mouth to speak, but his father would not allow him. "If you are not willing to understand or believe the prophecies then leave me," concluded Ibrahim softly, his voice tinged with anger, "for I must have peace."

Gideone stood there for a moment, then turned and walked away, but, when he came to the door, he turned and said, sarcastically, "I leave you to find peace, which is a thing easily found in the midst of war." He then walked away.

* * *

The house of the healers was dark and filled with the stench of blood and death, but what house in Zaren did not smell of death? Many men had been healed of their wounds, but some were so far gone that not even magic could save them. The moans of the dying filled the place. Orion sat there, in a dark corner, hunched over on the ground. He was half-asleep with exhaustion, and yet he was unable to fully sleep because of the pain that filled his body body. So, he simply sat there, silently, waiting patiently for a healer to come tend to him.

It was almost midnight before his wounds were tended to, for, terrible though they were, they looked not to be gruesome and went unnoticed by the healers, until Orion, growing impatient, finally drew attention to them. Often was Orion overlooked by healers, for his blood was not like the blood of other men. His was as clear as water.

He was sorely injured, especially on his arms and face, and it took nearly an hour for the healers to bind up his wounds. He remained silent, almost deathly silent, throughout the whole of that time and kept his eyes focused on his arms.

The healers finally completed their tasks, and the blue-eyed warrior walked out into the still and silent streets of Zaren. All was dark, for the sky above was covered with clouds, through which only the smallest glimpse of the moon and the stars could be caught. An air of darkness, terror, and grim expectation lay heavy upon Zaren, and, if men dared speak at all, they spoke with low murmurs; it seemed almost sacrilegious to do otherwise.

Nightfall was waiting outside, when Orion emerged. He opened his mouth to speak but fell silent when he saw the look of horror in his friend's eyes.

"I could have died," Orion said with a voice trembling with terror. He tried to say more, but words failed him.

"Orion," answered Nightfall, his head tilted to one side in confusion, "thou hast not died; thou hast conquered, and won glory unto thyself."

"And what does the glory of one day matter, when, upon the morrow, you lie dead?"

"Orion," the griffin said with as soothing a tone as his voice would allow, "death is not a thing to be feared. Is it not through death that one doth enter into great glory?"

"What would you know of death?" asked Orion bitterly as he turned away from him.

Nightfall drew himself up in surprise at Orion's harsh tone. "My father doth guard the gates of Lothiel."

"Think you that I care what your father guards? Leave me alone." With that Orion turned and walked away, leaving Nightfall to look in confusion after him.

Orion walked through the still and silent city until he reached the high walls. He walked slowly along them. The cool wind blew softly upon his face, and overhead the moon shone through the clouds. He stopped and looked down upon the vast army below, and, as he gazed upon it, the one thought that kept running through his mind was, "There lies my death."

Beneath his tunic he could feel Mystia's ring against his chest. He pressed his hand against it, and he found himself wondering what strange gem it was inlaid within her ring, for he had never seen its like before. He seemed almost to know what it was, but, just as the mist over his eyes began to clear, it settled again, and he remembered not what gem it was.

He stood contemplating the ring and the sight which was before him for he knew not how many minutes when his thoughts were suddenly interrupted by Prince Gideone who had walked quietly up beside him.

"'Tis a terrible sight, is it not?" asked the Prince.

"A terrible sight indeed, Your Highness," answered Orion.

For a long moment Gideone was silent, and, as Orion had done before him, he simply looked out over the vast Delovachian army.

"Think you that we shall be defeated?" Gideone asked. He was a far different man from the one who had celebrated during the feast of Pallath-gaon.

"I see no way by which we can triumph," answered Orion, then added as almost an afterthought, "unless Joretham desires not our deaths."

"I care nothing for Joretham," said Gideone, his tone suddenly dark. "Give me what can be seen and touched, not intangible spirits."

Orion remained silent, for what did he know of Joretham?

"We face destruction," continued Gideone, "but know I that you, at least, shall stay and fight and not run in fear."

Orion bowed his head in reply but said nothing.

Gideone looked out over the vast army spread before him and for a long moment was silent. Suddenly he turned back to Orion. A glimmer of hope was in his eyes as he spoke. "Orion, I know that the power of lesser Magics has no effect on you, but what of the magic of a sorcerer, or a mage, or a Power?"

Orion hesitated then answered, "There are none of the Realm of Earth who can touch me with magic, whether Power or otherwise."

"Then the Dark Sorcerer has no hold over you." The Prince's dark eyes were beginning to sparkle with the hope rising within him.

"Perhaps, Your Highness, but we speak only of magic power; perchance he is a better swordsman."

Gideone laughed and dismissed Orion's words with a wave of his hand. "No man can wield a sword as you do, Orion. You're a master swordsman who cannot be touched by magic. You are our savior."

"Your Highness!" cried Orion as he took a step back. The thought of having the entire fate of Zaren--indeed, the entire fate of Nor--resting upon his shoulders was a terrifying thought.

"Orion," said Gideone, seeing Orion's fear, "if you will not fight the Dark Sorcerer then Zaren will fall, for my father, though he prepares to do battle with him, fears the Sorcerer." There was shame in his voice as he said those last words. "He believes that his death at the hand of the Sorcerer has been fated and is inevitable. 'Tis a false belief, but it shall certes keep him from emerging victorious." He looked hard at Orion. "Orion, promise me that you will take my father's place and fight this dark and terrible man."

Orion looked silently down upon the ground. Slowly he raised his head, and, turning his eyes to Gideone, he finally answered. "You are my prince, and I am your servant. I will do that which you ask."

"Thank you, Orion. You know not what great a service you do for me and Zaren and, indeed, for Nor."

Orion said nothing in reply.

"Well, I will leave you now," said Gideone, when he saw that Orion would not speak. "Find sleep if you can, for tomorrow will be a terrible day."

"Yes, Your Highness."

Gideone turned and walked away, and Orion was left once more to himself.

* * *

The morning dawned, and a dark and ominous morning it was, for the clouds overhead were black and threatening. The men of Zaren came and stood atop the high walls of their city. Grim-faced men they were, with eyes flashing, weapons held ready, and none of the joy of battle, which had filled them upon the previous day.

Above the main gate of the city stood King Ibrahim, sorcerer's staff in hand. He looked out over the huge army on the plain below, but what he thought none knew, for his face was as unmoving as stone.

The Delovachian army, with the Dark Sorcerer at its head, advanced toward the city. With his lips curled in a sneer, he slowly looked over the men of Zaren, and his gaze finally came to rest upon King Ibrahim.

"So, the dog dares show his face!" cried the Sorcerer in contempt.

There came a low rumble of thunder.

"I do more than show my face, sorcerer of Delovachia," replied Ibrahim solemnly. "I challenge you to a duel. Let us meet before the gates of this city, and let our two armies bear witness unto that which we do. If you should win, then the city of Zaren shall surrender, but, if I should win, then you and your army shall return to Delovachia and trouble us no more. Is this not better than wasting the blood of thousands of men?"

"What care I of wasted blood, seeing that it's the blood of Norians that is wasted?" answered the Sorcerer, his strange and foreign accent only lending malice to his words. "And why should I meet you in single combat, seeing that my army is far greater than yours? Nay, I spit upon your challenge, cur, for it is the challenge of a fool!" Almost before he finished speaking, he threw his arms above his head and cried out fierce words in a foreign tongue.

Ibrahim held his staff up high and lifted his voice up in a chant. A huge flash of light, as bright as the noonday sun, filled the sky and swept over the armies of Nor and Delovachia. The men were thrown backwards to the ground by the overwhelming power of the magic blast. The great and terrible sound of something slowly cracking could be heard across the whole of that vast plain, but only the Dark Sorcerer and Orion, who had not been thrown backwards, witnessed the gate of Zaren slowly split down the center and fall to the ground. For a moment all was utterly silent. There was huge flash of lighting in the clouds above. Orion's eyes locked with those of the Dark Sorcerer, and they could only stare--Orion in amazement at the strength of the Sorcerer's magic and the Sorcerer in wonder that any man could withstand his onslaught. The flash of lightning ended, leaving the city and the plain in darkness. There came a loud rumbling of thunder which died away into the shrieking of the wind, and, beneath that wind, there could be heard the men rising to their feet; it was as if the dead themselves arose.

The sky was lit by another flash of lightning, and the army of Delovachia saw that the great gate of Zaren lay broken upon the ground. With a great shout they rushed forward upon the city. Orion's howl of anger was drowned out by a terrifying crack of thunder.

* * *

Far away, in the place of Nortath's Fury, Mystia lay flat upon her back in an almost trance-like state. Her black eyes were wide open, and she stared up at the cavernous ceiling overhead, but she seemed not to see anything. Her maid sat at her side and looked down in concern upon her. Queen Malcah also sat nearby, but when she cast a glance at Mystia it was more in exasperation than anything else.

Mystia gave a long sigh and said softly in fear, "It begins again."

* * *

Never, since the days of Balor, had the streets of Zaren seen battle, but they saw it now. The cries of men and the shrieks of harpies mixed with the rolling of the thunder. The lightning flashed and the rain poured down so heavily that, between the darkness and the light, one could scarcely tell friend from foe.

Orion stood upon a battlement, with crystal-bladed Ronahrrah in his hands. He gave a terrible battle cry that, while yet human, was at the same time like the roaring of a lion and the hissing of a terrible serpent. The soldiers of Delovachia swarmed all about, and Orion, swinging his sword madly about his head, waded into where they were thickest, crying as he did so, "Come, Nightfall! If we are to die, let us win everlasting glory as we do so!"

* * *

While Orion fought upon the walls, Gideone battled in the streets. His mouth was turned up in a smile, but it was not a smile that came from the joy of battle. He sent his sword smashing into the shoulder of a soldier. The soldier screamed in pain and looked down in horror at his arm dangling from a few strands of muscle and skin. No, his smile was filled with anger, disgust, and contempt. With a snarl Gideone finished him off, then turned to continue doing battle.

* * *

As the battle waxed hot, the Dark Sorcerer rode up and down the length of the city, searching for King Ibrahim. He caused bright, red, magic fire to spring up before him to light his way, and, in the midst of the pouring rain, the proud, high-walled city of Zaren burned.

* * *

"I can see it," whispered Mystia so softly one could barely hear her. "Zaren burns, and yet I have no tears to shed." Then, even softer, she moaned, "Joretham, it burns."

Through the many caverns of the Place of Nortath's Fury and through the huddled groups of women and children gathered there, one figure slowly walked. Tall he was, and handsome, clothed entirely in black, with eyes and hair as red fire. Upon his face, he bore the look of supreme evil. With an air of suppressed passion, he made his way ever toward where Mystia lay.

Mystia, who had, ever since the day before, lain upon the ground, suddenly sat up. Her eyes were wide open in utter terror, and she spoke in a choked voice, saying, "He comes... Joretham, no, he comes."

* * *

Orion, covered with blood and grime, still battled atop the walls of the city. It seemed that he, like the raging storm, only grew in strength and fury with the passing of the hours. None could stand against him, and any wound he was given seemed only to spur him on to greater madness. Some fled at the mere sight of him, when, as the lightning lit the sky, they looked up to see his flashing spectral blue eyes fixed upon them.

As Orion fought, he suddenly caught a glimpse of the Dark Sorcerer beneath him. He gave a fierce battle cry and scrambled as quickly as he could down off the wall and onto the street below. The rain had mixed with the dirt and the blood, and Orion found himself ankle-deep in mud. He ran as quickly as he could toward where he had seen the Sorcerer ride, but the ground seemed to do all it could to keep him from his end.

Suddenly, he felt as if his whole chest had caught on fire. Clutching at it, he fell to the ground and gave a howl of pain. In a stroke of insight, he pulled Mystia's chain and ring from about his neck. He held it up before him and looked with amazement upon it, for the ring glowed bright red and hot. As he stared at it, the mist cleared from his eyes, and he knew what it was--a soul stone. She had given him her soul stone.

He jumped to his feet and looked wildly about for Nightfall. As lightning illuminated the sky, Orion looked up and saw far above him the black griffin, battling harpies in the sky.

"Nightfall!" he bellowed, but had the roar of the battle not drowned out his voice the rolling thunder certainly would have.

He gave the most profane curse he could think of and ran back up onto the wall. Slicing all who stood in his path, he reached the highest battlement.

"Nightfall!" he roared as he jumped up and down and waved his hands furiously above his head. Perhaps Joretham was with him, for Nightfall looked down and, seeing him, turned and flew down to him.

"The Princess is in danger," Orion shouted over the noise of the storm and the battle. "Come." Almost before the words were out of his mouth, he was running down from off the wall and toward the stable where Nightfall's saddle was kept.

"Orion, art thou mad?" croaked Nightfall as he landed and galloped after Orion. "Why think thee the Princess is in danger?"

"Look!" Orion cried as he held up Mystia's soul stone. "Her soul stone glows."

Nightfall drew back in amazement as he beheld that precious thing which Orion possessed. Terror welled up in his heart, as it had already in the heart of Orion, for he knew, as Orion did, that a soul stone never glowed unless the one whose soul it belonged to was in mortal danger.

* * *

King Ibrahim sat upon his horse in the middle of a wide muddy street. The battle raged all about him, but he fought not. His head hung down upon his chest, and he seemed entirely devoid of strength.

There was a flash of lightning, and, as Ibrahim looked up, he saw the Dark Sorcerer upon his sable charger with his sword drawn and held ready. He said not a word, but the flashing of his eyes told Ibrahim all that was needed.

"Is it then time?" murmured Ibrahim as he raised his staff. He seemed to be so very weary, and yet, for all of his weakness, there was a look of determination in his dark eyes.

The two men gave fierce yells and dug their heels deep into the sides of their horses. They pounded toward each other and crashed together. The muddy ground and the force of their impact joined to send them plunging to the ground. The Dark Sorcerer rose with a snarl and, whipping his wet, mud-caked hair out of his face, turned toward Ibrahim who was still scrambling to his feet. Not allowing him the chance to fully rise, the Sorcerer fell upon him and almost sent him sprawling into the mud once again, but Ibrahim kept from falling and fought back with a strength that surprised the Sorcerer.

The air about them fairly glowed with the power of their magic as back and forth they battled--first one slipping and falling into the mud, only to rise and send the other reeling back--until Ibrahim's anger waxed great, and, holding his staff as though it were a club, he dealt the Dark Sorcerer such a blow as to send him sinking to his knees, where he could but look up in pain upon the King. Another blow sent the Sorcerer's sword flying from his hand, and another broke his arm. Ibrahim drew back his staff for the final blow, but, even as he did so, the Dark Sorcerer gathered all of his power into one last spell. As Ibrahim sent his staff crashing down upon the Sorcerer, the Sorcerer held his good hand up and caught the staff with an iron grasp. With one swift motion, he yanked it from Ibrahim's hands and rose to his feet. His strength returned to him, and with his magic he forced Ibrahim to kneel before him.

"Fool! Insolent cur to think that you could ever defeat me!" cried the Dark Sorcerer as he raised the staff above his head. Magic crackled all about him, and Ibrahim knew that his end had come.

"Kill me, Sorcerer of Delovachia, and let it be done with," growled Ibrahim.

* * *

Gideone stood upon the walls of Zaren and fought with all his strength, yet things went not well with him. Suddenly, he looked down and saw his father kneeling helplessly before the Dark Sorcerer. He gave an unintelligible cry of terror and fury and began to run madly along the wall in a desperate attempt to reach his father before the Sorcerer killed him, but, as he ran, a long, dark arrow suddenly struck him. He gave a cry of pain as it pierced through his armor and struck him just below his heart. He staggered and fell, and, as he fell, he saw his father struck down by the Dark Sorcerer. For a long moment no sound would come from his mouth, and he could only stare in silent horror at where his father lay. Suddenly, he caught sight of Orion upon Nightfall flying up out of the city. They rose into the air and flew away from Zaren.

"Coward!" shrieked Gideone as he jumped to his feet and turned upon his enemies. "Coward!" No other word would come. For a few moments, he fought like a furious demon, but his wound soon overcame him. He sank to the ground and did not rise.

* * *

Nightfall flew as he had never flown before, but no speed was fast enough to satisfy Orion. The storm raging all around seemed only to lend even greater urgency to his mission. He looked down upon Mystia's glowing soul stone and, with each passing moment, felt increasingly certain it would grow dim with her death.

* * *

"Joretham!" Mystia screamed. Her maid, not knowing what else to do, put a comforting hand upon her shoulder and tried to make her lie down once again. "Take your hands off me!" cried Mystia as she jumped to her feet. For a moment she stood looking wildly about her, then she turned and fled into the dark recesses of the caverns.

Even as she disappeared into the darkness, there entered and stood before Queen Malcah the dark man who had been making his way through the Fortress of Nortath's Fury. With a terrible growl he turned to face the guards who sought to bar his way, and, with not even a word, he struck them down with a powerful magic spell.

"Who are you?" demanded the Queen rising.

"Where is she?" he snarled, ignoring the question.

"How should I know?" answered the Queen.

"Insolent fool!" cried he as he struck her across the face with a large, clawed hand. She did not even scream, but gave only a small gasp as she fell to the floor, where she struck her head upon a rock and moved no more. The dark man stalked past her dead body and into the darkness where Mystia had run.

* * *

It took no more than half an hour for Nightfall to fly the many miles from Zaren to the fortress in the Caves of Nortath's Fury. Nightfall landed on a rocky ledge before the main entrance of the caverns, and Orion ran to a large group of women and children who were gathered about the body of Queen Malcah. It was doubtful that Orion even saw the dead queen, so overcome was he with terror for Mystia. It took him but a second to see that the Princess was not one who was gathered there, and he cried out, "Where is she! By the blood of Joretham, where is the Princess!" But, with his clothes and dragon-scale armor covered with the blood of his enemies, his long hair flying all about him like a savage, and his blue eyes looking wildly all about him, the already terrified women could only scatter before him.

It was a small girl, with huge green eyes open wide, who overcame her fear enough to point to the darkness of an adjoining cavern and say, "There, and he followed her."

Orion stopped not to ask who "he" was but whirled and leapt back into Nightfall's saddle. The griffin instantly jumped into the air and hurtled into the adjoining cavern, but Mystia was not there. Through cavern after cavern he flew, and, though the flight took but thirty seconds if that, it indeed was the longest flight he had ever taken.

He burst into yet another chamber, and, in this one, Orion's eyes were met by the sight of a tall, evil looking man forcing Mystia back against a wall. Mystia stood cowering before him. Her eyes were closed, great tears pouring from them, and her whole body shook with huge sobs of terror.

"Phyre!" cried Orion--for he knew that man--as he, with sword drawn, sped toward him. Phyre turned toward Orion, and as his eyes met Orion's his face twisted into a look of unimaginable hatred. He gave a cry unlike any a mortal man could make, and as he did so, his features distorted and he began to grow. He rose and rose, his body covered with billowing black smoke, until, finally, he completed his transformation and stood--a huge dragon, whose scales were as clear as crystal and whose innards swirled with raging smoke and fire. He gave a terrible, hissing roar and leapt toward Orion.

Mystia shrieked as Phyre's massive tail lashed out toward her. She bolted sideways but did not entirely escape the blow and was sent skidding across the hard stone floor.

Phyre did not even know he had struck her, for all of his rage was focused against Orion. He lashed out at the blue-eyed warrior, but was not quick enough, and Nightfall was able to evade him. The griffin flew along the length of the dragon's immense body; as he did so, Orion plunged his sword into Phyre's body and was able to give him a gash that stretched from his shoulder to the base of his tail. The fiery dragon lifted up his voice in a terrifying roar that threatened to split the very floor of the chamber, as fire began to pour from his wound.

"You dare seek her life!" cried Orion in fury as he struck Phyre again. "Dog!" He struck again and again, ever yelling as he did so, but his words were drowned out by Phyre's roars of pain and of anger. Finally, Phyre's great clawed forefoot met with Orion and Nightfall and sent them both tumbling through the air. The griffin managed to right himself and gain flight, but Orion struck the ground hard and lay as one dead.

"Fool!" spat the great fiery dragon at Orion's limp form. He then turned upon Mystia who lay dazed and terrified upon the floor. Slowly, with fire still pouring from his wounds, he took a painful step toward her. A screeching battle-cry and the dark form of Nightfall speeding towards him brought the dragon up short. With a terrifying roar he struck the griffin who fell to the ground and did not rise.

Phyre turned once again upon Mystia, but, before he could make another step toward her, Orion could be heard crying out from behind him, "Die dragon!" Even as the words left his lips, he drew back his sword, then, with all his might, hurled it toward Phyre. It flew through the air, spinning end over end. Phyre roared and tried to turn, but he was too late. Fire erupted as the blade smashed into the dragon's head, piercing through his crystal skin and continuing out the other side. He gave a terrifying, hissing roar of pain and leapt up in the air. For a moment he seemed to hover at the apex of his ascent, then he began to speed toward the earth. The cavern shook as with a thundering roar he crashed into the ground. Stones flew through the air as Phyre dug deep into the earth and disappeared.

For a moment Orion could simply stand, gasping for breath as he looked at the fiery tunnel left in the floor by Phyre. Though wounded, the dragon was not dead, and it would not take him long to tunnel back to his lair.

Taking one last breath, Orion turned and ran quickly to where Princess Mystia lay sobbing upon the ground. His face was hardened from the battle he had just fought, but the moment he came into her presence his features softened.

"Your Highness," said he, as he helped her sit up, "are you uninjured?"

Her whole body shook with tears, but she said, with what little pride she had left, "A giant dragon almost killed me. Of course, I'm uninjured." She threw her arms around his neck and began to sob even harder than when she had first begun. She was far too upset to notice how tense Orion became. However, no matter how embarrassed he was, he waited silently and patiently for her to cease her tears, and when she had done so he spoke. "Phyre is not dead, Your Highness, for he is a mighty dragon and likely to heal himself very quickly. It would be best if I were to take you from here."

"And where will you take me?" asked Mystia, voice still trembling. She waited for his reply, but Orion was no longer listening; he had caught sight of the limp form of Nightfall, lying upon the ground.

"Nightfall!" he cried as he ran over to his friend. Mystia followed him and also knelt beside the fallen griffin. Nightfall lay unmoving upon the ground; there was not even the slightest motion of breath. Timorously, Orion touched his hand to the griffin's body, and, when Nightfall did not respond, he took up the great eagle head of his friend and cradled it in his arms. Words could not describe the look of utter anguish that was in his face as he looked silently upon his dead friend.

Suddenly Nightfall's head began to move of its own accord, and Orion dropped it in his surprise. Nightfall gave a cry of pain as it hit the floor, but after a moment he murmured, "Please, hold my head again, for I found it most comfortable."

"Nightfall!" cried both Orion and Mystia together.

"I thought you were dead," said Orion, relief filling him. "Never frighten me like that again."

"Orion!" exclaimed Nightfall in indignation as he struggled to his feet, "Know thee not how hard the skulls of griffins are? I feel strong enough to fly through the whole of the Realms of Deithanara."

Orion laughed as he rose and place his arm around Nightfall's neck.

"Let us hope what you say is true," he said, "for we have a long journey ahead of us."

"Where are we going?" asked Mystia in a small voice.

"To the house of the sage Zenas in the Mountains of Lathinor. You will be safe there, for Phyre cannot enter that place," answered Orion.

* * *

The storm which had raged over Zaren ended even as the battle which had raged in Zaren ended. Stavros cast a sad look back at the smoldering city that had once been his home, and Vayan, who stood at his side, did the same. Together they had escaped the fury of the Dark Sorcerer, and they had managed to rescue Prince Gideone as well. Stavros turned his eyes from the far off city and down to the unconscious form of Gideone. He tore open the Prince's tunic and looked upon his wound. The place where the arrow had pierced him had already turned black and thin dark lines had begun to creep out from it. Stavros studied it for a long moment then gave a long groan of anguish.

"No," he moaned. "Joretham, let it not be."

Chapter 3
The Mountains of Lathinor

"Thou didst dare seek to raise thyself up over the whole of Deithanara, and for thine insolence it shall be that even that which thou dost possess shall be taken from thee. Thou art no longer the ruler of Lairannare, but another more fitting and worthy shall be found to take thy place. And of this place in which thou didst cause such great death--of Lathinor: thou art forbidden to enter it, unless thou dost wish to hasten thine own death." So did Nyght, Queen of the Realm of the Heavens, curse Phyre King of the Realm of Earth.

The wind whistled past Mystia's ears as Nightfall flew through the air. The Princess' eyes were squeezed tightly shut and her skin was almost deathly pale. She sat in front of Orion, her back pressed against his chest. His arms were wrapped loosely around her waist.

She gasped as Nightfall flapped his wings, making himself rise slightly.

"Hold me tighter!" she cried.

Orion tried not to groan. His body hurt all over from his battle with Phyre.

He leaned forward slightly and spoke in her ear, "Worry not, Your Highness, I will not let you fall."

"Still..." she said after a slight pause, "hold me tighter!"

Wincing in pain, he did as she asked. After a few minutes, he slowly began to relax his grip until he was holding her as loosely as he had to begin with. He could feel her trembling. She clutched his legs tightly, and he was thankful for his armor for, without it, he was certain her fingers would have dug deep into his skin.

The sun was fast setting, and, even had Nightfall not been tired from the battle and weighed down with an extra person, it could never have been hoped that Zenas' house would be reached before the fall of night. As the sun was setting he was forced to land in the Forest of Althoros. They made their camp in a small glade surrounded by tall, stately trees. The murmuring of a brook could be heard as it wound its way through the forest. It would have been very picturesque had the season been summer. It was, however, still winter. The trees were laid bare of their leaves, and, though there was no snow upon the ground, the night was still chilly.

Orion, who was exhausted by the fighting of the day, silently made a fire and, leaving Nightfall to guard and Mystia to do what she willed, rolled up in a blanket and fell instantly to sleep.

Mystia sat and ate a piece of bread as she stared into the shifting flames and thought silently. There was little mystery to the course her reflections took; her kingdom had been destroyed, her mother murdered, and she herself almost killed, and, for the time being, she could think of little else. Occasionally her body would tremble slight, either with a silent sob or a sudden shudder of fear; however, she made no noise, and when she had finished eating, she, like Orion, covered herself with a blanket and tried to sleep.

The night passed slowly. Clouds covered the sky, blocking the moon from sight. Sometimes, as they moved across the sky, they would part enough for the moon's silver rays to shine down upon the countryside, only to hide them again in the next moment. The forest was almost dead with the winter, but there were some animals still in residence. Occasionally, their soft sounds would pierce eerily through the trees.

The hour of midnight was drawing nigh when Mystia rose and walked to where Nightfall sat, head held high and white eyes alert, guarding the camp. He was surprised to see her there, for he had thought her long since asleep.

"Thou sleepest not, Highness?" asked he.

"I find the ground a harder bed than that to which I am accustomed," said Mystia as she sat down, and Nightfall thought that beneath her veil she smiled wanly.

"Highness, lean upon my side. I cannot be harder, perhaps might be softer, and, at any rate, can be no colder than the ground."

"Thank you, Nightfall," said she as she leaned against him. A moment of silence passed, then she stirred.

"I have spoken to Orion very rarely in the last two years," said she, "for loath my mother was that I should ever have contact with one such as he. You, however, have ever been his closest companion, and perhaps you can tell me how he fares."

"In some matters he seemeth well, Highness; in others he seemeth not well," answered the griffin. "He doth take both command and rebuke in silence. He doeth all which he is asked. He is the model of a servant and a soldier. Yet he is very silent and very sad."

"A far cry from the wandering warrior who once did save me from the hands of Kozan....

"Tell me something, Nightfall. You yourself say that Orion is sad and silent, and I have seen as much with my own eyes. Why then, seeing the burden he carries, does he continue in his service to Nor?"

"Dost thou not remember the vow he took that he would serve and protect the royal house of Nor, though that service may claim his very life?"

"But why made he such a vow at all, seeing that it has made him so unhappy?"

cried she.

"Thine enemies are his enemies, and thy wars are his wars. That is why, Highness."

"And is the shedding of blood his only reason for serving Nor?" asked Mystia. Her large black eyes seemed to plead for a certain answer, but Nightfall was a griffin young in years who had yet to truly learn the ways of humans--much less the ways of women--and so her silent question escaped him.

"Am I a seer to search and know all that transpireth in the heart and mind of a man?" asked he.

"So you know nothing?"

"I know only what Orion hath told me, and the answer to thy question is something which he hath kept to himself, or, if he hath enlightened anyone, it hath not been me."

"Then so be it," said Mystia has she leaned back against Nightfall's side.

"He is a strange man; is he not?" she added softly. "With eyes like those of a specter and blood as clear as crystal but with a heart more noble and courageous than many a human in Lairannare. A man who cannot touch magic and yet who cannot be touched by magic. Certes he is a strange man."

She said no more that night but fell asleep, with her head resting upon Nightfall's warm, soft side, as the griffin kept watch over the small camp.

Mystia and Orion awoke at the break of dawn. It was a beautiful morning. The sun shone brightly through the trees, and the forest was alive with the sounds of the birds that remained throughout the winter.

They ate a light and hurried breakfast and prepared to leave, but, before they continued on their journey, Orion drew the Princess away from the camp to a place where, though Nightfall could still see them, he could not overhear their words.

"Your Highness," said Orion, "what in the Three Realms possessed you to give me your soul stone, and why did you not tell me what it was you gave? I deserve no such gift as this, and 'tis dangerous for me to possess it. I am a man of war, and were I to be overcome, your stone could fall into the hands of ones who ought not possess it. Please, Your Highness, take it back, for I have no desire to be the means by which it falls into the hands of those who do evil."

"Do you truly wish to return it?" asked she.

"I am your servant and will do whatever you command me," answered Orion.

"Then it would seem we are rather at an impasse, seeing that I would have you decide, but you would have me," said she with laughter in her voice, then more seriously, "Please, keep it, for I wish you to have it."

Orion paused for a moment, and looking into her eyes, said quietly, "You lie very poorly, Your Highness."

"Think you that I lie!" cried she, with the tone of one who had just been gravely insulted.

"I think that you speak not the truth," answered Orion slowly, "though I pray your forgiveness for having insulted you, for I meant not to do so."

For a moment neither spoke.

"Ask not for forgiveness, Orion," she said, suddenly contrite, "for it was the truth you spoke and I who spoke unjustly." She became solemn as she continued. "In sooth, it is not left to you or me to decide what becomes of my ring, for One higher than either of us has already determined that. Joretham desires that you have it, and Joretham's wish is my wish also. Keep it always with you; give it not to others for safekeeping, for that also is the will of Joretham."

It was clear by his expression that Orion wished not to keep the ring--just as it was clear by Mystia's voice that she wished not to give it--yet he bowed his head and replied, "I will do as you command. I shall keep your stone and do all that is within my power to keep it from falling into the hands of wicked men."

Without further words they returned to Nightfall who had stood patiently by as they had conversed, and once more they began their journey to Zenas' home in the Mountains of Lathinor.

Far did they fly over hills and plains, lakes and rivers, saying nothing as they went, for both were wrapped up in their separate reflections. What precisely Orion thought cannot be known, but they were troubling and kept his features grim and solemn.

For Mystia's part, she had finally worked up the courage to open her eyes. Once she did so, she could not keep from looking down upon the ever-changing landscape beneath her. She had but once before been outside the country of Nor, and that had been during the summer. Now, however, winter yet reigned and afforded her a chance to see things, which she had hitherto only dreamed of. Never before had she seen entire forests laid bare of all their leaves and covered with a blanket of snow. Never had she seen lakes frozen over with ice or whole plains of snow sparkling in the light of the sun. She was freezing to be sure--the cloak she wore did little to hold back the cold--but she barely noticed it, such was her wonder.

The sun was several hours past its zenith before Mystia's amazement and Orion's grim thoughts were arrested as the Mountains of Lathinor appeared on the horizon. They stood tall and imposing, bathed in the light of the sun. They were, by far, the tallest of the mountain ranges in Lairannare, but, had they not been the tallest, yet would they have been the most grand, for, with nary a hill to announce their beginning, the mountains shot up thousands of feet almost perpendicular to the ground.

It was said that once, thousands of years ago, those mountains, like all the land about them, had been smooth and level. In those days there arose a great prince named Balor who possessed magic power unlike any who had ever come before him. He was the greatest man in the whole of Lairannare and the ruler of many countries. Even the greatest kings and queens paid homage to him. Balor followed in the paths of wickedness. He was not content to rule only that which he had been given authority over or to wield merely such power as had been seen fit to give him--no matter that both were extensive. He searched out the darkest and most mystical forms of magic--magic so evil that few dared work it.

His power grew until none could stand in his path and yet live. He raised an army so great that its like had never before been seen in Lairannare, and he crushed all beneath him. He filled the Realm with war and forced all to bow before him as their king.

But he was not satisfied to hold Lairannare in his hand and have the blackest of magic at his fingertips. He turned his eyes to the Realm of Magic and the Realm of the Heavens--to Keiliornare and Belunare--and in his heart he lusted after them and all the power they could bring him.

Yet no matter how greatly he desired it, Keiliornare and Belunare could not be taken by his mere army of the Realm of Earth. Great his army may have been, but even it was not that strong. But Balor's desire would not be appeased; he would rule Belunare and Keiliornare.

Filled with a knowledge and power he should never have possessed, he went and stood upon the Plains of Adalrick. His vast army stood behind him, and the wind rushed over him as, using words he should never have spoken, he called forth the dead from Elmorran--fool that he was! The spirits, freed from their torment, rushed forth from the pits of darkness. Terrifying, twisted creatures they were--dead and yet alive, with only one desire: the death of all. Balor cried out commands for them to follow him, but who was he to think that they would obey him? They turned and began to wreak havoc upon Lairannare.

Think not, however, that during the whole of that time in which Balor had conquered and ruled over the Realm of Earth, not one man had risen up to oppose him. Vallendar--a child of the hated race known as the Shallee--rose up against Balor. He gathered together a mighty army, and, even as Balor, with his army, journeyed to the Plains of Adalrick to call up the dead, Vallendar brought his army there to do battle with him.

The two armies stood stretched out over the whole of that vast plain--the wind rushing over them, their weapons glinting in the sunlight. The soldiers of Balor stood tall and proud and hurled curses and insults at the followers of Vallendar, but Vallendar and his men stood, grimly and nobly, and looked in silence upon their enemies.

Suddenly, Balor threw out his arms and shrieked the fateful words of sorcery, which summoned the dead, and, as the spirits of all of those who had fallen into Elmorran rose up out of that dark and evil place, terror fell upon the hearts of the warriors until even the mightiest of them fled. Vallendar alone remained, the only one who dared challenge the accursed spirits. One against many was he, but, though they had all the power of evil at their command, he, a child of a hated race, held within him the power of Joretham.

Firmly did he stand and fight against them, and, though they struggled with all their might, he defeated them and sent them back whence they had come. Then he turned upon Balor who had fled in terror at what he had brought about, and he--Vallendar--slew him.

Thus was Balor defeated and the spirits of Elmorran banished once again from the Three Realms, but evermore would the Plains of Adalrick bear the scars of that great battle. Nevermore would that place be called Adalrick but would instead be named Lathinor--"struggle"--for thereon had the greatest of all struggles been waged.

As he approached the mountains, Nightfall lifted up his voice in a shrieking cry of triumph. He rose high into the sky, and seemed to hang, with Orion and Mystia upon his back, momentarily at the apex of his ascent, before he went hurtling with breathtaking speed back down. Mystia was in terror, holding tightly to Orion, but she was laughing with joy, for she, like Nightfall, felt the air of victory imbued in Lathinor. It was as though nothing evil or unjust could ever enter that place again.

Nightfall sped through the tall mountains, until he came to one that was in the midst of all the others. From high atop its cloud-covered peak there poured a waterfall. It was by no means a broad waterfall, but it was high beyond imagination. Mystia could only look in awe upon it, and it was not until Orion had begun to slide off of Nightfall's back that she realized they had landed.

"Orion," said she softly when he had helped her to the ground, "never have I seen anything as wondrous as this place.

"Of course," she continued when she had thought for a moment, "I have seen precious little of Lairannare."

"Far and wide have I traveled over Lairannare, Your Highness," said Orion, "and to me has the privilege to look upon Keiliornare been granted. But, for all the things I have beheld, Lathinor is the greatest, save for one place."

"And what is that one place which is more grand than that in which we now stand?" asked Mystia as she gazed up at him.

"The place in which the rulers of Deithanara gather together in the Council of the Three Realms."

Mystia, for a moment, was struck dumb with her amazement. Orion, for his part, spoke as if he laid claim to no great thing. He, in fact, did not even look at her but instead continued to gaze at the panoramic view before him.

"You have seen where the Council meets?" breathed Mystia in awe.

"Yes, Your Highness," he replied as he looked down upon her. "Twice, in fact--once when I was a child so young that it's a wonder I still remember it, and once when I was eighteen years of age.

"But enough of this, for I see that you're cold. 'Tis time we met Zenas."

He led her though a small door, which, up until that point, had remained hidden in the stark shadows caused by the bright light and the tall mountains. Mystia found herself in a wide, open cavern, and, though she searched with all her might, she could find no sign of life.

"Zenas!" Orion cried. His voice echoed off the stone walls, but there was no answer. He shouted the name again, but still there was no reply. He opened his mouth to cry a third time, but stopped short when, from one of the dark recesses of the cave, a voice could be faintly heard. The voice grew steadily nearer until the words could be discerned.

"...but wake ye up from your afternoon nap seekin' shelter," said the voice. "And never with so much as a 'please' they walk right in an' make themselves comfortable in front o' yar fire and fill their fat stomachs with yar food, and then without so much as a 'thank ye' they leave, takin' yar best horse while they're at it."

An old man came into view around a large stone. Small was he, and the fact that he was hunched over with age did nothing to increase his stature. His hair was entirely silver, and his beard flowed down almost to his waist. His garb was completely gray save for the black belt fastened around his waist. In his hand he held a thick wooden staff.

Zenas--for that was who the old man was--continued on with his muttered complaints during the entire time it took him to cross the cavern, and it was not until he came within three feet of Orion and Mystia that he actually looked to see who it was that had called his name. When he did, his entire demeanor changed.

"Orion, m' boy!" he cried out in delight. "How be ye?! By the Powers I have missed ye!" He turned to Mystia and said in a voice somewhere between awe and delight, "And ye brought a woman with ye too! And what a woman." He bowed low--no small task when one considered how bent he was already--and said, "Welcome, m' lady. Though ye cover yourself with a veil, still do yar eyes--so dark and radiant--betray a beauty which shines above that o' all other women. The greatest poet in Deithanara could ne'er find words t' give ye half the justice ye deserve. How then can I, a simple man, find words t' describe your beauty?" Suddenly, through some working of magic, he held a dark red rose in his hand. "Please, m' lady, take this as a token o' my esteem, though yar beauty far outshines this simple flower."

"Thank you," Mystia said as she curtsied and took the rose. "Few times if ever have I received such a fair gift." Neither Zenas nor Orion could see that beneath her veil she was laughing silently.

"Tha' is th' greatest compliment I have ever received," Zenas said as he kissed her hand. He could have praised Mystia for hours had not Orion interrupted.

"Zenas," the warrior spoke, "we need your help."

"Anything t' help so beautiful a woman as this," Zenas said.

"This is Princess Mystia of Nor...."

"Your Royal Highness," Zenas said as he bowed even lower than the first time and gave Mystia another rose. "Honored I am by yar presence."

"Princess Mystia is in..." Orion began, but Zenas continued speaking.

"It has always been rumored that ye were the most beautiful woman in Deithanara," Zenas told her, "but I ne'er believed it 'til now."

"Phyre is..." Orion said louder, but still Zenas continued speaking.

"Now I see that what I have heard does ye no credit. Ye truly are..."

"Zenas!" Orion exclaimed. "Please stop this! The Princess is beautiful and none deny it, but this is not the most auspicious time to speak of it! Please, let me continue."

"Ye have m' utmost attention, lad," Zenas said, not turning his eyes from Mystia.

"I have no time to tell you the tale in its entirety," Orion began, "but suffice it to say that the dragon Phyre desires to kill her, and 'tis my duty to see that the he does not have her. I, however, have certain tasks, which I must fulfill without delay. She can't accompany me as I do them, and I need someplace safe for her to..."

"She can stay here," Zenas said, even before Orion had finished his sentence. "By all means let her stay here."

"Thank you," Orion said in relief.

"Yes," Mystia said softly, "thank you."

Zenas turned his eyes from Mystia and looked at Orion. "Will ye be needin' any food?"

"If you have any to give it would be appreciated," Orion answer.

Zenas laughed. "O' course I have food t' give. Especially when ye're th' one I'm givin' it to."

Zenas turned around and began to walk back the way he had come. Orion and Mystia followed, and the old man led them behind the large rock he had come from and into a small room. A cheery fire burned in the fireplace, which had been cut into the rocky wall, and the whole room was lit with flickering oranges and yellows. From a metal hook within the fireplace, hung a large iron pot, in which boiled an unknown substance. Zenas crossed to the larder and pulled out a loaf of bread, some cheese, and some fruit. He then wrapped them all up in a large cloth and gave it, along with a skin filled with water, to Orion.

"I have nothin' t' give Nightfall," Zenas said. "I hope he isna too hungry. I feel bad enough already that he canna even fit through the cavern door, but now I canna give him anythin' t' eat either."

"Those of the griffin race are a hardy folk. Nightfall is able to fend for himself," Orion assured him as he took the napkin of food Zenas held.

"I hope ye're right."

"I regret I can stay no longer, Zenas," said Orion, "but I have much to do and little time in which to do it."

"I quite understand, lad," said Zenas, as he sat down at the table, "and I wish ye the best o' luck." He would have said something more, but he suddenly realized that the contents of his metal pot were boiling over into the fire.

"Confound this bleedin' thing!" he cried as he rushed over to rescue it before any more was lost.

"What a curious man," said Mystia laughingly, as they walked back to Nightfall.

"He is rather absent-minded and no small bit eccentric, Your Highness," admitted Orion, "but he has strong magical powers and great knowledge. Phyre can't enter these mountains, and I think that Zenas is strong enough to protect you from any other enemy which might discover your presence here."

"Thank you, Orion. During the time that you have been with us of Nor you have ever proven yourself to be the best of servants and the greatest of friends."

Orion smiled and bowed his head to her. He could think of nothing to say in reply to such treasured words.

Silently they walked out into the cold mountain air, and silently Orion mounted Nightfall.

Before they could leave, Mystia opened her mouth and spoke again. "Where are you going, and how long will it be until you return?"

"I go first to seek help for Nor from Queen Eagle, and after that I want to return to Nortath's Fury and learn the extent of Nor's defeat," answered Orion. "I know not how long it will take, but I do know that I shall return as soon as I possibly can."

"I wish you luck, Orion, for that is all I can do."

"You are too kind to me, Princess," he told her.

"Nay," she said, "if anything, I am not kind enough."

Then, before he or she could say another word, Nightfall leapt into the air. As they flew away, Orion looked long upon Mystia, and he thought then that there was nothing he would not do for she who was so noble and beautiful.

Chapter 4
Times of Trouble

In times of peace friends abound, but in times of trouble few are found.

--Vallendar

The country of Kerril was not truly a country at all but rather a very large forest. It was ruled by one of the three most powerful people in Lairannare, namely, Tnaka who was one of the two Lesser Powers. He was a wood elf who ruled a kingdom of wood elves, but she who sat at his side upon the throne of the queen was young Eagle of the sky elves. Eagle may have sat upon the throne, but she did not help her husband rule the country. She sat silently and humbly, and let her husband do the ruling, which he did right well.

The night had already fallen upon the forest kingdom when Queen Eagle entered her chambers. She came alone, for she disliked being waited upon.

The main room of her chambers was very plain with a simple, blue carpet upon the floor and a wooden table in the center. There was a large fireplace, and upon the wall there were a few paintings, but, for the room of a queen, it was very un-adorned. When Eagle entered she set silently about lighting the many candles, which rested in various brass holders and wall sconces.

The queen had a very beautiful face, what with her long blonde hair, large gray eyes, soft pink lips, and the small delicate features, typical of the elven races. But, comely, though she was, she was also very sad, and her sadness was made but more pronounced by the fact that she was only nineteen years of age-- a time which should have been filled with joy.

Many a tale was told of the sad, young queen of Kerril--most involved cruelty on the part of her much older husband, necromancy, murder, adultery, and plots of insurrection, but all of which were false in one way or another.

Eagle had just begun to light another of the many candles in her chambers when she heard a sound behind her. She spun around and found herself looking up at a terrifying man with long, wild, auburn hair, armor made of blood-red dragon scales, and eyes like those of a magic beast. She opened her mouth to scream but stopped short when, instead of attacking her, he knelt down before her and said reverently, "Your Majesty."

"Who are you, and what are you doing in my chambers?" Her voice was sharp with fear and her gray eyes were wide, as she backed away from him.

"Men call me 'Orion', Your Majesty," said he as he rose. "Fear not, for I come not to harm you but to seek your aid. I come on behalf of the country of Nor and of Prince Gideone."

She stood still and stared at him, each moment the fear growing less and less until finally, her face was a stony mask of impassivity. She opened her mouth and said coldly, "What mean Gideone and Nor to me?"

"Are you not she who once spoke so boldly against the Powers? And are you not she who was once betrothed to Prince Gideone? And are you not she who, even now, leads a secret group of people in rebellion against the Powers?" answered Orion.

Eagle was silent, as she regarded him closely.

"True it is that I once spoke against the Powers," she finally said, "and true it is that I was once betrothed to Gideone, but what makes you think I lead a rebellion against the Powers? Is not my husband a Power? Perhaps you have been sent by one of my enemies in order that you might find something that would turn my lord against me."

"I have not come from your enemies, Majesty."

"'Tis only a fool who takes a man at his word. Prove to me that you come from Gideone."

"I know that about the Prince's neck there hangs a golden amulet which is in the shape of the feather of an eagle. Inlaid within it is a small diamond. The Prince showed it once to me, saying as he did so that it was you who gave it to him."

She looked upon him unconvinced so Orion continued. "I know also that once, several years ago, in the county of Sha-Lalana, on a night when the moon shone full, you were given a second name by a man who loved you."

She drew a sharp breath but recovered herself and said coolly, "And what was that name?"

"'Honoria', for he who gave it did say you were a woman of honor."

"And if, as he did say, I am a woman of honor why ask you succor of me?" she asked as she turned back to lighting her candles. "For it would be dishonorable of me to aid the enemies of my lord."

"That keeps you not from doing it," replied Orion.

Eagle turned sharply and looked at him. "And how would you know what I do?"

"Since your earliest days in the court of your father word of you has spread throughout Lairannare. There are few who know not that at one time you opposed the Powers.

"Many times have I been sent by Prince Gideone to look upon you and to see if you do well, for the corridors and secrets of Tnaka's palace are not unknown to me. I have watched silently and have learned much, and I am convinced that a woman such as you would not turn her back upon all that she deemed right and honorable simply because her husband had not the same beliefs as she."

She turned away from him and after a moment said coldly and softly, "What have the people of Nor ever done for me that I should lend them aid in their hour of trouble?"

"Is not Prince Gideone the one you love, Majesty?"

"And what did loving him bring me?" she asked as she turned back to him. Her voice was still soft but there was a tinge of anger to it. "Nothing, for how can one who is empty give anything? He spoke of love, but his words were hollow. I promised him my heart, and in return he would not even say a word in protest when I was given to Tnaka. Now he has not even the courage to come to Kerril himself, but sends some servant in his stead. I will not help a spineless dog such as he."

"Prince Gideone is not a spineless dog, Your Majesty," protested Orion. "He is one of the bravest men I have ever met."

"Then you have met precious few men."

"On the contrary, Majesty, I have met many men both great and small." He paused for a moment then continued, saying, "I can but speak for my own actions and know not the reasons for those of others, but I know that Prince Gideone loves you more than words can describe. Perhaps he had some plan by which he had meant to rescue you, but which was defeated before you learned anything of it; I know not, but this I do know: Prince Gideone does love you, for he has said as much to me, and many times have I seen him with his face turned toward the south where he knows you abide."

"What are words and what are looks when no actions spring from them?" asked she bitterly. "I will not help him." She walked to another candle stand, and, as she lit the candle, she said almost as an afterthought, "Even were I desirous to lend him aid, and even had I the means to do so, I could not, for my lord and I shall shortly journey to Jocthreal that we might visit Queen Provenna."

Orion began to speak again, but she cut him off with a voice that only hinted at the despair beneath her cold exterior, "I serve the Powers now. Leave this place quickly, else I shall be forced to call the guards."

"Yes, Your Majesty," said Orion as he bowed. Silently, he turned and left by whatever means it was he had entered.

* * *

"She will not help us," said Orion to Nightfall, when he had rejoined the griffin.

Nightfall glanced about them at the deep shadows of the Forest of Kerril. "Where go we now?" he asked.

"We go to the Caves of Nortath's Fury, for I would see whether the fortress there has fallen. Come," he cast his eyes upward to the sky, "it may be night, but it would be best to leave this place as soon as possible."

They flew for several hours, until they crossed over a wide river, which snaked its way through the forest, at which point they landed and made their camp at the edge of a small glade. Orion set about making a fire as Nightfall prowled throughout the trees in search of food. Orion proved to be far more successful in his venture than was Nightfall in his, and soon they both sat beside a warm fire.

For many minutes they sat there in silence. Orion made no movement to eat or to lie down and sleep. He simply sat and stared into the fire.

After a long moment, Nightfall broke the stillness. "Orion," said the griffin, with his head tilted as it always was when he was about to ask a question, "I know why I eat not, but I do not know why thou dost not."

"I have no stomach for food," answered Orion dully.

Nightfall blinked his large, white eyes and said, "And why hast thou no stomach for food?"

Orion was silent for a moment as he looked mournfully into the fire, but he spoke presently, his voice trembling with anger and sorrow. "What am I to say to the Princess when it comes time to tell her that there are none who will fight to keep her country from falling and her people from being sold into slavery?"

"Thou couldst tell her the truth," answered Nightfall, not knowing what else to say.

"Would that there were another man to tell her, for I wish not to be the one to cause her sorrow."

For a moment he was silent.

Orion's eyes were still turned to the fire, but he seemed to be looking at something very far off. He spoke again, in a very soft, sad, and longing voice, "One as fair and innocent as she should not be made to feel the cold harshness of war or the baseness of men."

"Thou speakest truth," the griffin answered with a sad nod of his head. "Would that it were so, but this land is a dark and imperfect place where that which is just and true doth not always reign." He brightened a little. "One day, 'tis said, the Realms of Deithanara shall be made perfect once again when He who madeth them doth return, but until then we have but the promise that those who chaseth after wickedness shall be banished to Elmorran upon their deaths, while we who do follow after that which is righteous shall enter into Lothiel."

"Lothiel," said Orion with a bitter and angry laugh, but after doing so he became very silent and thoughtful.

"Tell me of this place called Lothiel," said he, after a moment. "Certes you must know more than many, for have you not said yourself your father guards the gates to that place?"

"Yea, have I said so," answered Nightfall, "and, because 'tis thou who dost ask and none other, I shall tell thee that which thou art desirous to know."

His shiny black coat gleamed in the orange glow of the fire, and his croaking eagle voice, rising and falling with a melody all its own, rose through the still and silent night. "Never have I seen it, and never shall I until my death, but my father spaketh once of it to me. It lies not in Deithanara but is indeed outside the Three Realms. 'Tis a place of glory and majesty that no mortal can truly comprehend." And thus did Nightfall begin. It would be impossible to repeat his words. He spoke of a place so beautiful and peaceful and glorious that it made Orion's heart ache with longing, but, throughout the whole time the griffin spoke, Orion would not allow his face to betray any emotion. He sat and stared deeply into the flickering fire, and not once did he move.

He stayed like that for a long time after Nightfall ceased to speak, but finally he raised his eyes to the griffin. He gave a slight smile. It was filled with sadness, and yet it bore also a hint of hope--if only very small.

"'Tis a fair place of which you speak," he said softly, "and it is good that one as noble and beautiful as Princess Mystia will one day abide in a place that is so worthy of her." His eyes returned to the fire, and he smiled that sad yet hopeful smile once again. "And who knows," he continued, "but that I also might one day gaze upon that place." Nightfall could only tilt his head and blink his eyes in confusion, for he dared not ask Orion what he meant by his words.

The warrior said nothing more but silently wrapped himself in a blanket and went to sleep.

The light of the early morning sun shone through the trees and fell upon Orion and Nightfall where they slept, side by side. They awoke presently and silently went about preparing for their departure. Nightfall still asked no questions, and Orion seemed disinclined to speak upon his own.

Soon all was made ready, and Nightfall, with Orion upon his back, once again leapt into the air. They continued on their journey to Nortath's Fury. It was a long flight, and throughout it neither said a word, for both were wrapped in their own silent thoughts.

Twilight was turning to night when they arrived at the Mountains of Shem-Joloch. Concealed by the long shadows of the mountains Orion and the griffin were able to creep up unnoticed to the Caves of Nortath's Fury. In front of the main entrance to the Caves there could be seen two soldiers standing guard, and through the cool night air there drifted the sound of raucous celebrating.

"Wait here," said Orion softly to Nightfall, as he took from out of the packs a dark, gray cloak. He turned and walked silently away.

He did not make his way toward the main entrance of the Caves but instead began to edge around and to the left of it. There were many ways into the Caves of Nortath's Fury, and Orion knew most of them. He was hindered by the shadows, however, and it was only after several minutes and many bruises that he found himself in front of one of those hidden entrances. Silently, he took off his red dragon-scale armor and placed it in a small crevice in the rocks. He put on his long, gray cloak, so as to hide his face beneath its cowl, and, after taking a deep breath, he entered through the small opening and into the darkness beyond.

It was practically impossible for him to see even his hand in front of his face. Fortunately, he knew the Caves of Nortath's Fury well enough to be able to grope his way through the darkness to where he knew an opening to one of the larger caverns was. His journey through the blackness began well enough, but, after he tripped over some rocks, tumbled down a rather steeply slanting incline, and struck his head on a particularly large stalactite, he found himself wishing for a torch to light his way. He had just begun to mutter some rather strong words when he tripped over yet another object which lay across his path. It was during the time that he was saying some more-than-strong words that the thing over which he had tripped began growling words even stronger than the those Orion was saying. It was then that the warrior realized how close he was to his destination.

"Sorry," he whispered to the Delovachian over whom he had tripped. "I meant no harm. Hold your peace."

The Delovachian, however, did not cease his snarls of annoyance and was just in the process of saying something about his armor when Orion tripped over that also. As he fell to the floor, he uttered the strongest word that either he or the Delovachian had said up until that point.

Orion picked himself up, offered a quick word of apology for disarranging the man's armor, then began to once more grope his way forward.

He suddenly stopped and thought for a moment. With one quick motion he turned around, drew his dagger, and stabbed the man in the heart. The only satisfaction the Delovachian could have found from Orion's gesture was that, as he died, he said a word far stronger than anything Orion could have hoped to say.

Orion thought nothing of what he had just done but simply wiped his knife off and re-sheathed it. He then proceeded to put on the Delovachian's armor, methodically adjusting each piece by feel in the darkness of the tunnel. It never even occurred to him to wonder why he had bothered to apologize for tripping over the Delovachian and his armor when, in the next minute, he had returned, killed the Delovachian, and stolen his armor. He merely completed his disguise by picking up the large battle-axe that had lain next to the armor, then continued along the passage.

He ran into only two more stalactites before he reached the entrance to the large cavern, which had been his goal. The light of countless, smoking torches revealed that the cavern was filled with soldiers of Delovachia who were riotously celebrating their slaughter of Nor. All were drunk, and Orion knew he would not learn anything of value from them. As his gaze wandered over the drunken crowd it came to rest upon two soldiers who seemed to be having a serious discussion. One of them was obviously a man of high rank, but Orion could not tell whom or of what rank the other was. Whoever the other was, he appeared to be a Magic of some sort, for he was clothed in a long, flowing black cloak, the cowl of which was drawn up to hide his face. Only his flashing green eyes could be seen.

Orion made his way through the throng so that he could hear what was being said between the two men. As he neared them he heard the cowled man say "...Abiel, the son of King Kozan, and yet you dare question my words, General?"

"But, Highness," said the General who was unfortunate enough to come under Abiel's withering glare, "th' Dark Sorcerer left ye t' lead th' army in his absence, and if he returns and finds ye gone there's no knowin' what his anger'll be."

"And what care I for his anger? He can do nothing to me. I, on the other hand," Abiel added darkly, "can do a great deal to you."

"But, Highness," said the General in one last attempt to change his commander's mind, "I tell ye plainly: Gideone is dead. I was standin' almost right next t' him when ye shot him. I saw him fall."

"But before he fell I saw him fight with a strength and a fury far greater than any Delovachian's, and I saw him being dragged off the battlefield by soldiers who took every precaution to see that he was not struck again. I won't believe that Gideone is dead until I hold his severed head in my hands."

"Very well," returned the General sullenly. Then, seeing that further argument was useless, he turned and sulked off.

Orion turned to go as well.

"You!" cried Abiel as he laid a hand on Orion's shoulder.

"Who? Me?" asked a startled Orion as Abiel spun him around.

"Why are you not getting drunk like everyone else?" demanded Abiel. Orion paused for a few seconds and waited for his mind to catch up with this sudden turn of events.

"Sir," he finally said, "I would not say that they are 'getting drunk', for I would say they are drunk already. So, seeing that they are all ready drunk, I cannot now be 'getting drunk' with them."

Abiel opened his mouth to say something in reply, then stopped. He had been looking intently at Orion and had just caught a glimpse, through the holes in Orion's helmet, of the bright blue of Orion's eyes.

"Orion!" cried he in surprise. He reached out and tried to pull Orion's helmet from his head, but his hands closed upon thin air, for, even as he reached forward, the auburn-haired warrior, suddenly disappeared in a swirl of blue and gold dust. Abiel and the others who had witnessed the sight were left staring in surprise at the empty spot where Orion had stood.

"There is dark magic afoot here," murmured Abiel, frowning, "and methinks it holds but evil for Delovachia."

Despite his grim foreboding, he turned quickly and departed; not even magic of the strangest kind would keep him from taking revenge upon his greatest enemy, Prince Gideone of Nor.

Chapter 5
The Forest of Raia-Torell

And thus spoke Abiel, "Run where you will, Gideone, but you cannot hide. For I swear by the blood of Balor that I will have my revenge."

The morning upon which Gideone awoke was cold and heartless. The sky was gray and overcast, and a cold, relentless mist filled the air. Gideone found himself lying upon the ground surrounded by tall trees that looked gray in the dull light. He took a deep breath and groaned as his chest began to throb with pain.

"Your Highness?" he heard a voice beside him say.

"Stavros?" said he when he saw to whom the voice belonged.

"How feel you, Your Highness?" asked Stavros.

Gideone gave a groan as he remembered all that had happened to him. "I have just fought the worst battle of my whole life. I have seen my father killed, my people slaughtered, the man whom I thought to be my bravest and most trusted servant run in fear, and I myself was shot. I feel wonderful."

"I am sorry, Your Highness."

"You are older than I, Stavros," said Gideone as he struggled to sit up. "Surely by now you must know that is the way of war."

With Stavros' help he was able to finish the process. He looked around slowly and saw Vayan, standing nearby next to three horses.

The Prince placed his hand over his wound and said, "When that arrow pierced me, I thought surely I was a dead man. How is it that I still live?"

There was a moment of troubled silence before Stavros spoke, "In sooth, I know not why, Your Highness, for the arrow which struck you was enchanted and sorely wounded you. It's obvious that there is some type of magic at work here, protecting you, but..." His voice trailed off, and his troubled look told Gideone that there was something important left unsaid.

"What is it?" demanded Gideone.

"Whatever the magic which keeps you alive is, it is slowly being overcome. The spell placed upon the arrow, if not placed by a Power, was placed, at the least, by an arch-mage." Stavros took a breath and continued, "If you find not someone with the power to remove the spell, you will die."

Gideone was silent as the full meaning of Stavros' words sank in.
"I am dying, and none but a Power or an arch-mage can save me?" asked he.
Stavros nodded his head grimly.
"Then I must find an arch-mage," said Gideone, more to himself than to Stavros and Vayan.
"A difficult task, considering all of the arch-mages serve the Powers, and one which would perhaps prove fruitless, considering we know not whether even an arch-mage has the power to heal you," said Stavros, ever the optimist.
"And what would you have me do?" cried Gideone. "Surrender myself to death?"
Stavros said nothing.
There was a brief pause as Gideone turned his options over in his mind. He then spoke, "Tmalion is an arch-mage, perhaps he will save me."
"But, Your Majesty!" cried Stavros. "He's aligned with the Powers!"
"All the arch-mages are aligned with the Powers. Tmalion, at least, was once our ally, and perhaps he'll be moved by pity at the sight of our state and offer us aid."
"More likely, Your Highness, he'll take you and give you over to the Powers," replied Stavros with vehemence. "Out of all who might be able to save you I would trust him the least."
"Who else would you have me turn to?"
Stavros opened his mouth to answer, but Gideone cut him off, saying, "Tmalion may be aligned with the Powers, but perhaps he is not as loyal to them as one might think. Or forget you that I was once to marry his daughter?" He said those last words bitterly and continued, saying, "Stay here if you will, Stavros--I wish not for any man to be forced to accompany me--but I, myself, will journey to the Mountains of Scalavori."
"I f'r one would travel with ye wherever ye go," declared Vayan who had been only a silent spectator up until that point.
Gideone turned to look upon Vayan then cast a sly look back at Stavros and said, "Well, Stavros, it seems that Delovachia can provide me with better servants than can Nor."
"I never said I wouldn't go with you, Your Highness," replied Stavros, "but I think it foolish to hope that we'll ever be allowed to enter Scalavori--elves are a horribly solitary race--and, even if we do, Tmalion is certain to kill me and Vayan and take you captive that you might be given over to the Powers."
"You have the better part of the bargain I would say."
Stavros only sighed in response.
"Well," said Gideone as he rose, "our country has been destroyed, our people slaughtered, I, the heir to the throne of Nor, am mortally wounded, and we are now embarking upon what, most likely, is a suicide mission. I see nothing to keep us from being optimistic."
"I see much," muttered Stavros under his breath. Gideone cast him a look but

merely said, "Come on."

He began to walk toward the horses but stopped and, turning, said, "By the bye, where are we?"

"The Forest of Raia-Torell," answered Stavros as he too walked toward the horses.

Many stories were told of the Forest of Raia-Torell--most of them contradictory. Some would have people believe that the forest was inhabited by the most noble and benevolent of wood elves. Others claimed that the forest was an abode of utter evil. Evil or no, it was a large forest, and Gideone, Stavros, and Vayan could not afford the time it would take to make their way around it so they were forced to go through it.

The day remained cold and wet, and Gideone was right glad that he had not only a warm tunic but a warm cloak as well. It was as he was thinking that that he realized the tunic he wore was not his own. He looked over at Stavros and for the first time noticed that beneath his cloak he wore no tunic.

"Stavros," cried Gideone, "you gave me your tunic."

"I thought it only right, considering 'twas I that tore the one that you wore," answered Stavros.

Gideone could think of no answer save "Thank you," which he said right heartily.

They rode for the whole of the day, and the further they went the more certain did Gideone become that the forest was watching them. It had all the sights and sounds of any normal forest--the trees appeared to be normal and the birds sang as they did in any other forest--but there was a certain air of silent curiosity that pervaded Raia-Torell.

"I dislike this forest," said Stavros grimly.

"'Twas you who brought us first here," replied Gideone.

"Aye, and I'm beginning to wish I had not."

"A forest is a forest; what could it possibly do to us?" continued Gideone, though, not a minute before, he also had been feeling not entirely comfortable beneath the eyes of Raia-Torell.

Their fears, however, seemed unfounded, for they traveled throughout the whole day and not once saw anything seemingly unnatural. Night fell at last, and Gideone was glad, for, though he had spoken not of it, his wound hurt him considerably. They quickly set up their camp then sat down to eat.

As they ate their evening meal, they spoke and jested and laughed, for it was a way to keep their spirits up. Gideone tried to join in--he was not used to letting Stavros, who could be quite humorous when he so chose, tell a funnier story than he--but, though he tried, he did not entirely succeed. Vayan did not seem to notice, but Stavros, who, since the day of the Prince's birth, had been with him, could tell that all was not as well as Gideone would make it appear.

Vayan was chosen to take the first watch, and Stavros and Gideone promptly lay down to go to sleep. Stavros made sure to say a few words about what ill he was sure would befall them during the night, and Gideone, though silently believing every word Stavros said, made sure to say that Stavros was out of his mind.

The forest that night was a grim and eerie place filled with a dark magic that seemed to creep and twist its way through the dark, hidden paths between the trees until it came upon the three men and completely surrounded them. It was in the midst of all this that Gideone slept and dreamed.

He found himself once more upon the high walls of Zaren. The cries of men rose to him, and the stench of blood and death filled the air. The fires of the Dark Sorcerer rose into the sky, and the rain poured down upon all that was there. The Prince looked down upon all the horror laid out before him, and suddenly, as a bolt of lightning tore through the sky, he saw his father kneeling before the Dark Sorcerer.

"No!" Gideone cried as the sword of the Dark Sorcerer fell through the air and cut through his father's body, and then Gideone found himself standing, not upon the battlements, but beside his father's dead body.

His mind screamed for him to awaken, but he could not do so, for the dream was not yet over. He raised his eyes to the sky above, and, as another flash of lightning lit the sky, he could see Orion upon Nightfall fleeing from the battle. He saw Orion turn his head toward him. The warrior's cold, blue eyes were filled with spite, and his mouth was turned up in a cold, cruel smile.

"Coward!" the word fairly screamed itself in Gideone's mind.

Gideone awoke with a start. His heart was pounding. He was covered with sweat, and his wound had begun to ache terribly.

"Highness," said Vayan in concern, "Are ye all right?"

"Yes," answered Gideone, trying to make his voice sound as normal as possible. "I am quite fine." With that he rolled over and tried to fall asleep again.

* * *

On that cold, dark night, fury raged not only in Gideone's dreams: Abiel, the dark prince of Delovachia, sat tall and proud upon his sable charger. A menacing figure made he with his long black cloak whipping in the wind. His face was hidden from view and only his flashing green eyes could be seen beneath his cowl. Before him stood fifteen of Delovachia's finest warriors and Magics.

"It has been said that you are the greatest of all the warriors of Delovachia," said Abiel, anger evident in his voice, "and it has been said that you are the strongest of the magicians of Delovachia." His voice was rising. "Why then know you not where Gideone and the vermin with him are?!"

The fifteen magicians could only hang their heads; for none dared say that Abiel had told them too little for them to know where Gideone had gone.

"Fools!" he fairly screamed. Then, almost as though he were reading their minds, he cried, "They went to the north! What more need you know? I am the son of Kozan; how dare you not do that which I command! I order you--again--bring me the head of the swine Gideone!"

"Now go!" he shrieked when his men did not instantly do his bidding. The fifteen warrior-magicians bowed and galloped off to the north.

* * *

The sun rose, casting it warm light upon Gideone, Stavros, and Vayan. The darkness of the previous night was replaced by the most cheerful of mornings, and in the light of day, Gideone's spirits rose until they were quite high. He made up for his failure the night before to tell a more humorous story than Stavros. Indeed, he made up for it ten times over. One would not have thought that the merry group winding its way through the forest was composed of men fleeing for their lives from a vast and terrible enemy.

Gideone was in the middle of telling about an encounter he once had with a troll when Stavros interrupted.

"You speak of trolls, Your Highness," said he. "Methinks we will shortly meet one face to face."

Gideone turned and looked upon what Stavros spoke of. Before him he saw a river cutting directly through the forest path, over which was a small bridge wide enough for only one man to cross at a time.

"Stavros," said Gideone, "I see a river and a bridge, but I see no troll."

"Bridges over rivers always mean trolls, Your Highness."

"You can smell a troll a mile away. I smell nothing."

"Perhaps he has learned the advantages of bathing, Your Highness." Gideone found the thought of a troll bathing particularly amusing, and he started to laugh.

"Laugh if you will, Your Highness, but I still think a troll is there."

Gideone only laughed some more and dismounted. Stavros and Vayan also dismounted.

"And still think I that there is no troll there," said Gideone as he began to walk to the bridge. He did draw his sword, however.

"We shall see," said Stavros calmly as he leaned against a tree.

When Gideone had reached the middle of the bridge, they did indeed see, for at that moment the largest, ugliest troll that any of the three men had ever seen jumped out from beneath the bridge and opened his mouth in an utterly horrifying roar.

Stavros drew his sword and began to walk toward the beast, and, as he did so, he could not help but notice that, though the troll was very ugly, his fur was quite clean.

"Give me all your gold, and I might let you live," snarled the troll.

"We have no gold," answered Gideone truthfully.

The troll drew back at Gideone's answer, for this problem had never before presented itself. Gideone could only raise his eyebrow in an amused look as he watched the troll's demeanor go from fierce and terrifying to something far less than either.

"Give me all your armor then," growled the troll, as he once more became menacing. Gideone and Stavros looked at each other then turned back to the troll.

"What?" said Gideone with the most incredulous look that anyone could ever have held. "So that we'll be all the easier to roast on a spit?"

The troll drew back again, for he could never before remember having this problem. Most travelers cowered at the mere sight of him and were on their knees begging for mercy at the smallest glimpse of his razor-sharp teeth. Of course, he had been hibernating all winter. Perhaps he was merely out of practice. At any rate, he was quite hungry and was not about to let his first meal of the season slip away.

"Now I have an ultimatum for you," said Gideone as he swung his sword about nonchalantly. "You must either let us pass, or we shall be forced to kill you."

The troll decided that now was the time to put his foot down. He bared his teeth and opened his mouth in the loudest, most terrifying roar that had ever rung throughout Raia-Torell.

Gideone jumped back and barely missed being sliced by the troll's long claws. Stavros and Vayan ran forward. The troll gave another roar and charged toward them. Gideone tried to strike him, but, even as he swung his sword, the troll struck him hard across the head.

With a cry, Gideone tumbled to the ground. For a moment, he could simply lie there and hold his hand to his head. He heard a loud cry followed by a huge splash, and struggling to his knees he saw Vayan bobbing up and down in the river.

He looked over at where Stavros and the troll battled. Blood was streaming from Stavros' arm, but it seemed not to bother him. With a cry he sent his sword slicing through the troll's neck. The troll's head rolled from his neck, and his body fell limp to the ground.

Stavros stood up straight and for a moment simply looked around him, breathing heavily. Catching his breath slightly, he looked down at his wound; it was rather bloody but far from dangerous. He ran his hand over it, and it immediately closed up, leaving only a thin, white scar.

He walked over to where Gideone sat and asked, "Are you uninjured, Your Highness?"

"Stavros," said Gideone, "I have just had my head boxed by a creature who was, at least, two and a half times my weight; of course I'm fine."

Stavros placed his hand on Gideone's head, and held it there for a few moments. When he removed it, Gideone said, "Yes, that is definitely much better. Thank you, Stavros."

"'Tis only my duty, Your Highness."

Almost before he had finished speaking, there could be heard a loud splashing as Vayan tried desperately to pull himself out of the river. Luck, however, seemed not to be with him, for the river was deep and had a strong current, and the rocks were so slippery that, scarcely did he manage to pull himself up, he fell back in again. He made such a comic figure that Gideone and Stavros could not help but laugh.

Stavros made his way over to the river, and, holding out his hand, he said, still laughing, "Come on, son." He hauled Vayan out of the water, and for a moment Vayan could only stand there shivering with his arms crossed as he looked at the still laughing Gideone and Stavros with an expression that was a cross between the indignant and the amused.

They had little time to loiter, however, and quickly started on their way again. Their brief encounter with the troll had raised their spirits even more than they already had been, and nothing that day could lower them. They made excellent headway, all the while laughing and talking, until the sky grew gray then, finally, dark with the coming of night.

* * *

Abiel sat upon his horse beneath the gray sky and looked darkly out over the surrounding countryside. His magicians--fools that they were--had yet to bring him any news of Gideone's whereabouts. The frustration and anger welling within him was almost more than he could bear. He could not let Gideone slip through his fingers.

As he looked out over that which surrounded him, he suddenly became aware of the figure of a dark bird flying in his direction. He was in the midst of contemplating whether he ought to take his frustration out on the creature, when, to his surprise, instead of flying over his head, the bird dove down and landed before him.

"My Lord," said she, spreading her wings and bowing before Abiel, "I hold knowledge which I believe you are desirous also to hold."

"Who are you?" spat Abiel. "And what makes you think you possess knowledge which I desire?"

"My Lord, I am the raven Redeye." (The raven's right eye was indeed red.) "I am a prophetess, and to me has been given the gift to read the minds of men. Know I that you seek Prince Gideone, and know I where he can be found."

"Where?!" demanded Abiel.

"Upon the main path of the Forest of Raia-Torell," she answered simply. Abiel gave a cry that seemed a cross between fury and victory, and he dug his spurs into his horse's sides. His horse reared up then almost trampled Redeye beneath his feet as he shot off toward Raia-Torell.

"Come to me! I know where Gideone hides!" cried Abiel. His words carried across the whole of the surrounding land until they reached the ears of his magicians who turned and spurred their horses on that they might return to their dark prince.

* * *

For Gideone, Stavros, and Vayan the night came on quickly, and they were forced to dismount and make camp. When dinner was over, Gideone rose and declared that he would take the first watch. He had expected Stavros to object on the grounds that he was wounded, but in this he was pleasantly surprised, for Stavros said nothing in objection. In fact, all he did was murmur "Good night, Your Highness", roll over, and fall asleep.

The night was very peaceful, and in the stillness and darkness Gideone found his thoughts turning from his duty of guarding the camp toward all of the things, which had so recently taken place. He had pushed those thoughts to the back of his mind, but now, in the stillness of the night, they came rushing to the forefront. His father was killed, his kingdom destroyed, and his mother and his sister were no doubt taken captive by Kozan.

Well did he remember the day when, seventeen years before, he had gazed upon his newborn sister as she lay sleeping in her cradle. His father, King Ibrahim, had stood next to him and had spoken. "Son, look well upon your sister. Many will hate her, and, princess though she is, few will love or protect her. Help her, guide her, protect her, for she is the Princess of Nor." But he failed in that trust his father had laid upon him, and Mystia, if she was not now dead, lay in the hands of the enemy.

His hand went to his chest and through the cloth of his tunic he could feel the amulet, which hung from a chain around his neck. It brought to mind the other woman he had failed. He did not need to look upon the amulet, for well did he know its features. It was made of the purest of gold, which was beautifully and perfectly wrought into the shape of an eagle's feather, and inlaid in it there was a beautiful diamond, which sparkled in the light. Even better than its form, knew he the features of she who had given it to him--the love of his youth. She also had been lost to him.

He took the amulet out from beneath his tunic and held it up in the light. With the moon and the trees to bare witness he spoke softly. "I swear upon this amulet and by the one whom I love more than any other in Lairannare that I will lose nothing more. I will build another army, and I will regain her and my sister and my country. And if I do not do all which I vow to do may death take me." He brought the golden amulet to his lips, and, after he had kissed it, he hid it once more beneath his tunic.

Even as he leaned back against the tree, a large owl flew through the air and swooped down toward him. He started and jumped to his feet. It caused such a noise with the flapping of its wings that Stavros and Vayan awoke. As Gideone looked at it, it suddenly seemed that it opened its beak and spoke. "Run," it cried. "Run for your life."

Gideone's mouth fell open with astonishment.

"Run for you life," it cried one last time as it faded into the darkness of the forest shadows.

In less than a second Gideone, Stavros, and Vayan were running to the horses and throwing the saddles on them. Gideone forced the bit into his horse's mouth and began to mount, but he was too late, for, even as he did so, the sound of galloping horses could be heard. Through the shadows there could be seen the dark figures of almost a score of riders. They drew up before Gideone, Stavros, and Vayan and held up their swords. Gideone dropped back down to the ground and, drawing his sword, turned to face them.

"Fifteen of them and three of us," said he. "The odds are almost in their favor."

"You always were one to jest, Gideone," said a cloaked figure, scornfully, as he pushed himself to the front of the men. Gideone recognized him immediately.

"And you, Abiel, could not jest if your life depended upon it," replied Gideone with a sneer.

"You dare mock me?" cried Abiel.

"I would hardly call it daring; 'deigning' is a much better word."

"Mock this!" Abiel threw back the hood of his cloak to reveal a terrifying, hideous sight. His whole face was a mass of scars. It was as if his skin had bubbled like boiling water and was then suddenly frozen in that shape. A long, deep, lurid scar stretched from one end of his forehead to the other, and his mouth was perpetually twisted in a hideous grin, the ghastliness of which was only heightened by the evil glint of his green eyes. Beneath his right eye the skin was shriveled and stretched so thin that one could clearly see the bone beneath it.

"'Tis almost an improvement over your former looks," said Gideone when he had finished looking upon Abiel. Stavros could only wince at what he knew was certain to follow an insult such as that.

"You did this to me!" shrieked Abiel. "And by Balor you shall pay!" He motioned with his hand and there sprang up on the ground before him a wide circle of fire. Immediately, everything about it began to also catch fire, save for that which was in the center. The red glow of the dancing flames cast a sinister red light on all which surrounded it.

"Enter into the ring of fire, Gideone," said Abiel, with a look of evil anticipation upon his face, "and let us duel." He drew his sword, jumped down from his horse, and took his place in the fiery ring. The light of the flames played off his twisted features and made him look like some terrible creature risen from the pits of Elmorran.

"Enter into the Circle," he hissed.

Gideone started forward, but he was stopped by Stavros who grabbed him by the arm and said, "No, Your Highness. 'Tis wickedness."

"Unhand me," cried Gideone as he pulled his arm from Stavros' grasp. He once more began to enter the Circle, but, even as he did so, a huge cry broke out from within the forest, and scores of arrows were suddenly shot from the cover of the trees. Abiel screamed in fury at this unexpected attack and ran toward the trees.

He had almost reached them when he was suddenly thrown back by some unseen magic force. He gave a snarl of rage and hurled himself once more toward the trees. He was struck back again with such force that his head struck the ground, and he was knocked unconscious.

"To the trees! To the trees!" unseen voices cried, and Gideone, Stavros, and Vayan did as they were urged.

In the darkness of the forest cover they looked back out, and, in the light of the fire which still burned, they saw the fifteen magicians, sorely pressed by their unseen attackers, pick up their unconscious leader and ride away as quickly as possible.

As the enemy disappeared, the three men turned and looked about them for those who had lent them aid. For a moment all was absolutely still and silent. Then, slowly and with scarcely a rustling of leaves, figures walked out from the darkness of the shadows into the soft light of the moon. Scores and scores of them there were. Their faces were small and delicate, their eyes large and light-colored, and their ears were pointed. The tallest of those people measured only slightly more than five feet. Their long, light-colored hair moved slightly in the soft breeze.

One of them stepped forward. From his long, light brown hair there hung the claws and teeth of a dozen different woodland animals. He looked upon them with eyes that were the lightest, clearest color of blue imaginable. With a voice, though soft, could be clearly heard, he said, "I am Chzaros, king of the elves of Raia-Torell. Welcome to my kingdom."

Chapter 6
The Council of the Three Realms

And this is the law which Joretham set forth: It shall be that when a creature of one Realm wrongs a creature of another Realm the Three Realms shall gather together in council and pass judgment over him who has done wrong.

To be sure, Orion was rather startled to find himself disappearing in a swirling cloud of blue and gold dust, but he was far less surprised than any other man in his situation would have been. In fact, he was not even surprised that it had happened--he had expected it would. He was merely startled at the suddenness with which it had begun.

The same could not be said of Nightfall, who had not expected to suddenly disappear in a swirl of dust, and who was far more than merely startled; he was scared witless. When Orion first set eyes upon him, the fur on the griffin's back was sitting straight up, and his eyes were as wide a those of a cat who had a huge pack of dogs bearing down upon him. He looked wildly about him until his gaze fell upon a rather amused Orion. He suddenly realized that he looked completely foolish, and in less than a second he went from an utterly terrified griffin to one who was calmly preening himself as though he had not a care in the world.

"I say, Orion, where are we?" he asked nonchalantly.

"Why do you not leave off trying to save face and look for yourself?" answered Orion with a slight smile. Even as the warrior spoke, Nightfall looked up, and his eyes instantly grew even wider than they had been when he was terrified, for he found himself in a cavern so immense that it defied description. The ceiling stretched hundreds upon hundreds of feet above the floor, and the walls were every bit as far from each other as was the floor from the ceiling. That alone was enough to stagger the mind of any, but the fact that everything was made entirely of crystal added to the beauty and magnificence so much that one thought they were in a dream.

Every single piece of crystal pulsated with an inner fire, which cast a faint, red light upon all that surrounded them. The magic of the place was indescribably strong. Indeed, it was so strong that Nightfall knew the place in which he stood could not be of the Realm of Earth.

"The Crystal Caves," he whispered in awe.

There was not one creature of Deithanara who had not heard of the legendary

Crystal Caves, for they were the place in which the Fire of Magic burned and where he who had once been the King of Keiliornare lived. It was a place that Nightfall had never dreamed of ever seeing.

"A beautiful sight is it not?" Orion asked.

"Yea, it is," breathed the griffin in awe.

For a long moment the two simply stood there and looked upon all which was about them.

"Are ye finished gazing?" a rich, deep voice suddenly asked, interrupting their reverie.

Nightfall started and turned quickly, but he found himself unable to see who it was that had spoken. Even Orion, who knew what it was he searched for, was hard pressed to find the source of the voice.

Finally, Nightfall was able to discern whom it was that had spoken. Curled up in the corner, there rested a dragon who was formed entirely of crystal. He was immense; his foreclaws alone stretched greater than six feet. He gazed down at them with large, unblinking, blue eyes. For a moment, the griffin could only look in amazement at how blue the dragon's eyes were, and then, in disbelief, he turned and looked at Orion's. He cocked his head, blinked his large, white eyes, and turned back to the dragon who gave a rich deep laugh at Nightfall's shocked expression, then turned to Orion and said, "Orion, thou wert ever a scoundrel and a fool-hardy scoundrel at that, but it seemeth that thou hast entered into an extraordinary amount of trouble even for thyself these last few days."

"War has a way of making that happen, Lyght," answered Orion.

The dragon opened his mouth to reply but was interrupted by Nightfall's amazed cry of, "Thou art Lyght?"

The great dragon turned and looked at him and said, "Yea, I am Lyght, but I know not what thy name is. Please, enlighten me."

Nightfall bowed low before Lyght then began to speak quickly, "Lord, honored am I that one as noble and exalted as thou shouldst ask of me, lowly griffin that I am, my name." He nodded his head in a short bow. "I am called 'Nightfall'." He ended by bowing even lower than he had at the start and staying in that position.

"Nightfall," repeated Lyght. "Thou art the son of Elavorn the white griffin."

The griffin straightened. "Yea, I am."

"'Tis good that one such as thou shouldst keep company with my son."

"Thy son?!" Nightfall cried in surprise. Orion remained still and silent.

"Find thee that so strange?" asked Lyght of the griffin.

"Exceedingly strange!"

Lyght laughed again and said, "'Tis a strange place in which we live. Perhaps thou shouldst stand by thyself and ponder that further, for I would speak privately with my son."

"Y-y-yes, my lord," stuttered Nightfall, who then bowed once more, and ran quickly toward the far end of the vast, crystal cavern.

Lyght lowered his head so that he could better look upon Orion and said in a soft voice that Nightfall could not discern, "Orion, thou hast caused for thyself much trouble. Phyre already hated thee, and now thou hast caused his anger to wax so great that he will not be satisfied until thou art destroyed."

For a long moment Orion could not answer but only stood there with his hands clenched as he stared at the floor.

"I know," he finally answered--nothing could hide the despair and fear in his voice, "but what was I to do? Was I to simply stand by and allow Phyre to murder the Princess whom I have sworn to serve?"

"Curse that woman!" growled Lyght in anger. "And curse the day thou didst swear to defend her, for she hath brought thee nothing save trouble!"

"How can you say that?" cried Orion, forgetting his fear. "'Tis not the Princess' fault that this has happened but Phyre's, for 'tis he who seeks her life."

"Think thee not that this princess hath given Phyre a reason to desire her death?"

"Of course she's given Phyre a reason to desire her death, for she is the most beautiful, noble, virtuous woman who has ever walked the face of Lairannare; she is everything Phyre hates." His voice was filled with anger and despair.

Lyght was silent for a long moment. Then he spoke, saying, "If this woman is as virtuous as thou dost claim why dost thou not simply allow Phyre to have her. What harm will come from it? For she will die and enter into Lothiel, and Phyre will be appeased."

"What?!" cried Orion. "You would have me be a party to murder?"

"I would only have thee save thine own life," answered Lyght angrily. "For no matter what thou doest this woman will die. Thou mayest either stand aside and allow Phyre to have her, or Phyre will kill thee and then take her. I for one would have thee follow that first path, for at least thou shalt then live."

"But how can you..." Orion began.

"Orion!" Lyght silenced him. "Dost thou truly hold this woman so high that thou wouldst give thy very life for her? Thou and I know how great a price that is; is she worthy of that?"

For a very long moment Orion could only look upon the floor as he wrestled silently with himself. His jaw was clenched, and his hands were balled into fists. His whole body seemed to tremble slightly.

Finally, he slowly raised his head and said with a voice of agony, "I cannot renounce her. I..." he could find no words to express that which he thought and felt so deeply and could only repeat, at length and almost to himself, "...cannot renounce her."

"Then so be it," answered Lyght.

* * *

Mystia stood outside in the cool mountain air and looked up into the sky as it turned from pink to purple to black. She was glad to have a moment of solitude, for, though she had found Zenas to be as kind and courteous as any man could be, his continuous words in praise of her great beauty had grown rather tiresome. She smiled silently at the thought of him.

It was good that Orion had brought her to that place, for it was peaceful. It was a place that offered the solace needed to heal the scars brought on by war, yet, comforting though it was, Mystia longed for the time when Orion would return and take her back to her people. Her thoughts were turned ever toward him, and at that moment she desired so very greatly to know where he was and how he fared.

* * *

Orion stood in the meeting place of the Council of the Three Realms. His glittering, crystal sword was strapped to his side. He wore a new tunic of fine red cloth, and over this he wore his red, dragon-scale armor, which Lyght had transferred along with Orion and Nightfall to the Crystal Caves. Orion's auburn hair flowed freely over his broad shoulders, and around his head was a thin circlet of fine crystal. His arms were crossed and his feet planted firmly apart. He looked to be the proudest, most noble man in the whole of Deithanara.

It was a beautiful place in which he stood--a wide and open glade surrounded by very tall and stately trees, which seemed to sparkle with gold and silver when struck by the light. Overhead, the black sky was filled with a myriad sparkling stars all reflected in a large, circular pool of water in the very center of the glade. Placed at regular intervals along the edge of the meeting place were large, clear, crystal stones which glowed with the same inner fire as did the stones in the Crystal Caves. The air of the place hung heavy with the most powerful of magic.

To Orion's right stood every manner of creature. Each seemed to be a legend sprung from the pages of lore, for they were all creatures of the Realm of Magic. At the forefront stood the three Powers of the Realm of Magic. The supreme of these was the Greater Power Haunnar, a gargoyle, sinewy of body and proud--though noble--and grim of face. Beside him stood the two Lesser Powers, the gargoyle Ranaush and the dryad woman Ramainyne.

To Orion's left there stood a great crowd of creatures of the Realm of the Heavens--afrits, incubi, ghouls, poltergeists, fiends, and many other creatures both dark and terrible--and before them stood a huge dragon whose scales where made entirely of the purest crystal and whose innards swirled with a great cloud of blackness. She was Nyght, Queen of the Realm of the Heavens.

Both those of the Realm of Magic and those of the Realm of the Heavens were gathered there, but of the Realm of Earth not a single representative was present, for Provenna the Greater Power hated the Council and, after having once appeared before it, declared that the Powers of Lairannare would never again have anything to do with it.

"Where is the accuser?" asked Nyght when she had looked about and found him not. "Where is he who hath caused this great Council to be gathered together?"

Even as she spoke, there appeared in the middle of that vast meeting place a swirling cloud of sparkling red and gold dust. All the creatures there scattered as Phyre appeared, spun around in a circle, and hissed menacingly at all who were gathered there. There was along the length of his body a scar caused by the liquid crystal, which had welled up and hardened over the wound Orion had dealt him. The same had also happened to the wound upon his head.

He turned his eyes to Orion who stood calmly by, and as his gaze fell upon the red dragon-scale armor Orion wore he shrieked, "Murderer! Killer of my daughter!" He charged toward Orion. "I swear thou shalt die!" Nightfall jumped one way, and Orion jumped the other way, drawing his sword as he did so. Lyght gave a low, menacing growl and sprang to meet Phyre.

"Stop!" bellowed the gargoyle Haunnar. "Is this not a sacred place? How dare you profane it with thoughts of murder. Now take your place or leave, but fight no more."

"He murdered my daughter, desecrated her body, and now he has the insolence to wear her scales in front of me!" screamed Phyre. "I want justice!"

"Justice has been done!" declared Haunnar roughly. "Your daughter deserved her fate, and I would suggest that you quietly take your place, or you shall be joining her."

For a moment Phyre could only stand trembling with rage, but slowly his anger left him and was replaced with a look of pride.

"No matter," he spat at Orion as he turned to take his place, "thou shalt soon be mine."

"If I were you, Phyre, I would not speak so rashly to one who possesses greater magic than do you," warned Orion. "Or do you forget that I am the prince of the Realm of Magic and that my power is greater than is yours? In the Realm of Earth I cannot use it, but here, where the three Realms meet, I am entirely capable of wielding it." He spoke softly, but behind his eyes there burned the anger and the hatred of a deadly beast.

"We shall see, little man; we shall see," answered Phyre softly and menacingly. He turned to the assembly and, raising his voice, spoke. "People of this Council, listen to my words. There is in Deithanara a race of people. To those of Lairannare they are known as 'High Elves'. To those of Keiliornare they are known as 'Noble Fairies'. To those of Bellunare they are known as 'Arch Fiends'. And they themselves taketh as their name 'Shallee'.

"Ye know how, in days of yore, these people rebelled against Joretham, and ye know how Joretham cast them down from their lofty position and made them to wander as outcasts throughout Deithanara. Ye know how these High Elven people were ever thorns in our flesh, and ye know how the agony and strife they caused culminated in the great wars in which millions of us--the people of Deithanara who had not rebelled and whom Joretham had not cast out--were slaughtered without mercy."

A murmur of anger at wounds which few there had ever felt and memories, which almost none truly possessed but which had been handed down from generation to generation over the many centuries, filled the starlit meeting place. Spurred on by this, Phyre continued, with even greater boldness of spirit and strength of word. "Remember ye not how, when the great wars were over and we gazed upon the barrenness that surrounded us, we declared that never again would the High Elves be allowed to wax great? Nay! We swore by the Heavens and the Earth and by Magic that we would hunt down the High Elves and destroy them completely."

The creatures there lifted up their voices in a cry of triumph, and as Orion saw them rejoicing over deeds they had not done--indeed, deeds they had not even seen--anger filled him, and he cried out, saying, "Lying serpent! How dare you profane this place with your words!"

"Speak not, little man," snarled Phyre as he turned upon Orion, "thou who dost break the ancient law and serve High Elven filth."

A gasp of surprise and horror escaped from the assembly, and Lyght looked in shock upon his son and hissed, "Mystia is a Shallean?"

Orion did not hear his father or the assembly. His blue eyes flashed with fury, and his whole body trembled as he looked upon Phyre and said slowly and softly, "She is not filth."

* * *

The night had entirely overtaken the Mountains of Lathinor, and the stars and their pale mistress lighted the sky with all their spectral glory and sent the mountains into sharp contrasts of darkness and light. The wind blew strong and cool. It was a night that could have sent one running back in dread to cower in their house, or it could have sent one running madly with the wind at their back for the pure joy of it.

It was not the first feeling but the second, which took hold of Mystia's heart. She took a step toward the edge of the outcropping of rock upon which she stood then another. The wind swirled madly about her. She took another step and another and another, until, finally, she stood at the very edge of the rock outcropping, and there she stood with arms outstretched and face lifted to the sky as the wind swirled around her and sent her dress and her veil and her long, flowing black hair dancing madly to its song. For one moment every care lifted itself from her heart, and she was free.

* * *

Phyre gave a terrifying roar and drew back a clawed forefoot to strike Orion a blow from which he would never recover. Even as Orion jumped out of the way, Phyre was thrown backward to the ground.

"Be still, dragon," said Haunnar whose eyes seemed almost to glow with the magic he had just put forth, "for now is not the time for killing."

"But Mystia is of the Shallee," growled Phyre, "and Orion doth deserve to die for serving her."

"That remains to be seen," answered Haunnar roughly. "Now get you back to your place."

Phyre gave a hissing snarl and took his place once more.

"She is of the Shallee?" Lyght whispered in horror again to his son. Orion did not answer but simply turned and gave Lyght a look that fairly challenged him to speak further. The crystal dragon became silent, but it was clear he burned with anger.

"Great kings and queens, lords and ladies," came a voice, "may I be allowed to speak?"

All eyes turned to where the voice had come from, and their gaze fell upon the figure of a griffin. She was young and sleek and obviously very strong. Her fur and feathers were as red as blood, and she looked up with eyes as dark as night upon those gathered there.

"Speak, child," said Haunnar.

"Great and noble rulers," said she, "I am young 'tis true, but I pray that will not keep ye from listening to my words. Ask I ye this: are truth and wisdom to be spoken by none save the aged?

"'Glorious Dawn' am I called, and I am the daughter of she who doth guard the gates of Elmorran. Many people enter into that place--elves, humans, fairies, incubi, Shallee... Elmorran's eyes are blind to everything save whether a person believeth in and serveth Joretham. Nightfall," said she as she turned to the black griffin, "thy father doth guard the gates of Lothiel. Is it not true that as all races enter into Elmorran so also do all races, including the Shallee, enter into Lothiel?"

"Yea, it is true," answered Nightfall.

Glorious Dawn turned back to the assembly of creatures and, raising her voice, continued, saying, "Ye people of this great assembly tell me if in death the Shallee are thine equal why so not also in life? Who hath given ye the right to say that an entire race and any who dare look kindly upon it should be murdered?"

"Fool! Cur!" snarled Phyre. "What knowest thou? Thou didst not see them descend like wild beast upon thy home! Thou didst not see the ground turned red with the blood of thy slaughtered brothers and comrades! Thou didst not see the whole of Deithanara laid waste! What right dost thou have to speak on behalf of the High Elves?!" His voice had been ever rising, until, he practically screamed his last words.

The red griffin cowered beneath the fury of his words, but she refused to allow herself to run in fear. She drew herself up and, in defiance, snarled, "Who hath made thee judge?" She turned to the creatures gathered there, and her voice, filled with passion, rang throughout the meeting place. "People, why listen ye to the lies this serpent doth tell ye? Fear ye the truth, or do ye not know it?

"Lyght," tears were pouring from her eyes as she turned to the great crystal dragon and implored him, saying, "thou wert there at the dawn of history. Tell them how not only the Shallee but all the races of Deithanara rebelled against Joretham. Tell them how, upon that great and terrible day, Joretham did curse that which he had created. Tell them how Deithanara itself was torn asunder. For they will not listen to me, but perchance they will to thee."

The great crystal dragon stood with his head bowed and did not answer. Glorious Dawn could only stare in brokenhearted disbelief at him.

"See ye?" cried Phyre to those gathered there. "By his silence, he doth proclaim that my words are true."

"No!" shrieked Glorious Dawn.

"The High Elves are evil and deserving of death!"

"No!"

"They must be destroyed completely!"

"No!" the red griffin's scream rose above Phyre's voice for one moment then was lost amid the cheering cry which rose from the lips of the hundreds of creatures assembled there.

"As must those who loveth the High Elves," added Phyre as he turned slowly and menacingly toward the red griffin. His words had not risen above the cries of the creatures, and Glorious Dawn had but the slightest of warnings before he drew back his great clawed forefoot and sent it crashing down upon her. She jumped to the side but did not entirely escape the blow, and one of her hind legs was crushed beneath his claw.

"No!" shrieked Nightfall as he leapt into the air and sped toward the fallen Glorious Dawn. He stood over her and stared up at Phyre, with wide, unblinking, white eyes, which were filled with hatred. He gave a low growl. Phyre gave a terrible hiss and drew back his forefoot, but, even as he drew it back, Orion's voice rang out, as he cried, "Phyre, strike him and you'll die!" Phyre gave a roar of fury as he spun to face Orion.

* * *

The night, so terrible and beautiful, was filled with the wild and mystic song of the wind shrieking through the Mountains of Lathinor. Mystia had never felt as free as she did in that moment as she stood with arms outstretched and empty space beneath her.

Suddenly, with no warning, she was pulled from the edge of the cliff and held in a tight grasp. "Hello, Princess," a man said mockingly.

She screamed and in terror wrenched herself from his hands. She turned and found herself facing a man clothed entirely in the blackest armor. He looked upon her with cold brown eyes that betrayed no sympathy. For a long moment neither he nor she said anything but simply looked upon each other as the wind whipped around them.

* * *

Phyre's terrifying roar died away and left all the common creatures trembling in its wake.

"Thou darest threaten me?!" he spat. "I am not the one who hath broken the law of the Three Realms! I am not the one who doth consort with High Elves! I am not the one who doth even now affront this sacred Council by wearing about my neck the soul stone of a High Elf!"

At his words a great murmur spread throughout the crowd and every creature gathered there strained his neck to see if what Phyre claimed was true. Orion's hand flew to his chest where he felt the cold, hard form of Mystia's ring beneath his tunic. He could only look up in amazement upon the fiery dragon, for how did he know Mystia's stone hung from his neck?

"Fool!" spat Phyre, seeing Orion's shocked look. "'Twas I who tore her soul apart to begin with! Think thee not that I would know where it is?"

"Beast!" cried Orion as he drew his sword.

"Is this true what Phyre doth say?" demanded Nyght, the great dark dragon, before either Orion or Phyre could say anything more.

"And what if it is?" snarled Orion.

"Then thou dost admit it!" cried Phyre, before any others could speak.

"What is there to admit?" Orion demanded as he turned angrily upon Phyre and pulled the ring out from beneath his tunic. "Of course I wear it!"

A great cry went up as the crowd recoiled in revulsion.

"Then thou must die!" Phyre spat.

* * *

High within the Mountains of Lathinor, as the wind blew with tremendous force, the full terror of the night took hold of Mystia's heart, and she screamed with a fear she had never felt before.

* * *

The beast-like look in Orion's eyes waxed ever brighter as his anger burned hotter and hotter.

"Who are you to claim that I must die?!" he snarled with a malice to match Phyre's. "I am not the one who has brought death and suffering wherever I go! I am not the one who is the chief of all the sinners in the Three Realms!"

* * *

Mystia ran in terror towards the entrance of the cave, as the wind blew ever stronger.

* * *

"Thou hast knowingly and willingly served a High Elf!" shrieked Phyre. "And thou hast dared profane this sacred place with a High Elven soul stone!"

"She is not even a full Shallean!" cried Orion as his whole body trembled with an anger that he still fought to hold back.

"And, as for this stone, Princess Mystia gave it to me, and I will wear it proudly wherever I go!"

There came a great uproar from the creatures gathered there.

"Hear ye that?!" shrieked Phyre.

* * *

Zenas appeared at the door of the cavern and blocked Mystia's way.

"Let me in!" she cried. "Let me in!" But he stood in her path and would not let her pass.

In pain Mystia fell to the ground as she was struck from behind by the magic of the sable man.

"Zenas, how could you?" she whispered as she lay upon the ground.

Zenas merely stood above her and looked down with no emotion in his face.

* * *

"So thou dost serve this High Elven woman, and dost wear her favor?!" cried Phyre.

"And what of it?!" cried Orion in defiance.

"So thou dost admit to cherishing this woman?!"

* * *

The sable man picked Mystia up from where she lay helpless upon the ground, turned to Zenas, and said, "Your debt is paid. Live in peace."

"Demon," Mystia hissed at the old man.

He said nothing in return but only looked at her with unfeeling eyes.

* * *

"Yes, it was Princess Mystia who gave me this stone, and, yes, I do protect her, and, if you call 'serving' 'cherishing', then, yes, I do cherish her willingly and wholeheartedly."

"Then you must die!" shrieked Phyre, and the vast crowd of creatures gathered there began to chant, "Death! Death! Death!" over and over and over again.

* * *

Zenas turned his back upon the Princess and her captor, but in his mind echoed Mystia's word of demon, demon, demon. Over and over and over it echoed.

* * *

The cries of death grew louder and louder until Orion could stand it no longer. He lifted up his voice in a cry unlike anything a human should have been capable of uttering. It rose above the cries of the creatures gathered there and made them all stop with the pure fury it contained. Orion was left standing there, looking more like a beast than the many other creatures gathered there-- with his specter eyes flashing with a fury no human could hold.

"Look to yourself before passing judgment on me!" he snarled, and the fury of his voice sent many of the creatures scurrying away in fear.

"Today in the Council of the Three Realms we have heard lies the like of which have never seen their equal, but none save a griffin child have been able to answer them!" he cried. "And why is that?! It's because Phyre," and with that he pointed an accusing finger at the dragon, "has lied and killed and ever worked to destroy the knowledge of the people of Deithanara so that, when all has been forgotten, he might reign over the Three Realms! Already has he..."

"Lies!" hissed Phyre in rage. "They are all lies!"

"It is the truth!" cried Orion. "It was you who made war with the Shallee so that you could gain more power than you already possessed! And..."

"I fought that war so that the perfection which Joretham created might not be destroyed!"

"And it is you again who has started this war so that you may regain you lost power!" Orion continued. "You..."

With a great shriek Phyre drew back his great clawed forefoot and swung it at Orion, but the warrior jumped back out of the way and was not struck.

* * *

Mystia, her hands tied tightly in front of her, struggled desperately against the Sorcerer, as he dragged her roughly after him, across the rocky ledge. She yanked with all her might, then gave a cry as she pulled herself from him and went tumbling to the ground.

Slowly, she began to sit up, but, as she raised her head, she stopped moving and a gasp escaped her lips. Before her stood two fearsome black horses--tall and sleek, each with a pair of large, black wings. Their eyes burned with fire, and they looked more like creatures of the Heavens than creatures of the Earth.

* * *

"How dare you try to strike me!" cried Orion. "You cause hatred, strife, and blood wherever you go and now you dare even profane this place! You will die for your insolence!"

He was like one possessed by the spirit of a madman as he turned upon Phyre and cried out words in a strange tongue. His sword glowed with magic fury and his eyes seemed to spark fire. Phyre gave a hissing growl.

* * *

The Dark Sorcerer placed Mystia upon one of the horses and mounted the other. The horses spread their wings and leapt into the air.

The wind seemed to whisper, "demon, demon, demon," as Zenas stood and watched them disappear from sight.

* * *

Phyre slowly backed away in terror from Orion as Orion continued to chant.

* * *

"Demon, demon, demon," whispered the wind.

* * *

Lyght looked down upon his son and knew not what to do.

* * *

Zenas spat in defiance and returned to his cave.

* * *

Phyre stood cowering against the wall, as Orion's chant grew louder and louder. Finally, with a shriek of hatred and terror the great, fiery dragon disappeared in a swirl of red and gold dust a second before Orion's spell was completed.

Orion stopped short and, for a moment all the creatures gathered there simply stared at where Phyre had last stood.

"The accuser is gone," said Haunnar simply. "The Council is ended." With that all of the creatures gathered there began to disappear in swirling clouds of sparkling dust until none save Orion, Lyght, and Nightfall were left.

Lyght, his eyes flashing, turned toward Orion and cried in fury, "Why didst thou not tell me she was a Shallean?"

"Why think you I didn't tell you?" answered Orion angrily. "The Princess is hated by enough people, and I wished not to add you to their number."

Lyght, not even hearing Orion's words, continued, crying, "How canst thou simply turn thy back upon the law of Deithanara and serve this unholy woman?!"

"Why should I heed the law of Deithanara?" snarled Orion. "What has it done for me save tell me I am a wretched man filled with unrighteousness? I will not turn my back upon the only honorable creature I have ever known simply because the law tells me I should!"

"Orion! Dost thou forget whom it was who saved thy life when thou wert but a babe? Thou wert to be killed, but I made thee my son and delivered thee from death; for that was I cast down from my place as King of the Realm of Magic. And how dost thou repay me for my sacrifice but by serving a woman of the Shallee!"

"Lyght," started Orion. His anger began to disappear, leaving in its stead only sorrow at the unfairness of all that had happened, "all my life I have been told to live honorably. True, the meaning of 'honorable' changed with each person who told me to live thus, but the message was still the same. I did not live honorably, for there was no reason for me to do so. But now I have a reason. Now I live as you wished me to live, but, now that I do so, you no longer want me to be thus.

"I see not why you grow angry at me for serving this woman. You were once the King of the Realm of Magic; there were none greater than you, yet you sacrificed your position and the power it held so that you might save me. Princess Mystia is hated, her life is sought, and there are none to protect her save me. Why is what I do for her so different from what you once did for me?"

"But she is a Shallean!" cried Lyght, his voice filled with despair and anger. "How canst thou give up thy life for a Shallean?"

"To you she is a thing to be hated, but to me she is a goddess," answered Orion stormily.

His voice became, once again, filled with despondence as he said. "Why do you hate the Shallee so? They are no more evil than any other creatures in Deithanara. Why do you wish them all dead?"

Lyght looked down upon his son then turned his head away and said softly, "Whether they live or die I care not, but I wish to have no more dealings with them." He was silent for a moment, and then continued, sorrow in his voice.

"We are all caught up in a tapestry woven of conflicting powers and passions, and my thread hath crossed that of the Shallee far too many times. Follow this woman; give thy life for hers, but ask not of me my acceptance."
He turned his back to Orion and said very softly, "Now go."
He gave Orion no chance to speak but immediately transported him and Nightfall back to the Realm of Earth. As they disappeared in the swirling blue and gold dust Lyght whispered, "Thy goddess is in danger."
Orion and Nightfall found themselves standing outside the Cave's of Nortath's Fury.
"My goddess is in danger?" repeated Orion. In horror he turned to Nightfall as he suddenly realized what his father had meant.

The night was filled with a beauty that few who lived then would ever see again, but Orion cared nothing for it. His heart was pounding as he jumped upon Nightfall's back, and Nightfall jumped into the sky. They sped through the night faster than one would have thought possible, but still it was not fast enough for Orion. With each passing moment his fear for Mystia waxed greater and greater until it threatened to overcome him.
The hours it took to cross the vast expanse between the Mountains of Shem-Joloch and the Mountains of Lathinor seemed to last a century and no amount of urging on Orion's part would make them pass any quicker. He found himself cursing every second of that journey, until finally he and Nightfall arrived at the Mountains of Lathinor.
Even before Nightfall had fully lighted upon the ground, Orion had jumped off and drawn his sword--the crystal blade shone strangely in the pale light of the moon--and had begun to walk toward the waterfall. With his sword held ready he walked quickly into the cave, but, though he expected someone to attack him, there was no one there.
"Zenas?!" he called, "Princess Mystia?!" But there came no reply.
With each step toward Zenas' cave, the dread of what he might find there grew until his foreboding became so great that he had to stop just before he rounded the large rock which lay beside the door to Zenas' cave. It was during the second when he paused outside the entrance to Zenas' cave that he heard Nightfall shriek in anger and fury. Orion spun and began to run back to Nightfall, but as he reached the cave entrance he found his way barred by two men with drawn swords. He gave a great cry of fury and hatred as he realized what was happening.
Faster than one would have thought possible he sent his sword slicing down through one man's neck and through the other's arm. He heard a noise behind him, and he turned--not bothering to finished the second man--and faced those who stood behind him. He swung and, though one of the men held his sword up to ward off the blow, Orion's sword cut right through it and deep into the man's flesh. More men began to pour through the entrance into the cavern, but Orion

was filled with the blind wrath of a dragon thirsty for blood. Some fled at the very sight of him, others ran at his savage war cry, and those who dared stand and oppose him were cut down with no mercy.

Orion exploded through the cavern entrance. Nightfall, caught in a large net, lay on the ground. Above him stood a man with a sword held to his neck. Nightfall struggled with all the magic within him, but the man who stood above him held him back with a stronger power.

"Drop your sword or the griffin dies!" the man ordered.

"Drop yours, or I'll make you eat your tongue as I tear your stomach from your body!" snarled Orion, with such hatred that the man was taken aback and for one moment wavered, but one second was all that Nightfall needed. With a shrieking cry and a great blast of fiery magic, he broke his bonds and sent all the men who were there flying either back against the side of the mountain or over the edge of the cliff into the emptiness below. The man who had stood above him screamed in pain as the griffin dug his claws into his face and chest. Orion ran back to Zenas' cave as fast as he could go.

"Princess?!" he cried. Only Zenas was there. He looked up in terror upon Orion and suddenly turned and tried to flee.

"Where is she?!" the warrior shouted as he grabbed Zenas and threw him against the wall. The old man fell crashing to the floor and did not rise.

"What did you do with her?!" Orion screamed. It was a wonder that in his rage he did not simply cut the old man in two.

Zenas tried to rise, but he was overcome with a fit of coughing, and he fell once more to the floor.

"Where is she?" Orion demanded, and, though his voice was soft, there was more hatred and menace in it than there had been when his voice was raised.

"I told Kozan tha' she was here," Zenas answered between his coughs. "Th' Dark Sorcerer came abou' sunset an' took har an' left these men t' capture you. They should soon reach Nolhol."

Orion gave a cry of rage and despair, and, throwing the old man into the wall, ran from the cavern. Nightfall, his claws and beak dripping the blood of his enemies whom he was devouring, raised his head from his bloody meal and looked upon Orion's face. Orion, filled with anger, looked wildly about him, but it was doubtful he saw a thing. There in the darkness of the night, with the moon and stars overhead, he raised up his voice and cried with all the fury within him, "Joretham, I curse you!" He fell to the ground and in anguish cried once again, "Joretham, I curse you."

Chapter 7
City of Darkness

"Nolhol shall not always be dark and filled with evil, for one day I shall return in power and destroy he who does now sit upon my throne, and I shall reclaim that which is rightfully mine." So once did Darus, rightful king of Delovachia, declare.

The dark horses of Mystia's captor--ever turned toward Delovachia and the terrible city of Nolhol--galloped like the wind. The Dark Sorcerer had only allowed them to fly that they might escape Lathinor; after that, he had made them run. Why he had done so Mystia neither knew nor cared. Her breast heaved with great, silent sobs of anguish, and she turned to cast one more look upon the mountains she had been taken from. Even as she turned, her captor spoke in his strange, foreign voice, saying, "Bother not to look behind you, for you shall not see the mountains. These horses, which Kozan himself gave me, are of the line of Daemielle and long ago left Lathinor behind them." Mystia looked nonetheless and found it to be exactly as he said; there was no sign of Lathinor.

With another sob, she turned her face once more to the north. The countryside flew by as she stared down at the mane of her horse and tried not to burst into tears. The minutes passed, and slowly she regained her composure.

"Who are you who are so great as to merit such steeds as these?" she asked softly.

He turned to her and with a sneer said, "I am the Dark Sorcerer, the greatest and most powerful of all Kozan's warriors and Magics." At his words, fear welled up within Mystia's heart, and she turned her face from him so that she would not see his dark and terrible eyes gazing down upon her.

For many hours they rode, and, as the time passed, Mystia's terror grew until it seemed she could feel nothing else; she was so weary that she had not the strength to combat it.

It was the time of night just before dawn, when all was yet dark, that the horses climbed to the top of a very large hill, and Mystia and the Dark Sorcerer, looking down, saw Nolhol stretched out before them.

The dark city lay spread out for mile upon mile of rolling hills. Its tall, black towers rose high into the dark night sky, and, upon the highest of the hills, the terrible temple of Balor loomed over the rest of the city. It stood ominously black against the horizon with naught behind it save the silver moon and the sea, which lay at the foot of the tall cliff upon which Nolhol was built.

"Welcome to Nolhol, Mystia," sneered the Dark Sorcerer.

Mystia choked back another sob and closed her eyes that she would not have to gaze upon the terrifying place. Never had she felt such fear as that which gripped her tighter with every step her horse took toward that city of evil. She bowed her head and tried to keep from breaking down, but a single teardrop escaped. It glistened for one moment in the light of the silver moon, then rolled down her cheek and was gone.

The road leading up to Nolhol was terrible to behold. The men of Morannah had, as had Nor, risen up against Kozan, and, forming a great army, they had marched against the city of Nolhol. Kozan slaughtered them mercilessly, and, as one final act of savagery, caused both the dead and the living to be impaled and set up around his dark city.

The road was lined on either side with thousands upon thousands of bloody and rotting bodies. The stench was almost overpowering. The skin of some had been torn from their skulls to reveal the bloody bone beneath. Their faces were contorted into expressions of the most horrible pain, and their eyes stared out before them but saw nothing.

As Mystia looked up at the thousands of men whose faces were forever twisted in silent screams of agony, she burst into tears of terror and anguish.

"Cease your whimpering!" hissed the Dark Sorcerer as he slapped her across the face. Mystia could not stop her tears and could only try desperately to quiet them as much as she could.

As they reached the gate of the city someone high above them cried out, "Who goes there?"

"It is I, the Dark Sorcerer!" the Dark Sorcerer cried back.

Without further questions, the two doors of the city gate slowly swung open, and the Sorcerer and the Princess rode into the city. Just before the gate closed Mystia gave one last long look out at what lay beyond the city walls. Her whole body shuddered as, with an echoing boom, the doors closed.

Slowly she and the Sorcerer began to make their way through the winding streets which led to Kozan's palace. How any city of that size could be as silent as Nolhol was that night is impossible for one to ever know. The sound of the horses' hooves striking the ground and the sound of Mystia's quiet sobs were all that could be heard.

Up through those dark, silent streets Mystia and the Sorcerer rode, ever making their way to Kozan's palace. Finally, they reached the high wall that surrounded the palace.

Again they were challenged, and again the Dark Sorcerer identified himself. Immediately, the doors swung inward, and the Sorcerer and Mystia rode through.

City of Darkness

As she looked up at Kozan's great palace towering above her, terror pierced Mystia to her very heart. Every muscle of her body was tensed, and as she continued to gaze upon the dark, massive structure, she saw that there was no hope of escape from that palace or from its dark king's grasp.

The Dark Sorcerer dismounted and had to fairly drag Mystia from her horse, for she was so filled with fear that she could barely move. An old man, so shriveled and bent with age that he long ago had lost the appearance of being human, came and led the two horses away.

Across the long, empty courtyard, into the dark palace, and through the long echoing corridors they walked. The slaves who passed them cast a dull look in Mystia's direction but continued on their way without a pause.

Presently, they reached a large pair of doors, in front of which stood two grim, unmoving guards. The Sorcerer stopped and, pulling out a long dagger from his belt turned to Mystia. Mystia's eyes grew wide and she took a step back, but the Sorcerer grabbed her arm and pulled her to him. With one swift motion he cut through the ropes binding her hands. Then, without a word, he turned and knocked loudly upon the door. The hollow, echoing sound was the first thing Mystia had heard since entering that dark palace, save for the soft tread of her own feet. The two doors opened silently, and the Dark Sorcerer walked in, pulling the Princess along with him.

Mystia found herself in a large, splendid chamber. The floor was laid with rich carpet and the walls were covered with the most exotic of tapestries and works of art, all of which were lit by dozens upon dozens of candles. In the middle of the chamber, at a large wooden table, sat the dark king of the palace. His golden crown and the rubies inlaid within it flashed in the light of the many flickering candles. His long, brown hair flowed down over his shoulders. His lips were turned up in the smallest, most empty of smiles, as with cold, brown eyes he gazed upon her. From his left ear dangled an earring of some strange twisting design which Mystia had never before seen, but, though she knew not what it meant, she felt that it could bode naught but evil.

"Welcome, Princess, to Nolhol," said Kozan with scorn. Mystia was too petrified with fear to say a word in response.

Kozan glanced up at the Dark Sorcerer and the two servants who stood by the door, and they, understanding his unspoken command, walked from the room, leaving the king alone with Mystia.

"Really," said Kozan, with the faintest of Delovachian accents, as he rose, "I've spent years searching for a way to meet you, and, now that I finally have, you greet me with silence? I think that hardly polite."

Mystia took a deep breath and in a trembling voice spoke. "You have kidnapped me and brought me here to you. What do you expect me to say? Am I to beg to return home? That's all I wish to do."

"'Return home,' you say," said Kozan as he took two golden goblets and began to pour wine into them. "Perhaps I would return you to your home if you had one, which you do not." Mystia could scarcely keep from bursting into tears.

"Ah, yes, how sad it is to be without a home," continued Kozan, as he picked up the two goblets of wine and walked toward her. "However, if you so choose, you could once again have this thing which you so desire." He handed her one of the goblets, which she accepted and held tightly with both hands for fear that she would drop it.

"What mean you by that?" she asked softly.

"Simply this: your father and your brother are both dead." Even through her fear, Mystia's eyes flashed with anger at those words.

"You do not believe me?" he asked.

"No, I do not."

"Then perhaps this shall change your mind." He walked over to a dark corner of the room and returned bearing in his hands a long object wrapped in a black cloth. "A messenger brought this to me not two hours ago; methinks you shall find it particularly interesting."

Mystia looked silently on as Kozan went about loosening the cords, which bound the cloth to the object beneath. Fear began to well up within her as she saw that it was a long wooden staff. Kozan pulled it fully from its dark covering, and for a moment Mystia could only look in horror upon it. It was a staff--beautifully carved--with a small crystal stone embedded in its head.

"No," she whispered as she stepped back, away from Kozan.

"'Tis your father's staff," said Kozan as he held it out to her.

"No," she said again, her voice trembling, as she took another step backward.

"Your father is dead; the Dark Sorcerer himself killed him," said Kozan as he stepped toward her.

"No!" she screamed as tears began to fall from her eyes. Her golden goblet fell from her hands, spilling wine all over the floor. Her legs would no longer support her, and she collapsed beside the fallen goblet.

"Get up," Kozan said in disgust as he took her by the arm and pulled her close to him. Looking intently into her eyes, he continued, saying, "You are the sole, surviving heir to the throne which once belonged to the country of Nor. I rule that county now, but there are many who dispute my ruler-ship. Were I to marry you..." His voice trailed off, as, with an evil glint in his eyes, he looked down upon her and waited for her answer.

As Mystia looked up at him, her black eyes filled with anger, and she cried, "Pig! Do you actually think I would ever marry you?" She slapped him hard across the face and, wrenching her arm from his grasp, tried to run from him. He gave a snarl of rage, and, even as she fled, he shot his hand out and grasped her arm once again. With another growl he yanked her back to him. She gave a scream and tried to pull away, but he held her even tighter against his body.

"Miserable wench," he hissed--even through her veil his breath was hot upon her cheek--"I gave you the chance to be my wife, for what man would not be raised in greatness who had a wife such as you? But think not that I care one bit about your honor. I will have you wife or no."

"Let go of me!" she screamed as she struggled against his strong embrace. He threw her, shrieking and sobbing, to the floor where he held her tightly and tore her veil from her. As his gaze fell upon her face he suddenly started and scrambled to his feet and for a moment after could only stare down in shock upon her. Her skin was smooth and pale, and her lips dark red. Her features were soft and delicate, and she looked up at him with tearful, black eyes that were wide with fear. Beneath her long, black hair, which tumbled down about her, he could see small pointed ears. She was so very Elven, and yet so much more beautiful than any elf of Lairannare that it was immediately apparent what she was.

Kozan opened his mouth to speak, but the only words to be heard were, "High Elf?"

He looked at her for a moment longer then turned and cried out, "Sorcerer!" Immediately the Dark Sorcerer entered. His gaze fell upon Mystia, and he too was filled with amazement and horror.

"Take her to the dungeon," said Kozan softly then turned his back on them both.

Silently the Dark Sorcerer brought Mystia through the corridors of Kozan's palace and down a long endlessly twisting staircase into the dark, gloomy, stench-filled dungeon.

They were met at the bottom by a dirty, grim-looking warder who held a wicked looking whip in his hand.

"Why're ye here?" he asked gruffly. "Upstairs is where the pretty women go."

"The king wants her here," answered the Sorcerer.

"It'll be a pleasure," said the warder as he leered at Mystia.

Mystia shrank back, then suddenly looked up in confusion as the Dark Sorcerer snarled, "Listen, dog, High Elven maids are not for your pleasure, and if you so much as touch one hair on her head, the pain you will feel by my hand will be beyond your ability to comprehend."

"Aye, sir," said the warder, suddenly quite meek. Quietly he turned and led the way through the darkness.

The cell he brought them to was dirty beyond belief. The walls and floor were covered with slime, and in the corner was a small bit of moldy straw in which the rats made their nest.

"No," Mystia said with a strangled sob as the Dark Sorcerer pushed her into the cold dark cell. She spun around to run out, but she was met with the hard wood of the door as it slammed shut.

"No," she sobbed as she heard the sound of the key turning in the lock.

Hugging herself as tightly as she could, she stood in the middle of the cell and cried. For a full hour did she stand in the middle of that slimy, rat-infested place, but with each passing minute exhaustion took a stronger and stronger hold on her.

Finally her body could take it no more, and, collapsing to the slime-covered floor, she allowed sleep to overtake her.

* * *

The Dark Sorcerer stormed into the room where Kozan stood.

"You never said she was a Shallean!" he cried.

"I never knew," Kozan snarled in reply. "How was I to? How was anyone?"

In fury and what could almost have been despair the Sorcerer struck the solid stone wall with his fist and snarled something in his native tongue.

"She is only one Shallean woman," said Kozan rather startled at the Sorcerer's outbreak of rage.

"Will you kill her?" the Sorcerer demanded as he turned suddenly to face Kozan.

"I want you to stay here in Nolhol," said Kozan, not answering the Sorcerer's question. "Nor has been defeated, and there is no need for you to personally oversee the ferreting out of the few rebels that remain."

"Will you kill her?" the Sorcerer asked again. The look in his eyes made it clear that he would not cease asking until he had received an answer.

Kozan hesitated then said, weakly, "The Law of Balor requires it." There was a pause and he said even weaker, "What else am I to do?"

As if to strengthen his words, the long, low, mournful sound of Balor's Horn echoed across the vast city of Nolhol, signifying that yet another creature had been sacrificed upon Balor's bloody altar.

Chapter 8
In the Company of Wood Elves

Then Vallendar smiled and answered her, saying, "You ask me why it is I give not up hope? Because, though few good men are found in times of trouble, there are yet some, and they are the most noble and courageous of all those in Deithanara. They are not those who let fear keep them from following after what they know to be good and just. Though the whole of Deithanara stands against them yet are they willing to give you succor and to stand by you in your darkest hour. That is why I do yet hope."

When Chzaros introduced himself as the king of the elves of Raia-Torell Gideone, Stavros, and Vayan were quick to kneel before him. At this Chzaros laughed and spoke, saying, "Methinks you should be more careful to whom you show reverence, for, though I did save your life, you know not what I intend to do with it."

He laughed again at the expressions his words drew from them and said, "Rise, my friends, and worry not, for, unless you find the thought of feasting and sojourning with the children of Raia-Torell unpleasant, you have naught to fear."

"You are most kind, Your Majesty," said Gideone as he rose. "Not only did you provide us with much needed aid in our fight with Abiel, but now you open your house to us who are perfect strangers."

"'Tis but a small service which we, who have been blessed with so much, can give to three weary travelers," said Chzaros lightly as he, followed by his elven warriors, began to lead the way through the forest, but he then grew more serious. "The forces of evil wax great these days, and desirous am I that there would be at least one place of refuge left in Lairannare, though I fear that soon even Raia-Torell shall be overcome.

"Oh, but I make sorry conversation," said he, once again lighthearted. "Darkness may come tomorrow, but that does not mean I should not rejoice in the sun today."

He looked at them. "So tell me, good sirs, what are your names?"

"Stavros, Vayan," said Gideone motioning to each in turn, "and I am Gideone."

Chzaros laughed and said, "Honored am I to be let so quickly into your confidence, for, were I a prince fleeing from my enemies, I would not be so quick to give my true name to strangers no matter what aid they had lent me."

Gideone was amazed beyond measure that Chzaros was able to so easily discern his true identity, but he was unwilling to show his surprise.

"And did I judge so wrongly in believing that you are a noble person who can be trusted?" he asked, speaking lightly and easily. Though his voice sounded natural, his hand, which was pressed against his heart, betrayed that he felt not entirely well.

"Nay, not at all, but, still, 'tis best to show prudence in times such as these."

Chzaros looked and saw how Gideone pressed his hand so tightly against his chest and, turning to him, spoke in alarm. "Prince, I knew not that you were wounded in the battle."

"I was not wounded in the battle," answered Gideone, "only wearied."

"Sit down, sit down. You're in no condition to walk." Gideone's face had by that time turned astonishingly pale.

"No, I can walk," he insisted, though he was not too stubborn to refuse Stavros' support.

"What happened to you?" Chzaros asked in concern.

Gideone motioned for Stavros to answer the Elven king's question, which Stavros did as they continued to make their way through the forest. He was just concluding his account of the poisoned arrow when the group of men and elven warriors emerged from the forest and found themselves in a wide glade. In the center of the clearing there was a large fire about which were gathered many elves, some singing and some engaged in conversation.

"Welcome to my home," said Chzaros as, with a sweeping gesture, he motioned toward the open glade.

The elves who had been gathered about the fire became aware of the return of their king and made their way toward the group of elven warriors who stood at the edge of the trees.

Chzaros raised his voice and said to those who had gathered there, "My friends, we have triumphed; the evil has been driven from our forest, and, what is more, we have brought back three guests to sojourn among us." As the elves gathered around Gideone, Stavros, and Vayan and welcomed them to Raia-Torell, Chzaros turned to a young elf and asked, "Where is Wild Rose?"

"Here I am, lord," came a soft female voice. She walked out from the midst of the crowd and stood before him. "What do you require?"

"We have a wounded man with us," answered Chzaros as he motioned toward Gideone who had by then sank down upon the grass. Then he turned and, raising his voice, spoke to the elves, "I want our guests to be treated with the greatest of hospitality. See that they want for nothing."

As Stavros and Vayan were being led away Chzaros helped Gideone to his feet. The small party of Chzaros, the Prince, and Wild Rose began to make its way across the wide glade into the trees on the other side, and during the brief walk, Chzaros quickly told Wild Rose all that Stavros had told him of the origin and nature of Gideone's wound.

Amidst the trees were the small, well-built huts of the forest elves. Wild Rose led them into one that was filled with all manner of balms and potions used in the art of healing. She had Gideone take off his tunic and lie down upon one of the beds there. When he had done so, she went about unbinding and examining his wound. Her brow became deeply furrowed as she searched it, and for a long time she remained silent. The thin, black lines originating from the point where the arrow had pierced him had crept even farther across his chest since Stavros had last looked at it.

Finally, in a troubled voice, she spoke. "I have seen such wounds as this before, and I can say with certainty that it was given by a far greater magic than ever I will hope to be. You are not wrong in believing that none save an arch-mage or a Power can heal it." She turned her blue eyes up to him. "'Twas the Dark Sorcerer who gave you this wound, was it not?"

"I don't think it was the Dark Sorcerer himself who shot the arrow," answered Gideone slowly. "Though it does stand to reason that 'twas he who cast the spell upon the arrow."

"Well," broke in Chzaros, "whether or not the wound was given by the Dark Sorcerer, the fact still remains that none save an arch-mage or a Power can heal it."

"Aye," said Wild Rose. "The only thing which has kept you from being overcome already is that amulet which you wear about your neck." Gideone turned his eyes to the golden feather Eagle had given him.

Wild Rose paused then continued, "but the power of the amulet will soon be defeated by the power of the dark magic unless something is done to stop it." She rose and walked to a shelf, which stood against the wall, and, taking a small, ornate jar from it, she turned back to Gideone and said, "This is the strongest of all my many healing balms. I know not how long it will keep you alive, but I pray that it gives you enough time to find one who can heal you fully."

She rubbed some of it over Gideone's wound, and immediately all the pain the Prince felt subsided. He took a deep breath and slowly rose to his feet.

"Thank you," said he with a slight bow of his head. "I am in your debt."

"You are welcome," answered she with a slight smile. Then, turning to Chzaros, she said, "Lord, if it be your will, I shall see to it that Prince Gideone is properly quartered and attended to."

"So be it," answered Chzaros.

When Gideone awoke the next morning he felt more refreshed than he had in many a day. It was beautiful outside, and he was drawn away from the glade where the elves made their home and into the solitude of the surrounding forest. He did not walk very far before he came upon a river; it was, in fact, the very same river over which he, Stavros, and Vayan had had their adventure with the troll. It was a very peaceful place with the water swirling silently by, the tall trees casting cool shadows down upon the ground, and with only the soft chirping of the birds to break the stillness.

Here Gideone stopped and sat upon a large rock at the river's edge. He was soon lost in reflection over all that had happened, and all that he feared would yet come to pass. He was so deeply lost in thought that he did not notice that Chzaros, who had walked through the forest in search of him, now stood very near. For a moment the elven king simply looked upon the Prince, but finally he broke the silence, saying, "You seem very troubled, Prince."

Gideone started, then regained his composure and, turning to him, replied, "If I seem troubled, Your Majesty, 'tis because I am."

"And what troubles you?"

"Death and that which comes after and the fact that I shall, in all probability, soon be in possession of first-hand knowledge of both experiences."

"I wish that I could help you," said Chzaros sadly. "There was a time when I had the power to overcome the might of the Dark Sorcerer, but he has grown strong, and I have grown old. Such is the way of things."

"My only solace," continued Gideone, "is that, in the thirty summers which I have breathed the air of Lairannare I have lived a far fuller life than many a man," then, as almost an afterthought, he added rather sadly, "Though it could have been fuller still."

"You speak of Eagle do you not?"

"Yes, I speak of Eagle. It seems rather fitting; the Powers have taken away my country, my family, my love, and now myself--everything I have ever held dear."

They were silent for a moment until Gideone suddenly said, "Have you ever loved?"

"No," answered Chzaros with a thoughtful smile, "I have never loved." He gave a laugh and continued, "Noble women hold me in derision, and common women exalt me to a place I should not hold. I have never yet met one who viewed me as an equal." He sighed. "But such is the lot of one who was born a king with a commoner's heart."

He was silent for a moment then spoke again. "'Tis true I have never loved, but I do know that one should never give up hope too quickly. It is possible to regain that which you have lost. The Powers are not immortal. You are not yet dead, and there are those in Deithanara who have the power to heal your wound. You have yet the chance to defeat the Powers and regain your kingdom, and who knows but that you might also regain the one whom you love."

"I feel very reassured, Your Majesty," said Gideone in a voice which said he was anything but.

"Whether I reassure you or not, I still speak the truth, Prince Gideone. But perchance this shall reassure you more: should you or any of those who follow you require aid--be it small or great--you have but to ask the children of Raia-

Torell, and we shall give it most willingly."

"Thank you," answered Gideone. "In that I truly do find assurance."

Chzaros simply smiled then turned and left.

Several hours passed, but Gideone did not leave the riverside. It was there Stavros found the Prince, in the mid afternoon, still sitting upon the large rock, looking down upon the flowing water, with the cool breeze blowing across his face.

"Your Highness," said Stavros interrupting Gideone's reverie.

"Yes?" said the Prince as he turned to face Stavros. Then, after seeing the expression Stavros wore, he said, "Stavros, you look worried. Whatever is wrong?"

Stavros took a short breath then said, "Your Highness, forgive me if I seem too bold, but I desire to know why it is that Abiel bears such a great hatred for you; certes something terrible must have happened between you and him that would cause you both to enter into the Ring of Fire."

Gideone paused, considering for a moment whether he ought to tell Stavros, then he answered. "Abiel and I first met each other several years ago, during the time that I was wandering throughout Lairannare. He loved a woman who loved me." The Prince gave a wry grin. "The amusing thing is I didn't care a whit for the maid. That, however, did not matter to Abiel who felt that I had personally affronted him. He challenged me to enter into the Ring of Fire, which I did." He gave a laugh. "Sadly for him, I was a much better swordsman than he. I threw him back into the fire, and he was so wounded that he could not rise. Until now, I believed him to be dead, but, evidently, he survived and, being the incredibly vain man that he is, has come to seek revenge for his marred face, which I never thought was particularly comely to begin with."

"That is the reason for your quarrel?!" cried Stavros. "A face scarred during a duel fought over a woman you didn't even love? For something as small as this you're willing to break the law of Joretham and enter into the Ring of Fire?"

Gideone laughed and cried, "Stavros, what does it matter? Methinks you put too much weight upon ancient laws written by mythological personages. Fire is fire; 'tis the same whether it's in a ring or a hearth, whether someone is dueling in it or cooking food over it. If Abiel wishes to fight in a ring of fire then far be it from me to keep him from doing so. If the one who is killed truly is feasted upon by the dead then so be it; I still will not fear."

"But, Your Highness," cried Stavros, "how can you say such a thing?"

Gideone, laughing at Stavros' horrified expression, answered, "'Tis easier than you might think." Then, more seriously, he added, "I fail to see why this troubles you so. Give me one good reason why I should not enter into the Ring of Fire."

"I will give you two, Your Highness," answered Stavros gravely. "Firstly, Joretham forbids it, and, secondly, I, who have ever been the most faithful of your servants, ask you not to do so."

Gideone was silent for a long moment as he thought upon what Stavros had said. He cared nothing for Joretham, certainly, but he suddenly thought of Stavros, with no tunic, walking through the cold, wet forest of Raia-Torell. He gave a sigh and rather grudgingly answered, "Very well, it shall be as you wish; I will not enter into the Ring of Fire."

"Thank you, Your Highness," said Stavros as he bowed his head.

"Thank not me," answered Gideone with a grin. "Thank whatever it was that possessed you to give me your tunic." With that, he stood up and walked away, leaving Stavros to stare after him.

The day passed quickly, as times of joy and peace seem always to do, and, as twilight fell upon the forest, the Elves and their three visitors gathered around the great fire in the middle of the glade. There they feasted, conversed, laughed, and sang, for such was the way in which the children of Raia-Torell bade farewell to those who left their midst to go to war or seek adventure.

The feast was not as long as some would have liked, but Gideone, Stavros, and Vayan needed to leave early the next morning so the merrymaking was cut short. After but a few hours, Wild Rose appeared, bearing in her hands a large, golden goblet filled with a sparkling, amber-colored liquid.

"Your Highness, good sirs," said she, turning to Gideone, Stavros, and Vayan in turn, "'tis the custom of the elves of Raia-Torell to have their warriors drink from this cup before they depart for battle. You are neither elves nor go you off to battle, but the road ahead of you is dangerous and we wish to honor you as though you were one of us. So drink, and may Joretham give you strength to complete your journey."

To each in his turn she walked, and, curtsying, she handed him the goblet, from which he drank, and received it back again when he had finished. And thus did the feast end. The elves and men quickly retired, and for one last night Gideone slept under the watchful eyes of Raia-Torell.

Chapter 9
The Night of the Feast

Jocthreal was, perhaps, the greatest of all the countries of Lairannare, for it was ruled by the greatest of all the people in the Realm of Earth--namely, Queen Provenna, the Greater Power. Of all the cities of Jocthreal Leilaora was the greatest, for it had beauty such as no other city could rival. It was the City of a Hundred Temples, and the golden towers and spires rose high into the sky and shone gloriously in the light of the sun.

To the north and east, a large forest grew, which, indeed, reached to the very walls of the city. It was composed of all manner of deciduous trees--maples, oaks, birches, and many others. During the summer they would have been a sight to behold as they reached tall and proud into the sky with their branches, covered with lush, green leaves, waving softly in the wind. As it was, however, they had yet to regain their verdant crowns.

A broad road led up to the gates of the city. The forest grew thick on its eastern edge, but, on the other side, it thinned out very quickly so that, on the western side of Leilaora, there was a large open plain broken only by a few small hills and a couple of trees. Nearly a mile away the forest began again, stretching both to the north and to the south, and, if one traveled but a few miles in either direction, one would find that it eventually curved and joined with the forest on the other side of the road.

Upon the road, there could be seen the most joyful of processions. It was a large group of Elven-folk all dressed in the most festive of clothing. At its head rode King Tnaka upon a milky white horse. For an elf he was tall--almost five and a half feet. He had a very handsome face which some would say had grown only more distinguished with the passing of years. His hair, which was blonde-- as was the hair of many elves--fell only to his shoulders, which was unusually short for the style of the day, but it suited him well. His gray eyes, which were at that moment filled with laughter, betrayed great intelligence. If one had seen him without knowing who he was, one would never have thought him to be a Power, for the Powers were supposed to be the most wicked of all those who walked the face of Lairannare, but he seemed almost incapable of doing evil.

To his right there rode his wife, Queen Eagle, upon a gray palfrey. She neither spoke nor laughed but was an attentive spectator of all that went on about her.

To Tnaka's left, mounted upon a large brown horse, rode the only human in that company of elves. He was a lad of no more than sixteen years, with long brown hair and bright green eyes. On his face there was a mixture of expectation, awe, and anxiety, which only intensified the closer they drew to Leilaora.

At the gate of the city was assembled a small group of people also mounted upon horses. Foremost among these was Queen Provenna herself. She was a beautiful woman with large, flashing green eyes and soft, white skin. Entwined within her long, red tresses were more than a score of milky pearls, and upon her head was a delicate and beautiful crown of gold. Her dress was made of the finest purple and gold silks, and, while it was modest--for she was a queen--it failed not to remind all who looked upon her that she was, indeed, a woman. Her face was alive with an excitement and anticipation, which only grew as the Elven procession drew closer. By the time they reached her, she was fairly glowing with joy.

"Tnaka, my friend," said she, "welcome once more to Leilaora. Long have I awaited this day."

"You have not waited in vain," answered Tnaka, with a smile. "Receive him for whom you have so long waited: your son." He motioned toward the young man who sat beside him.

"Hello, Mother," said the youth rather softly and shyly.

"Aeneas," breathed Provenna, and, such was her joy, she could say no more.

"I pray you are pleased with him," said Tnaka.

"Need you even ask?" replied Provenna, still smiling. "I gave you a boy and have received back a man." She took Aeneas' hand in her own and said, "Welcome home, Son. Long have we in Leilaora desired your return."

"And long have I desired to return home, Mother," answered Aeneas with a small smile. "Hardly a day went by in which my thoughts did not turn to this city. When I left it I thought it was beautiful, but now that I return I find it ten times so."

Provenna laughed. "If you think it is beautiful now, awed you will be beyond measure when you stand upon the walls of the palace and look out over it."

"That is a pleasure I eagerly anticipate."

"Methinks for you to ever have the chance we must first return to the palace." Then, turning to all those assembled there, she said, "Come, my friends; tonight we shall feast in celebration of the return my son, Prince Aeneas."

With Aeneas upon her left hand, Tnaka and Eagle upon her right, and the whole elven procession behind her, Provenna rode through the golden gates and into the beautiful city. The streets were lined with people all straining to see the four royal personages who led the grand procession up through the glittering city to the palace.

As they rode, Provenna could talk to none save Aeneas; she wanted to know every detail of his life and training under Tnaka's watchful eye, and Aeneas, though rather in awe of all which was happening to him, answered all that his mother asked.

Tnaka, for his part, was smiling, perhaps even more than Provenna herself, as his gaze passed back and forth between the overjoyed mother and his own young wife, who remained a silent, though not uninterested, spectator of the whole scene.

As they reached the outer gates of the palace, Provenna turned to Tnaka and said, "You have taught Aeneas well, and I doubt that I will ever be able to convey the depth of my gratitude. This truly is a time for rejoicing."

"Your approval is payment enough," replied Tnaka. "And, as to this being a time of rejoicing, all I can say is that I could not agree more heartily."

Provenna laughed and said, "Tnaka, methinks that I, who am the mother receiving back her son, should be the most joyful of all who are gathered here, yet you bear a smile upon your face such as few could match."

"We all have something which makes us joyful beyond measure."

"And what is that which raises your spirits so?"

"Seven months hence I shall be the father of a child."

Provenna's face became fairly alive with excitement. "Tnaka, that is wonderful!" Then, turning to Eagle, she said rather conspiratorially, "Tell me he is not lying."

"What my lord speaks is true," answered Eagle.

"Then this is a day of double rejoicing," declared Provenna. "Tonight we shall feast not only in honor of my son but also in honor of Tnaka's child."

With that, the procession made its way into the beautiful marble palace of Queen Provenna.

The banquet hall of Provenna's palace was truly a sight to behold. It was immense, and its walls were decorated with the most beautiful and exotic of tapestries. It was filled with long, exquisitely carved wooden tables, which were piled high with foods of staggering variety. The smell of veal, boar, bread, and a dozen other types of food not readily distinguishable wafted through the room.

The hall was alive with the hundreds of guests gathered there. The sound of laughter and conversation filled the air, and the merry music of the minstrels rose and mixed with it.

Between the tables, many servants made their way, refilling wine goblets, replenishing the platters of food, and, in general, making sure that all ran smoothly and no one lacked for anything.

Upon a dais there stood the table at which sat those who were most noble of rank. At the center sat Provenna, with Aeneas at her right hand. To her left sat Tnaka, and to his left sat Eagle. Provenna and Aeneas had not ceased conversing since the beginning of the feast. Tnaka and Eagle, however, had remained rather quiet, which was more because of Eagle than himself. Provenna, however, was too overcome with joy at the return of her son to notice how silent her friend and his wife were.

Suddenly, with a laugh, she raised her goblet and cried, "A toast! A toast!"

Everyone became silent and waited for the Queen to speak.

"A toast to..." began Provenna, but, even as the words were leaving her lips, the guards in the corridor began to cry out. All eyes turned as the doors to the banquet hall were suddenly thrown open. Murmurs of surprise escaped the lips of those gathered there as their gaze fell upon King Kozan. A dusty cape was thrown over his shoulders, and his hair was disheveled from a journey of hard riding.

His cold brown eyes flashed with scorn and hatred as he marched up through the hall to the dais. He crossed his arms, planted his feet, and glowered at Provenna. For a long moment, Provenna could only stare back at him.

"What are you doing here?" she finally asked, her voice trembling with rage.

"That," said Kozan with a loud voice as he mounted the dais, "is not the question." He took Provenna's goblet from her hand and, after drinking, looked out over the hall and continued. "This is a marvelous feast. You know I have always loved feasts." He turned back to Provenna. "Why did you not invite me?"

Her green eyes were flashing with anger as she looked up at him and said softly but dangerously, "I commanded you never to show your face in Jocthreal again. Why then have you come?"

"To see my son of course!" cried Kozan, slamming his goblet down so hard that a few drops of red wine flew from it and fell upon Provenna's dress.

Kozan turned to Aeneas and looked him over well.

"You have grown much," he said after a moment. "I would scarcely have recognized you." He tilted his head to Provenna and added, "Though that is no fault of my own; your mother has kept me away from you for so long."

Aeneas, his face pale, looked up at Kozan. When no one else spoke, he said nervously, "I hope you are pleased with me."

Kozan took a step back and surveyed Aeneas more closely. "Well, you certainly are better than Provenna's other son—deil that he is--but I'll not be fully pleased unless you can handle a sword well."

"Are you finished?" Provenna asked coldly.

"No!" cried Kozan as he turned to face her. "I am not finished!" His voice became softer as he continued. "Since the day of his birth, I have seen Aeneas but once; I hardly think that fair. Now that he has returned from training under Tnaka--" he gave the elven King an ugly look--"you should send him to Nolhol to learn the art of war from one who can truly teach it."

"Who? The Dark Sorcerer?"

Kozan's eyes flashed at her insult, but Provenna ignored his reaction and continued, "Aeneas will never journey to Nolhol; I will never allow you to take him from me. I had two sons once, but one left me. Aeneas is all I have left. You, on the other hand, have dozens of children, and, if you find their number lacking, I am certain Mystia can provide you with still more."

Kozan's cold brown eyes sparked with rage as he looked upon Provenna and growled, "I do not love Shalleans." With that he turned and stormed from the banquet hall, leaving all to stare in surprise after him.

"What?" said Provenna, clearly confused. For a moment, she stared at the doors through which Kozan had disappeared, and then suddenly she realized what Kozan meant.

"Mystia is of the Shallee?!" she cried in amazement.

"Apparently," answered Tnaka as he too stared after Kozan.

The throne room of Provenna was a place to strike awe into the heart of even the most dispassionate of men. It was wide and open and filled with light. The walls, the pillars, and the large tiles of the floor were made entirely of fine, white marble. Along the walls, there were beautiful stained-glass windows, each depicting a hero of the golden days of old. The warriors, savage and impassive, gazed down from their pictures, silent spectators of all which went on in that great room.

Provenna and Tnaka were the only two to fall beneath the gaze of the ancient warriors that night. Provenna sat upon her beautiful crystal throne, and Tnaka stood before her.

"Provenna," said the elven king gravely, "something must be done about Kozan. He grows more insubordinate by the day."

"And what would you have me do?" asked Provenna in despair. "This problem is unlike anything any other Power has ever faced. Never before has a Lesser Power been at such odds with the Greater Power. If I kill him our strength will be cut off with his death, and punishing him in some other way will only serve to anger him more."

"But something must be done. You know as well as I that Kozan seeks in some way to set himself up as the Greater Power and make you subject to him. If I had not warned you, this would already have taken place; Aeneas serves as a constant reminder of that."

At Tnaka's words, Provenna's countenance grew ominously dark. "The pig deserves to die. You know it. I know it. The whole of the Realm knows it. Yet fate has made it so that I cannot destroy him without destroying myself." In frustration she slammed her fist down upon the arm of her throne.

For a long moment after that she was silent, and when she finally did speak, her voice was filled with hopelessness few could fathom. "The burden of ruling this land is all but unbearable. At times I feel as though I were not even meant to be the Greater Power. 'Tis almost as though at some time in the past, the true Greater Power died, and I was set up in his place." She laughed bitterly, "But that is mere wishful thinking on my part; how I wish that there were someone else to carry this load, but it's for me and me alone to bear. I am the Greater Power and have always been the Greater Power, and ever shall I be the Greater Power."

Tnaka gazed at the queen in silence for a moment.

"Provenna," he said at length, "I know not what to say, or what to do. You know that I provide you with all the advice and support that I can, but I can only help you so far as the tangible is concerned. When you enter in to the realm of the mind and the will I cannot help you. That is an inner struggle, which only you can overcome.

"However, though this will give you little comfort, I must say that I, at least, think you rule right well."

Provenna gave a small smile and said, "Thank you, Tnaka. That does give me comfort.

"But, please, go now," she added, glancing away, "for I have much to consider and would be left alone to think in peace."

"Very well," said Tnaka, inclining his head respectfully.

Then he turned and walked silently away, leaving the Queen alone beneath the gaze of the impassive, stained-glass warriors.

* * *

Eagle stood outside Aeneas' chambers and knocked upon his door. It was quickly opened by a slave, and Eagle was permitted to enter. Aeneas stood in the middle of the room and looked darkly at her.

Eagle turned to the slaves, motioning for them to leave Aeneas' chambers. When they had left she turned to the young prince and said, "This has been a rather interesting day."

"'Rather interesting'?" Aeneas repeated. He stared at Eagle for a moment then burst out, "This day has gone from being the most anxiety-ridden, to the most happy, to the most disgusting, worthless day of my life, and the only words you can find to describe it are 'rather interesting'?" He became calmer and said, more to himself than to Eagle, "At least 'twas only my father who came here and not my brother as well. Joretham, it would have been decidedly worse had I had to contend with him also."

He suddenly shook his head. "But I'm forgetting my manners." He led her to a chair. "Please, sit down. Would you care for some wine?"

"Please."

Aeneas walked over to a small table upon which stood a carafe of wine.

"Aeneas," said Eagle, as the young prince poured the wine, "this is the second time this night which I have heard mention of your brother. In the past also I heard of Provenna's other son, but never did I learn more than that he simply existed."

Aeneas gave a bitter laugh and said, "If you want to learn of my brother I would suggest you talk to one of the slave-girls. Certes they know more of him than does anyone else." He walked over to Eagle, handed her a goblet, and said rather bitterly, "He is a painful memory, and we speak little of him."

"I am sorry," said Eagle. "I meant not to pry into things of which you have no desire to speak."

"No, no," answered Aeneas. "'Twas not improper of you; 'tis quite understandable that you would be curious of him.

"There is a reason little is known about my brother. When he was ten years of age he, like I, went to Kerril to learn under Tnaka, and he didn't return until six years later. He remained in Jocthreal for only one more year before he ran away for some foolish reason or another; 'twas probably to seek adventure."

"Certainly you must know more than simply that, for he was your brother."

"You wish to know more?" Aeneas' voice rose, and the bitterness and anger in it were unmistakable. "Very well. My brother was a wicked, cruel thief who gave not a second thought to killing a fellow man. He was a terrifying, savage barbarian who treated everyone around him as though they were his slaves. That is what I know of my brother."

"Certes he could not have been as bad as that."

"He was worse than that, Eagle," answered Aeneas. "It was as though he had not a shred of conscience within him." His voice became soft once again, yet the bitterness and anger lingered on. "But despite all of that, my mother still loved him best. You can't imagine how happy I was when he finally left. And by Joretham, if he ever returned I swear I would kill him."

Eagle could only look up in amazement at him, for never before had she heard him speak with such anger and such deadly earnest.

* * *

The sky was black, and the moon shown over the dark and terrible city of Nolhol. Orion stood upon a hill and looked down upon the city. He was dressed in the armor of the Delovachian he had killed, and in his hands he held the large battle-axe, which glinted evilly in the light of the silver moon. His blue eyes sparked with anger, and he whispered with fury, "Kozan, ravishing dog, you'll pay for your folly." With that deadly promise, he made his way toward the dark city, leaving Nightfall to stare after him through the darkness.

Chapter 10
Escape From Darkness

Mystia lay alone in a cold, rat-infested cell in Kozan's dungeon. How long she had been there she knew not. Whether it had been a day or a week, it did not matter; time had no meaning in that dark place. She had not eaten since she had been brought there, for she could not bring herself to touch the maggot-ridden bread the guards had served her. She was so cold she felt as though she had been pierced to her very heart with ice. Her whole body was racked with terrible coughs. She was so tired that she did not even sit up but instead lay crumpled upon the slime-covered floor, yet sleep refused to come to her.

Suddenly, the door to her cell was thrown open, and a guard, carrying a huge battle-axe, strode in. He paused just inside the cell, seeming to tower above her. She gave a gasp of fear and scrambled into the corner, sending the rats scampering in all directions as she did so.

"Your Highness!" the guard cried as he dropped his axe and started toward her. She did not hear his words but pulled herself tighter against the wall and, with a strangled sob, cried, "Stay away from me!"

"Your Highness!" the guard exclaimed, "'Tis I: Orion." Even as he spoke, he fell to his knees and pulled his helmet from his head to reveal his long auburn hair and his bright, blue eyes. For a moment Mystia could only look in disbelief upon him.

"Orion!" she finally cried, as, bursting into tears, she threw her arms around his neck. Even as she did so she was taken by a sudden fit of coughing. Orion could only hold her as her whole body convulsed violently.

When her coughs had abated he looked at her intently and said, "Did Kozan hurt you?"

"No," she breathed, her voice still trembling with emotion. She gave a slight sob and, holding him tighter, rested her head against his shoulder, as she repeated, "No, he did not hurt me."

The relief that filled Orion was quickly overcome with concern, as he perceived that, while the Princess shivered with cold, her skin seemed almost on fire. Even as he noticed that, her body shook with another cough.

"Your Highness," he said mournfully, "had I come but sooner for you." He silently cursed the whole of the two days it had taken him to find her.

"Trouble not yourself, Orion," she whispered, "for I did not think you would come at all."

"Of course I would come, Your Highness. I swore to serve and protect you. I would give my life for you. Of course I came."

"'Twould have been better had you not," she said so softly Orion could barely hear her, "for now Kozan shall capture you as well."

Orion suddenly realized that she was drifting into unconsciousness.

"Your Highness, wake up," he said as he shook her gently. She awoke with a start and was suddenly taken by another fit of coughing.

"I have to get you away from here," he said when she had caught her breath. "Can you walk?"

"I suppose I will have to," she answered with a wan smile.

Orion put his helmet back upon his head and, after picking up his battle-axe, turned back to Mystia and helped her rise. It was only his strong grasp that kept her from falling back down to the floor. His heart sank; how was he to lead her out of Kozan's palace when she could not even stand by herself.

She placed her hand against the stone wall for support and said, "Let go of me, Orion." He did as she commanded, and for a long moment she simply stood there, breathing deeply, as she tried to gain her strength and balance. Finally, taking her hand from the wall, she turned to Orion and, with a brave look, said, "Now, Sir Guard, take me where you will."

Out of the cold, small cell Orion led Mystia, past the jailer who lay dead from a wound Orion had dealt him, and up into the dark corridors of Kozan's palace.

That there was only one guard with a prisoner would have immediately drawn the attention of any soldier, but only slaves walked through those darkened corridors. Whether they knew or cared that Orion and Mystia were escaping could not be known, for they looked with dull, unseeing eyes upon the two and went silently about their business.

For many minutes Orion and Mystia walked, with only the sound of their footsteps to break the silence. Presently, they reached a long corridor, which was empty save for one, lone woman. Her back was to them as she stood and looked out of a window into the beautiful night beyond. Her hair was long and golden and adorned with many pearls. Her flowing, blue dress was made of the costliest of material, and the bracelets upon her bare arms were made of gold and inlaid with the most precious of jewels. She was clearly no mean slave-girl, and the closer they drew to her the stronger grew the sinking feeling within Orion that he knew her. For a moment his steps faltered as he realized he did indeed know her; she was Lareina the second wife of Kozan.

She turned her head to look at them. Upon her face, there was a look of complete peace. She smiled and, giving a slight nod to Orion that he might pass, she turned back to the window.

Orion breathed a sigh of relief and walked on.

They continued forward, but scarcely had they rounded the corner when Mystia stumbled and fell to the floor. Orion was almost instantly kneeling by her side. She tried to rise, but her body was racked with another fit of coughing.

"Orion," she said, her voice tinged with fear, "I can't get up."

"Yes, you can," he answered. Even as he said so he took her about the waist with his right arm and pulled her to her feet. Supporting her with his right arm and carrying his axe with his left hand, he continued down the corridor. They had not gone far before he saw two guards coming down the corridor toward them.

"Hide your face," he whispered to Mystia. She bowed her head and turned her face so that her cheek was to Orion's shoulder. Her long, black tresses fell down and almost completely hid her features.

The two soldiers, who staggered slightly as though they had been drinking, looked with amusement upon the spectacle walking up the hallway toward them, for it was not every day that they saw a fully armored knight holding a huge battle axe in one hand and supporting a half-fainting woman on the other.

"Soldier," said the larger of the two guards as he stepped in front of Orion, "where are ye takin' this tender morsel?" He eyed Mystia greedily.

"Where I'm takin' har is none o' yar concern," answered Orion, with a flawless Delovachian accent. He tried to shove past the guard, but the man stuck out his arm and held him back, saying as he did so, "So ye don't want t' say where yar takin' har? I'm wagerin' I can guess. And I'm certain thar's enough o' har t' go around."

"Haven't ye ever larned no' t' cross paths with a man carryin' a battle-axe?" asked Orion, his voice lowering.

Before Orion could move, the guard gave a snarl of anger and struck him hard across the chest. Orion reeled backward, nearly losing his grip on Mystia. She gave a gasp, and her head flew up. For the first time, the two guards could see her face.

"A High Elf?" the first exclaimed as he jumped back, even as the second cried for the guards.

Orion gave a cry of fury and, releasing Mystia, took his axe in both hands and lunged toward the two guards. The first guard reached for his sword, but, even as his hand was closing on the hilt, Orion raised the axe and sent it crashing down upon the guard's head. The man had not time to even scream before he fell lifeless to the floor, blood pouring from his head.

Orion turned upon the second guard. The man, his eyes wide with terror, tried to flee. He gave one last desperate cry for the guards before Orion, with another howl, jumped forward and sent his head rolling from his body.

The sound of many footsteps filled Orion's ears as he ran to the Princess and pulled her from the floor. He fairly dragged her behind him as he ran through the halls of Kozan's palace.

Mystia cast a quick glance behind her and saw no less than a dozen guards charging down the hall, slowly but surely gaining on her and Orion.

She and Orion rounded a corner and found themselves upon a balcony overlooking Kozan's great banquet hall. They ran the length of it until they reached the open staircase at the end. Mystia gave a shriek as she stumbled. Orion lost his hold upon her, and she tumbled down the stairs. The blue-eyed warrior raced down the stairs and was at her side in a moment. The guards were close behind him. With one swift motion, he pulled Mystia up off the floor, and, as the guards began streaming down the stairs, he began running toward the main doors of the banquet hall.

Before he reached the doors, they were suddenly thrown open, and more than a score of guards stormed in. Orion skidded to a halt and slowly began to back away from them, looking wildly about for a means of escape, until he stood in the very middle of the room, surrounded by long wooden tables.

"Give up," ordered the leader of the guards. "Thar's no escape."

"When I finish with you there will be," snarled Orion. Letting go of Mystia, he pulled a dagger from his belt and shoved it into her hands. Then, with a cry, he ran forward to meet the guards even as they fell upon him. Mystia, left suddenly unsupported, fell to the ground, her body racked with coughs.

"Orion, stop," she cried as she gasped for breath, for she could see that all hope of escape was gone. Orion did not hear her cry but continued to battle, though he was sorely outnumbered. Already crystal blood was pouring from a dozen wounds, but it seemed that with each blow he was dealt his strength and fury increased until he became not a man but a raging beast.

"Orion, stop!" she screamed again, but still he did not hear her. As the fighting drew closer, she crawled beneath one of the tables to escape the fray. There exhaustion, pain, and fear finally overcame her, and she began to sob uncontrollably.

The doors to the banquet hall were thrown open once again, and Kozan stormed in, the Dark Sorcerer at his back. If anyone could match Orion in anger it was the King of Delovachia.

Orion cried out his name and tried to run across the room toward him, but the guards were thick and held him back.

Kozan paid him no heed. He looked around the room for Mystia until, at last, his gaze fell upon her. He stormed over to where she lay weeping beneath the table.

She saw him coming, and anger overcame her fear. She crawled out from beneath the table, and as he reached her she lashed out at him with her dagger. He dodged out of the way but not quickly enough. Blood began to flow from the gash Mystia left upon his cheek.

With a snarling cry he struck the blade from her hand and pulled her roughly to him. Spinning her about so that she faced Orion, he hooked his arm under her chin and cried, "Drop your sword, Orion, or I'll break her neck."

His words worked like a magic spell. Instantly, all fighting ceased, and the banquet hall became utterly silent. Orion stood for a moment, breathing heavily, clutching his battle-axe, and simply looked at Kozan and Mystia. Mystia returned his stare in terror.

"Drop it now!" Kozan growled as he held Mystia tighter. Still Orion did not move.

Mystia struggled to breath.

"Orion," she whispered. Tears were falling from her eyes.

Slowly Orion uncurled his fingers from about the handle of his axe and let it drop to the ground.

Kozan took his arm from beneath Mystia's chin but still held tightly to her arms.

In the silence that ensued, one of the soldiers walked up behind Orion and struck him hard across the head with the pommel of his sword. Orion fell unconscious to the floor.

"No!" Mystia cried and tried to run to him, but, though she struggled, Kozan held her fast.

"Take him to the dungeon and chain him fast," ordered Kozan. "And as for you!" he cried as he spun Mystia to face him, "Be thankful I don't kill you right now!"

He threw her from him, and, as she hit the floor, her body was taken by another fit of coughing.

The Dark Sorcerer looked down upon her, as she gasped for breath. What he thought no man knows. After a moment he turned to Kozan and said, "'Twould be pity were she to die before she could be sacrificed. Permit me to take care of her."

Kozan looked upon Mystia in disgust and said, "Do what you will. I care not." With that he stormed from the banquet hall.

The Dark Sorcerer knelt and picked Mystia up--she was too weak to resist him--then he carried her from the banquet hall, turning not once to look upon the floor, which was covered with the blood and dead bodies of men.

* * *

Screams of agony filled the torture chamber of Kozan's dungeon, mixing with the groans and creaks of terrible machines of torture. The bloodstained walls shone eerily in the flickering, red light of the torches. The floor was strewn with moldy straw mixed with slime and blood. In some of the darkest corners there could be seen bones and the rotting remains of men--the only creatures to find peace in that terrible place.

"Chain him," ordered Kozan.

Orion snarled and struggled against those who held him. It took four strong guards to drag him to the whipping post and bind him there. Sweat poured from his body as he strained to break his chains.

His armor had already been stripped from him, and now his tunic was torn away also.

"What is this?" Kozan asked, as his gaze fell upon the golden chain hanging around Orion's neck.

As the King stepped forward Orion gave a low growl, his blue eyes wide like those of a cornered beast.

As Kozan reached out to take the chain from Orion's neck, the warrior tried to bite his hand. Kozan gave a cry of rage and struck him hard across the face. Then, with one swift motion, he took the chain and pulled it up over Orion's head. For a moment he simply stared at the ring, which dangled at the end of the chain. "How nice," said he with sneer, "a soul stone." His fingers closed over it, and he held it tightly in his fist.

* * *

Mystia lay upon a soft bed in a peaceful, dimly lit room. The Dark Sorcerer thoughtfully looked down upon her sleeping form. Suddenly, her eye flew open, and she opened her mouth and began to scream uncontrollably.

* * *

Kozan hung the chain around his own neck, then, turning to the chief torturer, said, his lips turning up in a wicked smile, "Begin." The torturer drew back his whip, and one more voice was added to those filling the dark chamber with cries of agony.

Chapter 11
On the Road to Juassax

Gideone looked upon the blonde-haired elf and said, "What does it matter who I am or where I've come from? The past has no meaning to men such as I. I've left my home and come in search of adventure, and you, sir, are the first person I have met who might be able to provide me with that."

It was a strange yet beautiful scene Gideone, Stavros, and Vayan found themselves in. Above them, the sky was covered with gray clouds, from which fell a gentle, soaking rain. But to the east the sky was clear, and the sun shone down and cast its rays not only upon the countryside beneath it, but also across that which surrounded Gideone, Stavros, and Vayan. It had the effect of making the landscape wonderfully beautiful and mysterious, for it was not often that the sun shone as the rain fell.

Gideone gave a laugh. He was soaking wet, but what did he care?

"'Tis a beautiful day!" he declared. His horse gave a snort and shook its head, sending water flying all about.

"It seems your horse begs to differ," observed Stavros.

"That is only because he has not spent the last four years of his life trapped in a castle, forced to be the prince of a whole country, when he would much rather be off wandering throughout the Realm as a commoner.

"Besides, what does it matter if my horse disagrees with me? Am I no longer allowed to think the day is beautiful simply because a dumb beast does not?"

"The day may be beautiful, Your Highness, but I doubt it's good for your health. I would be far happier if we were at an inn and you were sitting warm and dry next to a crackling fire."

"But if I were sitting in an inn in front of a warm, crackling fire I would miss this beautiful day."

"Your Highness..."

"Faith, Stavros, you put yourself into a such a pother over things which are entirely out of your control."

"I think it wise to at least notice the problems which you face, Your Highness."

Gideone rolled his eyes, and sighing, turned to the older man. "I am not blind. I see the rain, and I know that a man who is soaked to the bone can easily catch his death. But I also know that I must ride through the rain whether I wish to or not, so, I might as well enjoy myself.

"If a man must die upon the morrow does that mean he's not allowed to eat, drink, and be merry upon the night before? Or must he spend the night in worry and despair over that which is inevitable?" He was silent for a moment, then added, "I see not why you should worry at all--especially over things which are beyond your control--considering the God you serve is reputed to be the most powerful god in the whole of Deithanara."

Stavros sighed and did not answer. He had learned long ago that whenever Gideone brought up the subject of Joretham it was only so that he could go around in circles for the next hour arguing over whether or not the god existed. The Prince found some sort of amusement in that--an amusement Stavros could never understand.

When Gideone saw that Stavros would not answer, he looked around once more at the countryside and, with a laugh, said, "Well, rain or shine--or perhaps I ought to say rain and shine--'tis still a beautiful day."

They rode on in peace and relative quiet for the space of a half an hour, when, upon the end of that time, they came upon a stranger: A woman. Her back was to them, and she sat upon a small, brown horse, which made its way slowly down the road in the same direction Gideone, Stavros, and Vayan were heading. Her bright garments were entirely soaked as was her brown hair, but she sang to herself as though she were the most happy, content person in Lairannare.

At the sound of their horses, she turned. She was young--no more than twenty years of age. She had a very homely face, but her eyes, which were soft and brown, were alive with such a life and joy that her lack of beauty was hardly noticeable.

"Good day, sirs," she said with a smile.

"Good day," returned Stavros with a nod of his head and a slight smile of his own.

"Aye," said Vayan with a grin, "a beautiful day."

Gideone looked guardedly at her for a moment.

"Hello," he finally said, with no trace of his former smile left upon his lips.

She laughed and, turning to Stavros, said, "My, you certainly have a suspicious friend here."

"In days such these, suspicion is an advisable trait," answered Stavros. "In sooth, surprised I am that you yourself show less of it."

She smiled. "Perhaps I have no reason to fear. Perhaps I'm a powerful Magic. Perhaps I'm Provenna herself in disguise." She suddenly held her hand to her mouth and exclaimed, "Oh! I should never have said that; now you'll think I really am Provenna."

"Well, I don't think ye're Provenna," said Vayan.

"Nor do I," said Stavros. "However, I do wonder why it is that you, who are but a maid, are riding alone; 'tis a dangerous thing to do at any time but especially in dark days such as these."

"Sir, I am a bard and storyteller of sorts. I have no family so I travel throughout Lairannare, spreading my songs and my stories as I go, and trusting in Joretham to keep me safe. Perhaps it was He who is responsible for you and I meeting. We are all riding in the same direction, and if I were to travel with you I would no longer be in danger."

"You imply, of course," interrupted Gideone, "that we are men whom you can trust and men who will allow you to ride with us, neither of which are certain."

She turned to him and, with a laugh, said, "You really are a very suspicious man, sir."

"What's your name?" asked Stavros of the maid, before Gideone could say more.

"Phautina" answered she.

"Ah, Phautina..." He looked intently upon her. "You have a good face."

"Stavros, Vayan," said Gideone (his commanding tone was unmistakable), "come here." He turned his horse and rode a short distance away. Stavros and Vayan followed him.

"What do you think you are doing?" Gideone hissed. "That woman could easily be an enemy."

"Your Highness," answered Stavros, "she could just as easily be exactly what she claims, and if we simply leave her here we'll no doubt arouse her suspicions."

"I think we've already roused har suspicions," said Vayan as he looked back at Phautina who was looking at them.

"Your Highness," continued Stavros, "I fail to understand why you've taken such a disliking to this woman."

"I know not," answered Gideone. "But there is something about her that seems not right. I know not how I know, but I am certain she is more than what she appears."

Stavros hesitated and looked back at her.

"You feel she is an enemy, and I feel that she is a friend," said he slowly. "Methinks that in either case it would be wise to bring her with us for if she is an enemy we can watch her, and if she is a friend she could, perchance, give us aid."

Gideone was silent for a moment, but, finally, he answered. "Very well, she may come with us, but only as far as Jwassax. Once there she is no longer our concern."

"Very well, Your Highness."

"I suppose you ought to call me Gideone for the time being. ('Tis a common enough name.) We wish her not to know who we are."

"Very well."

On the Road to Jwassax

The three returned to where Phautina stood patiently waiting. She looked up expectantly at Stavros.

"We shall reach Jwassax sometime tomorrow. You may journey with us that far," he told her, "but after that I know not what will happen."

Her face lighted up. "Oh, thank you, sir. Thank all of you."

They continued on. Introductions were made and conversations begun, though Gideone, whose spirits had been so high less than a few minutes ago, said scarcely a word.

The rain fell for a little while longer then stopped. The clouds dispersed, allowing the warm sun to shine fully down upon the countryside, and by the time the night fell, the clothing of the four travelers was completely dry.

They stopped and made camp for the night. They built a small fire around which they sat and ate of the given to them by the elves.

When it came time to sleep, Gideone declared that he would take the first watch. Stavros would have none of it; Gideone was already weak from his wound, and Stavros wished him to get a good sleep so that he would not become ill as a result of having been drenched. But Gideone was determined to have the first watch. He and Stavros argued hotly, and it was only after Vayan and Phautina took Stavros' side that Gideone, who was exhausted, was overruled. He sullenly rolled himself up in a blanket and tried to sleep.

* * *

The moon and the stars shone eerily down upon the dark countryside. All was still and silent. Abiel sat upon his dark charger and looked out over the peaceful scene before him.

"You have escaped me thus far, Gideone," he hissed, "but rest assured you'll pay for what you have done. And when I have finished with you, I'll return to Raia-Torell and punish them for their insolence."

He turned to his magicians who, mounted upon their black horses, formed an uneven row behind him. Dark and impassive they were as they sat and awaited the words of their leader.

"Go!" Abiel commanded. "And this time, make sure Gideone does not escape!"

The fifteen magicians bowed their heads, then dug their spurs into their horses' sides and galloped off across the moonlit countryside.

* * *

Gideone awoke to the chirping of birds. Whether it was a beautiful morning or not he could not tell nor did he care. He was even more exhausted then when he had gone to sleep, and he felt worse than he could say.

Every night he was haunted by dreams; they filled his mind until he could find no escape. Sometimes he found himself standing in the Ring of Fire battling Abiel. Other times he found himself standing among the guests at Tnaka and Eagle's wedding--forced to watch the woman he loved be given to his enemy. But most often he found himself standing once again upon the walls of Zaren. The battle raged all about him, as he saw his father cut down by the Dark Sorcerer. He screamed out in disbelief, and then he looked up to the sky to see Orion fleeing from the battle.

He was filled with anger at the mere thought of Orion. How could he have misjudged the warrior so? He had taken him to be the bravest of all men, but instead he was the greatest of cowards.

"Gideone, are you well?" Stavros' words broke into the Prince's thoughts.

"Do I look well?" Gideone snapped. Then before Stavros could say anything in reply he said, "Hurry up, we have to finish packing."

It took not long to prepare everything for their departure and soon they were once more upon their way. It was embarrassingly silent, for Stavros rarely talked unless there was a reason to, Gideone was in no mood to talk, and neither Vayan nor Phautina thought it their place to speak.

Vayan looked around him for a while and finally got up the courage to say, "Phautina, ye said ye be a storyteller. Why d' ye no' tell us a story?"

At his suggestion, her face lighted up and she turned to Stavros and Gideone. "What do you say, sirs? May I tell a story?"

"By all means," said Stavros.

"If you feel like doing so," muttered Gideone as he massaged his temples.

"Very well," said she. "I shall tell you a tale of the darkest, most wicked of creatures, a tale of the great war waged between good and evil, a tale which stretches back to the very beginning of time.

"Thousands upon thousands of years ago when Deithanara was yet whole and all was beautiful and perfect there was a creature. Many names and titles has he had over the centuries--L'iranon, The Keeper of the Earthly Fire, and Aidan--but his oldest and truest name is Norenroth. He was the king of the whole Realm of Earth and one of the three greatest creatures in Deithanara.

"Among the creatures of the Three Realms, there was a race named the Shallee. They were dark and beautiful, strong and filled with fire. They were poets and artists, builders--creators. They served Joretham with their whole hearts, and He loved them and raised them up on high.

"Norenroth looked upon them and was consumed with anger and envy, for was he not greater than they? Was he not the King of Lairannare? Yet Joretham took a lowly people and made princes and rulers of them.

"With a jealous heart and crafty intentions he went among the Shallee and whispered lies in their ears. Were they not a strong and beautiful people? Surely they deserved more than the pittance Joretham gave them. Joretham ruled over them, but who had set Him up as King? When had the people of

On the Road to Juassax

Deithanara ever risen up and with one voice cried out for Joretham to lead them? Never!

"Slowly, Norenroth turned the hearts of the Shallee against Joretham, and as he did so his lies spread throughout the rest of the Three Realms. He filled the hearts of the people with anger at the wrongs they believed Joretham had committed and with longing for the glory they believed Norenroth could bring them.

"Joretham made His home in a beautiful white marble palace beside the sea. And there, as one, the people rose up and formed a great army to wage war against Him. Human, elf, fairy, goblin, ghoul, Shallean--they stood there, with their heads held up in pride and their faces filled with hatred.

Their number was so great they stretched as far as the eye could see in every direction. The steel of their armor and their weapons flashed brightly in the light of the sun. Their long hair blew in the wind. At their head stood Norenroth himself, strong and proud and filled with fury; he cried out curses against Joretham, his King; his Creator.

"Suddenly, there was a blinding flash of light, and every creature in the whole of the vast army was thrown backward to the ground. Slowly, in pain, they rose once more to their feet, but as they did, they found themselves looking up into the face of Joretham. He stood before them, bearing no sword, wearing no armor, but one look at him spoke of the power He embodied--the power that, with a word, could have destroyed the whole of that vast army, a power that not any weapon within the whole of Deithanara could have harmed. But, for all His strength, His green eyes were filled not with fury and hatred but only with sorrow.

"At the sight of Him, every creature there could do nothing save sink to their knees. Joretham looked sadly out over them. His people had turned against Him, and there was a price that had to be paid for their sin. They look up at Him, sadly, silently, begging for mercy, but mercy he could not then give.

"While they had been able to freely stand together and walk throughout the Three Realms, the lies of Norenroth had spread quickly, and the people of Deithanara had been able to band together. With a word Joretham tore his beautiful world apart, dividing it into the Realm of the Heavens and the Realm of Earth and the Realm of Magic. No longer could the creatures of Deithanara pass freely among the three. No, they were cursed to stay in their own Realm, to never step out save only at great peril, and to never love a creature of another Realm.

"Then Joretham turned and created a place that stood outside of the Three Realms. When He had finished making it, He tore from it everything found within Himself--honor, nobility, peace, joy, comfort, love, life--and there was left only want, degradation, torment, hatred, and death.

"He turned back to the people of Deithanara and said in sorrow and anger, 'You wish not for Me to be your lord? Then this is your kingdom! 'Tis called

Elmorran, for it is utterly devoid of Me. Gaze upon it in awe and thanksgiving, for is it not a beautiful place?

"'Weep not, for you shall not be long in entering into it. Death will take you in the night, when you expect it not, and you will enter in forever to this glorious place.'

"The people filled with terror and cried out, 'No, Lord, spare us! We have sinned. Forgive us! Let us return to You!' But Joretham stood firm, for they had broken the law which ruled Deithanara--the law which He had set up and which they knew full well--and they had to bear the consequences of their actions.

"Then He turned to the Shallee. Tears fell from His eyes as he spoke. 'I loved you most of all, yet still you turned against Me.

"'You are cursed. You will have no Realm to call your home. You will have no place to rest. You are free to travel as you will throughout the Three Realms, yet you will be outcasts among all.'

"The Shallee could say nothing, for they knew theY deserved their fate. They hung their heads in sorrow, for they could not bear to look upon Him--He who had loved them and he whom they had betrayed.

"He looked upon them and their silent penitence for a long moment then said, 'But, though all others will hate you, I still will love you, and it is through you that the redemption of Deithanara shall come.'

"They bowed their heads in thanks.

"Joretham then turned to Norenroth and said, 'Will you admit your sin? Will you ask for mercy?'

"And Norenroth snarled, 'I submit to You?! Fool! I spit in your face! Mark well my words, I will rule Deithanara; it will not ever be yours again!'

"Joretham said. 'You are no longer a son of mine but a creature damned. You and your offspring are cursed to enter into Elmorran and never find redemption. And, at the moment Deithanara is redeemed your fate will be sealed.'

"Joretham set up sacrifices through which the people of Deithanara could find temporary redemption--animals died in the place of the people who had sinned-- but they were not enough to undo that which had been done. It would take a far greater sacrifice than any person of the Three Realms could offer.

"Joretham left Deithanara and created for Himself the place called Lothiel. He took with him the few who had not rebelled against Him--the Torelli they are called--but they were not enough to comfort Him.

"The years passed and turned into centuries. Norenroth worked ever to erase the memory of what had happened, and with each new generation he succeeded a little more, until there were few who remembered and even fewer who would tell others.

"He turned the hearts of the people against the Shallee, and he waged war with them. He was determined to destroy them, for it was through them that Deithanara would be saved, and if that ever happened Norenroth would be condemned forever to Elmorran.

"Three great wars were fought against the Shallee, the results of which served only to inflame even greater the hatred felt for that despised race, for the Shallee fought with passion and shed much blood in their defense. However, though they fought with all their might, they were slaughtered almost to extinction.

"But a few remained, and from these there emerged the one called Jaidev. He was Joretham himself who had come down from Lothiel to save the people of Deithanara from Elmorran. Through His veins there coursed the blood of all three Realms. He was perfect and without sin.

"He willingly allowed himself to be killed. He, the one who had been sinned against, became the sacrifice that was great enough to buy the permanent redemption of Deithanara." Phautina began to laugh. "'Twas Norenroth himself who killed Jaidev. He knew that Jaidev was Joretham, and he thought if he could but kill his former Lord he would become the ruler of Deithanara. But instead by killing Him he brought about the redemption of Deithanara and sealed his own fate as he did so.

"Jaidev did not remain dead, for He was Joretham. His nature was all which is good and righteous, but death came about as a result of--and can only contain-- that which is evil; it had no power over Him.

"He returned to Lothiel. And one day, I pray soon, He will return and completely destroy evil, but until then, by following after Him, the people of Deithanara can find a path to life.

"Norenroth was filled with fury. He had been beaten, but he had not yet been destroyed. He sought to become the king of all Deithanara, and in that way he hoped to gain enough power to destroy Joretham, or at the least to take as many people as he could with him into Elmorran.

"There was born a prince called Balor. He possessed great magic power, and to this Norenroth, who was at that time still the King of Lairannare, added such strength that Balor was able to defeat the whole of the Realm of Earth.

"Most know the story of how Balor then freed the spirits from Elmorran so that he might conquer Keiliornare and Bellunare. And most know how he was defeated by Vallendar. But most do not know that it was Norenroth who gave Balor such knowledge and power.

"When Balor was defeated, so also was Norenroth. He was thrown down from his place as King of the Realm of Earth, and his power was taken from him.

"It was prophesied that it would be through one of Vallendar's descendants that Norenroth would meet his doom. So now Norenroth, weakened, overthrown, but far from destroyed, prowls throughout Lairannare, searching for the one who will bring about his destruction and seeking ever to regain his throne and the power he once held.

"And that is all I can tell you of this tale, for the ending has yet to come. What say you?"

"'Twas a very interesting' tale," said Vayan who had listened closely to every word.

"Interesting it was," said Stavros, "but it seems hardly a tale a bard would tell."

"Oh, I know many other stories," answered Phautina, "but that's the one that many times I tell first, because it's a true story and an important story but a story few in these days know."

"I thought it was a foolish story," said Gideone, "untrue and unimportant, and far better left alone than brought out and remembered."

Phautina turned to him. "In my experience, sir, the men who speak that way are the ones who most need to hear it."

Gideone gave a not too soft "hurumph" then said. "If Joretham truly loved the Shallee so He would have protected them and not allowed them to be massacred."

Phautina opened her mouth to reply, but even as she did so Stavros, who was looking behind them, interrupted. "Your...Gideone, look."

Gideone turned and saw, riding furiously toward them, a group of perhaps ten black riders. They were yet several hundred feet from them, but the distance was rapidly being closed.

"Abiel!" he exclaimed.

The four turned and dug their heals into their horses' sides and charged off down the road.

They heard a cry of fury arise from the lips of one of their pursuers. Suddenly, the space in front of them erupted into a wall of flames. Their horses reared and plunged, and, in the chaos, Gideone was almost thrown to the ground.

As soon as they brought their terrified horses under control, they turned and galloped hard to the right. The wind whipped against their faces as they thundered across the uneven countryside, with Abiel in hot pursuit.

Suddenly, Phautina gave a scream as her horse stumbled and fell, throwing her to the ground.

Stavros and Vayan turned around and began galloping back to her. Even Gideone, with a growl of anger, charged back to rescue her.

Phautina scrambled back on all fours as Abiel and his men bore down upon her. The dark prince, his black cloak whipping in the wind, his eyes flashing with rage, stretched out his hand as if it would bring him closer to those he pursued. His mouth opened in a howl of unimaginable fury. The earth shuddered beneath the hooves of his great, black horse.

Suddenly, Phautina cried out a long stream of foreign words. The ground began to shake violently. All at once, the earth between her and Abiel began to crumble away. The horses of Abiel and his magicians reared back and, as quickly as they could, scrambled backward. One of the horses did not back up quickly enough. It shrieked and its rider gave a cry of terror as he found himself upon sinking ground. The horse desperately tried to escape, but it was no use, and in a moment it had disappeared beneath the sinking ground.

For a moment, Abiel and the remaining magicians could do no more than stand and stare in shock and horror at the chasm Phautina had created. Then, with a cry of fury, the dark prince turned his gaze to her, but before he could do anything Phautina was upon her feet. She held out her hand and cried out more strange words. The ground began to shake, and Abiel and his men quickly backed up as the chasm began to widen. Yet the ground was crumbling more rapidly than they could retreat, and four more magicians were sent plunging into the darkness of the pit. With a snarl, Abiel wheeled and, followed by the remaining magicians, galloped away.

Phautina was still gazing after Abiel when Gideone, Stavros, and Vayan galloped up to her.

All was silent for a moment.

"You never told us you had magic powers," Gideone accused.

She turned in surprise to him. "You never told me you were being chased by an evil magician!"

"She has a point," said Stavros to Gideone.

"Truth to tell," said Phautina, calming down, "I can't use my powers all the time, and the times I can use them I can't use them to the same degree. So I didn't think it important to tell you."

Her gaze fell upon her horse and she suddenly cried out, "Oh! Merja!" She ran over to where her horse lay thrashing upon the ground. She tried to come close but could only stand at a distance for fear of being struck by one of the flailing hooves.

Stavros and Vayan quickly jumped from their own horses and, being careful to avoid being struck by Merja's hooves, approached the fallen horse. She had been sorely wounded by her fall, but it was a thing easily fixed with magic. Stavros and Vayan were able to quickly heal her, and soon Phautina was covering her with kisses.

"Much as it pains me to interrupt this touching moment," said Gideone, "I think I ought to remind you all that Abiel is far from defeated so we ought to quickly make our way to Jwassax before he returns."

Though far from being politely spoken, the Prince's words were true. The other three quickly mounted their horses, and soon the small party was making its way once more to Jwassax, with the bright sun shining down upon them and the cool breeze blowing across their faces.

Chapter 12
The Dungeon of the Palace

Mystia lay upon a soft bed in a dimly lit chamber. The Dark Sorcerer sat at her side and looked silently down upon her. Her skin was deathly pale, but her breasts rose and fell evenly with her slow, deep breaths. The pain, which had pierced her soul when Kozan first came into possession of her ring, had subsided to a dull ache, and she had slept in relative peace for the last two days.

With a sigh she slowly opened her eyes and, for a moment, simply stared into the empty space above her. With another sigh, she began to look dully about her, until her gaze fell upon the Dark Sorcerer. She gave a gasp of surprise and fear and sat up with a start. She tried to scramble out of the bed and stand up, but, before she could, the Dark Sorcerer took her by the hand and said, "Lie back down, Princess. I am not here to hurt you."

"Let go of my hand," she demanded as she pulled it from his grasp and drew away from him.

She looked warily at him for a moment then said, "Why am I here?"

"I asked Kozan to allow me to heal you," he answered.

"How long have I been here?"

"Two days."

"Two days!" she cried her black eyes growing wide. "What's happened to Orion? They could have done anything to him by now." She tried again to scramble from the bed.

"Calm down," the Sorcerer ordered as he took her by both shoulders and looked into her eyes. "Orion is alive."

"What have they done to him?" she cried, growing hysterical. "Where is he?"

"He is locked in the dungeon."

"What have they done to him?" she demanded, beginning to cry.

The Sorcerer faltered, then said, "I think you should lie back down again."

"No!" she cried as she pulled away from him and stood up. "Tell me what has happened to him."

She gave a gasp, as she suddenly grew dizzy. She reached out to the bed to support herself, but even as she did her legs buckled, and she fell to the floor.

"I told you not to rise!" cried the Sorcerer as he ran around the bed to where she lay. He reached out to pick her up but stopped short at the sight before his eyes. Mystia's hands covered her face, and her whole body shook with great sobs.

The Dungeon of the Palace

"They've tortured him," she cried.

"Yes," said the Dark Sorcerer, "they have tortured him. Now, please, Princess, you need to rest."

"I want to see Orion," she whispered through her tears.

"You can't even stand. I doubt you could walk all the way down to the dungeon."

Her eyes flashed with anger and determination as she grabbed hold of the bed and forced herself to rise. Breathing heavily, she turned to the Dark Sorcerer and said, "I can stand."

"Dungeons are not places for women," the Dark Sorcerer muttered.

"Fool!" she shrieked as she struck him across the face. "Did that keep you from taking me there before when I didn't want to go? Now I do want to, but you refuse me! I want to see Orion!" She burst into tears and pounded his chest with her fists, until she fell once more to the floor.

For a long moment the Dark Sorcerer simply looked down upon her sobbing form. Finally, with a growl of disgust he said, "Get up. Put on a clean dress. I will take you to Orion." With that he turned and walked from the room.

Mystia heard a low, menacing growl come from within Orion's cell as the door was pulled open. She stared uneasily into the darkness beyond but could see nothing.

"Orion?" she said as she stepped into the cell. The Dark Sorcerer closed the door behind her.

Slowly, Mystia's eyes adjusted to the darkness, and in the corner she could see Orion. He sat upon the floor, his arms and neck chained to the wall. He stared up at her, his blue eyes dull.

"Orion!" she cried as she ran and knelt at his side. She gave a gasp as, even in the darkness, she saw the wounds he had sustained. Everything--his face, his arms, his chest--was covered with massive bruises and deep gashes, and his skin was dotted with masses of blisters where a torch had been held to him. He was covered with sweat, slime, and crystal blood.

He chains rattled as he held out a scarred and blistered hand and touched her cheek. His voice was filled with pain and sorrow. "Are you some beautiful spirit that has come to bring me comfort in my hour of affliction?"

Her black eyes filled with tears as she answered. "No, I am no spirit, and I have no comfort to bring--would that I did. 'Tis I, Mystia. Do you not recognize me?"

His hand fell away from her. "I had hoped it would not be you."

"And why did you hope that?" she asked with a trembling voice.

He closed his eyes and was silent for a long moment, and it was only when she saw his body shudder that Mystia realized he was crying.

Tears poured from his eyes and fell down his broken and bloodied face, and his whole body shook with great sobs as he said, "I lost your soul stone, and now Kozan has it. You told me to keep it always with me. I failed you."

She wanted to reach out and comfort him, but touching his wounded body would only hurt him more.

"Orion, weep not." She quickly brushed a tear from her cheek. "'Tis but a stone, and any pain that comes to me through it is nothing to be filled with agony over. You have not failed me; you never could."

For a long moment he said nothing but simply sat there as his body shook with silent sobs. Mystia longed to reach out and comfort him with a touch, yet she could not, and, though she yearned to speak, words failed her.

At length, he turned his eyes to her, and they were filled with a terror the like of which Mystia had never before seen.

"Help me," he whispered. "The pain is unbearable, but the thought of death is even worse. I..." He struggled to find the words to express all that was in his heart, but they would not come.

"What can I do?" asked Mystia, struggling to keep from bursting into tears.

"'Tis too late to do anything," he answered. "I once thought I could find a measure of happiness before I died, but 'twas only a foolish dream."

"Orion..." She gave a sob and could say no more.

His chest heaved in another sob of pain.

He was silent for a moment, and his thoughts seemed to drift far away.

"Princess," he said, "let me call you Mystia."

"You can call me anything you wish," she said as her tears fell.

There was another pause.

"Mystia, let me kiss your hand."

"Kiss my cheek." She leaned forward, but even as she did so the door to the cell was thrown open. Mystia started and turned, and Orion never got to kiss her.

"'Tis time to leave, Princess," said the Dark Sorcerer. Mystia, tears still pouring from her eyes, rose and walked to the door.

"Mystia." At Orion's voice she turned back to look at him. His blue eyes were filled with pain and terror.

"Pray to your God for me," he said softly with a broken voice.

"I will, Orion," she sobbed. "I always have."

She turned and walked from the cell.

Behind her she could hear the Dark Sorcerer shut the door, and she could hear the click of the key turning in the lock.

"Come, Your Highness," he said. As he said that, Mystia began to cry uncontrollably. The ache of her soul seemed to grow worse as she held herself tightly and wept for more than a minute.

The Dark Sorcerer stood silently by and waited, until, at length, her tears had subsided.

His voice, softer and gentler than it had been since he had first spoken to Mystia, broke the silence. "Do you love him?"

The Dungeon of the Palace

Mystia looked up at him. "What sort of a question is that?" she demanded as her tears began again.

He said nothing more but led her back to her chambers. There, Mystia collapsed upon her bed, and for the rest of the day she lay where she had fallen, neither moving nor saying a word. It was as if the life had been taken from her.

Chapter 13
The Garden and the Inn

"You speak proud words, sir elf," said Gideone, "and you need to be taught a lesson."
"I am not the arrogant one," replied the elf as he drew his sword. "Nevertheless, I accept your challenge."

Eagle sat upon a marble bench in the garden of Provenna's palace, gazing eastward across the towers and spires of the city. Behind her the sun was sinking low in the sky. The evening was cool but not cold, which was common in the late days of winter and the early days of spring.

Her face bore a far-off rather sad and longing look as she stared into the already dusky eastern sky, but even in that moment of solitude, when she kept her thoughts and feelings least guarded, it was difficult, if not impossible, to tell what it was that truly went on behind her large, gray eyes.

She heard a rustling of the leaves behind her and turned to find herself facing Tnaka.

"Your Majesty," she said as rose and curtsied. She did not see the look of pain that flashed across his face at her words.

"Hello, Eagle," said he as he took her hand. "You look beautiful this evening."

"Thank you, Lord."

There was a slight pause then she said, "To what do I owe the honor of your company?"

Tnaka sat down upon the bench and pulled her down beside him, saying as he did so, "Eagle, you are my wife, yet you always act as though I must have some great, underlying reason to come and talk with you. Perhaps I simply want to be with you."

Eagle was silent for a moment then said, "I suppose you are right, but it certainly helps the conversation along if you have a reason for coming to see me."

Tnaka gave a laugh and, leaning against a tree that stood behind the bench, said, "Are you purposely being difficult?"

"No, Lord."

He did not hear her answer, for as he had leaned back he found himself staring up at the very sky that Eagle herself had been gazing upon but moments before. He suddenly became silent and thoughtful.

The Garden and the Inn

"'Tis a beautiful picture," said he presently, then, turning to Eagle, "Tell me, what is it you think of when you sit out here and stare up at the sky?"

"Many things, Lord, though not the sort of things which can be put into words."

"Oh, I believe not that," said he as he sat up. "Certes some of what you think can be put into words."

She said nothing in reply but simply looked at him and waited.

He took her hands in his. "Look up at the sky."

She turned and did so.

"Now tell me what you think," he told her.

She looked silently at the scene before then finally said, "'Tis a beautiful sight. The stars are bright and the clouds beautiful...the sky dark and..." Her voice trailed off.

"Are the only thoughts which run through your head critiques of the picture?"

She was silent for a few moments then continued. "The sky is very wide open....'Twould be a wonderful place to ride an eagle, and certain am I that Ruffian would love it beyond measure." During her days in the palace of her father, Ruffian had been the eagle she had ridden and her closest companion.

Tnaka drew close to her and, putting his arms around her waist, gazed up at the sky. After a long moment he spoke. "You miss your home, and you miss the eagles and the tall mountains do you not?"

"Yes, Lord," she answered softly, a slight tremble to her voice.

He said nothing in answer to her words, and for a long, long time they simply sat and stared up at the darkening sky and thought their own private thoughts.

"Tell me," said Tnaka--his voice was a mixture of longing, hopefulness, and something Eagle could not quite discern-- "do you think of him often?"

"Think of who, Lord?" asked she as she turned to face him.

"Gideone."

She pulled away from him. "Are you accusing me of harboring unfaithful thoughts?"

"No," he exclaimed, "not at all. I simply wanted to know."

"Well, Your Majesty, now that you have spoken of him, of course my mind is turned to him, but when left to myself if I think of him at all 'tis only a passing thought and not in the light you would construe it to be."

He gave a wan smile. "Do you truly mean that, or are you lying?"

"Joretham forbids us to lie."

He looked at her intently; that same longing and hopefulness which had been in his voice was now in his gaze. "Do you love me?"

She was taken aback by the question, but she answered. "You are my husband."

"It is possible to be married to someone and yet not love them. Do you love me?"

She bit her lip and said, "I am your queen, your wife, your lover, the mother of your child; is that not love?"

The hopeful look in his eyes fell.

"Twas a foolish question," said he as he rose, "and one I should not have asked." He looked around him. "The hour grows late. Do you wish to return with me to the palace?"

"I would rather stay here for a while longer," she answered quietly, "but if Your Majesty commands me I will willingly come with you."

"No, stay here as long as you wish. It matters not to me."

He took her hand in his and, bowing, held it to his lips.

"Good night, Eagle," said he with a sad smile.

"Good night, Lord," she said.

He wanted to say more, but the words would not come so he turned quickly and walked away.

Eagle watched him walk away, and when he had gone she turned once more to the dark eastern sky. She held herself tightly and rocked back and forth. She had lied to her husband; ever since Orion had come asking her for aid her thoughts had turned often toward Gideone, and right then she wanted more than anything in Lairannare to know where he was and how he faired.

* * *

Gideone gave a fierce cry and sent a chair crashing down on the head of one of his attackers. As he looked at the fracas going on all about him he decided that the Inn of the Wild Boar had been aptly named.

He, Stavros, Vayan, and Phautina had reached the town of Jwassax a mere two hours earlier. Considering the Inn of the Wild Boar was the only place of public lodging in the vicinity, they were forced to lodge there, and Abiel and his magicians had had no trouble in finding them.

As a result, the whole of the common room was in an uproar. Every one, whether or not he had a reason, was fighting. Broken tables and chairs lay overturned, and shattered glass covered the floor. Several kegs of beer had been broken, and the warm, sudsy liquid had poured out all over the floor.

The owner of the inn stood behind the bar and cried out for the fighting to end. There was a loud crash as the balcony rail above him was broken. He barely missed being crushed beneath the man who was thrown down.

Stavros battled a short distance from Gideone. They had been interrupted in the middle of dinner, and Stavros was still famished. As a result, with his right hand he wielded his sword, and with his other, he held a leg of chicken, which he was calmly eating.

Gideone dodged out of the way of a sword-blow and looked around quickly for his sword. He found it lying on the floor but a short distance away.

At the same instance, he could sense an attacker behind him. He dove for his sword, barely avoiding the slashing blow as he did so. With one swift movement he grabbed his sword, then rolled and twisted, so that he ended up on his knees facing the direction from which he had come, his sword held before him. His attacker, who had run after him, ran straight into the blade. Gideone gave it a hard twist and pulled it out from the man's stomach. The man gazed down in shock at his wound then fell dead to the floor.

Gideone jumped up, gave a cry, and flipped his sword around in the most stunning of spectacles, then with a grin lowered it at his enemies. He rushed at them, and they scattered before him.

"Stavros," he cried over the din of the fight, "how's the chicken?"

"It could use some wine," answered Stavros who was being backed against the wall by three strong warriors.

Gideone picked up a bottle of wine which sat on a nearby table and threw it to Stavros who, catching it, grabbed it by its neck and sent it smashing into the face of one of his attackers even as he dodged the blow of one of the other men and kicked the last hard between the legs. The first screamed out in pain and clutched at his eyes. The last doubled over and fell to the floor.

"What a waste," said Gideone. "And I thought you believed in fighting honorably at all times."

"Under the circumstances..." began Stavros as he took the part of the bottle he still held and rammed the jagged ends into the face of the only attacker who still stood; the man screamed in agony and, clawing at his face, fell to the floor, "...the loss of some wine and some dignity seemed a fair exchange." He quickly finished off his three attackers.

Gideone laughed and turned around, only to find himself face to face with two huge men. He jumped back, barely missing being cut down by a pair of blades. He scrambled into a defensive position, but, before the two men could attack, a heavy wooden chandelier fell from the ceiling, crushing them beneath it.

Vayan, not even giving the two men a second look, jumped off the chandelier, which he had ridden down on, and cried, "Hurry up! Phautina's go' th' horses ready, an' I gotta ge' back an' help her!" With that he began fighting his way to the door. The moment he reached it, he dashed out into the night beyond.

Gideone and Stavros turned to follow him, but even as they did so Abiel suddenly appeared, stepping through the threshold to block their way. His hood was thrown back to reveal his hideous features, and upon his face he bore a look of utter hatred and contempt.

Gideone and Stavros skidded to a halt.

"Leaving so quickly?" spat Abiel. "You forget, Gideone, that you and I have unfinished business to attend to." He stepped forward and motioned with his hands, and around him there burst up a ring of fire. Immediately, the fire began to spread across the wooden floor to the chairs and the tables and the walls.

Terrified cries filled the room as those within scrambled to escape the flames.

Abiel wore a hideous grin of anticipation. "Come, fight within the flames, or is it too hot? Are you afraid you'll burn yourself?"

Stavros cast a warning look at Gideone.

Gideone's lips turned up in a sneer, and he said, "Judging by our respective looks, I am not the one who ought to be afraid of the fire." With that he turned and began to walk away.

"Come back here you coward!" screamed Abiel. "For ten years have I sought to do battle with you, and I will not be refused!"

The fire raged throughout the whole room.

Gideone looked back over his shoulder and with a condescending smile said, "I only duel those who are decent swordsmen; it provides better sport for me and a fighting chance for them." With that he continued to walk away.

"Fool!" shrieked Abiel. "Cur! Coward who dared not even stand against Tnaka when he came to make your love his wife! You said not a word in protest but ran home to the safety of the high walls of Zaren! You're no man! The lowest slave-girl in my father's palace is more a man that you!"

Gideone stopped and began to turn to Abiel. The fire raging all around only added to the flashing of his dark eyes.

"Your Highness," said Stavros lowly but forcefully, "you promised me you would not."

With a growl Gideone turned back and continued toward the door.

"Your cowardice lost her!" Abiel cried. The flames rose high throughout the room, casting a terrifying red light upon his face. "'Tis not your arms that hold her, or your lips that kiss her!"

A table crashed to the ground as the flames consumed it.

Gideone slowed.

"'Tis not your bed she shares!" Abiel jeered.

More tables and chairs began to fall as the fire took them. Smoke was filling the room.

"Your Highness, come," growled Stavros as he took Gideone by the arm and pulled him along.

"Eagle is with child, and it's not your child!" sneered Abiel.

Gideone yanked his arm from Stavros' grasp and turned to face Abiel. The fire, which rose within his heart and swirled behind his dark eyes, burned far hotter than that which danced about him.

"You lie!" he snarled as he dashed forward and leapt into the Ring of Fire.

Gideone's sword clashed with Abiel's, sending sparks flying about them. The Prince, filled with fury, sent blow after blow raining down upon Abiel. In terror, Abiel stumbled back and tried to escape.

The inn was falling all about them.

Abiel leapt out of the Ring of Fire and disappeared amidst the flame-filled room. Gideone started to run after him, but even as he did so, he was pulled roughly back by Stavros. A huge, flaming beam crashed to the floor where he would have been had Stavros not pulled him back.

"Come," ordered Stavros.

The Garden and the Inn

They ran out of the flaming building.

Vayan and Phautina stood outside beside the four horses, desperately fending off more of Abiel's magicians.

"Hurry!" Vayan cried. He was covered with blood.

Gideone and Stavros ran to the horses and quickly mounted, as Vayan and Phautina did the same.

One of the magicians reached out to grab the reigns of Gideone's horse, but the Prince kicked him hard in the face. Then with a loud "Hiya!" he dug his heels into his horse's side. He raced off toward the road, with Stavros, Vayan, and Phautina following closely.

"Stop them!" Behind him, Gideone could hear the voice of Abiel. He turned his head and saw a dark figure--silhouetted by the flames of the inn--stumbling after them.

He started to turn his horse, but Stavros rode up along side of him and kept him from doing so.

"Stop them, you fools!" he heard Abiel shriek.

Suddenly Phautina, who was riding behind him, gave a cry of pain and would have fallen from her horse had Vayan not reached out to steady her. She turned to see a long, dark arrow sticking out of her shoulder. Her face was twisted in pain, and tears were falling from her eyes, but she kept her seat and urged her horse on.

Vayan cast a look behind him. The red flames of the burning inn rose high into the dark sky, and the cries of men carried across the whole of the town. He could see no one pursuing them.

Phautina gave a choked sob of pain.

"Ye'll be all righ'," said Vayan. "No one's chasin' us, an' we'll be able to stop soon an' look a' yar wound. We're safe for now."

Chapter 14
Conflicts of Interests

Mystia sat upon the pillows in the window seat of her chambers and stared listlessly out across the dark city of Nolhol. Dark and imposing against the evening sky stood the great Temple of Balor, with naught but the swirling sea behind it. Her eyes were turned toward it, but she seemed not to see it, but rather to look through it. Thus had she sat for two whole days. She had neither eaten nor drank during the whole of that time. She had wept much and slept little. Though the slaves spoke to her, their words fell upon deaf ears.

Finally, in desperation, the Dark Sorcerer was called for.

He entered and, after sending all the slaves away, stood for a moment, looking down upon Mystia. Whether she was aware of his presence he knew not, for she continued, unmoving, to stare out at the Temple of Balor.

"My magic has returned you your strength, Princess," he said, at last breaking the silence, "but if you do not eat it will soon abandon you again."

"Think you that I care?" she asked dully, not turning to him.

"Few have ever willingly given up their lives."

"But I do."

"And why are you willing to throw away as good and noble a life as the one which you possess?"

"And what would you know of my life--whether it is good and noble or false and crass?"

The Sorcerer gave a sigh and said, "I will not argue over whether you are good or whether you are evil. I wish simply to know why you are so willing to kill yourself."

It took a moment for Mystia to respond, then, even as she opened her mouth to speak, the long, low, mournful sound of a horn rose up from within Nolhol and spread out across the whole of that dark city.

She gave a bitter smile. "The city answers for me." She touched her hand to the glass window--it was cold--and looked long upon the Temple of Balor.

"Every day that horn sounds," said she softly, "once in the morning, once at mid-day, and once when the sun sets. Tell me, what is that horn and why is it winded?"

"'Tis the Horn of Balor," answered the Dark Sorcerer. "And it is sounded whenever a sacrifice is made to Balor."

"And tell me, what is it that is sacrificed to Balor?"

"Pigs."

"And what else?"

The Sorcerer hesitated but finally answered. "The people of the Shallee."

"And what am I?" she demanded as she turned to face him.

"A Shallean," he answered, clearly loathe to do so.

"Yes," she said as she began to cry, "a Shallean. I may be a princess who has lived but seventeen years upon this land, but this much I know: my blood will join that of the blood of the countless Shalleans who have been sacrificed upon the altar of Balor before me, unless I do something." Though tears streamed down her cheeks, there was a look of deadly determination in her eyes as she looked up at him. "I will not let Balor find a good and pleasing sacrifice in me. Escape is impossible so I can but kill myself."

She turned away from him and looked back out the window, and he silently looked down upon her and tried to think of what to say.

"I may be a soldier who has few dealings with women," he finally said, "but in battle I've learned never to give up too quickly. Kozan will not...sacrifice," (He hated to use that word), "you until the Day of Chanar. Much can happen between now and then."

With an angry look, Mystia turned to him and demanded, "What do you take me for--a fool? Do you think I will so easily forget that it was you who kidnapped me and brought me here in the first place? Speak not to me as one who would comfort a friend; you are a captor."

The Dark Sorcerer began to lose his patience, and he growled, "Then as the captor I command the captive to eat."

"No," Mystia answered, her black eyes sparking with anger and determination.

"Princess, I will warn you I am no noble man," he said with anger growing in his voice. "I was born a child on the streets, and I respect no man or woman. Now eat."

Tears began to fall from her eyes, but she still glared defiantly up at him.

"Listen to me, little wench!" he cried as he took her by the arm and shook her roughly. "In this chamber, I am king!"

Mystia gave a scream and tried to wrench herself from his grasp.

"Let go of me!" she cried as she slapped him hard across the face with her free hand. He released her arm, and she fell sobbing to the floor.

For a moment he simply stood and glowered down at her. But suddenly, he grew calmer.

"Through all of this, you have thought only of yourself," he said, a threatening tone to his voice, "but there is another that you have forgotten."

She looked up in confusion.

"Even now he lies in the dungeon."

A horrified look of realization appeared upon her face.

"The torture Orion has suffered up until now is like Lothiel compared to what I can make him feel." His strange and foreign accent only leant malice to his words. "I know methods of torture that are beyond your ability to comprehend, and I will not hesitate to use them, unless you stop acting the fool and eat."

For a long moment she was silent. Then softly she said, "You leave me no choice."

He said nothing more but turned and began to walk away; however, he turned back when he heard a sob escape Mystia's lips. She looked up at him, and her black eyes were filled with anguish.

"How can you do that to him?" she sobbed. "How can you treat any man the way you treat him? How do you live with yourself?"

"You would not understand," he said then turned and walked quickly from the room.

* * *

Deep within Kozan's dungeon Orion lay, still chained to the wall. He had long ago given up struggling against his bonds, for he could not break them. The pain, which consumed him, was more terrible than anything he had ever known. He had screamed his throat raw, but the pain had not ended. He had wept in agony, but pain did not stop. He had lashed out against those who tortured him, but they had only beaten him more. There was nothing he could do and no one he could cry out to.

The pain was too great to let him sleep, but he was too exhausted to remain awake, so he sat against the wall with his eyes open, yet not seeing, with his mind unconscious, and yet not dreaming. He was living and yet dead.

The door to his cell was suddenly thrown open, and a woman walked in. Orion raised his eyes and stared dully at her. How he longed to see the black eyes and beautiful features of Mystia, but the woman who stood before him had blue eyes and her hair was blonde, and her face, though beautiful, was not the face of a Shallean but that of a simple human. She was Lareina, the second of Kozan's wives.

Slowly, she approached him and knelt before him. Tears rolled down her cheeks as she gazed into his blue eyes and reached up to touch his bruised and broken face.

"Orion," she said, her voice quivering with tears, "I knew it was you. The moment you passed me in the corridor I knew it was you. Oh, how I wanted you to escape, but now...here you are. Please, is there something--anything--that I can do to help you?"

He gave a long groan, arising from unspeakable agony of spirit and, turning his face, whispered, his voice hoarse and filled with pain, "Look not upon me in that way, woman; I never looked upon you like that. And feel no sorrow for me; Kozan may torture me for unjust reasons, but I still deserve the blows."

She reached out and gently turned his face back to her. "What care I if you have never looked upon me as I look upon you? And what care I if you deserve the blows you are given? I love you, and I want to help you."

"Lareina," he said with a groan, "go away. There's nothing you can do. "Forget me. I loved you not then. I love you not now, and never will I love you in the future.

"Leave me. You serve only as a reminder of the wickedness I have committed in my life."

"Nay, it was not wickedness; it was a thing of beauty. You treated me as no man ever treated me and loved me as Kozan could never love me. You were the one bright star in my world of darkness."

"Lareina..." he began.

"Orion," she cut him off, "let me help you escape; I can do that, I swear by Joretham. Let us return to what we once had."

"Lareina..."

"Do you not remember what it felt like?"

"Lar..."

She pressed her lips to his.

He started and turned his face quickly from her, saying as he did so, "Has Kozan sent you here to torment me more? Leave me, woman. I love you not, and, even did I, escape would still be impossible; even you must see that."

She was silent for a long moment as she gazed upon him. Then she stood up. Her blue eyes were filled with tears.

"Is there nothing I can do for you?"

"The one thing I would have you do," answered he softly, "is the one thing you never would do. Leave me alone and let death take me, for once Mystia is gone I will have nothing left."

She looked at him for a moment longer. Tears were falling from her eyes. Then silently she turned and walked from his cell.

With a hollow, echoing boom, the door slammed shut, and Orion was left once more in solitude.

* * *

Kozan sat at the table in the same, dark room in which he had first greeted Mystia. Before him sat a golden goblet and a pitcher filled with wine.

He was just in the process of pouring himself another cup when the door was thrown open and the Dark Sorcerer strode in.

"You called for me, Your Majesty," he said as he bowed.

"Aye, Sorcerer," answered Kozan as he raised the goblet to his lips, "I did." He took a drink then continued. "You have shown great concern for Mystia ever since you first brought her here--nursing her back to health when she was so ill. Balor's Law is very lenient, but there are sins even he will not forgive."

The Dark Sorcerer looked at him blankly for a moment, then, realizing what his words implied, said, "Are you accusing me of harboring feelings of love for this woman? I assure you, Lord, I wish only to keep her alive and healthy that she might make a more pleasing sacrifice to Balor."

Kozan, who had taken another drink as the Sorcerer spoke, set his goblet down and said, "Let us pray that that truly is all you desire, for I would hate to see the most trusted of my servants fall into sin."

"Yes, Your Majesty."

Kozan took a final sip then said, "You may go."

The Dark Sorcerer bowed and walked from the room, leaving Kozan alone to finish his wine.

* * *

Provenna and Tnaka sat alone in a beautiful, spacious room. The morning sun streamed through a large, clear, glass window and flooded the whole chamber with light. It was a very beautiful room with ornate carpets upon the floor and beautiful tapestries hung from the walls. In the middle of the room there sat a beautifully carved table upon which there was set all manner of fruit, bread, and drink.

Both Aneas and Eagle had been invited to break their fast with Provenna and Tnaka, but both had politely declined, which perhaps was good, for it allowed Provenna and Tnaka to talk about things they would otherwise have not been able to speak of--Kozan, insurrection in Lairannare, and, in general, the many different problems they were facing. But, as they were finishing their breakfast, the topic turned to Eagle.

"So tell me," said Provenna, "how goes it between you and Eagle?"

Tnaka's whole body sagged and a look of weariness and frustration filled his face. He gave a sad smile and said, "As well as it has ever gone."

"Nothing has changed?"

The elven king stared down at the table and shook his head. "No, not a thing." He was silent for a moment then continued. "There was the briefest of times when I thought perhaps she harbored some fond feelings for me, or at the least did not dislike me as much as she had in the past, but that was wishful thinking on my part. She is as distant from me as she ever has been."

Provenna was silent for a moment as she thought. Finally, she said, "Are you certain the fault is solely with her?"

Tnaka looked at her blankly. "What?"

"You cannot deny that the last two months have, in particular, been rather strenuous where ruling the Realm is concerned. A person could easily find himself ignoring the people most important in his life.

"Let us look at it from Eagle's point of view. 'Twas an arranged marriage--a marriage she wanted no part of. I know that if I were married to a man I wished not to be married to, 'twould take some time for me to even think of liking him. If I finally did start to love him only to then have him get so caught up in affairs of state that he had not time for me, that would certainly cause a resurgence of coldness on my part."

"Do you truly think that is all which is wrong?" Tnaka asked.

"It makes sense does it not?"

"Yes." He sounded doubtful. "Yet, still, 'tis not you we speak of, or any other woman, but Eagle."

Provenna reached out and, placing her hand over his, opened her mouth to speak. Even as she did so, there was a knock at the door.

"Enter," she said, straightening.

The doors to the chamber opened and one of the chief servant-women walked in. She curtsied low before Provenna and said, "Forgive me, Your Majesty, for this interruption, but a messenger has just arrived. He claims his message is of the utmost importance and must be delivered immediately."

"Very well," answered the Queen, "show him in."

The servant-woman left and quickly returned, ushering in a grimy, sweaty man who had obviously ridden a long way very quickly.

He bowed.

"Yar Majesty," he said with an unmistakably Delovachian accent, "I bring a message from th' Dark Sorcerer." He produced from a pouch a piece of paper, folded and sealed and, bowing once again, handed it to her.

Provenna opened it and silently began to read. Her expression did not change, but, as she read, her face suddenly flushed with anger.

"Bring me a quill and some paper," she ordered the servant-woman softly, her green eyes fairly sparking with anger.

The servant left and quickly returned, bearing with her all that was needed to write a letter.

Quickly and with cold efficiency, Provenna wrote, signed, folded, and sealed her letter. Then, handing it to the servant-woman, she said, "Take this, give it to Gareth. He is to take the fastest horse in the stables and ride as quickly as he can to Nolhol, and there he is to put this letter directly into the hands of Kozan. To any who would stand in his way he is to give the message that he has been sent from Provenna herself, and the consequences will be dire to any who stand in the way of the fulfillment of her commands."

"Yes, Your Majesty," the woman said as she curtsied then turned and walked from the room.

"You," Provenna continued turning to the messenger, "will stay here and rest, and tomorrow you will begin your journey back to Delovachia."

She clapped her hands together and a slave entered.

"See that he is properly quartered," she ordered.

"Thank ye, Yar Majesty," said the messenger as he bowed. Then he turned and followed the slave out of the room.

Only when the door was safely shut did Provenna's cold expression melt into one of complete anger. She rose from the table and turned away from Tnaka, her whole body trembling.

"Provenna!" Tnaka exclaimed as he jumped to his feet, "What is it?"

Her voice was cold and soft and filled with barely contained rage as she answered, "Kozan has Orion."

"What?!" Tnaka cried as he snatched up the letter from where it lay upon the table and began to read it.

"I swear one day that pig will pay," Provenna hissed.

Tnaka walked through the gardens of Provenna's palace. It was a beautiful, early-spring morning, but he did not notice it. His mind was filled with dark and troubling thoughts such as he had rarely entertained before.

"My Lord, whatever is troubling you?"

The king started as a voice broke into his thoughts, and he turned to find Eagle sitting upon a bench nearby.

"Eagle," he breathed, "you nearly killed me."

"Please, Your Majesty, forgive me," she said as she rose. "I meant no harm."

"No, Eagle, there is no need to apologize," he told her as he took her hands in his.

He looked down at her. Her long blonde hair was bound up in the most elaborate of braids, which were wrapped tightly around her head. A few strands had escaped and now fell fetchingly over her forehead. Her cheeks were turned rosy by the crisp, cool air.

"No," he said again, "there is no reason to apologize. Had I been paying attention but a little I should have noticed you."

There was a troubled look in her gray eyes as she gazed up at him, and there was genuine concern in her voice as she spoke. "Lord, you look so troubled. Whatever is the matter?"

He looked upon her and gave a sad smile as he thought, *Must I always be this troubled in spirit to elicit a response from you?*

He sank down upon the bench, drawing her with him as he did so, and after taking a deep breath, proceeded to tell her the whole tale.

* * *

Kozan stood atop the walls of his palace. A cool breeze blew across his face. The city spread out in all directions from the palace, but the magnificence of the view was lost to him. Rather, he stared down at Provenna's letter held in his hands.

The Dark Sorcerer stood nearby and watched silently and without emotion as he saw his master's face twist in rage.

"The shrew!" Kozan cried as he crumpled her letter. "Meddling woman! Pig!"

He snarled more insults, most of a vulgar nature, then growled, "If she thinks that I will do as she commands then she is mistaken. I captured Orion, and I am not about to let that woman take him from me! Nor will I give her the Soul Stone."

"Your Majesty," the Dark Sorcerer broke in, "I think it not wise to contradict Provenna at this moment in time."

"What care I what you think?" snarled Kozan. "For sixteen years has Provenna lorded over me, but no longer. What makes her think she can rule me? She was born nothing more than a peasant girl. I was the Emperor of the Seas!"

The Dark Sorcerer was silent for a moment. Then he spoke, saying, "Your Majesty, permit me to speak."

Kozan calmed slightly, then gestured for him to continue.

"I know not why you dislike Orion so; truth to tell, I did not even know you knew him. What I do know is you have spent more than sixteen years planning the destruction of Provenna. Are you willing to risk throwing all that away simply so that you can kill Orion?

"I see not how or why you have anything to fear, for if she kills him it merely accomplishes your own intentions. And if she does not, you can simply wait until all is in place and then sweep down and destroy her and kill Orion as you do so."

Kozan's fists were clenched and his face twisted in rage as he looked out across his dark city and searched to find some reason, no matter how small, to disregard the words of the Sorcerer.

"Orion is clever," he said haltingly. "He could, perhaps, find a way to escape during the journey to Leilaora; then he would escape me completely."

"I myself can take him to Leilaora and see that he does not do so," the Sorcerer answered calmly.

Kozan could find no fault with the Dark Sorcerer's words, hateful as he found them. With a snarl he took the chain from which hung the Soul Stone and handed it to the Sorcerer.

"Go," he said softly, his voice trembling with anger.

"Yes, Your Majesty," said the Dark Sorcerer who then bowed and turned and walked away.

* * *

Orion looked weakly up as the door to his cell was thrown open and two guards walked in. He gave a low groan and turned his eyes away as the cell was filled with the red light of a torch.

He was too weak to struggle against the guards as they came and unchained him and tied his hands tightly in front of him. They dragged him out of the cell--he had not the strength to walk--but, instead of taking him to the torture chambers, they took him up from the dungeon, through the twisting corridors of Kozan's palace, and out into the courtyard.

Orion blinked in pain, for, though the sky was gray and overcast, the light, at least to his eyes, was still far too bright.

He was taken across the courtyard to where the Dark Sorcerer stood beside two black, winged horses. At a command from the Sorcerer, Orion was placed upon one of them. He blinked his eyes and struggled to breath as he clutched the horse by the mane and concentrated with all his might on not tumbling from the saddle.

Without further words, the Sorcerer mounted the other horse and, taking his own reigns in one hand, and the reins of Orion's horse in the other, began to walk from the courtyard.

Orion looked in confusion at him. "Where are you taking me?" he asked, his voice so hoarse he could barely speak.

The Dark Sorcerer turned to him and said, "Perhaps to death, perhaps to life. We shall see presently."

With that, he said nothing more but led Orion from the courtyard, through the gates of Kozan's palace, and out into the dark city of Nolhol.

* * *

"Aeneas," said Eagle softly--her voice was filled with concern.

They stood in the gardens of Provenna's palace. The bright sun shown down upon them, and tall trees surrounded them.

"I think there is something you should know," she said.

He looked at her, first in interest then in concern as he saw the furrow of her brow and the troubled look within her eyes.

"What is it?" he asked.

She took a deep breath then said, "Your brother will soon be coming to Leilaora."

"What!" Aeneas cried in disbelief as anger welled up within him.

"Provenna has called him here."

He was too stunned to speak but simply stared at Eagle. The look of horror in his eyes was unlike anything she had ever seen before.

Suddenly, he turned and simply walked away, leaving Eagle to stare after him. She reached out her hand and opened her mouth to call out to him but hesitated then let her arm drop. Nothing she could say or do would change what he felt. She understood his need to be alone.

Chapter 15
Hatred, Anger, and Despair

The dark, thick woods surrounded and hid from sight Gideone, Stavros, Vayan, and Phautina. The silver rays of the moon shone down through the spaces between the leaves overhead and dotted the ground with pale light. Phautina lay on her stomach upon a soft, grassy spot of earth and tried to keep still as Stavros and Vayan examined her shoulder.

Stavros looked utterly exhausted. There were dark circles beneath his eyes, and it seemed to be taking all his energy simply to concentrate on Phautina's wound.

Gideone sat on a nearby fallen tree. His head was in his hands, and he moaned to himself, "He lies. He has to be lying."

Phautina's left sleeve had been cut off so that Stavros and Vayan could work more freely. The shaft of the arrow stuck out and angled slightly toward her spine, and the head was firmly embedded in her shoulder. Though Stavros touched the area around her wound as gently as possible, she gave a sob of pain.

"It appears nothing vital was struck," Stavros said after a moment.

Gideone's brow was furrowed in anger. "Abiel must lie; Eagle promised herself to me."

Stavros cast an annoyed look at Gideone, and then turned back to Phautina. "The arrow pierced deeply," he murmured. "If the arrow is pulled out we run the risk of having the arrowhead break off inside the body."

"Abiel will regret that lie," Gideone growled as he stood up.

"I could use some silence," Stavros said as he scowled at Gideone, but Gideone either did not hear, or did not care, for he continued talking to himself.

With a sigh of annoyance, Stavros turned back to Phautina. "I'm going to have to push the arrow all the way through your shoulder and out the other side."

"Tnaka will pay too," Gideone said he, his voice growing louder as his anger waxed greater.

Stavros gave a loud sigh and, opening his mouth, turned to Gideone, but before he could speak Phautina said with a groan, "Hurry up and just do it."

"He never deserved her," the Prince growled.

"This is going to hurt," Stavros said, still clearly angered by Gideone.

"As if it doesn't hurt already," Phautina muttered, still fighting the pain.

"Does he think that simply because he's a Power and I only a prince that he is more worthy of her than I?"

Stavros reached out and took the shaft of the arrow in both hands. He realized he had forgotten to tell her that, before the arrow could be pushed through, the feather had to be broken off.

"I swear I'll make him pay," Gideone cried.

Stavros cast another angry look at the Prince.

"All three of the Powers will pay!"

"Would you be quiet!" Stavros suddenly snarled as he snapped the arrow in two. Phautina gave a cry of pain.

"Do you realize how much sleep I have had since we left the elves?" Stavros demanded as he jumped to his feet and faced Gideone. "Practically none! Why? Because, despite your bravado, you needed to sleep so I took your bloody watch. I have had no sleep for the last fourteen hours. I am out here in the middle of a forest in the middle of the night, trying to tend to a wounded woman, and all you can do is stand by and snivel over an insult thrown out in the midst of battle by a man who is barely worthy to bear a sword? What is wrong with you?"

"How dare you talk to me like that!" cried Gideone.

Phautina gave a sob of pain and said, "Vayan, can you finish this?"

"Aye," he said as he knelt down where his father had been. He took the arrow in both hands.

"Abiel is a worthless cur," growled Gideone. "Why should I not be angry at his lies?"

"All right," Vayan murmured to himself, "I can do this." He had never hurt a woman before.

"His lies?!" Stavros cried.

"Yes, do it!" Phautina groaned.

"If it's lies that anger you, Gideone, did it ever occur to you that Tnaka and Eagle have been married for three years? I doubt Abiel is lying."

Gideone gave a cry of fury and sent his fist slamming into Stavros' jaw. Stavros reeled back.

Phautina screamed as Vayan pushed the arrow through her shoulder.

"It's all right. It's all right," Vayan said soothingly has he helped her sit up and pulled the arrow free.

"What is she still doing here?" Gideone growled as he turned to face her.

Stavros, holding his hand to his chin, picked himself up off the ground.

Vayan put his hand over Phautina's wound, and immediately it was healed, leaving only a small scar. Even as he did that he turn and, his jaw clenched, looked up at Gideone.

"I thought I said she could only come as far as Jwassax," snarled the Prince.

"What's wrong with ye?" Vayan demanded as he jumped to his feet. "Ye've hated har since th' momen' ye set eyes on har, but she's saved yar life twice already."

"She never saved my life!"

"Do ye actually think we could o' outrun Abiel's men on th' road to Jwassax?

Do ye forge' tha' less than an hour ago had she no' been ridin' behind ye, you would o' been th' who was shot?"

Gideone took a step back and looked wildly at Stavros and Vayan. "First Orion betrayed me, and now you!"

"How dare ye say tha'!" Vayan cried. "Orion's my friend, an' I know he'd never betray anyone."

"He betrayed me," Gideone snarled as he drew his sword. "He escaped, but you won't!" He rushed at Stavros and Vayan. They drew their swords to defend themselves.

"Stop!" Phautina's cry rose loud and clear through the night. Her brown eyes flashed, and her homely face bore such a look of nobility and command that the three men could not help but draw up short.

"Stavros, you are exhausted," she said. "Gideone, you are wounded and exhausted. Both of you will sleep, and Vayan and I will stand watch."

"No!" Gideone cried weakly as he stumbled forward. His face had suddenly turned ashen, and his hands had begun to tremble. He fairly gasped for breath as he said, "I will stand watch over the..." His sword fell from his hands, and, with a groan, he sank to the ground.

Stavros rushed forward, but, before he could reach him, Phautina was already at the fallen Prince's side. She looked up at Stavros, and there was something in her eyes that made him stop and step back.

She held the Prince's head in her arms and looked down at him, and with his dark eyes, he stared weakly back up at her.

Softly--so softly that neither Stavros nor Vayan could hear her words--she spoke. "I know why it is you wish to stand guard. These dreams, which haunt your sleep, and make you long for the light of day, are brought by no man save yourself. They are your hatred, and your anger, and your despair which fill up your heart and consume your mind and from which you cannot free yourself. They will drive you to insanity if you find no deliverance from them, but that day has not yet come. This night Joretham will give you peace that you might sleep, and perchance upon the morrow you will awake a wiser man."

He said nothing in reply. His eyes closed, and she lay his head back down upon the earth.

"What have you done with him?" Stavros demanded as he rushed forward.

"'Twas but a small sleeping spell," she answered as she turned to him. "I suggest you check his wound, for it has obviously worsened. Then you should also sleep."

"Thank you," he breathed and gave a slight smile. "I swear you must be sent from Joretham."

She smiled in return and said, "Perhaps I am."

Abiel did not attack them again that night, and both Gideone and Stavros slept in peace as Vayan and Phautina took turns standing watch.

When Gideone awoke in the morning, he was much subdued. Rested he may have been, but it seemed as if the life had been taken from him; the magic of the arrow continued to slowly overwhelm his body--the web of black lines now reached even to his shoulder--and the argument the night before had left him deeply affected.

Here, in the light of day, he knew that neither Stavros nor Vayan had turned against him, but their actions the night before brought to mind the man who had betrayed him. The anger that welled up within him at every thought of Orion was so powerful he could barely stand it, and yet he had to bear it, for he could not free himself from it.

The words of Phautina echoed in his mind; "They are your hatred, and your anger, and your despair which fill up your heart and consume your mind and from which you cannot free yourself. They will drive you to insanity if you find no freedom from them."

But what did her words mean to him? She was nothing more than a poor bard whom he allowed to journey in his company. She knew nothing of his thoughts or his dreams. He knew that once he destroyed his enemies and made Eagle his wife, his anger, hatred, and despair would depart, and he would have peace.

* * *

The pale rays of the early morning sun shone out across the golden city of Leilaora, and already the towers and spires of the castles and temples and cathedrals sparkled in the light.

Though early, the streets were already filled with people, and through this throng the Dark Sorcerer, with Orion riding beside him, made his way. The Sorcerer sat tall and proud upon his horse and did not even deign look upon the people who crowded the streets.

All strength was gone from Orion. His long, dirty, hair, washed in his own blood and sweat, hung down and nearly covered his face. He sat slumped forward in his saddle and had not even the strength to raise his eyes and look about him.

As they rode through the streets of Leilaora the people's eyes turned toward them. They looked in awe upon the dark magnificence of the Sorcerer and in pity upon his prisoner; who was this man who seemed so bowed and broken?

Orion could feel their stares upon him, but he did not return their looks. He could not bear to look back at the people, or gaze upon the city that he had left ten years before. He had once sworn that he would never return, but now he was being dragged there against his will.

Beside him he heard someone gasp in astonishment and fear, and he could not help but turn to see who it was. His gaze met that of an elven woman. Her long, blonde hair fell wildly about her, and her blue eyes were filled with terror. She nearly tripped and fell as she turned and tried to run from him.

Hatred, Anger and Despair

Shame filled his heart. He knew not her name, neither had he any recollection of her face, but he could imagine why she ran in fear. The wounds and the dirt which covered his body and the space of ten years had made him unrecognizable to everyone else, but he had no doubt that she would remember him until the day she died.

Now it was not only in weakness and exhaustion that he raised not his eyes, but in shame as well. He could still feel the eyes of countless people turned toward him. Once he had gloried in the stares of men, now he could only writhe beneath them.

Up through the glorious city of Leilaora he was brought by the Dark Sorcerer, but he did not look upon the beauty. Through the pearly gates of the palace he was led, but he did not see them either.

They stopped in the middle of the quiet courtyard of the palace. The Dark Sorcerer stepped to the ground and practically had to pull Orion from his horse.

Orion was so weak that he fell to his knees, and it was only then that he raised his head. He found himself gazing up at a small group of people who looked down in astonishment upon him and seemed at a loss as to what to do for him.

His eyes first turned to Tnaka. What the elven king thought was impossible to fully discern. There was amazement and horror upon his face, but there was another look that swirled behind his gray eyes that was indescribable.

At his side stood Eagle. She looked down at him with large, sympathetic eyes. Behind her stood a young man with brown hair and green eyes. His arms were crossed and his face twisted in a scowl of fury.

Finally, his gaze turned to Provenna where she stood in front of the other three. Her face was filled with horror at his condition, and yet there was a hopeful expectation within her eyes.

His lips turned up in a sad half-smile and he breathed, "Hello, Mother." Then, with a sigh, he fell forward, unconscious.

Provenna rushed forward. Even as she did so, the Dark Sorcerer knelt to help the fallen man. Slaves were quickly called, and Orion was carried away to a private room where the palace healer was called to tend to his wounds.

* * *

Provenna stood in a spacious, dimly lit room and looked down upon Orion who lay asleep upon a large, soft bed. His wounds had been washed and bound, and he had been made to feel as comfortable as possible, but he did not seem to be entirely at ease. His mouth was firmly shut, and his brow was slightly furrowed in a frown.

Provenna reached out and touched his forehead.

"Orion," she said, "I doubt you can hear me--perhaps 'tis better you cannot, for you were ever one to frown upon family affection--but I cannot help but speak. I missed you so much, and I doubt you will ever know how overjoyed I am that you are once again here in Leilaora.

"I wish I could have spared you the pain you suffered at the hands of Kozan. One day, perhaps very soon, he will pay for his insolence. Perhaps it will be you yourself who takes revenge.

"'Twas funny," she said with a laughed, "for ten long years I prayed that you would return to me, and when you finally did I could only stand, unmoving, there and in horror look upon what Kozan had done to you.

"'Tis now night, and you have been unconscious since you were first brought here, but I would be a fool if I could not see that you have changed much over the years you were gone. I looked into your eyes for but a few moments, but I could see in them an experience and a profoundness that they never before held."

She laughed. "Oh, but listen to me rambling on while you cannot even hear me."

She bent and kissed his forehead.

"Goodnight, Orion. I love you, Son."

With that she turned and walked from the room.

The Dark Sorcerer stood in the corridor outside. He had obviously been waiting anxiously for her.

"Your Majesty," he said and started toward her, "please forgive me. Had I known he was your son I would have written to you the moment Kozan captured him."

She smiled softly. The anxious expression upon his face made him look far more like a schoolboy who had been remiss in his lessons rather than the powerful sorcerer and warrior that he was.

"Trouble not yourself, Sir Sorcerer," Provenna told him, "for how could it be expected that you would know Orion was my son. And worry not, for, as you have probably seen, he is not entirely human, and, now that he can rest, his body will quickly heal."

"But I feel so terrible."

"No, you have no need to. You have done no wrong. Indeed, I wish only that I could have honored your request to have Mystia brought here as well, but that would have angered Kozan far more than I could deal with at this moment." Her features darkened at the thought of her former lover.

"I understand, Your Majesty."

Provenna suddenly brightened and, smiling, asked, "Will you join me at the feast in celebration of my son's return?"

"I would count it a great honor, Your Majesty," the Dark Sorcerer answered as he inclined his head to her. He offered her his arm, which she took, and they began to walk down the corridor toward the banquet hall.

Her gaze fell upon the ring, which she wore on her finger. The Dark Sorcerer, in his letter, had asked that she demand that ring from Kozan. It was a very beautiful ring to be sure--the stone was unlike any she had ever before seen--but she could not understand why the Sorcerer found it so important.

"Sir Sorcerer," she began. He turned his face to her.

"All day," she continued, "I have meant to ask you what this ring is and why you found it important enough to ask me to demand it of Kozan."

He looked at the ring for a moment then said, "The ring itself is unimportant, Your Majesty. As near as I could tell, it was a gift to Prince Orion from Mystia. Both of them held it precious, and I thought it deserved to be kept by one more worthy than Kozan. Perhaps when the Prince has recovered you can return it to him."

"You can rest assured I will treat it with care, and, when he has recovered, return it to the one to whom it was given."

"I did not doubt you would, Your Majesty," he answered.

* * *

Queen Eagle sat alone in the palace gardens. Darkness had but recently fallen upon Leilaora, and the night was yet warm. The silver moon shone down upon her and cast the whole garden in a beautiful light. She sat upon a marble bench and leaned her back against a tree as she looked up at the stars. The faint sound of music drifted across the garden from the palace where Provenna celebrated, and occasionally she could hear the merry voices of people who walked along one of the paths which winded it way through the trees and shrubs.

As she sat there she suddenly had the feeling that she was being watched, and turning, she found Tnaka standing in the shadow of a tree and gazing silently upon her. Realizing he had been caught, he stirred and, walking forward, laughed and said, "I knew I would find you here. Not a day has passed since we first arrived in Leilaora that you have not come to this place."

"I am honored that you would count that knowledge worthy to obtain, Lord," she said as she rose.

He took her hand and, smiling, said, "I would count any knowledge of you worthy to obtain." He raised her hand to his lips.

She hesitated then said, "You seem quite merry this night, sir."

He laughed and said, "I not only seem it; I am." He sat down upon the bench.

Eagle looked confused and, as she also sat down, said, "I pray you will not think this too forward of me, Lord, but I fail to understand why you're so lifted up in spirits now that Orion has been brought here, when just yesterday you were so troubled by the thought of his arrival."

"'Twas not Orion's arrival that troubled me but how Kozan would react to it. Kozan bears Orion an enormous grudge, and it wasn't clear what he might do if the Prince was taken from him. But, now that Orion has been brought here, the danger is passed."

He was silent for a moment and grew more thoughtful.

"I am also happy because now Provenna is reunited with the son she has missed for so long," he said. "Perhaps now at least some of the anger and bitterness within her will disappear.

"Orion is an intelligent and capable man, and perhaps he will find a way to deal with Kozan. And perhaps, with Kozan destroyed and Provenna appeased, the wars which tear this land apart will be ended, and I will no longer have to conquer but, instead, will be able to return to Kerrill and live out the rest of my days in peace."

"Those are three very large perhapses, Lord."

Tnaka was no longer smiling but had grown more thoughtful still.

"Yes," he said with a sigh, "I know. Large perhapses they may be, but still they are my wishes."

He took her hands in his and looked intently into her eyes as he said, "I wearied of war before it ever began, and throughout the years of conquering the countries of Lairannare for Provenna I have wished only for peace." He gave a small smile. "Eagle, I have waited so long, and at times I despaired of anything ever changing, but now in my heart I feel that soon everything will indeed be changed. The day I have so longed for will come, and I await it with open arms."

Eagle was silent for a moment then said, "I await it too, my Lord."

Tnaka smiled again, but this time it was not in joy. Eagle was taken aback, for, though he had been laughing and merry but a moment before, his eyes suddenly bore a look of pain and sadness.

"Lord, what is it?" she cried as she reached out and touched his arm.

He gave a wry smile and said, "Eagle, must you always call me Lord or Master? I swear, you must address me so in every single sentence you speak to me."

"What would you have me call you, Lor...?"

"Eagle, must you even ask? Do you not know?" He rose to his feet and, with arms opened, turned and faced her. "For three years have we been married, and in that time you have called me by every title under the sun--sir, lord, majesty, your majesty, my lord, good sir, kind sir, and a myriad that slip my mind--but you have never called my by the one thing I wish to be called. Why have you never called me Tnaka?"

She paused for a moment before answering. "Sir, you are the King of Kerrill. I am a citizen of Kerrill, and your humble servant. 'Tis not my place to call you anything but Lord and Master."

"Eagle," he cried, "you are my wife. If you are not in a place to call me by my name then who is?"

She paused again and bit her lip. "Is it not the place of a wife to honor her husband?"

"You can honor me without calling me by titles."

She could think of nothing to say in reply, but she could not simply stare up at him and so, instead, gazed down at her hands.

"Eagle," he began but then stopped. He searched to find words to convey that which filled his heart.

She turned her face to him.

"Eagle," he said again as he sat once more down beside her, "there was a time--it seems like a lifetime ago--when you were the proudest most noble woman in the whole of Lairannare. You had knowledge and wisdom far beyond your years. Your wit, your skill in conversation and argument, and your un-tamable spirit were renowned throughout the Realm, and you had a courage that would put many a man to shame. That was the woman I thought I married."

She was silent for a long moment as she looked upon him. Her gray eyes were filled with sorrow.

"Lord, you speak of things as they once were." Her voice was filled with bitterness. "They are no longer that way. Everything changes. Kingdoms rise, wax great, and eventually fall. The merry spring turns to the lazy summer and eventually becomes the long, bitter winter. The babe is born, matures, and finally grows old and dies.

"Ask me not to be Princess Eagle of the Sky Elves who was young, impetuous, foolhardy, who fought with swords, rode eagles, and who believed ideals could be realized." She fought against her tears. "I am Queen Eagle of the Wood Elves whose spirit has been tempered, who speaks her mind less impetuously, who tries to serve and support her husband faithfully, and who long ago gave up swords and eagles and the skies of Scalavori."

She rose quickly and walked a few paces away but not before a sob escaped her lips.

Tnaka waited for a moment then quietly rose and walked to where she stood. He placed his hand gently upon her arm and said, "Eagle, I came to you this night to give you something. I pray you will accept it."

"What?" she said in a trembling voice as, brushing the tears from her eyes, she turned.

"Here," he said, a hopeful look upon his face, as he held out his other hand.

Her eyes grew wide with awe as she saw what he held. In his hand were three beautiful flowers. The pure, white petals had only begun to open and did not yet reveal the silvery-blue pistil within. The long, silver stems curved gracefully beneath the flower's weight and shimmered in the soft light of the moon.

"Lumellia," she breathed as she took them. "The flowers of the snow." She could feel the silver stem against her hand. "And they're real." She looked up at him in amazement. "Wherever did you get them?"

He smiled and said softly, "That is my secret."

He held up his other hand and in it he held another flower. He reached up and began to fasten it in her hair. She tried to turn away, but he stopped her with a whisper. "Eagle."

He quickly finished with his work and stepped back from her.

"Stand there," he said motioning with his hand. Hesitantly, she walked to where she thought he motioned.

"Yes," he said when she looked up questioningly at him, "right there where the moon shines full upon you."

She straightened and stood still and silently as he looked upon her.

After a long, long moment he spoke. "You truly are a child of the snow and the mountains. You were meant to soar with the eagles not sit at home all day among the trees of the forest.

"Noble woman, ever have your eyes been turned toward your native country, and ever has your heart yearned after the home of your youth, but never once did you complain when I saw not the look which was so plain upon your face." He took a step toward her. "When my business with Provenna is completed, you and I shall travel to the Mountains of Scalavori. You will see the father from whom you have been so long absent, and you will ride the eagles you have so longed for. We shall stay there a month, a year, as long as you desire, and, after we have left, we will return far more than we have in the past three years. This I promise you."

"Oh, Lord," she said with a voice trembling with the tears that threatened to fall, "thank you. With all my heart I thank you."

He walked to her, and put his hands around her waist.

"'Tis but a small thing to do for the wife I love."

He kissed her brow.

"I love you, Eagle," he told her softly. "But," he continued as he took a step back, "I think I have neglected you. 'Tis a sin for which I pray you will forgive me, and I want you to know that I will do my utmost to let it not happen again."

She looked up at him. Her large, gray eyes were filled with gratitude. Her long, blonde hair fell down about her, and the moon lighted her soft, beautiful features. As Tnaka looked down upon her, he could say with certainty that he knew of no woman more beautiful or noble than she.

Chapter 16
The Falling Darkness

Thus shall you know the Scion of Vallendar, the Child of Magianna: his blood shall be as dark as the rose of Bellenira.
--The Book of the Prophecies

Mystia sat at a table in the main room of her chambers. The darkness of the room had just begun to fade away as the sky outside the window grew light with the early morning. She did not see this, for she lay asleep at the table, her head cradled in her arms.

All night had she stayed awake and prayed to Joretham for herself and her country, but mostly for Orion. The nameless terror that welled up within her heart at the thought of Orion being killed was unlike anything she had ever known before, but she knew not why the thought of his death frightened her so, for would not his death simply free him to enter into an eternity of peace?

Her prayers had finally ceased as exhaustion overcame her, but, even in sleep, peace did not come. She found herself once more kneeling beside Orion where he sat chained to the dungeon wall. His blue eyes were filled with terror as he begged her to pray to Joretham for him. She reached out and touched his face; she could feel it broken and scarred beneath her fingers. She opened her mouth to speak, but no words would come.

A hand suddenly shook her roughly. She awoke with a start and looked wildly about. She found herself staring up at a woman, nobly dressed, with long blonde hair, and clear blue eyes. Her face bore a cold yet sorrowful look, and her voice was tinged with anger and anguish as she spoke. "Come with me."

"Who are you?" Mystia demanded as she rose and took a step back.

The woman gave a sigh of annoyance. "My name is Lareina. Kozan has gone to the Temple of Balor to offer up the morning sacrifice. Now is your chance to escape."

"And why give you succor to me?"

Her voice was filled with bitterness. "If I were you, I would simply praise my God that I was being helped and not quibble over the reasons. Now come." Lareina turned and began to walk away, and, after a moment's pause, Mystia silently started after her.

They walked out of the door and into the corridor. Two guards stood there--one on either side of the door--but they did nothing to stop the women as they went past.

Through the dark and twisting corridors of Kozan's palace they made their way. Mystia's heart was racing, but she did not let her terror overcome her.

As they walked through the palace, she came to the realization that Lareina was the queen, for every time they passed a guard he would stand at attention and salute her. This calmed Mystia's fears somewhat, but it also filled her with confusion, for why would one of Kozan's wives help her?

At last, Lareina led her out of the palace and into the garden, and, in spite of the fears that still held her, Mystia found herself looking around at the trees and the bushes, for the lush greens of the garden were a beautiful and welcome sight after the darkness of the palace, and indeed, the darkness of the whole of Nolhol.

She started as the sound of Balor's Horn pierced the air.

"We must hurry," Lareina said, "for Kozan will soon return."

They began to make their way quickly along one of the narrow paths that wound its way through the garden. Small statues, which oftentimes stood almost buried in the dark green foliage of the bushes, stared out at the two women as they walked past. Every so often the cry of a bird would pierce the silence, as if telling them to hurry.

They rounded a corner, and Mystia almost ran into Lareina as the queen suddenly slowed her pace. Before them, in the shadow of a tree, stood a harpy. She was beautiful, with light skin, black wings, and dark hair that tumbled down over her shoulders, and upon her head she wore a small, very ornate, golden crown. Mystia realized the she must be Nirreloyn, Kozan's first wife.

The harpy was looking down upon a statue of a dwarf, a thoughtful expression upon her face as she ran her fingers over its head. As Lareina approached, she looked up.

"What are you doing here?" she demanded, as she looked them over.

Lareina took a quick breath and said, "Before the Dark Sorcerer left, he asked me to take Mystia for a walk in the garden, for he thought it wise that she be given some fresh air."

Mystia shrank back as Nirreloyn took a step toward her and Lareina.

"Do you actually expect me to believe such a feeble lie as that?" she demanded.

"I speak no lie," Lareina answered. "Now let us pass." She began to walk around Nirreloyn who barred her path, but as she did so, Nirreloyn suddenly grabbed her by the arm and threw her to the ground.

Lareina scrambled to her feet and with a cry of fury flung herself at Nirreloyn. The two went down in a kicking, clawing, screaming pile. The harpy managed to get on top of Lareina. The blonde queen gave a scream of pain as Nirreloyn dug her long nails into her face.

Mystia ran forward and grabbed Nirreloyn--whose back was turned toward her--by the hair close to the skull. The harpy gave a hiss of pain as Mystia gave a hard tug and pulled her from Lareina.

"Guards!" Nirreloyn shrieked. "Guards!"

"Be quiet," Mystia ordered, as she pulled the harpy's head back.

"Break her neck!" Lareina snarled as she scrambled to her feet.

"No," Mystia exclaimed, repulsed at the very thought.

"Kill her!" Lareina screamed as she rushed at Nirreloyn.

Mystia let go of Nirreloyn's hair; crying as she did so, "Stop!"

Nirreloyn wasted no time, but spread her wings and leapt into the air, eluding Lareina's grasping hands.

"Guards!" she screamed, and her voice carried across the whole of the garden. "A prisoner is escaping! Guards!"

"Coward!" Lareina shrieked as she jumped up and down, trying to grab the harpy. "Come down here!"

Nirreloyn gave a wicked smile and, with a hiss, swooped down at Lareina. Lareina gave a scream as the harpy slammed into her, and she went flying back.

Mystia began to rush forward to the fallen woman, but Nirreloyn swiftly turned on her, blocking her way. Mystia jumped off the path, avoiding the harpy's long, pointed nails as she flew past. Nirreloyn gave a hiss as she turned and flew at Mystia again. Once again the Princess leapt out of the way.

Nirreloyn gave a snarl of anger as she swooped a third time toward Mystia; this time she would not miss. Mystia stood unmoving and watched intently as the harpy sped toward her. Finally, at the last moment, Mystia jumped to the side, reached out with her arms, and grabbed Nirreloyn around the waist.

Both women fell to the ground. Mystia, fighting against the pain of the fall, struggled against Nirreloyn and managed to get on top of her.

"Guards!" Nirreloyn screamed one last time just before Mystia drew back her fist and slammed into her face.

The Princess gave a groan of pain as she stepped up and away from the unconscious harpy. She looked around, and saw Lareina lying on the ground nearby. The blonde-haired woman, who had not been knocked unconscious but had only had the wind knocked out of her, also gave a groan as she sat up. She looked up at Mystia, then down at Nirreloyn, then back up at Mystia. She said nothing, but her eyes were filled with surprise.

Suddenly they heard the sound of men running through the garden, and they looked up just in time to see a guard come running around a tree.

"Hey, Larkin!" he cried. "I found them!"

As Mystia and Lareina looked at him, their hearts sank.

* * *

Kozan stared down at Lareina, where she knelt before him on the floor. A table stood beside him, and behind that stood Mystia, silent and passive as she looked on.

Kozan stared darkly at Lareina for a full minute before he finally spoke.

"Why," said he, his voice soft but filled with rage, "did you try to help Mystia escape?"

She stared up at him with her most cold and spiteful look and refused to speak.

"Answer me!" Kozan fairly screamed.

Still she refused to speak.

"Answer me, wench!" he cried as he struck her hard across the face.

Mystia gave a gasp and took a step toward Lareina. Kozan spun and stopped her with a look.

Lareina did not scream in pain but remained absolutely silent. Then, as she looked up at Kozan, the sneer upon her face grew, and she opened her mouth to speak.

"Strike me, Kozan," she hissed. "Strike me, a woman who kneels defenseless before you. Strike me and tell the whole of Nolhol so that when you ride through the streets the crowd can cry out, 'Brave warrior! Noble king! We bow before you who struck a defenseless woman!'"

"Silence!" Kozan cried as he struck her again.

She looked at him with a hurt expression and said, "But I thought you told me to answer you."

"I told you to answer me, not mock me," Kozan growled.

She sneered. "When speaking to you 'tis the same thing."

He gave a snarl of fury and struck her once again.

"Why did you betray me?" he demanded. "You are my wife, my love!"

"Your love?" Lareina cried. "How can even you be such a hypocrite? How can you say I am your love--you who have just struck me thrice? What would you know of love? Is love having another wife besides me? Or is love giving yourself over to who knows how many concubines? Is love striking me and despising me and ignoring me?

"You know nothing of love!" she snarled, her voice rising with anger and bitterness. "But I know what love is! Love is being faithful to one man, though he may care nothing for you. Love is being willing to die for him. Love is helping his accursed woman escape the clutches of his worst enemy!"

Kozan looked upon her in furious amazement as he realized what she was saying. For a moment he could not even speak, so great was his anger.

"Orion!" he finally cried. "You helped her escape because of Orion!" He had to clutch at the table beside him to keep from falling, and even then he barely remained standing.

"He stole Rhianna from me, and now I find he stole you also. Why?!" he cried. "Why?"

"Fool!" she spat. "Why do think? He was strong and handsome and courageous and passionate! He held me as you never did and loved me as you never could."

"No!" he shrieked as he struck her with all his might. She gave a scream of pain.

"Kozan!" Mystia cried as she rushed forward.

"No!" he cried again as he struck Lareina once more.

Lareina fell back and remained still. Kozan, wide-eyed and gasping for breath, could only look silently down upon her.

Mystia knelt beside the fallen queen and took her up in her arms. She looked down at Lareina's lifeless face then up at Kozan. Her black eyes were wide and accusing. "You killed her!"

For a moment Kozan knew not what to feel--whether horror or satisfaction. He could only stare down, unblinking, upon Lareina's lifeless body.

He suddenly could feel guilt and terror taking hold of his heart.

"What of it?" he cried, less to Mystia and more in rebellion against his conscience, as he rushed forward and pulled her from the floor. She gave a cry of surprise. Lareina's body slipped from her arms and fell in a heap.

Kozan looked deeply into her eyes and said menacingly, "I kill who I will, when I will. Just thank your God I did not kill you as well."

Suddenly, there was a pounding on the door.

"What?" Kozan snarled as he turned his face to the door. The door opened and a guard walked in. He opened his mouth to speak, but he suddenly saw Kozan holding Mystia tightly and Lareina's dead body lying on the floor. He hesitated.

"What?" demanded Kozan as he thrust Mystia from him.

"Your Majesty," the guard said as he bowed awkwardly, "we captured this High Elf in the palace." He motioned with his hand and two more guards walked in, dragging between them a man dressed in the armor of a palace guard. They threw him on the ground at Kozan's feet. The Elf's long black hair fell wildly around him, and he look up with fearless black eyes at Kozan.

"And I assume you were trying to rescue my prisoner as well," Kozan said coldly.

The Elf said nothing in reply, but cast a quick glance at Mystia.

The Princess looked in pity upon him. He reminded her of Gideone.

Kozan slowly circled the Elf, looking furiously down upon him as he did so. "I am the Power-king of Delovachia. When I demand an answer you will give it. Now, tell me, were you trying to rescue my prisoner?"

The High Elf kept his mouth clenched shut.

"I said answer me!" Kozan cried as he kicked him hard in the stomach. Mystia gave a gasp of terror. The Elf's eyes bulged and he doubled over in pain, but still he refused to speak.

"Kozan..." Mystia whispered. The dark king scowled at her then turned back to the prisoner.

"Very well," said he when he saw the Elf would not speak. "Guards." The three guards stood at attention and awaited their orders. "Take him to the dungeon. Perhaps the torturer can loosen his tongue, but see that he is not killed. No, that pleasure will come tonight. 'Tis high time that Balor's altar feasted on something other than pigs."

"Yes, Your Majesty," said the leader of the three guards. They bowed and dragged the Elf from the room.

Kozan turned back to Mystia who stood silently by, and as he did so his gaze fell upon Lareina's body. He gave a growl of anger and contempt and turned his eyes from her.

"Three separate times has someone attempted to rescue you," he said to Mystia, his voice trembling with anger. "I will not allow a fourth. From this day until the day you lie dead upon Balor's altar, you will not leave my side."

* * *

It was late in the afternoon when Provenna and the Dark Sorcerer walked along the palace walls and conversed together. The cool wind gently caressed their faces, as the warm rays of the sun shone down upon them.

Provenna looked beautiful. She wore a silken, green dress embroidered with gold. Her arms were bare, and upon her right wrist she wore a single, small, golden bracelet. Her long, red hair flowed freely over her shoulders, and a small, golden crown rested upon her head.

The Dark Sorcerer, for his part, looked more than a little austere by contrast, what with his simple costume all of black, and his long, brown hair combed and fastened securely behind his head, but he also looked very handsome.

"Once again, Your Majesty," he was saying with his strong foreign accent, "I wish your son the quickest of recoveries."

"Thank you," Provenna answered. "You know not how much that means to me." She smiled. "You know, Sir Sorcerer, you are one of the very few people who has ever shown any concern over the troubles with which I am faced."

"I think it's sad that there are so few who would show you compassion."

She gave a sigh. "Such is the price of being a Power--or any Magic of great strength; people believe you to be invulnerable."

There was a moment of silence then she spoke again. "So tell me, how soon shall you return to Delovachia."

"Tonight," he answered. "Indeed, with Your Majesty's permission, I wish to leave within the hour."

"So soon?" she asked in surprise, coming to a halt. She paused for a moment then said, "The few times you have come here, you've left quickly. Why do you not stay longer and give us the honor of your presence?"

"Kozan dislikes it when I am gone long from his service, and, as his servant, it is my duty to return to him as quickly as possible."

"And am I not far greater than Kozan?" Provenna asked. "Should you not do as I bid?"

The Sorcerer was silent for a moment before he answered. "If you require me to stay here then I must, but if you do not then I will return to Nolhol, for there is much there that I must do."

"So you will not willingly stay?"

"Nay, I will not."

Provenna turned and looked out over the city stretched out in all directions before her. It was truly a city of gold, with its gilded temples and palaces and towers of greatness. Even the massive, granite monuments shone red-gold, for the setting sun cast its warm rays over the vast city, setting the tops of the buildings and the tips of the spires and towers shining brilliantly with its light.

Her hair moved softly with the wind as she spread her hand out over her city and spoke. "Look long upon this city, sir Sorcerer. 'Tis the jewel of the Realm of Earth. Is it not a city of splendor? Is it not a city to be lifted up in pride over? This is my city--my beloved city. This is the city from which the Realm of Earth is ruled.

"It has stood for more than five thousand years. Battles great and terrible have raged here. Blood has flowed like rivers through the streets, yet it still stands. 'Tis said that Joretham himself once walked here.

"Look well upon this city. See you how far it stretches? Do you see how the sun shines upon it and makes it yet more glorious?" She turned and looked at him. "Is not my city far greater than that of Kozan?

"What does Kozan's city hold? Darkness, terror, lewdness, oppression, death.

"But what does my city give? Life, hope, beauty, peace." She gazed up at him with pleading eyes. "Leave him and join with me. You will be great, the greatest prince in all my realm. This city of golden splendor will be your city."

The Sorcerer looked silently down upon Provenna as she looked up at him, her green eyes filled with a pleading he never knew she felt. In her face he saw a sorrow and a longing he knew she had betrayed to no one else. He turned his face quickly toward the buildings and towers stretched out before him, for he felt he had seen something no man should ever have seen.

"'Tis indeed a magnificent city," he said softly. The longing welling up within him was like nothing that had ever possessed him before. He took a deep breath. "And perhaps the day will come when I can return to it and live in peace." He bowed his head, "but now I must return to Nolhol, for there is much I have left undone.

"And now, if I may leave...?"

Provenna lowered her eyes and nodded. In silence, the Dark Sorcerer turned and walked away.

Never before had he desired something as much as he desired to stay in that beautiful city. He would have given up all his dreams to do so. Had he looked back and beheld Provenna as she stood there with a look of utter despair upon her face, or had she simply called out to him, all strength of will that yet remained would have left him, and he would have run back to her and never parted again. But he did not turn, and she did not speak.

Provenna watched him until he disappeared into the tower at the end of the wall, then she also turned and walked away. Were one to have looked upon her face, one would never have guessed what had transpired upon that wall above that beautiful city, for her features were as unmoving as stone.

* * *

Far to the south, the sun was also setting upon the city of Nolhol, and the time of the evening sacrifice drew nigh. The streets were lined with thousands upon thousands of people all lifting up their voices in savage cries of praise to Balor.

Up through those streets rode Kozan, upon a massive, black stallion, followed by a huge entourage of priests. Before him walked the chief torturer who drove the High Elf in front of him. Up through the streets they made their way toward the temple of Balor, which stood dark and ominous against the gray sky.

Mystia, veiled, sat upon a black mare and was forced to ride beside Kozan. She looked down in pity and silent horror upon the Elf as he stumbled and fell. His hands were tied tightly in front of him. His black hair, which was soaked with sweat and blood, hung down in front of his eyes, and his face was broken and bleeding.

The crowd jeered, and the torturer cracked his whip across the High Elf's back. The Elf's eyes widened in pain, but he made not a sound. He struggled to his feet and continued on.

He was scorned and mocked, whipped and spat upon, but, though his pain was evident, he made no noise. Blood and dirt covered his body. Occasionally, as he stumbled forward, sticks and stones were thrown at him. His face twisted in agony, but he forced himself to move forward.

Up through the streets of Nolhol, Kozan and his entourage made their way until they stood at the very foot of the steps leading up to the Temple of Balor.

The thundering, furious screaming of the crowd abated slightly as the High Elf suddenly fell to the ground and lay as one dead. Slowly, Kozan dismounted and walked to the fallen man. The Elf's hand moved slightly--proof that he still lived.

"Rise, dog," Kozan growled.

The High Elf struggled to obey, but he rose not quickly enough. Mystia watched in terror as Kozan drew back his leg to kick him.

"No!" Mystia's mind screamed.

Kozan suddenly drew short, and his head snapped around as he turned to look at her. Mystia slapped her hands over her mouth as she realized she had cried the word aloud. The dark king's eyes flashed as he gazed at her, then, without a word, he turned back to the Elf.

"I said rise!" he growled.

The High Elf's eyes filled with pain, and he struggled to regain his breath. Slowly, and with great effort, he clambered to his feet, and the frenzy of the crowd increased as they mocked and sang and cried out in exultation to their god.

Kozan turned to Mystia. "Come." It was more than simply a command; it was a promise--a promise that her insolence would not go unpunished.

She dismounted. Her head was spinning, her legs felt weak, and she felt that at any moment she would faint, but she managed to force herself to walk to him.

Up the many steps of stone, which led to the temple, rose Kozan, Mystia, and the High Elf. Behind them, in two long lines, came the priests of Balor, dressed in long robes of flaming red. They formed two rows, which stretched from the very top to the very bottom of the steps.

Kozan, Mystia, and the High Elf reached the top of the steps and stood in front of the massive door, which led into the temple. It was guarded on either side by the never-sleeping statues of the Baltuil. Thousands of years ago, Balor had set them up to guard his temple. It was said that in times past they had spoken-- prophesying and giving the commands of Balor--but, if that was true, they had long since fallen silent.

They stood as tall as the largest of horses, but their bodies seemed lithe and muscular like those of demon cats. Their paws--both forefoot and hind-foot-- had long, sharp claws attached to them. Their granite faces, like those of panthers, were carved into grotesque and evil grins, and their jeweled eyes glowed red.

The High Elf was made first to walk beneath their terrible gaze. He limped forward, his shoulders hunched with pain, but he looked up in scorn upon the stone creatures as he passed under them. Kozan followed, his dark robes sweeping behind him as he did so.

Mystia took a halting step then stopped at the threshold of their gaze. She dared not go farther.

The cries of the people pounded against her ears.

"Come, woman," Kozan growled, "or Balor shall receive a double sacrifice."

Trembling, Mystia forced herself to take that last fatal step. The Baltuil grinned leeringly down at her. As she passed beneath them, the fiery red light of their eyes flared, and there arose from the depths of those unmoving, granite creatures the most terrifying of hissing cries, like millions of voices screaming up from the pits of Elmorran.

"Blood!" they cried. "Give us blood! Give us the blood of Vallendar!"

The cries of the vast crowd rose, but they no longer screamed in savage joy. There voices were filled with fear and wonder.

For a moment Kozan could only stare in amazement at Mystia as she stood still in terror beneath the eyes of the statues. He regained himself and in less than a second was at her side. He yanked her inside out of sight of the crowd.

He stared at her in utter confusion, until, after a moment, a look of realization dawned in his eyes. He pulled a dagger from his belt, and, before Mystia could pull away, he drew the blade across the palm of her hand. She gave a cry of pain and tried to wrench her hand from him, but he held her fast. Amazement filled his heart as he gazed upon her palm. The blood, which poured down her hand, was not the bright red of normal blood but dark red, so dark it was almost black. He looked down upon her and for a moment knew not what to do or say.

"You are the one?" he whispered, agony written upon his face.

Her whole body shook. "Please let go of me," she pleaded.

Suddenly his features became stony. "But no, you can't be."

In one quick motion, he let go of her hand and spun around.

"Prepare the altar," he ordered the priests who stood nearby.

Tears of pain fell down Mystia's face as she held her wounded hand tightly to her. With a trembling voice she whispered a few words in a foreign tongue. Immediately, the gash on her hand closed itself and left only a faint scar. She brushed her tears away and looked up in time to catch a glimpse of the High Elf as he was being dragged away. Even with such a brief glance, she could see how intently he looked upon her.

Kozan walked to the door of the temple and looked out upon the huge crowd of cheering people. He raised his arms and cried out in a voice like the thunder, "Rejoice! Rejoice! The blood of the High Elves flows from Balor's altar!"

At his cry the cheers of the crowd swelled in fury and intensity until the whole of the Temple shook beneath it.

He turned and walked back into the Temple and, with Mystia at his side, entered the inner sanctum. Hundreds of red torches lit the massive sanctuary, but it was darkness which reigned supreme. In the flickering light, the black walls, streaked with blood, could just be made out. In the center of the vast room there rose a tall pyramid of steps, and at the very top stood the altar of Balor. A priest dressed in flowing robes of crimson stood beside it, holding a bottle of oil in one hand and a long, intricately carved dagger in the other.

The High Elf, chained hand and foot, lay upon the altar and looked down upon Kozan and Mystia as they ascended the many steps.

As they reached the uppermost step, Mystia gave a gasp, for at the foot of the altar lay her father's staff. Kozan saw what she gazed upon and with a sneer said, "I put it there as a constant reminder that the magic of a High Elf is nothing compared to the power of Balor." With that he turned and walked to the altar.

He looked down with a mocking smile upon the High Elf. The cries of the crowd echoed throughout the Temple as Kozan began the ceremony.

"Hear us, Balor!" they cried. "Bless us, Balor! Powerful is Balor!"

"Powerful is Balor," began Kozan softly, "and mightily he conquers nations." He stretched out his hands over the High Elf. "Feel the fire of his power." Mystia choked as the Elf's body contorted in pain. She started forward, but Kozan suddenly turned his head and fixed her with a murderous look. She stopped where she was and could only look on in agony upon the Elf, who still refused to cry out.

Kozan took the jar of oil from the priest who stood silently by. "Balor, we cleanse your enemy of his filth."

The cry of the people still echoed through the sanctuary. "Hear us, Balor! Bless us, Balor! Powerful is Balor!"

The dark king poured oil upon his hand and ran his fingers across the High Elf's brow. "Clean of mind."

He touched his hand to the Elf's lips. "Free of blasphemies."

He turned and took the dagger from the hands of the priest, and then turned back to the High Elf. Mystia shuddered at the sight of the blade shining evilly in the light of the torches.

"Great Balor," Kozan said, "we give you the blood of your enemy."

He reached out with his left hand and forced the Elf to turn his head so his right cheek was exposed. Mystia, her body trembling and her eyes wide, looked on in horror as Kozan carved the symbol of Balor into the Elf's cheek.

The cry of the people still shook the temple and echoed throughout the sanctuary. Suddenly it was joined by the sound of hundreds of different voices lifted up in a terrible singing chant. The Princess looked down and saw that the whole of the sanctuary beneath the towering pyramid was now filled with crimson-robed priests who lifted up their voices in their savage song of praise to their god.

Kozan raised the dagger high and prepared to plunge it into the High Elf's heart.

"No," Mystia whispered, but no one heard her voice. The cries of the people and the song of the priests filled the sanctuary.

Kozan opened his mouth to say something more.

"No," Mystia sobbed, but still no one could hear her.

Kozan's words were drowned out by the people and the priests.

Mystia could stand it no longer. "No!" she screamed as Kozan sent the dagger flying down toward the High Elf. She rushed toward the king and ran into him with all her might. He reeled back and almost went tumbling down the many steps to the floor far below.

The singing of the priests suddenly stopped. Kozan regained his balance and rushed toward Mystia. He struck her hard across the face and sent her sprawling to the floor. Mystia screamed out in pain and terror as he followed her down and struck her again and again, crying as he did so, "How dare you strike me!"

"Villain!" a hoarse voice cried out. "How dare you beat her! How dare you treat any woman so!" It was the High Elf.

Kozan turned in surprise and looked at the Elf, but the Elf paid him no heed. He looked down at Mystia and said softly, "Weep not over my death, lady, for both you and I know I go to a far better place than this. I die happy for, not only will I enter into joy, but I have gazed upon the Scion of Vallendar, the Child of Magianna, the one who will finally deliver our people from Norenroth."

The long mournful sound of Balor's Horn suddenly pierced the air and filled the Temple.

"How touching," spat Kozan. He rose, walked to where the Elf lay chained to the altar, and plunged the dagger into his heart. The High Elf gave a soft sigh, and, as the last note of Balor's Horn died away, he gave up his life--the small hints of a smile upon his rugged features.

"And thus it is done," hissed Kozan. He turned to Mystia. "Come, wench."

With that he walked from the Temple. Mystia, weeping softly, slowly followed him. As they rode back through the streets of Nolhol, the setting sun sank behind the horizon, and darkness fell upon the land.

Chapter 17
Reunion

The night was cold, and not a sound could be heard, as Vayan stood watch over the small camp. Gideone, Stavros, and Phautina were all sleeping peacefully, and there seemed to be no evil about, yet Vayan could not shake the feeling that there was something out of the ordinary about the night. He looked at the tall trees that rose all around him, and tried to peer through into the darkness behind them. He gazed back down at the three sleeping people then rose and turned his eyes once more toward the trees. He hesitated, cast one last look down at Gideone, Stavros, and Phautina, then turned and began to slowly make his way through the forest.

He walked as quietly as a wood elf, and, though he knew not where he was going, he confidently made his way through the trees. By and by, he found himself at the top of a small gully. He lay down upon his stomach and peered down over the edge. What he saw made his eyes open wide in wonder.

Below him there stood three of the most beautiful people he had ever seen. They were all dressed in flowing, white robes, and they seemed fairly to shine with glory. They were strong, and behind their eyes lurked power and passion unlike anything Vayan had ever seen before. They could have been the most deadly and terrifying of enemies, but there was a love and humility they exuded which filled Vayan with peace. They seemed more perfect and more glorious than any creature in the whole of the Three Realms.

What they did there Vayan knew not. He could only lie and look down upon them in wonder.

Suddenly, he heard the sound of someone approaching. He turned quickly, and found himself looking up at Phautina. She smiled softly and, lying down beside him, looked down into the gully.

"Torelli," she whispered. "The Unfallen."

Vayan gaped at the figures below. "Are ye sure?"

"Aye."

"What're they doin' here?" he asked as he turned his face to her.

"I can't say," she answered, as she stared intently down upon the beautiful figures. "'Tis said the Torelli travel all throughout the Three Realms, doing the bidding of Joretham. They fight in wars and help the weary travelers. They comfort those filled with sorrow and lend aid to those in trouble. One can never be certain if the stranger one meets is truly another creature of Deithanara or if he is of the Torelli.

"Usually when the Unfallen travel throughout the Realms they do so in the guise of those who have fallen, but these do not so, and why they don't I cannot say."

Vayan was silent for a long moment as he continued to gaze down upon the Torelli. As he watched, one of the beautiful creatures disappeared into the forest.

His heart began to pound as he suddenly realized something. "They can heal Gideone!"

He jumped up only to see the second of the beautiful creatures disappear. Vayan started charging down the gully's slope.

"Wait!" he cried, but even as he did so, the third also disappeared, leaving the gully empty.

Vayan reached the bottom and looked around, desperately trying to catch at least a glimpse of the Torelli.

"Da..." he started to swear then caught himself when he heard Phautina behind him.

He turned to her, a look of frustration upon his face, and demanded, "Now wha' do we do?"

"The only thing we can do: return to camp."

Vayan cast one last, disappointed look around him then started climbing up the incline to return to camp. "They could have saved him."

"Obviously that was not their purpose in coming here," answered Phautina, as she too climbed the slope of the gulch. "But, just because they came not to heal Gideone, does not mean they are not helping Gideone. Perhaps Joretham, though he wished Gideone to be healed in a different way, has sent those three Torelli to protect him from Abiel."

Vayan said nothing, but her words made him feel better.

They reached the top of the gully then began their way back through the trees to the camp.

Vayan found the camp to be just as silent as when he left it, and, after what he had just seen and been told, it felt far safer. Stavros lay fast asleep, and there was a look of peace that Vayan had never thought he would see upon his father's stern features.

Gideone also slept, but peace did not come to him. Beads of sweat had formed upon his brow, and his face was twisted into a look of hatred. Vayan saw that Phautina looked sadly down upon him. No, peace would not come to the Prince that night.

* * *

Orion lay asleep in a soft bed covered with warm blankets. His body ached slightly, but his wounds were, for the most part, healed, though many scars were left.

He gave a sigh and rolled over. The last thing he wanted to do was wake up-- it was so peaceful in his dreams--but his stomach was fairly growling with hunger, and even sleep had its limits. He rolled over again, and, giving another sigh, slowly opened his eyes.

The room was dimly lit, but still it took a moment for his eyes to grow accustomed to the light. Even after they did, he still simply lay there silently and stared up into the empty space above him.

"Your Highness, you're awake."

Orion sat bolt upright and looked wildly around. His gaze fell upon a beautiful slave girl. Her long, blonde hair was pulled away from her face and out of her soft, green eyes but was allowed to tumbled down over her shoulders and back. Her arms were bare, and the necklace she wore served only to accentuate the fact that her dress was entirely too low-cut.

He stared in shock for a moment before he recovered and tried to rise. Even as he threw back the covers, the slave girl was at his side.

"Please, Your Highness, forgive me," she said. "I meant not to startle you. Now please, calm down and rise not so quickly. You are still wounded, and 'tis not wise to move so suddenly."

She reached out and took him by the arm. He started at her touch and jumped to his feet.

"Leave me alone and stop calling me 'Your Highness'," he said as he pulled his arm away from her.

"But you are the Prince. What am I supposed to call you if not 'Your Highness'?"

Orion crossed his arms. "If you would leave me alone, you would not be faced with that problem."

When he crossed his arms, he realized, much to his annoyance, that his chest was bare, and, looking down, he found he was wearing nothing save his trousers.

"Sadly, Your Highness, I cannot do as you ask," the slave-girl said. "Queen Provenna was most strict in ordering me to stay beside you and see that you're properly bathed and fed."

"I'm twenty-seven years old," Orion answered, annoyance evident. "I think I can properly bathe and feed myself without the aid of a half-naked slave-girl."

"Most men can, but they find it not nearly as enjoyable as when I help them," she said, with a demure smile, as she took a step toward him.

"Get out," Orion ordered, stepping back. There was a look in his eyes that told her he was deadly serious. For a moment she simply stood and looked up at him, then, after giving a small curtsy, she turned and walked from the room.

Orion scowled at her back as she passed through the door, then turned and went off in search of a bath and some clothing. He found both and, less than a half-hour later, returned washed and dressed in the finest garments Leilaora had to offer. He was thoroughly uncomfortable. He far preferred the simple garb of a soldier to the finery of a nobleman. The boots in particular he disliked, for they were new and already were rubbing against his heels.

He wandered into the main room of the series of chambers, which evidently, at least for the time being, were his. The room was amply proportioned and made of gray stone so light as to be almost white. Dozens of candles lined the walls, lighting the room almost as well as sunlight would have. Beautiful tapestries also decorated the walls at various intervals. Much of the floor was covered by a large, light blue rug, and, in the center of the room, sat a wooden table upon which a hearty breakfast had been laid.

Orion stopped suddenly, when his gaze fell upon Provenna. She was sitting next to the table. She looked up at him, a hopeful, expectant expression upon her face. As Orion stared back at her he felt anger well up within him.

"Hello, Orion," she said, not certain what else to say.

Orion remained silent for a moment then said coldly, "Hello, Mother."

She continued to look up at him, hoping he would say more, but, when he did not, she motioned to the table and said, "Please, Orion, come and eat, for certes you must be hungry. You've not eaten since you were first brought here."

He stared at her for a moment longer, then, without a word, made his way to the table and sat down across from her. He picked up a piece of bread and began to eat it, concentrating on the plate before him.

For a long, awkward moment Provenna simply sat there and looked at him, until, finally, she burst out, "Orion, have you nothing to say to me, your mother? For ten, long years have you been gone from this place, and now that you've returned all you can do is sit and stare down at your plate?"

He raised his eyes and looked at her. "What would you have me say, or what would you have me do?" His voice was soft, but it was filled with anger. "Should I come give you a kiss on the cheek and say 'Hello, Mother, 'tis so good to return to Leilaora, though I have spent almost a decade running from it and the life I led here.'? Or ought I ask you how your many wars are faring, and whether Nor has been completely overcome? Mayhap you have taken a new lover--no doubt one who will be the cause of as many problems as your last two." Provenna's face flickered with hurt at those words, but Orion did not stop. "Or perhaps I ought to inquire whether the Arch-Deacon has any sage advise on how to torture your prisoners; certes that is something that ought to be told in a cathedral dedicated to the worship of Joretham. Or perhaps I should simply forget about everything and everyone and lose myself in the embrace of an excessively ugly slave-girl whom you sent to wait upon me."

"I thought you would have liked Eluned," Provenna answered, thankful that she could contradict one thing in his list.

Orion's eyes narrowed. "I disliked her immensely, and I never want to see her or any other slave-girl again."

Provenna laughed. "Methinks you would not be so heavy in your hatred, nor so quick in your expression of it, if you truly did find Eluned displeasing."

"Think what you will, Mother," he muttered as he rose and began to walk away.

"Orion, wait."

Slowly he turned to face her.

"Orion, forgive me," she pleaded. "Leave not so quickly. Twould be sad if, after ten years, we did not exchange a few kind words."

"And what kind words can be exchanged between enemies?"

"Orion...I am your mother."

"What does that matter?" Orion demanded. "Did you keep my country from being conquered, my people from being murdered, or my Princess from being taken captive by Kozan?" His voice was rising. "No! You did not! You stood silently by, and there is no doubt in my mind that, in fact, you encouraged it! Kill me or set me free but expect no kind words from me."

"I think that hardly fair," Provenna answered. "Do you think I want Kozan to be free to conquer what he wills when he wills? Goodness knows I would stop him if I could--"

"Then kill him!" Orion cried.

"Kill him?" Provenna exclaimed. "Orion, 'tis not as easy as that. You know as well as I that if I kill him my power will die with him."

"And what care I of that?" Orion snapped, as he turned and began to walk away.

"Orion, stop!" she cried. "I need your help."

"What?" he demanded as he turned back to her.

"Orion," she said, her green eyes filled with emotion, "return to me. Become the Prince of Jocthreal once again. Kozan fears you; he cannot touch you with magic, and you are a far greater warrior than he could ever hope to be. If you stand by my side, Kozan will not dare oppose me."

Orion was silent for a long moment and simply looked at her.

Finally, he opened his mouth and said, "Have Princess Mystia taken from Kozan and brought here to Leilaora."

"But...Orion, how can I..."

Orion gave a bitter laugh. "I have no power over Kozan, and you don't think that I do, else you would not fear to do as I ask. You want me at your side not because I can help you oppose Kozan, but because I am your son, your firstborn, and you cannot bear the thought of having me as an enemy.

"But I am your enemy. Free me or kill me, but think not that I will return to you." With that he turned and walked from the room.

Provenna stood and stared after him, her face filled with anger and bitterness. She opened her mouth as if to speak, then shut it, and, turning, walked quickly from Orion's chambers.

* * *

Mystia stood beside Kozan's great, golden throne and looked out over the vast crowd gathered in his throne room. It could have been considered by some to be beautiful. Large tapestries, each depicting a separate dark and gruesome picture of Balor's history, hung from the walls. The tall, stone pillars supporting the ceiling were covered with elaborate, gold ornamentation. A rich, red carpet ran up across the floor to the foot of the dais upon which Kozan sat. It was, however, a dark room, lit only with the flickering, red light of torches, which sat in black wall-holders shaped like dragon heads. The red light reflected off their fearsome features, giving them a demonic aspect.

There came the sound of movement in the corridor outside. A moment later the heavy, oaken doors were thrown open, and a servant announced, "The king, Rolfaren, of the country of Mornland."

Through the doors there walked a man dressed in robes of royal purple, with a golden crown upon his head. His long, brown hair was streaked with gray, and upon his face he bore a proud, ruthless look. He turned his eyes neither to the right nor to the left as he made his way up through the throne room to King Kozan. He was followed by a huge entourage of people--noblemen, soldiers, and slaves--and with them there were brought three huge, wooden chests.

Mystia could feel Rolfaren's cold gaze upon her, and she turned her eyes to the floor. Beneath her veil, her cheeks flushed.

When Rolfaren reached the foot of the dais, he knelt, with his right knee touching the red carpet and his head bent.

"Rise, my friend," said Kozan. "I welcome you to Nolhol."

"Thank you, my King," said Rolfaren as he stood. "As every year, I come to worship Balor and to show you honor. By Balor's might have I crushed all my enemies, and I now offer you gifts from the spoils." He motioned to the first large chest, which slaves opened. "Gold." He motioned to the second chest. "Silken cloth and precious gems." He motioned to the third chest. "Foreign weaponry." Then, with a sweeping gesture, he turned and motioned to a group of people who stood behind him. "And slaves--both men trained in and capable of teaching you the art of using their foreign arms, and women trained in arts far more gentle." He bowed low before Kozan.

Mystia looked down upon the slaves who stood there. With their short stature and olive skin it was evident they were from a land far away. Their dark eyes burned with hatred as they looked at Kozan and fairly challenged him to try and break their spirits.

"I accept your gifts, Rolfaren," Kozan said, the corner of his mouth turning up in the slightest of smiles. Mystia turned her gaze to Rolfaren as he rose.

"The Day of Chanar draws nigh," Kozan continued, addressing himself to all who were in the room, "and tonight we shall feast in honor of Balor." At his words the people gathered there began to murmur in muted excitement.

King Rolfaren said nothing. He smiled and bowed low, but not before he had looked once more up at Mystia.

The great banquet hall of Kozan's palace was filled with the sound of music and singing and the laughter and cries of drunken people. The long, wooden tables were covered with all manner of meats--deer, pig, bear, sheep--all smoky from the fires they had been cooked over and all covered thick with spices. Shoved in among the steaming platters of meat were all types of fruits and breads. In addition, there seemed to be an endless flow of wine, of which everyone made certain to partake.

Mystia's head throbbed as the laughter and shrieks of the people pounded her ears. Kozan had made her stand beside him and pour his wine. All night had she been forced to listen to Kozan and Rolfaren laugh and exchange coarse jests and speak of wars and women. The longer the night went on, the more drunk they became and the lower their conversation sank.

The Princess was near tears. Throughout the whole of the night, Kozan had not ceased to stare at her. He was so drunk she knew not what he would do, and the glint in his cold, brown eyes terrified her.

Rolfaren held up his golden goblet, and Mystia turned and began to fill it. He had not ceased eyeing her since he had first seen her in the throne room.

Before, something had told him not even to speak of her to Kozan, but now, however, wine so clouded his mind that, as she bent forward to refill his goblet, he reached out, grabbed her by the arm, and pulled her close to him. She gave a gasp of fear and surprise, and the pitcher she held went tumbling from her hands.

"Let go of her!" Kozan snarled, suddenly, as he took her by the waist and yanked her away from Rolfaren. She stumbled back, tripped, and fell onto Kozan's lap. She struggled to rise, but he held her fast and, glaring at Rolfaren, growled, "Never touch her again!"

Rolfaren may have been drunk, but even he could see how fiercely Kozan's anger burned.

"Let go of me," Mystia sobbed as she struggled to free herself.

Rolfaren licked his lips nervously and, without saying a word, nodded. His eyes were wide.

Mystia was crying uncontrollably. When Kozan let her go, she stood up and tried to run away, but, drunk as he was, he managed to grab her by the arm and pull her back.

"Pour my wine, slave," he growled. She looked down on the table where the overturned pitcher lay, with the spilled wine spreading out from it.

"I have no wine," she cried.

"Pour my wine." His fingers dug into her arm.

"But I have no wine." Her whole body was shaking with giant tears.

"I said pour my wine!" Kozan snarled as he jumped to his feet and drew back his free hand to strike her. Mystia screamed.

"Here!" someone cried.

Kozan stopped short, and both he and Mystia turned to see a young, wide-eyed slave-girl holding out a pitcher of wine. Still terrified, Mystia snatched the golden pitcher, and the girl, almost as frightened of Kozan as Mystia was, darted off and disappeared from sight.

Kozan released Mystia, and she, still trembling, filled his goblet.

Rolfaren did not dare so much as glance at Mystia, but the glint in Kozan's eyes grew, and often, as the night wore on, his hand brushed across her body. She could only pray to Joretham for strength and protection.

Kozan stumbled through the corridors of the palace, dragging Mystia after him. The Princess struggled to free herself, but he held her in an iron grip.

"Let go of me!" she cried.

He pulled her roughly to him and, looking into her black eyes hissed, "Let go of me."

She turned her head as much as to escape his cold, beast-like stare as to avoid the smell of alcohol upon his breath. She had no idea what he meant by his words.

He turned and, ignoring Mystia's sobs, began once again to make his way through the palace. Suddenly, he rounded a corner and almost ran into the Dark Sorcerer. He stumbled and lost his grip on Mystia who, in a second ran to the Sorcerer.

"Help me!" she cried.

The Sorcerer, whose clothes were still dusty from his long journey from Leilaora, looked down upon Kozan and Mystia in shock.

"Give her to me!" Kozan snarled as he tried to rush around him to Mystia.

"What are you doing?" the Sorcerer cried as he pushed Mystia behind him and away from the drunken king.

"Give her to me!" Kozan cried again.

"Your Majesty," the Dark Sorcerer said as he took Kozan by both shoulders and looked directly into his eyes, "you want her pure for the sacrifice."

Kozan gave a snarling cry and, before the Dark Sorcerer could react, pulled his arm away and struck him across the face. The Sorcerer could feel magic rushing into him, and he gave a cry as he was thrown back by Kozan's blow. His head struck hard against the wall, and he fell unconscious to the floor.

* * *

The Dark Sorcerer gave a groan as he awoke. His head pounded with pain as, slowly, he sat up. He breathed deeply, and after a moment the corridor stopped spinning. He looked around him and tried to gather his thoughts. It could only have a few minutes since he was knocked unconscious, considering no one had found him lying there.

With another groan he struggled to his feet. His head was still pounding as he made his way unsteadily toward Kozan's chambers. He could still feel the king's magic pulsing within him.

He reached Kozan's chambers. Ignoring the guard's cries to stop--they dared not forcibly hold him back--he walked into the room. It was dark, and it took a moment for his eyes to adjust. Even after they had adjusted, he could barely focus.

He gave another groan, held his hand to his head, and tried to concentrate.

When the room came into focus enough, he made his way unsteadily across the main room to the bedchamber. He opened the door and peered in. He gave a sigh of relief. Kozan lay passed out upon the bed; he would not wake until long after dawn.

Princess Mystia sat upon the floor, her knees drawn up to her chest. She looked pitifully up at him, and what part of her face was not veiled he could see was streaked with tears.

He gave a grimace of pain as he fought against his headache.

"You're safe for now," he told her. Then, without a word, he turned and walked away, leaving her to stare in disbelief after him. As he disappeared, she burst into tears.

He did not even hear her. He could barely think with Kozan's magic still struggling to overcome him. He had to lie down and heal himself, and then he would learn all that had transpired during his absence.

Chapter 18
The Darkness of Leilaora

Orion sat at the table in the main room of his chambers and gave a sad smile as he looked at the luxury all about him. Provenna had seen to it that his chambers were the most lavish rooms a man could want.

The main room was elegant and spacious with a pure white marble floor and beautiful pictures and tapestries hung on the walls. There were no windows, but the whole room was filled with the bright light of more than a score of candles, and, within a long, marble fireplace, there danced a merry, yellow fire.

Almost everything possible had been done for his comfort, and, had he chosen to make requests or commands, his every whim would have been answered, but he still had not his freedom, nor did Mystia have hers.

He suddenly heard noise in the corridor, and, as he looked over, the door to his chambers was thrown open, and Provenna walked in. He did not rise but simply looked, unmoving, up at her.

"Leave us," Provenna ordered the slaves who had followed her in. Silently, they turned and left, closing the door behind them.

Without a word, Provenna advanced to the table at which Orion sat and looked down upon him. Her face was hard and unmoving, and her green eyes were filled with intensity.

"Orion," she began--her voice held the same hardness and intensity that her face bore, "I need you to stand by my side and become the Prince of Jocthreal again."

"And what care I for your need?" asked Orion.

"You will be great--the greatest man in the whole of Lairannare. You will have power and wealth and everything you could possibly desire. When I die, you will be the King of the Realm of Earth, if only you return and become my son once again."

"What is power and wealth to me?" demanded Orion as he rose and looked down upon her. "I was once the Prince of Jocthreal. I was once your son. I once had everything that any man could possibly have, and what did it give me? Nothing!

"Nothing," he groaned, as he sank back into his chair. "Nothing save anguish, guilt and no reason to live. The only reason I didn't kill myself was because I feared death more than I feared life. But now, for the first time since I was born,

I have a reason to live; I serve Princess Mystia, and I will not forsake her that I might return to you."

"Orion, you need not forsake her to return to me."

"Fool!" Orion cried as he jumped once more to his feet. "I do!" His blue eyes were filled with emotion. "'Tis not a game we live in where all we must worry about is whether we win! Here, in this life, the path we take is as important as the end we seek. I will not forsake Princess Mystia!"

"Forget that Shallean wench!" Provenna cried. "What is she? Nothing more than a pig to be sacrificed upon Kozan's altar! Or nothing more than a ring upon my finger!" She held up her hand.

Orion looked in shock upon the ring on Provenna's finger. The crystal stone glowed and pulsated with soft, red light.

"Give that to me!" he cried as he jumped toward her and grabbed her wrist. His chair went crashing to the floor, and Provenna gave a scream as he twisted her arm, trying to pull Mystia's ring from her finger.

"Guards!" she shrieked. The door to the chamber was thrown open, and four guards rushed in. Orion growled in fury as he tried to pull Provenna to him and use her as a shield, but she managed to yank herself away.

He gave a snarling cry as the four guards descended upon him. He grabbed one by the head, but even as he snapped the man's neck the other three took him by the arms. He struggled against them, but they held him fast.

Finally, he stopped fighting, and simply stared up in anger at Provenna. Provenna walked around the dead guard and stood in front of Orion. She was breathing deeply, and her eyes were filled with fury as she drew back her hand and struck him hard across the face.

"I can find you twenty women as beautiful as Mystia," she snarled. "Now join with me!"

Orion laughed a scornful bitter laugh that could almost have been that of a madman. "Think you love is why I serve her?" Provenna looked down upon him as he continued to laugh.

"You fool!" he cried. "Be as noble and virtuous as she is, then will I serve you! Be as innocent and merciful as she is then will I serve you! Follow after Joretham as she does then will I..."

"Be quiet!" Provenna shrieked as she struck him with all her might. Orion's head snapped to one side, and he gave a sharp cry as her fingernails dug into his skin.

Provenna, trembling with fury, pulled her hand back and stood staring down at him.

Slowly, he turned his face back to her. Blood trickled down his cheek, and his face was twisted in rage. For a moment there was utter silence, then, with a howl, he lunged forward.

Provenna gave a gasp of terror and jumped back. Orion's fingers brushed the cloth of her dress but closed on air. The guards held him back with all their might, yet still he almost managed to escape them.

One of the guards drew back his fist and sent it slamming into Orion's head. The blue-eyed warrior gave a groan and fell limp. His hand twitched as he struggled for breath. He raised his head and glared at Provenna; however, he was too stunned by the blow to do her harm.

Provenna gazed coldly down at him.

"Take him to the dungeon," she order, furiously, "and torture him until he turns!"

Orion's face twisted with hatred and he opened his mouth, but, even as he did so, one of the guards struck him again. With a slight gasp, he fell unconscious.

Provenna, breathing heavily, watched two of the guards drag him from the room. When he had disappeared, she turned to the third guard.

"I want Zenas brought to me," she ordered, "and I want him brought as soon as possible." With that she walked from the room.

She stormed through the corridors of her palace until she reached her throne room. It was completely empty, and the sound of her feet striking the stone floor echoed off the walls. The warriors of old stared down from their stained-glass pictures and watched her as she walked up to the dais and took her seat upon the beautiful, crystal throne.

She looked down upon her hand and the ring she wore on her finger.

"Fool," she hissed. "Thief. Not for the whole of Deithanara would I save you from the hands of Kozan. Let him torture you, rape you, murder you; I care not. You stole my son from me and won my hatred forever."

She held her hand tightly over the crystal stone and whispered again, "Demoness."

* * *

It was the midday meal, and Kozan and Rolfaren sat in the banquet hall where they ate. There were a few others scattered throughout the room, but all was relatively peaceful. Mystia stood beside Kozan and held a pitcher of wine in her hands. Thankfully, Kozan called upon her far less than he had during the feast.

Suddenly, she gave a cry of pain. The pitcher fell from her hands and tumbled to the floor where the red liquid spilled out and made its way into the cracks between the stones. Giving another cry, she clutched as her heart and sank to the ground.

In surprise, the two kings turned and looked in confusion upon her.

* * *

Provenna looked out across her empty throne room. Her lips turned up in a scornful, bitter smile.

"Mother," a voice broke into her thoughts.

She started and turned and found herself looking at Aeneas.

"What?" she snapped.

"I came to ask a favor of you," he said as he bowed his head.

"What?" she asked more gently.

He took a deep breath and said, "Let me be the one to torture Orion."

She gave a laugh. "Torture him if you will; I care not. But see that you hurt him not beyond what he can heal himself of. I want him turned to my will not crushed beneath it."

"Yes, Mother," he said, trying to hide a smile. "Thank you."

He turned and walked from the room.

* * *

Orion strained to break the chains that held him to the wall. He had been stripped to the waist and already was covered with the dirt and slime of the dungeon. He gave a cry and pulled with all his might, but the bonds held fast.

Terror welled up within his heart at the thought of being tortured once again. He wanted to run; he wanted to hide, but the bonds would not break. He strained against them as he screamed out curses against his mother. His voice carried throughout the dungeon and mixed with the cries of the other prisoners.

The door to his cell was suddenly thrown open, and Aeneas, followed by a black clothed torturer, walked in. Orion gave a growl of fury and lunged toward him.

"Hello, dearest brother," Aeneas said with a sneer as he watched Orion struggle. "You know not how long I've waited for this day."

Aeneas' eyes may have been green like his mother's, but at that moment they looked exactly like Kozan's.

* * *

Tnaka ran through the halls of the palace, not caring about those who stared after him. He stopped only once to demand of a slave girl where Provenna was.

"I believe the Queen is still in the throne room, Your Majesty," the girl answered, and, scarcely had the words left her lips before Tnaka was running again.

He burst into the throne room, and the Queen, who had been sitting upon her crystal throne, rose in surprise, crying at the same moment, "Tnaka!"

He walked quickly across the empty floor to her and mounted the dais, saying as he did so, "Provenna, is it true that you've ordered Orion tortured?"

"Why do you not simply go into the dungeon and learn for yourself?" she asked coldly.

"Is it true?" Tnaka demanded.

She looked at him, startled by the intensity in his voice, and, after a moment, said, "Yes."

"What do you think you're doing!" he cried. "This is madness; stop it!"

"Who are you to tell me what I should and should not do?" she asked, her voice cold and her eyes filled with fury. "I am the Greater Power, not you. I torture who I will when I will, and were I you I would simply be glad 'twas not me."

"Provenna, this is not the way to turn him."

"Fool!" Provenna cried. "He tried to kill me!"

"But, Provenna, he is your..."

"I care not if he be Joretham himself! He tried to kill me, and he will suffer!"

"Provenna, listen to me. This is not right."

"And what care I for right and wrong?" spat she. "He chooses to serve a Shallean wench over me! He will turn even if it kills him, and when he does, if Mystia still lives, I will make him cut her down in front of me."

"Provenna--" Tnaka began.

"Leave me," Provenna ordered. Her green eyes flashed with such fury that he dared not disobey. He gave a stiff bow then turned and left her alone with her anger.

Chapter 19
Haflashon

It was a cold, misty, overcast day, and Gideone, Stavros, Vayan, and Phautina continued to press forward toward the Mountains of Scalavori. The trees, which had surrounded them throughout the whole of their journey, now slowly began to thin out. There were, of course, still many left--straight, towering, gray trees--and they would not fully disappear until a little past the town of Haflashon, which the four travelers soon would reach.

Gideone pulled his cloak tighter around him and tried to keep his teeth from chattering.

"Are you cold, Your Highness?" asked Stavros.

Gideone rolled his eyes and, with the most sarcastic tone he could muster, said, "No."

Stavros gave him a worried look, for he could not recall a previous time when the Prince had given a one-word answer when a longer one was possible.

"Your Highness," said he, "I think we ought to stop and rest for a moment."

"I need no rest," answered Gideone, crossly.

"Then at least let me look at your wound."

"My wound looks exactly the same as when you last examined it, and simply because your memory is too poor to remember does not mean I ought to be obliging and do as you ask."

"But, Your Highness..." Stavros began. He disliked how pale Gideone's face was.

"No," Gideone cut him off. "You may stop if you wish, but I, for one, will not rest until I reach Haflashon. We may be evading Abiel now, but I have no doubt that he still seeks us, and I intend not to sit still while he draws ever closer."

"Very well, Your Highness," said Stavros after a moment's pause.

They rode on in silence for several minutes until Gideone suddenly spoke. His voice was quiet, and he spoke his words as though they were a simple statement, but it was impossible not to tell it was a command. "When we reach Haflashon, Phautina shall part company with us."

"But..." Vayan began to protest.

Gideone cut him off. "She was supposed to have left us when we reached Jwassax, and 'twas only because I allowed it that she traveled with us further. Now her time with us has ended."

"But, Yar High..."

Gideone turned and gave Vayan a dark look. "I am the Prince. I am the heir of the throne of Nor. My word is the law, and you are expected to obey it."

Vayan looked as though he was going to protest again, but Phautina, who was riding beside him, put a staying hand on his arm and said, "Trouble not yourself Vayan. I have traveled all across the Realm of Earth--sometimes by myself and sometimes with others--and I have learned that even the best of traveling companions must eventually part ways. If Prince Gideone doesn't wish me to ride with you, than I shall do so no longer."

Vayan gave a sigh and fell silent, but it was clear he disliked the thought of her leaving.

They said nothing more as they pressed forward, the silence broken only by the occasional chirping of a bird and the sound of the horses' hooves striking the earth.

Stavros looked in concern upon the Prince. Haflashon would not be reached until late in the afternoon, but Gideone looked as though he would fall off his horse at any moment. His face was extremely pale, and his jaw was clenched tightly in an effort to keep his teeth from chattering. His hands trembled slightly, and there was a look of pain in his eyes which, though he tried desperately to hide, Stavros could see.

Those were themselves enough to make Stavros very worried, but there was another thing which filled him with even more concern. Ever since they had argued the night they had escaped from Jwassax, Gideone had grown more subdued by the day, but behind his worn and wearied exterior there lurked an anger that grew only stronger as the days passed. There was not a moment when his dark eyes were not clouded with hatred, as though some fell spirit lurked within him, threatening at any moment to emerge.

The hours wore on, and what faint shadows there were grew longer as the evening drew nearer. Gideone managed to stay upon his horse, but it was only through the sheer power of his will, and when they reached the town of Haflashon--late in the afternoon, close to the time of dinner--even that was barely enough to sustain him.

Haflashon was a very small town, peopled mainly by cheerful, rustic folk. Though the sky was gray and overcast and the air cool, children ran about and played in the streets, just as they would had the countryside been bright with the sun. As the four travelers approached, the children darted out of the way and stood at the edge of the streets, gazing up in curiosity at them.

Phautina laughed and waved at all whom she passed. Vayan smiled softly but said nothing. Gideone scowled at any child who dared look at him; indeed, he sent several of the younger children running in fear behind their older siblings. And Stavros kept a close eye on the Prince to see that he did nothing rash.

The town was so small that it had but one inn--the Ranger's Lodge--and to this the four travelers made their way. All arrangements were quickly taken care of, and Stavros and Gideone, who was so sick and weary that he could not even dismount unaided, went upstairs to their room, while Vayan and Phautina took themselves to the common room to have dinner.

* * *

Gideone lay upon a bed in one of the dimly lit chambers of the inn and stared up at the ceiling.

He gave a sigh. "Are you almost done?"

"Yes, Your Highness," came Stavros' reply as he finished examining Gideone's wound and began to rub some more of Wild Rose's salve upon it. The power of the salve--just as the power of the amulet before it--was slowly being overcome by the magic, which had taken hold of the Prince. The web of black lines had crept all the way to his shoulder, and soon they would reach even his neck.

Stavros finished rubbing on the salve, then quickly went about bandaging the wound. He remained silent as he worked, but as he finished he spoke hesitantly. "Your Highness."

Gideone turned his head to him.

Stavros took a breath then continued, "I think you ought to allow Phautina to continue with us."

"What!" Gideone cried as he tried to sit up.

Stavros put a staying hand to his shoulder. "Lie back down, Your Highness."

"I already said that she could come no further. Why then do you not accept my words?"

"Even a prince can be in error."

"Are you accusing me of being wrong?" demanded Gideone as he pushed Stavros' hand aside and sat up.

"No," Stavros said as he stood up. "I simply think you ought to reconsider your decision. Phautina has been nothing but an aid to us, and something tells me that she should journey with us all the way to Scalavori."

"What tells you that?"

Stavros was silent for a moment before he answered, "I know not what-- something, a feeling, a voice whispering in my head."

Gideone gave a sigh of disgust. "Give me what can be seen and what can be touched; give me not your feelings or your voices in your head."

"Your Highness, please we have had nothing but good luck since she joined. Abiel has not attacked us since Jwassax."

"Do you think I care if Abiel attacks us? If you would simply allow me to do so, I could destroy him once and for all. I am the greatest swordsman in Lairannare."

Stavros could not help but smile slightly at that. "The greatest?"

"Yes!" Gideone cried. "The greatest. I have never been defeated."

"Never?"

"Never!" Gideone declared with an anger and a vehemence that surprised Stavros. "Not even once!" His eyes were flashing. "I have no need of Phautina, and I am not going to let her come with me. Everyone else has turned against me, and I will not give her the chance to betray me also."

"I still stand with you, Your Highness."

"You do not. You stand with Phautina. Your pitiful excuse for a son stands by Phautina."

"Leave Vayan..."

Gideone did not allow Stavros to finish. "Orion, cur that he is, ran away. And Eagle..." He slammed his fist against the bed. "Eagle..." the words caught in his throat. "Eagle...you know what Eagle did."

He fell back on the bed and said dully, "Leave me alone."

Stavros looked upon him for a moment then, giving a sigh, turned and walked from the room.

* * *

The common room of the Ranger's Lodge was alive with merriment--not the revelries so often found in the inns of larger cities, but with simple, rustic gusto. There was not a person there not engaged in at least one conversation. Two rangers, who were sitting in the corner, were in the midst of giving a very animated telling of one of their adventures. Their voices and the shouts and laughter from their audience mixed with the sounds of the other conversations filling the room. Behind all of that there was the ever-constant sound of music, coming from the three musicians who sat in the corner opposite of where the rangers sat. The smoke of old men's pipes rose and wafted through the air and mixed with the smell of the smoked and spicy food.

Vayan and Phautina, sitting at a table against the wall, smiled and laughed just like everyone else. Many people had come up and spoken with them, but the two had been so famished that they had made sorry conversation. Vayan would have dug right into his venison had not Phautina stopped him and given a quick prayer of thanks to Joretham, during which Vayan had kept one of his eyes opened and turned toward his plate. Thankfully, Phautina was not one given to long, winding prayers, and, when she had finished, Vayan wasted no time in attacking his food. Phautina had not been able to keep herself from laughing at how much he consumed. He simply grinned silently and continued eating.

The night wore on, and even Vayan's hunger was appeased. Phautina was recovered from nearly choking on her ale (not only were the rangers excellent storytellers, but they were both comedians as well). The conversation had grown rather subdued, and it seemed that the night was winding to a close, when suddenly one of the rangers jumped up and declared that it was time to dance. Immediately everyone was on their feet, pushing tables and chairs out of the way. They formed two lines--women in one and men in the other--down the center of the floor. The musicians struck up a merry tune, and the laughter and shouting began anew. Those who were not dancing were stomping their feet and clapping their hands, and some were singing along to the music.

The first song ended, and Vayan's eyes were sparkling as he turned to Phautina. "Do ye want t' dance?"

She smiled and shook her head. "I'm quite content right here."

"But everyone wants t' dance!"

She laughed. "Not after the dinner I had."

"Phautina, ye had no' nearly as much as me." He took her arm. "Come on, it's yar last day with us."

She pulled her arm away from him. "No, you go dance, but I would rather just sit here and watch."

He gave a sigh. He was clearly disappointed, but he turned and took his place among the dancers, and after a couple songs he was almost as lighthearted as he had been before.

The time passed quickly, and it was Phautina who drew him away and reminded him that he ought to go to bed and get as much sleep as possible before the morning.

They stood outside the room Vayan shared with Gideone and Stavros, and as he looked down upon Phautina he could scarcely believe that it was actually time to say goodbye to her. He had never been one to say much, and now words escaped him completely.

"Well, Vayan," said Phautina, "I suppose it's time to bid you farewell. I have enjoyed traveling with the three of you, and I will pray that you reach your destination safely."

"Will I see ye tomorrow before we leave?"

"No," she said with a shake of her head, "I doubt Gideone would be pleased to see me, and it would probably plunge him into an even worse mood than he already possesses, which would hardly be enjoyable for you. So, I shall bid you goodbye tonight, and may Joretham be with you."

Vayan could think of nothing else to say, so he simply said, "Goodbye, and I wish you good luck, too."

Phautina bowed her head, smiled, then turned and walked quietly away, leaving Vayan to gaze after her.

* * *

Nearly a full day passed. Gideone, Stavros, and Vayan left early the next morning, and Phautina left shortly after them. Few noticed them, and, of those who saw them go, fewer still remembered them for more than an hour. By night, for most they were but a distant memory.

At that moment, the innkeeper was wishing he too had forgotten all about them--or, better yet, had never seen them to begin with. Only the flickering flames of a dying fire lighted the common room of the Ranger's Lodge, and the room was empty save for the innkeeper and Abiel. The innkeeper's hands were clasped tightly together, yet still they trembled as he looked upon Abiel's scarred and twisted features. The Delovachian prince paid no attention to the innkeeper, but, with his sword gleaming red in the light of the fire, he stared into the darkness and battled an unseen enemy.

"What can you tell me of four strangers who passed through this town?" Abiel's voice was soft yet deadly, and his sword arched through the air.

The innkeeper licked his lips and took a deep breath before saying, "There was one man, older than the others, who seemed to be the leader; a young man with a Delovachian accent; a homely woman who could not have been more than twenty years old; and a black-haired man who was sorely wounded."

Abiel gave an evil smile as he continued to battle. "That would be them. When did they leave, and where did they go?"

The innkeeper was trembling so that he could barely stand, as he answered with a weak voice, "The three men left early this morning and set out almost directly north."

Abiel concentrated on a point just in front of his blade. "And the woman?"

The innkeeper continued to look in terror upon the dark prince. "She left about a half-hour after the men and seemed to follow them."

"Good," Abiel said, an evil gleam in his eyes. "Very good."

He continued to fight in silence, and the innkeeper could only stand, trembling, and watch him.

Finally, Abiel gave a grin that only made his features more twisted and gruesome. "Do you think me ugly?"

The innkeeper searched for a reply, but before he could answer Abiel continued, "Most people do." There was a gleam of evil and hatred in his eyes. "I was not always this way--" the terrible grin was still upon his face--"but fire springs up quickly and burns hot."

The innkeeper swallowed.

"Do you know what it is like to lie helpless in the midst of a raging fire and watch your skin burn away before your eyes? And do you know what it is like to feel the creatures of Elmorran rise up out of the depths and fall upon you? Do you know the pain that takes you as your flesh is torn from your face?" Abiel gave a laugh. "I do."

The innkeeper's face was completely white.

"Now go," Abiel ordered. The innkeeper, all too happy to obey, exited as quickly as possible.

"To the north, ever to the north he goes," murmured Abiel as he continued to battle his unseen foe. "Where could it be that he goes? Surely not to Tmalion. Gideone would never be fool enough to do that. Tmalion stands firmly with the

Powers. Where could he go?" The dark prince gave a chuckled. "No matter. Wherever he goes he shall not reach it."

He gave another laugh and continued to fight. "Strike, thrust, parry, and three steps back, but this time it will be you who feels the pain of your body being consumed by the fire and the dead."

He spun and with a snarl sent his sword slicing deep into a wooden beam, which supported the ceiling.

"I will have my revenge!"

Chapᴛᴇʀ 20
ᴄ᷉ᴇᴍᴏʀɪᴇꜱ

Orion stood chained to the wall of Provenna's dungeon, his chest to the stone and his back to Aeneas and the chief torturer. He rested his cheek against the wall; the coldness of the stones against his burning flesh was the only comfort he could find. Long strands of dirty, blood-soaked hair fell in front of his eyes. His back was a mass of criss-crossing wounds from which blood poured.

How long the torture had lasted he knew not. The minutes and the hours and the days had all melted into each other to form one eternal present of torment. His features, twisted in agony, were lighted by the red glow of the few torches upon the walls and the pile of burning coals which lay within a circle of stones in the center of the floor.

He gave a choked cry as Aeneas slowly drew a knife, freshly held in the red-hot coals, down his back. The pain was excruciating, but he tried to force himself not to cry out or to move, for Aeneas drew the knife down in such a way that the less Orion moved the less he would be cut. But he could not keep himself from starting at the pain, and he gave a sharp cry as the blade zig-zagged across his back and dug into his skin.

Aeneas pulled the knife away, and Orion began to retch involuntarily; he would have thrown up had there been anything in his stomach.

"You're getting much better at this game," said Aeneas as he walked to the glowing coals in the middle of the room and held the knife to it. "You scarcely moved or screamed at all, which really defeats the whole purpose."

Orion's shoulders shook as he wept.

"Mystia," he whispered. He could barely say her name; his voice was so hoarse from screaming.

Aeneas gave Orion a scornful look then motioned to the chief torturer, who, whip in hand, was standing silently by. The torturer drew back the lash and sent it cracking across Orion's back. Orion gave a cry of pain, but no sooner had the sound died from his lips, when the torturer drew the whip back again and sent it once more biting into his flesh.

"Mystia!" Orion cried over and over with each strike of the whip. It was his prayer, his plea, his cry for help and mercy, but the torture continued. He wanted to run or to fight--to do anything to escape the blows. He strained against his bonds and clawed against the stones of the wall, but the chains would not break or the stones give way. Unconsciousness would not come to him, and he was left there, a creature half mad with impotent fury as he writhed beneath a torture he could not escape.

"Stop!" a voice suddenly cried.

"What?" Aeneas snarled as he turned. He found himself facing Tnaka.

"Fool!" the elven king shouted. "Provenna wants him alive not whipped to death"

Aeneas' face twisted in rage, but before he could say anything Tnaka said, "Get out. Now!"

Aeneas began to sputter in outrage.

"I said get out!" Tnaka cried.

The young prince gave an unintelligible cry and stormed from the room. The torturer followed him.

Tnaka waited until they had left then turned. Cautiously, he approached Orion, who stood resting his forehead against the wall. Orion wanted to lie or sit or even kneel, but his chains would not allow it so he was forced to stand even as his body screamed for rest.

"Orion?" Tnaka questioned, not certain if the warrior could hear him.

Orion turned his eyes toward Tnaka. His face was twisted with agony.

"Orion," said Tnaka as he gazed into the tortured man's face, "I have come here to beg you to please come back to us."

Orion gave a mirthless smile and said nothing, as he continued to stare, not at Tnaka, but through him--or into him.

"Orion, you need not betray those you serve. You need not turn from the path you have chosen for yourself. You can simply battle Kozan, rescue Mystia, and be free to live your life as you see fit."

Still Orion did not answer.

Tnaka hesitated for a moment. "Orion, can you hear me? Do you understand me?"

Orion took a slow breath and, with a hoarse voice, whispered, "I hear you."

"Then tell me you will return to Provenna."

"I follow after those who are righteous not evil."

"Orion, please," Tnaka begged, "come back. You can still serve Provenna and follow after righteousness."

Orion's face filled with pain as he took a breath. "How can I claim to follow after those who are righteous if I serve one who is evil?"

Tnaka hesitated for a moment, for he had no answer. "You can."

Orion gave a cold laugh.

"Orion..." began Tnaka, but Orion continued to laugh his bitter laugh filled with anger, despair, and contempt. It echoed off the walls and filled the room.

"Orion, stop!" Tnaka cried. "How hard can it be to turn?"

Orion's laughter died away, and he answered softly, "Not hard at all, but wrong nonetheless. I serve Mystia not my mother."

"Orion, listen to me!"

"Fool! I am listening to you, but I will not do as you ask. I once followed evil, and you begged me to serve righteousness. Now I follow righteousness, and you beg me to serve evil. I will not do so. I have chosen my path, and I will follow it."

"Even if it means death?" Tnaka demanded. "You know what a price that is!" He paused for a moment then continued, with soft intensity, "You have not the strength to resist and stand firm in your beliefs. You and I both know you will fall."

"You lie!" Orion snarled.

"No, I do not!" Tnaka cried. "And you know it! 'Tis only a matter of time before you surrender, and I would have it be sooner, while you still hold some of your convictions, rather than later."

"You lie," Orion said again, his voice trembling. "I will not turn. I will stand firm for Mystia."

"Forget that woman! Provenna herself said she would find you twenty women more beautiful than that one!

"Just return to us! All my life have I wanted peace, and all my life I have received war. Provenna has conquered and conquered and conquered. Now, if you simply turn, help her defeat Kozan, and become her son once again, she will be satisfied, and there will be peace."

"And what care I if you have peace?" asked Orion, softly but with fury. "I will not turn."

For a long moment Tnaka simply looked at the blue-eyed warrior and tried to think of some way to convince him, but there was nothing he could do. Finally, without another word, he turned to walk from the room, but, as he turned he stopped in surprise for in the doorway stood Eagle. How long she had been there the elven king knew not, but it was clear she was filled with questions.

* * *

Tnaka sat in his chambers with his head bowed and his hands folded and resting on the table in front of him. Eagle sat across from him. Her brow was furrowed, and she looked intensely at him as she asked, "Who is this man? You say he's Provenna's son, yet she has him tortured as though he is her worst enemy. He may be a warrior, but what good would he do against Kozan who is a Power? Why do you want so much to turn him to you?"

"Eagle," said Tnaka with a sad, weary voice, "ask me not why Provenna does the things she does, for I know not."

"Very well, why do you want Orion to turn?"

"I wish him not to turn at all, but I know he will so I wish him to turn now rather than later, when he will become so completely evil that he'll pull Lairannare into wars that will last far beyond my lifetime."

"And how can you claim to know the actions any man will take before they are taken?" demanded Eagle.

Tnaka gave a wry, half-smile and answered, "Because Orion is the son of Phyre."

For a moment Eagle could only stare, dumfounded, at Tnaka.

"What?" she finally sputtered.

"Just as I said, Orion is the son of Phyre, the one who was the King of the Realm of Earth, the one who first rebelled against Joretham."

"But how can that be?" she asked. "He cannot be the actual flesh-and-blood son of Norenroth."

"No, he is no longer the flesh-and-blood child of Norenroth; he has a far stronger, more evil tie than that."

Eagle looked at him in confusion. "What?"

Tnaka took a breath. "Perhaps I should simply tell you the tale in its entirety."

Eagle straightened and looked intently at him, as she waited for him to begin.

"As you know," began Tnaka, "Phyre was cursed by Joretham. After he had been cursed he sought, by every means he could, to defeat Joretham and overcome that curse. He started the wars with the Shallee and was defeated. He killed Jaidev and was defeated. He gave Balor strength and knowledge, and when Balor was defeated Phyre also was overcome and thrown down from his place as King of Lairannare. Ever since then, he has sought to regain his former position and the power that went with it.

"Forty-three years ago Provenna was born. She was a simple peasant girl in a quiet, little village unheard of even by most of the citizens of the neighboring cities, but Phyre--some way, somehow--learned not only of her existence but also that she was the Greater Power.

"He came to her village in the guise of a wandering knight--Aidan by name. She was young, and her family was not a good one; her mother was an invalid, and her father was an abusive drunkard. She was not suited to resist the wiles of so great and noble and generous a man as she deemed Aidan to be.

"Phyre hoped that through her he would be able to regain that which he had lost. But that hope ended when Orion was born. It was obvious, from the moment of his birth, that Orion possessed great magic power. The rulers of the other Realms had, with growing trepidation, watched Phyre, and with Orion's birth they could remain silent no longer. Phyre's evil was held in check because he was thrown down from his place as King of Lairannare and the Powers were given dominion over him, but Orion, who not only held great magic but was also the son of a Power, had no such checks. As Phyre's son he was cursed by the same curse Joretham had placed upon Phyre, and it was feared he would be just as evil as his father.

"The Council of the Three Realms was called together to deliberate Orion's fate. From the very beginning, the Council was turned against him. Some argued for his death, and others thought he should be thrown from the Three

Realms and made an outcast like the Shallee, but none stood with him. Provenna, fairly overcome with the thought of Orion being taken from her and murdered, begged with all her might for his life. I also argued and pleaded, with more eloquence and passion than I could ever hope to meet again. Even Kozan desired that Orion be allowed to live.

"But it was all for naught. The Council was determined that Orion could not be free to live completely unhindered. However, just before the sentence was to be delivered, Lyght, the King of Keiliornare, stood up and spoke, declaring that Orion would neither be killed nor thrown from the Three Realms but that he-- Lyght--would take him as his son and protect him.

"Queen Nyght was furious, for she had been most vocal in her call for Orion's death. There was, however, little she could do to keep Lyght from his intentions. She threatened to throw him down from his position, but still he stood firm and took Orion as his son.

"Nyght argued that at least some sort of staying power ought to be placed upon Orion, and it was not difficult to convince the other creatures in the Council of that. She demanded that Orion's magic strength be taken from him, and so they were; at least while Orion remains in the Realm of Earth he cannot use magic.

"But Lyght gave Orion perhaps an even greater gift than that which had been taken from him. He placed a spell so great upon Orion that no one--not even a Power--can touch him with magic.

"The Council ended and we returned to Lairannare. As the years passed, a terrible truth became clear. Lyght, through magic, had made Orion his flesh- and-blood son, but Orion still possessed the soul of Phyre. He was evil beyond imagination, and there was nothing we could do to hold him back. Lyght had made certain that magic would not touch him so we could only beg and entreat him to stop. You know not how relieved I was when he finally ran away and I was forced no longer to deal with him.

"I had hoped that he died," he gave a bitter smile, "but that proved not the case. When Provenna called him to the palace I was terrified at the thought. The wars seemed finally to be ending, and peace was close to becoming a reality, but I was certain that if Orion returned to the wealth, luxury, and power he once held he would desire them even more and plunge the whole of Lairannare into yet another war."

Tnaka leaned forward. "But when he came I looked into his eyes and saw within him something I never thought him capable of holding. The years had changed him and taught him what I never could--the ways of righteousness--and I allowed myself to hope that the evil I feared would not take place."

His gaze fell and his shoulders slumped, as he said in despair, "But the years taught him too well the ways of righteousness, and now he refuses to stand with us, all because of that foolish Shallean princess."

Eagle's brow became even more furrowed. "Lord, you fear the evil Orion is capable of doing, but what evil can he do by refusing to serve Provenna?"

"Do you not see?" Tnaka cried as he rose to his feet. "Orion still has the soul of Phyre; that is one thing Mystia cannot change. His most basic instinct is that of total evil, but because of the love of this woman he forces himself to turn against everything within him and follow after her. He refuses to bend--he believes that to be evil--but he will break beneath the torture he's forced to endure, and when that happens he will reject completely the ways of righteousness and become exactly what he was before--a man given over completely to evil."

Eagle looked intently at Tnaka. "Then free him before he is broken."

"How can I do that?" asked Tnaka in despair. "How can I turn against Provenna? Powers are not to be divided." He turned and walked to the window and said quietly, "Besides, were I to rescue him it would bring about the very thing I wish to prevent--war. Only it would be between me and Provenna, not Orion and whoever he claimed was an enemy."

"Powers are not to be divided against each other?" repeated Eagle as she rose and took a step toward him. "Kozan stands against Provenna, and he's a Power. He stands for what he believes in--evil and oppression. Why, Lord, can you not stand for what you believe in--peace?"

Tnaka turned back to her. "But if I turn against her I will bring war."

She looked at him and said, "Sometimes peace is only bought with war."

He said nothing; what could he say? He simply looked in despair at her.

"Leave me alone," he finally whispered.

She said nothing but curtsied low then turned and walked from the room.

* * *

Provenna sat upon her crystal throne and stared out into the empty space before her. Her throne room was empty, and she sat there as unmoving as stone. So had she come and sat every day since the Dark Sorcerer had left.

She started as there came a pounding on the doors to the chamber.

"What?" she demanded. Her voice echoed off the walls.

The doors to the throne room were opened and a servant woman walked in. She curtsied and said, "There is a man named Nuri who claims that you know him and who desires an audience with you."

Provenna was silent for a moment before asking, "Does he have white hair and very bright blue eyes?"

"Yes, Your Majesty."

She paused then said, "Very well, show him in."

"Yes, Your Majesty." The servant woman curtsied low then turned and walked from the throne room only to return a minute later, ushering in a very noble-looking, rather old man. The servant woman curtsied once again and left.

The man, with a slow, dignified gait, made his way up to the dais upon which the throne rested, where he stopped and bowed before Provenna. For a long moment, Provenna simply looked down upon him. His beard and his long, flowing hair were as white as snow, but he seemed not to be as old as from afar he appeared. He stood with quiet dignity and looked up at the Queen, and his spectral blue eyes seemed to pierce to her very soul.

"Hello, Lyght," said Provenna coldly. "Why have you come here?"

"Thou knowest why I come," answered Lyght. "I come to ask thee to release Orion and torture him no longer."

She looked at him for a moment then asked softly, "And what right have you to ask that of me?"

"As much right as anyone hath to seek mercy for a man who deserveth not his fate--more, considering I am his father."

"You," Provenna cried as she rose, "are not his father! You are nothing more than a meddling old fool who has ever worked to turn my son away from me and who stood idly by as a Shallean wench stole his heart!"

"And what know thee of what I did?" demanded Lyght, angrily. "Thou canst not see past the doors of thine own throne room, much less across the whole of Lairannare into the Realm of Magic where I make my home."

"If you had done something he would not serve her now."

"And think thee that he would do as I desire--I who, as thou sayest, am not even his father?" asked Lyght with scorn.

Provenna's eyes flashed with rage, but she could say nothing in reply.

Lyght looked intently at her and said, "Now, Provenna, release him. 'Twould be wrong for any man to so treateth him--how much more thou who art his mother?"

Provenna was silent for a moment then took a step toward him and began to speak. "I am his mother, and he is my son. Joretham commands him to obey me, yet he does not do so. What else am I to do save punish him? He has brought his fate upon his own head."

Lyght silently watched her as she circled him, and when she had stopped he said, "Thou speakest falsely, and thou knowest it. 'Tis wrong to treat any man as thou treatest Orion, but, unlike with other men, the consequences of doing so with Orion will be deadly. Now free him!"

"I will not!" Provenna snarled as she stepped back onto the dais and, eyes flashing, stared down at him. "He deserves no mercy!" Beneath the anger which filled her eyes and covered her face, there was pain that cut to her very soul. "Aidan turned against me. Kozan turned against me. The Dar..." The words caught in her throat. "The man I would have given my whole kingdom to forsook me. I will not let my son turn on me also."

"How canst thou say or do that?" demanded Lyght. "Three men have rejected thee, so thou dost take out thine anger against thy son? Thou art the ruler of the whole of Lairannare. Thou art to rule with wisdom and justice! What wisdom and what justice is found in thy treatment of Orion?"

"And do you think I want to be the ruler of Lairannare?" snarled Provenna. "I was born a peasant. I never wanted to be a queen or a Power, and often have I felt that I was not fate's first choice to be the Greater Power. But I am the Greater Power and I am the queen. My word is the law of Lairannare, and you will have to live with it!"

"Provenna," began Lyght.

"Be quiet," she said as she sat down upon her throne. For a long moment after she simply looked at him.

Finally, she gave a bitter smile and said softly, "They say that Darus, the true king of Delovachia, still lives and that he ever works toward the destruction of Kozan. You know not how much I wish that legend were true." She leaned forward. "I rule Lairannare because I must, because I am the Greater Power, because if I did not Kozan would, because if I stopped the people would kill me. But how I wish Darus were real and that he would go and kill Kozan. My Power would be destroyed with Kozan's death, but they say Darus is a good man, and I think that he would rule Lairannare well; and I think that he would not be a man to be feared; and I think that he would understand why I am what I am and would show me mercy." She leaned back again and gave an angry, bitter laugh. "But Darus is a legend and nothing more, and I will rule Lairannare until I die."

Lyght was silent for a moment, as he tried to think of what to say in response. He was just in the process of opening his mouth when there came a pounding on the doors to the throne room.

"Enter," snapped Provenna.

The doors were opened, and the servant woman walked in. She curtsied low and said, "Forgive me, Your Majesty, for this intrusion, but you wished to be told the moment Zenas arrived."

"Very well," said Provenna. "Have him brought here immediately."

"Yes, Your Majesty," said the servant woman, who then curtsied and walked from the chamber.

Provenna turned her eyes back to Lyght and said quietly, "I will not free Orion. Now leave."

Lyght remained still and silent for a moment, looking up at her, trying to decide what he should do next. Finally, he bowed then turned and walked away. The sound of his feet striking the hard, stone floor and echoing off the walls was the only sound in that solemn place. He reached the end of the room, where he stopped and looked back at Provenna then glanced up at the stained-glass pictures. Then without a word he turned and disappeared from the throne room. There was a hollow boom as the doors shut behind him.

Provenna sat upon her throne and forced herself to remain absolutely still and calm, but, though her face was an unmoving mask, darkness and fury raged behind her flashing, green eyes.

The doors to the throne room were opened once again and the servant woman, followed by Zenas, entered. Zenas hesitated and looked about him--wide-eyed with fear. The servant woman curtsied, gave Zenas a soft push in the direction he was to walk, then turned and left.

Slowly the old man made his way across the wide room. His head hung, and his shoulders were hunched over. He held tightly to his staff, but even so both his hands trembled. When he reached the dais, he stopped and looked up at Provenna. His eyes were like those of a man haunted--filled with fear and despair.

"Ye called for me, Yar Majesty," said he softly.

"Yes, I did," she answered.

"Here I am. What d' ye want?"

She was silent for a moment then said, "You are a very old man and a very wise man. I cannot begin to imagine the things you must have learned during your long life.

"You know Orion well, and Joretham knows you must know as much of him as I do." There was a bitter tone to her voice as she said that. She paused, then continued. "I want you to find a way to use magic on him."

"Do I have to?" Zenas asked in a pitiful voice.

"Yes," Provenna answered coldly.

"But..." began the old man, sorrow filling his voice.

Provenna rose from her throne and scowled at him. "I am the Queen of the Realm of Earth. Do as I order."

The old man fell to his knees and looked up in anguish at her. "Ask me t' do anything but tha'," he begged, "but please don't ask me to turn against Orion." His shoulders shook. "Please don't."

"Zenas," hissed Provenna, "you are nothing more than an old hermit whom Kozan would have killed had it not been for me. You owe me a great debt--a debt you have yet to pay."

"But she was such a pretty lass," he whispered in despair. "Such a very pretty lass."

"I care nothing about that. Now tell me how to use magic against Orion."

Zenas simply said there and said nothing.

"I will not ask again."

"I don't even know if it's possible."

"You will find a way."

For a long moment Zenas was silent, and when he finally did speak, he looked as though his heart was being torn from him.

"Very well," he whispered. "Tell me everything ye know about Orion."

* * *

Mystia sat upon the floor of Kozan's chambers. It was dark, for night had fallen and the silver rays of the moon, shining through the window, provided the only light.

Kozan sat at a small table and drank wine. It seemed to be all he ever did. He would sit there for hours on end, and as he drank he would stare off into space, with the most pained and anguished look upon his face, or he would fly into terrible rages that seemed never to end.

Mystia did not look at him, but she gave a wince of pain as she felt the bruise on her face. It hurt, but not as much as the ache in her heart, or in her soul.

She leaned back against the wall--she sat right beneath the window--and turned her eyes to the ceiling, as she prayed. She cried out silently--she dared not pray aloud--that Joretham would help her and give her strength and that He would protect Orion.

The mere thought of Orion was enough to almost make her burst into tears. Her shoulders shook with a sudden sob, but she forced herself not to cry. Even so, a single tear escaped. For one moment it sparkled in the light of the moon. Then it trickled down her face and disappeared beneath her veil.

"Are you praying again?" asked Kozan, mockingly.

Mystia started and turned her face to him.

"What makes you think that?" she asked with a soft, trembling voice.

He gave a sneer, and, as he spoke, the slur in his voice became evident. "Your eyes were vacant, and you were staring up at the ceiling as though Joretham were up there. You never think He's behind you or below you or in front of you. No, He's always somewhere up there." He waved his hand up at some vague portion of the ceiling.

Mystia stared down at the floor and said nothing.

"Perhaps He's standing next to me," said Kozan as he reached to pour himself another glass of wine. "Then you would have to look at me every time you prayed."

Still Mystia said nothing.

Suddenly Kozan gave a laugh. "Come here."

He looked at her, and, when he saw that she did not move, he growled, "I said come here."

Slowly she rose and approached him. Her black eyes were filled with fear, and when she came within six feet of him her steps faltered.

"Sit," Kozan ordered as he motioned to the seat across from him.

She hesitated for a moment then, eyeing him warily, silently did as he commanded.

"Look at me," he ordered, and, when he saw that she did, he said, "Now pray to your God."

"What?" she said in surprise as she pushed her chair back and tried to rise.

Kozan jumped to his feet and tried to pull her back, but she was too far away for him to touch. He growled in fury and fixed her with a dark stare. She screamed as unseen hands pulled her back down into the chair and forced her face to turn toward him. Her eyes were wide as in terror she stared up at Kozan.

"I said pray to your God!" he snarled.

She opened her mouth, but no words would come. Tears were streaming down her face.

He looked down in fury upon her, and his gaze locked with hers. For a moment he stood there, holding her gaze. Then suddenly he gave a cry and turned his face from her, snarling as he did so, "Stop looking at me."

The spell broke, and Mystia fell sobbing to the floor. Her chair went toppling over with her, and she gave a sharp cry as it fell on her hand.

"Would you be quiet!" snapped Kozan. "What sort of a God do you worship if you burst into tears every time you pray to Him?"

Even through her fear, anger filled her at his words and she jumped up, crying, "And what sort of a god do you serve? You, who murdered your wife, who have killed thousands of people, who strike innocent women, who know nothing of ruling a kingdom but sit in a drunken stupor and let your servants rule it for you?"

"Be quiet!" Kozan growled as he lunged forward and struck her across the face. She gave a gasp of pain and fell to the floor, where she scrambled back away from him as quickly as she could.

"How dare you defy me!" he cried. "I am a Power and a king and your master, and you are nothing more than my slave! My word is the law. How dare you try to insult my god!"

"Balor is no god," she answered.

His lips curled up in a sneer. "And I suppose Joretham is? Joretham, who has stood ever so faithfully beside you and your country, keeping your country from falling and you from being taken prisoner. Yes, what great power He has."

He rolled his eyes and added, "One would expect such power from a dead god."

"Joretham rose from the dead," Mystia told him softly.

Kozan laughed. "Do you actually believe the foolish stories made up for your religion?"

"Do you believe the stories of your religion?"

Kozan sat back down at the table, and his face was twisted in anger and scorn as he spat, "I do not need to put my trust in foolish stories created by long dead people in their pitiful attempts to lend credence to their failing religion."

He reached for his pitcher of wine, and as he poured himself another goblet he looked down at Mystia where she sat upon the floor. He grew very quiet as for a long moment he simply gazed upon her.

Finally, he spoke very softly. "I know a tale that few have ever heard; fewer still have been allowed to live once they have been told." He took a drink from his goblet, and there was a far distant look in his eyes as he spoke. "There once was a boy, many, many years ago--a pirate. How he became a pirate who can tell? For he himself remembered nothing of a life before the rocking of a ship and the ocean stretching endlessly in all directions.

"Pirates are an evil lot who prey upon all who are weaker than they, and this boy was very young and very weak." An angry look filled Kozan's face. "But this boy learned strength, and he learned power, and he learned ruthlessness. He learned that men were weak fools to be broken to his will, and he rose in greatness until, when he was barely a man, he became the greatest and most feared of all the pirates who ever sailed the seas.

"One day a storm sprang up suddenly, and he was caught in the very middle of it. It raged for weeks, and his ship was battered beneath it, until finally, as the fury of the storm became even greater, the vessel was broken. The boy was cast into the water, but how could the mere sea overcome one as great as he?

"He was tossed upon the waves until finally he was cast up upon the shores of an island. It was an island he had never seen nor heard of before. It was a dark, magnificent place filled with magic more potent than anything he had ever felt before, and in the very center of the island there was a great, towering temple made entirely of the blackest marble.

"The boy entered the temple, and there he was met by a man--a man who was more proud and terrifying and powerful than any man the boy had ever met." Kozan's eyes fairly flashed with evil. "That man was Balor, and that island was his sanctuary where he would stay until the time came for him to return and rule over Lairannare.

"He led the boy into the inner sanctum of the temple, and there he told the boy many things. That boy was great already, but he was destined to become even greater. He was destined to become the greatest man who ever walked the face of Lairannare. He was to rule the Realm of Earth, and he was to destroy the High Elves once and for all, and thereby open the way for Balor's return.

"There was another--a boy, a man, a woman, an elf; Balor did not say--and this other was a Power, but he did not deserve his Power. Balor showed the boy the most dark and ancient of magic spells, and together they cast it. The pain that took hold of the boy was unlike anything he had ever felt before--it was as though his body was being torn apart--but he was strong, and he endured, and, when he was finished, he held within himself the magic strength which had but moments before belonged to the unworthy Power."

Kozan gave a wicked smile. "Now that boy has but to destroy the fool of a woman who dares hold herself up as the Greater Power. Then all will be finished, and Balor will return and rule over Lairannare and, finally, over the whole of Deithanara." His brown eyes were flashing as he leaned forward. "That is the power of Balor--the power to take a person's magic strength--the very essence of a man--and give it to another, the power to set oneself up and reign on high over the whole of Deithanara. That is true power. What is Joretham compared to that?"

Mystia said nothing in reply. She simply sat upon the floor and looked steadily up at him. Kozan, for all the might of his god, could not bring himself to look into her eyes.

* * *

Far away, in the country of Jocthreal, in the city of Leilaora, Queen Eagle stood in the dark dungeon of Provenna's palace. She stood outside Orion's cell and covered her face with her hands. Aeneas had gone and the beatings had ended for the night, but still Orion cried out in a hoarse, pitiful, broken voice. His chains rattled violently as he strained with all his might to break them. Over and over again he cried out for Mystia--or to Mystia. And Eagle simply stood silently in the dark and dirty corridor and listened to him.

Darkness of Heart

Chapter 21
Darkness of Heart

Eagle stood outside the door to Orion's cell. The warrior's cries and struggling had ceased, and now not a sound could be heard.

"Open the door," Eagle ordered the warder who stood beside her.

"Are you sure, Your Majesty?" he asked. "He was making quite a stir earlier."

Eagle fixed him with a stormy glare and said, "I told you to open the door."

"Yes, Your Majesty," said the warder as he stepped forward and put a large, iron key into the lock. He gave it a hard twist then pulled the door open.

Eagle brushed past the warder into the darkness beyond. The cell was lit by only the faintest glow of the almost-dead coals, which lay in the center of the floor, and it took a long moment for her eyes to adjust to the darkness. When they finally did, she looked down to see Orion staring up at her. Aeneas had chained him so that he could sit upon the floor, but that tortured him almost as much as when he was forced to stand, for his back, which was a mass of open wounds, pressed against the hard, dirt-covered stone wall. His eyes were filled with agony, but he did not cry out; he had not the strength to do so.

Eagle looked down upon him, but she knew not what to say.

For a long moment there was silence. Finally, Orion took a slow, painful breath and said, scarcely above a whisper, "Have you also come here to torture me or try to make me turn?"

"Of course not," she said as she knelt down in front of him. "I came because..." Her voice trailed off, for she knew not why she came. Something--she knew not what--had forced her to come look upon this man who was treated so cruelly and who was the cause of so many conflicting desires. Sorrow welled up within her as she looked into his spectral blue eyes, which were so filled with pain and anger.

"Are you truly the son of Phyre?" she finally asked.

He said nothing, but his lips curled up in an angry sneer, and Eagle was certain she saw despair behind his eyes. "Is that why you've come? To satisfy your stupid, childish curiosity?"

"Why do you do this?" she asked. "Why do refuse to submit?"

"What does it matter?" he demanded.

"Tnaka believes you do so because of your love for Mystia."

He gave a bitter laugh. "Love. It must always be love. It must be love that upholds Deithanara and love that is the greatest feeling to be aspired to, and it must be love alone that would make a man faithfully serve a woman and refuse to be turned to evil. Fool!" Eagle started back at his sudden outburst. "What makes you think that I, who am the son of Phyre, am even capable of feeling love?"

What little energy he had was used up by his few angry words, and he slumped forward. His long, auburn hair covered his face and hid the look of anger and anguish filling his eyes, but it could not hide his shoulders, which shook with the sorrow he tried to contain.

Eagle looked down upon him and with a voice filled with sadness said, "Orion, please, forgive me. I should not have asked what I asked. I doubt I should even have come here. I wish only that I could find some way to comfort you."

Orion gave another bitter laugh and raised his head. He looked straight into her eyes as he said, "I am cursed to enter into eternal torment upon my death. I do not have Joretham's mercy or forgiveness to save me from this, so I must rely solely on my own actions to prove myself worthy to enter into Lothiel. Is there comfort for a man such as I?"

Eagle opened her mouth to answer but closed it without speaking, for what could she say? In anguish she looked upon him then silently rose and began to walk away. When she reached the door to the cell, she turned and cast one last look upon him.

"Forgive me," she whispered. Then she walked through the door and was gone.

* * *

Abiel, with his magicians close behind, charged through the thick forest. His way was lit by the red light of the sun, which had already sunk behind the trees and soon would disappear completely. The hooves of the horses cut up the ground as they flew over the underbrush. Gideone was not far; Abiel was certain of it. Every beat of the horses' hooves seemed to cry out for the blood of the Norian prince. Abiel's face was twisted into a terrible look of hatred and anticipation. Soon vengeance would be his.

* * *

Gideone sat upon the ground and leaned back against a tree. Every muscle in his body ached. He gave a long sigh and closed his eyes. He was completely exhausted.

Neither Stavros nor Vayan spoke more than Gideone. Vayan, who had been rather subdued ever since they had left Haflashon, was silently making a fire, and Stavros sat beside a fallen log nervously drumming his fingers on it.

They had made their small camp even further off the main path than normally they did, and Stavros had insisted that the horses be kept saddled and bridled, for he felt certain that something would happen that night; however, he knew not what it was or how else to prepare for it, so he was left to nervously tap his fingers against the fallen tree. He made scarcely a sound, but to Gideone, who sat close by, it was the most maddening noise he had ever heard. He opened his eyes, gave Stavros a dark look, and, "Would you stop it?"

Stavros gave him a confused look and asked, "What?"

"Tapping your fingers," answered Gideone with a sigh and a roll of his eyes, as though the answer were the most obvious thing in the whole of Deithanara. "'Tis dreadfully annoying."

Stavros bit back a response, but he could not hide his annoyance as he crossed his arms and began to drum his fingers against his skin.

"I told you to stop it," snapped Gideone.

Stavros' eyes narrowed as he turned to Gideone and said, "You may be sick, Your Highness, but there is still a fine line between what is proper and what is not. You crossed that line in your treatment of Phautina, but I allowed it because, though part of me wished her to continue with us, it would have put her in danger along with us. But cross not that line with me."

"Are you threatening me?" demanded Gideone.

"I am simply stating a fact, Your Highness. You would be wise to listen to it."

"You are threatening me!" cried the Prince as he jumped to his feet.

"You say it not I," answered Stavros as he too rose.

"Father, Your Highness," said Vayan nervously as he looked up at the two warring men.

"Stay out of this!" snarled Gideone as he rounded on Vayan and took a step toward him.

"Leave my son alone!" Stavros cried as he grasped Gideone by the arm and pulled him back.

Gideone gave a cry of fury and spun around, swinging his free arm at Stavros as he did so. Stavros ducked out of the way and struck Gideone hard across the jaw. The Prince gave another cry as he rammed his whole body into Stavros, sending them both tumbling to the ground.

The Prince managed to get on top of Stavros, and as he sent his fist slamming down toward Stavros' face he cried, "Traitor! How dare you stand against me!"

Stavros tried to dodge the blows and push Gideone off of him at the same time, but he was struck several times, and each time left him weaker and more dazed than the time before. Suddenly, even as Gideone pulled back his fist to deliver another blow, he was yanked off of Stavros.

The Prince spun around and found himself facing Vayan who was in the process of jumping back from the punch he knew was coming, but the young man was not quick enough. Gideone gave a cry, and his fist caught Vayan in the chin. Before Vayan could retaliate, Gideone sent his fist slamming into his stomach. Vayan clutched at his belly and doubled over in pain.

"Traitor!" Gideone snarled as he tried to strike again, but Vayan, still clutching at his stomach and trying to breathe, fell to the ground and rolled out of the way.

"You stand with Phautina and Orion and your father!" Gideone continued as he tried to kick him. Even as he did so, Stavros reached out and grabbed his tunic. Gideone lost his balance and fell to the ground. He scrambled to his knees.

"You all stand against me!" he shouted, as he lunged forward and fell upon Vayan.

Stavros tried to pull Gideone away, but he fell once more to the ground and was pulled into the fight.

"My, my, my," a cruel, mocking voice suddenly said. The three men started in surprise, stopped their fighting, and turned to find themselves looking up at Abiel. He sat upon his horse in the shadows of the trees and looked scornfully down upon them.

His mouth twisted up into an even greater sneer than it already bore as he looked down at where Gideone, Stavros, and Vayan lay. "I knew my father was perverted, but even he never went for other men."

Gideone's lips curled up as he pushed Stavros and Vayan off of him and rose, saying as he did so, "That was only because you were too busy with them yourself."

Abiel gave a cry of fury and dug his spurs into his horse's sides. Gideone drew his sword and rushed toward Abiel.

"No!" Stavros cried as he ran after Gideone.

Both of them gave a cry and jumped out of the way as Abiel's horse barreled down upon them.

Stavros tumbled to the ground then rolled to his feet and tried to run to Gideone, but even as he did so, Abiel's magician's rushed out from the darkness. He gave a shout of surprise and tried to draw his sword, but they were already upon him. He gave another cry, this one of pain, as the sharp steel of a knife cut into his arm. Everyone was yelling and screaming, and he could hear Gideone crying some obscene curses down upon Abiel. He struggled against the magicians who seemed to swarm about him and looked wildly about for the Prince and Vayan.

Suddenly, there was a huge crash, like the sound of thunder, and the whole forest seemed to ignite in flames. Stavros looked around in confusion. The horses were shrieking in terror, and everyone was running madly about as they tried to escape.

Stavros found himself free from the magicians, and, immediately, he rushed through the flames, which raged all about, and plunged into the darkness beyond. He ran for a short distance, and, when he thought he was alone, he turned and looked back at where the battle had taken place. He could only stare in confusion at it. The fire, which had so suddenly and mysteriously erupted, still raged. The orange flames rose high into the sky, but they did not spread to the surrounding trees. He had never been so astonished or puzzled in his life. "What happened?" he whispered. "Joretham, what happened?!"

* * *

Abiel ran through the forest as fast as he could go. His mind screamed out in fury against whatever strange and powerful force it was that stood against him. What had happened at the scene of the battle he understood not, nor did he care. All he knew was that Gideone had been taken from him even as he held the Prince in his grasp.

Abiel plunged through the trees. He would not let Gideone escape. The branches of the trees seemed to reach out and cling to him, and the roots seemed to rise up in his path. He stumbled and fell, and his cloak, which was caught by a tree branch, was torn from him, but he did not try to retrieve it. He rose and continued to stumble through the trees, which seemed to grow ever thicker the further he went.

Finally, he pushed through two trees and found himself in a small moonlit glade. There was not another moving, breathing soul to be seen, and silence reigned supreme. He stood there and simply looked about him not knowing what to do or what to expect.

Out of the shadows on the opposite side of the glade there emerged a figure, and, as it moved closer, Abiel saw that it was a woman. Her clothes were torn and worn from days of travel, and she seemed to be a very simple maid. Her face was homely, but there was an ethereal look about her.

She walked to the center of the glade where she stopped and beckoned for Abiel to come to her. He hesitated then walked out and joined her in the center of the glade, and, as he looked down at her, he recognized her as the woman who had been traveling with Gideone.

"Who are you?" he demanded. "What are you doing here?"

For a moment she remained silent. Then, with a voice that was soft yet clear she said, "I am Phautina, the servant of Joretham. I protect those whom he would have me protect, and minister unto those whom he wishes ministered to, and bring justice down upon those whom he would have brought to justice. It is I who have ridden with Gideone and protected him from you these many days, and it was I who caused the fire to spring up during your battle in the forest and scatter you and your men, for it is not Joretham's will that you should kill Gideone."

Abiel gave a scornful laugh. "And what care I for Joretham's will?"

She looked up at him with unblinking brown eyes and answered steadily, "Those are the words of a fool."

Abiel reached for his sword, but as he looked down upon her he found himself unable to draw it. He gave her a scornful, bitter look then turned and began to walk away.

"I have a message for you," she told him softly.

He continued to walk away.

"You are filled with bitterness and anger and hatred," she said, "but Joretham can give you peace."

Abiel slowly stopped and turned back and faced her. His scarred and broken face was twisted into a look of scorn and hate. "No one can do that."

"Joretham can, and he will but only if you allow him to do so. He does not want you to be filled with despair, and he does not want you to enter into Elmorran and eternal torment upon your death, but he cannot save you unless you let him. Forget Gideone, give up your quest for revenge, leave the path your father has shown you, and come follow Joretham. He stands with arms open ready to guide you, love you, and take away the bitterness and anger which fills you and give you peace in its stead."

Abiel said nothing in reply but simply stood there and looked down at her. The look of scorn never left his face, then without a word he turned and walked away, leaving Phautina to gaze sadly after him as he disappeared into the shadows.

* * *

Stavros walked slowly and quietly through the forest. He had seen neither friend nor foe since he had first run into the forest, and now he was slowly making his way back to the scene of the battle; he hoped that he would find Gideone and Vayan there.

His horse gave a soft snort. Stavros looked back at it and could only shake his head in amazement. As he had been walking through the forest, he had suddenly remembered that Wild Rose's healing balm was packed in one of the saddlebags of his horse. The chances of finding his horse in the midst of the dark forest were very slim, and he had been terrified by what would happen to Gideone were he to have no defense against the poison which filled his body. Stavros had done the only thing he could do--pray to Joretham--and as he had made his way back toward the scene of the battle he ran across his horse, which had been standing and munching quietly on the leaves of a bush.

Presently, he reached his destination. The fire, which had so mysteriously sprung up had burnt out, leaving only the charred remains of the trees. Stavros breathed a sigh of relief when he found Gideone, with a scowl upon his face, standing in the middle of the blackened trees.

"Finally," grumbled the Prince. "I thought you'd never come. What were you trying to do? Leave me here all alone so as to make it easier for Abiel and his magicians to attack and kill me?"

Stavros only gave a weary sigh.

"Or perhaps," Gideone continued, "you left me here so that that traitor Phautina could cast a spell on me."

Stavros looked at the Prince. "What does Phautina have to do with any of this?"

Gideone crossed his arms, and his scowl deepened as he growled, "The little cur followed us here. I knew she couldn't be trusted. And what's more, I saw her and Abiel conversing in the forest, and it looked not to be the conversation of enemies."

Stavros frowned and asked, "Are you certain it was her."

"Yes, I'm certain it was her!" Gideone cried, his dark eyes flashing. "What do you take me for--a blind fool?"

"Surely there must be some reason for..."

"Of course, there is a reason! She's a traitorous cur who, from the start, should not have been trusted!"

"Your Highness..."

"Be quiet! You..." the Prince's voice trailed off as he suddenly heard the sound of snapping twigs, announcing someone's approach through the forest. The two men stopped their arguing and quickly ducked into the shadows of the trees and waited silently to see whom it was that came.

After several moments, Vayan appeared, leading a horse behind him. He looked around and, when he found no one, said, "I don't mean to be impertinent, but after th' noise ye were makin' it seems rather poin'less t' hide."

Stavros gave a soft laugh, Gideone said nothing, and both emerged from the shadows.

"Joretham, I'm glad to see you," said Stavros. "Now all we need is a third horse then we can leave this place, hopefully before Abiel or any of his men find us. Vayan, you stay here and guard the horses while Prince Gideone and I search the forest for another one."

"Aye, Father," said Vayan with a nod of his head as he took the reins of Stavros' horse.

"Your Highness," began Stavros as he turned to Gideone, but the Prince was not paying attention to him but rather seemed to be listening to the forest around him.

"Your Highness?" questioned Stavros.

Gideone started and looked at Stavros. "What?"

"Shall we go?"

"Yes, of course," said Gideone who then turned and began to lead Stavros out of the charred circle of trees. They reached the edge of where the fire had burned and were just passing a tree around which there was a considerable amount of foliage, when, without warning, Gideone leapt to his right and ran around the tree. Even before Stavros or Vayan could move there came the sharp, startled cry of a woman.

"I knew it was you!" Gideone growled as he dragged Phautina from behind the tree and out into the open. Vayan started forward as the Prince threw Phautina roughly to the ground.

"Stay back!" Gideone, his dark eyes flashing, ordered Vayan. Then, turning back to Phautina, he demanded, "What are you doing here?"

Phautina picked herself up and as she brushed herself off answered, "I wanted to see how you fared and whether or not you had been harmed by Abiel and his men."

"Why? So that if you saw we'd escaped unscathed you could kill us for him?"

"Why in the Three Realms would I want to do that?" she asked as she took a surprised step away from him.

"I told you at Haflashon that you could no longer travel with us, yet you have followed me here, spied on me, and what is more I saw you speaking with Abiel!"

"Your Highness," Stavros broke in, "forget her. Just let her go and let us leave."

"Be quiet!" snarled Gideone and spun to face Stavros. "I am not about to let this woman go free so she can kill me!"

"Prince Gideone," said Phautina calmly as she spread out her arms, "I am unarmed. Search me and you will see. I came not here to threaten you."

"Then why did you come here?" demanded Gideone, furious.

Phautina paused for a moment then answered, "I came, just as I said, to see if you had been harmed by Abiel and his men."

"And what did you say to Abiel?"

"What was said between Abiel and myself is for but him, myself, and Joretham to know."

"You lie!" Gideone fairly shrieked with rage.

It was as if time almost stood still. Stavros saw Gideone reach for his sword. The sound of the blade scraping against the scabbard filled the air as the Prince drew it. Stavros, giving a great cry, rushed toward him. He slammed into the Prince, sending them both tumbling to the ground, but he was too late, for even as they fell, the blade of Gideone's sword caught Phautina right beneath her ear and sliced through her neck down to the shoulder of her other side. She fell to the earth, and her head rolled across the ground until it struck the root of a tree and came to rest a few inches from her lifeless, outstretched hand.

Vayan's cry mixed with that of his father as he rushed forward and fell to the ground beside the dead woman.

Gideone, pushed Stavros away, rose to his feet and slowly approached the place where Phautina lay, and as he looked down upon her his face twisted into a smile.

Vayan looked up in horror at the Prince and cried out, "You murdered her!"

Gideone laughed a cold, mocking laugh. It seemed to spread out across the whole of the forest, and, as the sound filled Vayan's ears, his shock and horror turned to rage.

"Murderer!" he snarled as he started up, drawing his sword as he did so, and rushed at Gideone, but, even as he did so, Stavros pushed Gideone out of the way and exclaimed, "No, Vayan! No!"

"But he killed her!" Vayan cried, his face twisted into a look of anger, horror, and agony.

"I know," Stavros said weakly. He was too overcome by horror and disbelief to say anything more.

Vayan, his eyes opened wide and his sword still held up, took a step backward then suddenly turned and ran off into the shadows of the forest.

All strength left Stavros, and he sank to his knees. His hands were trembling, and his face was deathly pale as he stared down upon Phautina's body, which now lay in a pool of blood.

"You killed her," he whispered in disbelief. "You killed her." But when he looked up, he saw no remorse in the Prince's cold, dark eyes.

Chapter 22
Darkness of Spirit

The hour of midnight drew near, and scarcely a sound could be heard within the dark forest save for that of the wind as it blew through the black branches of the trees. Stavros pulled his cloak tighter around his shoulders to shield himself from its bitter fury. He could hear the steady, rhythmic sound of the ground crunching beneath the hooves of the horses.

He looked back into the trees and the darkness that lay behind him and pressed his hand tightly to his chest as a feeling of utter sickness welled up within him. Vayan's cry of fury and anguish still rang in his ears, and the sight of Phautina's dead body covered with blood was burned forever into his mind.

He could not bring himself to look at Gideone; his revulsion was too great. The Prince's eyes still burned with evil glee, for he prided himself on having rid himself not only of Phautina, the evil sorceress and mistress of Abiel, but also of Vayan who was not only the ally of Phautina but also of the traitor Orion.

Terror welled up within Stavros at the thought of Vayan, who was all alone in the dark forest, accidentally crossing paths with Abiel or one of Abiel's magicians and being forced, alone, to defend himself. Disgust filled him as he felt Gideone's scornful gaze upon him; it was as though the Prince could read his mind and was silently mocking him because of his fear, but neither man said a word.

As they rode on through the darkness, the trees of the forest slowly began to thin out, and the light of the moon shone in ever-greater quantities through the branches of the trees and down to the ground.

Very abruptly, the trees ended altogether, and Stavros drew his horse up in startled horror. Many a tale had he been told of the Demesne of Elishauno, but nothing had prepared him for the sight that lay spread out before him. He looked out across the broken, blasted land, and nothing could describe that which filled him as his gaze was met with the sight of hundreds of thousands of bones all bathed in the cold, pale light of the moon.

Slowly Stavros started forward again and followed after Gideone who had not been stopped with horror. Piles upon piles of bones lay in silent testimony of the great battle, which had once been fought upon that land.

It was said that thousands of years ago, even before the time of Vallendar, the great and evil king Elishauno reigned. He commanded dragons and hideous beasts the like of which had not been seen in the Realm of Earth since the days of the wars with the Shallee. He conversed with the dead, foretold the future, and it was said he held the moon in the palm of his hand. He was so powerful and terrifying that even the Powers trembled beneath him. Some claimed that he was the son of Nyght, the dark, dragon queen of Belunare. Others claimed he was her lover, and some claimed both.

He ruled over his vast domain, and his darkness spread throughout it, and indeed past it. The people lived in terror, but no man is so powerful that none dare oppose him. The warrior Lemuel and his wife Niahm turned the terror of the people into courage, and together they raised a vast army that dared stand against the evil king.

The two armies met in the forest of Emaryl and fought one of the bloodiest battles that ever had been fought and ever would be. For ten days and ten nights it raged, and, when the sun rose on the eleventh, it fell upon the victorious Elishauno. He took the heads of hundreds of his enemies and set them up on spikes that all might look and tremble, and the other bodies he left unburied upon the ground. And it was said that he laid a curse upon the corpses of his enemies that their bones would never turn to dust but would instead remain until the end of Deithanara as a symbol of his greatness. The trees amongst which the battle had been fought withered and died, but the bones remained, and Lairannare never forgot the name of Elishauno.

For hours Gideone and Stavros rode through the dead and wasted land until, when the night seemed to be at its coldest and most still, they reached the greatest pile of bones they had yet seen. Hundreds upon hundreds of bones-painted white with the light of the moon and black with the shadows-were piled up to form a huge cairn that rose high above the two men.

Stavros could no longer contain his horror.

"This is a wicked place filled with evil magic," he said softly, his words seeming to fall to the ground the moment they left his lips. "Only infidels treat their enemies so."

Gideone's face twisted into an evil smile, and he answered, "I think it is magnificent beyond man's most terrible imaginings. To think, a shrine, which has lasted more than a thousands years, and which will serve forever as a testimony of his power. That is true greatness."

"Great it may be but evil nonetheless."

As Stavros looked up at the imposing tower, he could feel Gideone's gaze upon him. It was proud and contemptuous, and, as he felt it, anger welled up in his heart. He wanted to turn and scream at Gideone that it was he who had murdered Phautina, and it was because of him that Vayan, alone and in despair, wandered throughout the forest. Gideone had once been a prince devoted to nobility and chivalry. Now what did he honor? A pile of bones!

But Stavros did not turn, and he did not cry out in anger against the Prince whom he had sworn to serve. He simply tapped his heels against the sides of his horse and rode forward.

It was midday when they finally reached the end of the Demesne of Elishauno. The cool, fresh wind blew against their faces, and the sun shone brightly down upon the countryside. There was scarcely a tree to be seen in any direction, for before them lay gently rolling hills covered with the pale, yellow grass of the summer before and the fresh, new, green grass of the spring. Behind them rose the tall Plateaus of Scalavori, and beyond those, rising tall and majestic into the clouds, lay the Mountains of Scalavori themselves.

The sparkling river Nymun cut a winding path through the hills until it neared the plateaus where it was joined by the River of the Melted Snow which flowed down from the mountains and across the plateaus until it fell down in an impressive waterfall to the river which waited for it, and together they formed one great river which ran parallel to the cliffs of the plateaus and disappeared into the horizon.

Stavros took a deep breath. 'Twas good to be in the land of the living where it was wide and open and a man could feel the cool wind upon his face. The stench of death and the feel of evil had been far too strong in the place whence they had come.

He cast a look over at Gideone, and his relief suddenly turned to concern as he saw the Prince's face. Gideone's face was ashen, and he looked as if he was about to fall off his horse. Stavros, in alarm, reached out his hand to steady the Prince, but, even as he did so, Gideone slapped it away.

"Leave me alone. I'm not hurt," the Prince said with as much strength as he could muster, but there was pain in his voice.

"Pride is not seemly in times such as this," Stavros answered sternly. "Now, get off your horse and accept the help which I am offering you--the help, I might add, you do not deserve."

"'Twas but a passing lightheaded feeling and is already gone, and, moreover, Abiel no doubt closely presses us. Time is precious and we must waste as little of it as possible."

His face began to regain its color, but his jaw was tightly clenched in pain. He started forward, but, before his horse had taken five steps, he gave a cry of pain and clutched at his chest. He slumped forward and, giving another cry, fell from his horse, even as he tried to grab his saddle to support himself.

Stavros jumped from his horse and was at Gideone's side in a moment. Already was the Prince's face covered with a thin film of sweat. Stavros turned Gideone's face to one side and swore. The black web of lines had made their way above the collar of his tunic.

Stavros rose and ran the few paces back to his horse and began to search through the saddlebags for Wild Rose's healing salve.

Gideone gave a groan of pain and tried to sit up. He still clutched tightly at his wound, and his face was contorted in pain, as he looked up at Stavros.

Stavros finally found what it was he sought, and as he turned back to Gideone he saw the Prince's eyes leave him and focus on something behind him in the Demesne of Elishauno.

"Am I then so close to death that phantoms come to take me to the netherworld?" the Prince asked weakly.

Stavros turned back, and what he saw made his heart skip a beat. Eleven black-cloaked figures ran through the Demesne toward them.

"Those are no phantoms," said he softly.

Gideone sat straight up as he realized who the figures were. Then, with a cry, he scrambled to his feet and clambered back onto his horse, but instead of turning to flee he spun his horse around and started toward the dark prince.

Stavros jumped forward and grabbed hold of Gideone's reins, crying as he did so, "What are you? A fool! Do you forget your promise? Run!"

For one brief moment, Gideone hesitated. He looked down at Stavros then back up at Abiel. With a growl, he wheeled his horse around and set out across the hills toward the plateaus. Stavros ran, jumped on his horse, and went galloping after him.

From where he was within the Demesne of Elishauno, Abiel could see his prey escaping.

"Coward!" he screamed, but Gideone rode on, as though he had not heard. Abiel gave an unintelligible cry of fury and dug his heels deep into his horse's sides. The horse, his nostrils flaring and his body covered with sweat, strained with all his might to catch up with Gideone and Stavros.

The only place it was possible to ford the river was to the right before Nymun was joined by the Fallen Snow, and to this Gideone and Stavros attempted to ride even as Abiel desperately sought to cut them off. The hot noonday sun beat down upon them, as the horses traced a wide, sweeping arch across the grassy hills, and slowly, Abiel's horse began to draw closer to Gideone and Stavros.

Gideone turned his head often to look back at Abiel. There was no fear in his dark eyes. It seemed almost as if he urged Abiel on. Suddenly, Abiel's horse stumbled. Gideone winced then seemed to hold his horse back slightly so that Abiel could regain the ground he had lost.

Finally, Gideone and Stavros drew near to the River Nymun and halted. It was swollen with the melted snow, and it rushed past with tremendous speed and fury.

"Go!" Stavros cried, his voice barely rising over the roar of the raging river.

Gideone hesitated and cast another look back at Abiel. The dark prince was perhaps fifty yards behind them, and the distance was rapidly being closed. Gideone looked at Stavros then plunged into the water. Stavros followed him.

Gideone gave a cry as he was struck by the full force of the bitterly cold water. The water was up to his chest. His horse's nostril flared and his ears were turned back flat against his head as he struggled to keep his head above the swirling white waters.

Abiel reached the bank of the river and, without stopping, plunged in after Gideone.

He cried out with all his might, in a voice that could barely be heard above the roar of the river, "Sirrah! Cur! Woman! Come and fight!"

It was all Stavros could do to keep from being swept off his horse. He could not watch Gideone as well. He had just reached the opposite bank of the river when, above the roaring waters, he heard a furious cry. He turned and saw Gideone and Abiel in the middle of the river. Their hands were locked around the throat of the other, and they bore upon their faces the most primal looks of rage and hatred. The river swirled about them, and their horses were screaming in terror.

Stavros plunged back into the river. As he struggled to reach Gideone, Abiel's magicians raised their bows and took aim at him. He raised his eyes to them, and something in his gaze spoke to them of power unseen. First one then another lowered his bow, for none dared shoot this man who so foolishly and yet so bravely returned to defend his prince.

Gideone whipped his long, soaking-wet, black hair out of his eyes and tried to force Abiel's head beneath the water, but he had not the strength to hold the dark prince there.

Abiel escaped his grasped, and now it was Gideone who was pushed and held beneath the water. He grabbed on to Abiel's hands and tried to pry them from his neck, but he was not strong enough. His head was pounding, and all he could see was the white water raging all around him.

Stavros gave a cry as he saw what Abiel did, but there was nothing he could do to stop it; he was yet too far away.

Gideone's lungs screamed for air, but he could not free himself. In desperation, he pushed himself off of his horse. His horse gave a shriek as he lost his balance and disappeared beneath the water.

Stavros reached out to grab Gideone, but he could only feel the Prince's tunic slip from beneath his hand as Gideone was swept away by the current. Abiel was pulled off his horse by Gideone, and both he and his horse were also swept away.

The last sight that anyone could see was of Abiel desperately struggling to reach the shore, but he also was finally pulled beneath the raging waters.

* * *

Orion gave a strangled cry of pain. His throat was so raw from screaming that his voice sounded more like that of a wild beast than of a human. He was chained with his back to the wall, and as he struggled against his bonds the iron dug deep into his wrists.

Aeneas pulled his knife away from Orion.

"I told you not to cry out!" he snarled as he struck Orion hard across the face.

Darkness of Spirit

"What sort of a man are you? "

Orion gave a low growl. Long strands of auburn hair hung down in front of his face as he looked up, with wild, spectral, hate-filled eyes, at Aeneas. Suddenly, with a cry, he lashed out at the young prince, but his cry of fury turned to one of pain as his chains held him back.

Aeneas gave a laugh. "You really are quite pathetic." Then, more to himself, he said, "Now, if only I could think of some new, inventive ways to torture you. That imbecile of a torturer had nothing decent to suggest, and my mother has made it so difficult, what with her instructions to do you no permanent harm. She fails to understand that I am an artist who needs the freedom to express myself."

He was pacing back and forth as he talked when suddenly his gaze fell upon the pitcher of water and the hard crust of bread that lay upon the floor. He smiled at Orion, picked up a whip, and said, "Why do we not play a game. I know you're thirsty, and I am quite willing to let you drink if only you remain silent and do not cry out."

Orion sank forward and began to shake in anguish, fear, and exhaustion.

Aeneas drew back the whip.

"Mystia!" Orion cried with a hoarse voice as the whip bit into his skin.

Aeneas gave him a dark look as he continued to lash him.

"Mystia!" he sobbed. "Mystia!"

"Would you stop saying that woman's name?" Aeneas thundered suddenly. "What can she do? What sort of a man are you to break into tears and cry out to a woman? Stop it!"

"Mystia," Orion moaned.

With a snarl of fury Aeneas drew back his whip and struck Orion as hard as he could with it, but again Orion cried out to Mystia. Aeneas continued to whip Orion, but still he continued to scream her name. Over and over he cried out to his black-eyed princess, until, finally, Aeneas stuck him with all his might. Orion opened his mouth to scream again but managed to choke back his cry. Again Aeneas struck him, and again Orion kept from howling out her name, but still Aeneas would not stop.

The warrior looked wildly about him, and his voice rose into an unintelligible shriek of pain and rage. His gaze fell upon Aeneas, and his eyes were filled with the fury of a dragon. With all his might he strained against his bonds, even as Aeneas continued to beat him. His muscles bulged, and the sweat and the blood poured down his body. The chains began to creak beneath the strain, but Aeneas did not hear them, as he sent blow after blow down upon his brother.

Aeneas suddenly jumped back and gave a cry of surprise and fear as Orion's chains began to break--first the right arm, then the left, and then the right leg. The blue-eyed warrior started forward and reached out toward Aeneas but was pulled to the ground by the remaining chain.

Aeneas turned and ran to the door, but, even as he did so, Orion gave a great roar and tore his leg free. Before Aeneas could open the door, his brother rushed at him and threw him to the ground. Aeneas gave a cry of terror and tried to struggle to his feet, but he was no match for the dragon warrior.

Orion straddled Aeneas' chest and grasped the young prince by the throat. Aeneas' eyes opened wide in terror as he felt his brother's strong hands slowly tighten around his neck. He could hear footsteps and shouts in the passage outside the cell, and he fought desperately to stay alive until they could rescue him. His chest grew tight as he struggled to breathe, and he looked up in terror into Orion's inhuman eyes.

Orion gave a low growl. Then, without warning, he let go of Aeneas, jumped to his feet, and ran to the door. For a moment, Aeneas lay there gasping for breath. Then he sank into unconsciousness.

Orion ran out of the cell and barreled into the first man who stood in his way. The two went tumbling to the ground, and Orion, with a snarling cry, drew back his fist and sent it slamming into the man's face. The man gave a scream of pain and clutched at his face, even as Orion jumped to his feet and turned to face the other men who stood against him; there were five.

He gave a howl and ran at them, using the chains still hanging from his wrists as weapons. In terror, two ran away the moment he attacked. Orion slammed his fist into the side of one of the men's face, and there was a sickening snap as the man's neck broke.

There were only two men left, and of these only one had a weapon. Orion jumped out of the way as the armed man sent his sword arching through the air toward him. The swordsman gave a cry and ran toward Orion, but, before he reached him, Orion grabbed the weapon-less man and threw him at the swordsman. Both went tumbling to the ground, and Orion fell upon them, breaking both their necks.

He grabbed the sword from where it lay on the cold, black, stone floor and ran from the dungeon.

* * *

Eagle stood at one of the windows of her chambers and looked out upon the garden below. She pressed her hand against the glass and bit her lower lip as she tried not to cry. She could not hold back her tears. Her fingers curled into a fist, and she bowed her head as her shoulders began to shake with sobs. She could still hear Orion's cries of agony echoing in her mind, and she could still see the sorrow and the hopelessness in his blue eyes. She wanted to free him, but she had not the strength to stand alone against her husband or against Provenna.

Suddenly, she heard loud shouting coming from somewhere beyond her doorway. She looked up, and, when the cries did not immediately die away, she ran out of her chambers into the corridor beyond. She ran down the corridor and turned a corner.

There, her eyes opened wide, and she gave a gasp of surprise and fear. The corridor was filled with guards, servants, and slaves--some running, some fighting, but all crying aloud--and in the midst of them stood Orion, eyes wide and his mouth opened in a cry of rage. Blood and sweat were pouring from his body, chains hung from his wrists and his ankles, and in his hands he held a sword.

He was hopelessly outnumbered, but he fought like a raging beast. With snarling cries, he rushed at his attackers, and, though they ran before him, they never stopped fighting.

Eagle looked at Orion and saw a terror and anger in his eyes that cut her to her very heart. As his attackers rushed back in upon him, Eagle wanted to scream out for them to stop. She wanted to run forward and protect him from their blows, but the words would not come, and her legs would not move.

She sank to the ground and looked on in horror as Orion ran at some of his enemies only to be attacked from behind by others. With a furious roar he spun and turned upon those behind him even as those he had previously been attacking fell upon him.

With a cry of rage and frustration he spun around again. There was blood everywhere and dead bodies all over the floor, but his attackers had no end.

"No!" Eagle cried and reached a hand out as Orion suddenly stumbled and went tumbling to the floor. His attackers fell upon him, and, though he fought with all his strength, he had not the power to overcome them.

They held him tightly by the arms and began to drag him away, but still he struggled. Eagle gave a gasp and held her breath as he managed to break from his attackers' hold.

"No!" she whispered as he stumbled and fell once more to the floor. His attackers grabbed him again, and this time one of them struck him hard across the head.

Eagle jumped to her feet.

"No!" she screamed as Orion's body went limp.

She could stand it no longer. She turned to run away, but, as she did so, she almost ran into Tnaka. He took a startled step back when he saw the look in her eyes.

"Are you simply going to let them take him back to the dungeon?" she screamed.

"Eagle, please..." he began, but she was far too hysterical to hear him.

"No man deserves that kind of torture, much less Orion, who's cursed to suffer eternal torture! Free him!"

"Eagle, please..." Tnaka began again as he stepped forward and held out his hands to her, but once again she cut him off.

"Are you going to free him?" she demanded.

Tnaka took a breath and said, "Eagle..." But that was not the word she wanted to hear.

"Monster!" she cried as he slapped him hard across the face. Sobbing, she ran down the corridor, leaving the elven king, holding his hand to his face, to stare in concern after her.

* * *

The Plateaus of Scalavori stood tall and ominous, bathed in the silver moonlight and black shadows of the night. The countryside was utterly still and silent; there was not the stirring of a breeze or a single movement of an animal, but, as the hours of night grew long, there could be seen a man slowly ascending the face of the plateaus. It seemed an impossible feat, yet, hand over hand, foot over foot, slowly but surely, he was accomplishing it.

In the hours past midnight but before the first rays of dawn, he finally reached the top, and, when he did, he stood and lifted up his voice in a cry of fury and maniacal joy. The night rang with his cry.

"Here stand I, Gideone!" he cried. "Where lie you? Dead! Let the waters carry you, but I live!"

His laughter, the laughter of an insane man, spread out across the vast plateaus and the rolling hills below. Abiel's men, in their camp, and Stavros, in his, looked up as the sound of that dreadful laughter filled their ears.

Softly, Stavros spoke, "Abiel lives, but what of Gideone?"

Defeat

Chapter 23
Defeat

Aeneas sat alone in his chambers. He tried to pour himself a goblet of wine, but his hands were trembling so that he dropped the pitcher. It tumbled back to the table, then rolled off onto the floor, spilling wine all over the carpet. He stared down at the mess and cursed himself silently.

He reached up and held a shaking hand to his throat. He could still feel Orion's hands around his neck; they were tightening, cutting off all air. He struggled against them, but they were as strong as iron. Whenever he closed his eyes, he found himself looking up into Orion's terrifying, beast-like gaze.

"Why?" Aeneas' mind screamed. Why had Orion not killed him? There was no way Aeneas could have escaped. He had been completely at Orion's mercy, and Orion could have snapped his neck as easily as a dry twig, but he had not done so. Why had he not?

Aeneas held his hands tightly together and breathed deeply, trying to slow his racing heart.

Why Orion had spared his life he knew not, but of one thing he was certain: he would never set foot in that dungeon again.

* * *

Provenna sat upon her crystal throne and looked down upon Zenas. The old man stood before her with his head bowed. He held tightly to his staff, and his shoulders were bent as though beneath a heavy load.

"Well?" asked Provenna coldly. "My servants tell me that you have learned that which I desire to know."

Zenas took a deep, trembling breath and asked, in a voice that rose scarcely above a whisper, "Do I have t' tell ye?"

"I am the ruler of the whole of Lairannare," Provenna answered, unmoving-her voice filled with pride. "That alone is reason enough to tell me what I wish to know. You, however, must also take into account the fact that, were it not for me, you would have been killed by Kozan."

Zenas raised his head and looked at her. His wrinkled features were twisted into a look of anguish, and his voice rose into a shriek, "Ye never saw! Ye never felt! Ye never gave up th' most innocent, goodly lass in the whole of Deithanara to a fate worse than death! Ye never had her look up at ye with a look o' utter hatred and anger and terror...." He could not finish. His legs would not uphold him, and he sank to the floor, his shoulders shaking with his sobs.

He took another ragged breath and with a trembling voice continued in despair, "Ye never had t' look up into Orion's eyes when he learned tha' she had been taken from him. He looked as though he'd had his soul torn from him. And ye di' no' hear th' scream of rage tha' rose from his lips. And ye di' no' hear him, who had everything taken from him, cry out in fury and curse Joretham.

"Now ye want me t' betray him once again. How can I do tha'?" He clutched his head with his trembling hands and with a groaning voice said, "He bears th' curse of Norenroth. His love has been taken from him. He has nothin' left, except tha' which ye want t' take from him. Please, don't make me tell ye."

Provenna was silent for a long moment, as she looked down in contempt upon him.

Finally, she spoke, and her words were like ice, piercing him through the heart. "You owe me a great debt. I saved your life, and all I ask in return is that you to tell me how to use magic upon my son. If you refuse to pay me, then I will simply have to do what I kept Kozan from doing those many years ago."

For a long moment Zenas, with head bowed and shoulders bent, sat unmoving upon the floor.

Finally, he whispered so softly Provenna could scarcely hear him, "Very well."

He took a deep breath and, with a voice filled with agony, said, "'Tis th' power o' Lyght which flows through Orion an' which must be overcome if ye are t' use magic upon him. So, t' touch Orion with magic ye must find someone with strength a' least equal to that o' Lyght. The Powers, as ye know, are not as strong as the original rulers o' th' separate Realms. So, as far as I know, th' only ones capable o' usin' power upon him are Lyght himself, Nyght--the Queen o' th' Heavens--and..." His voice wavered.

"And...?" Queen Provenna asked.

"And perhaps if ye found a Shallean; their power, like themselves, is outside th' Three Realms. But I don't know tha' for certain.

"Now, please," he begged, "le' me leave. Le' me go home."

"What?" Provenna cried as she rose to her feet. Zenas started at her sudden outburst.

"Do you actually think that pitiful bit of information is worth enough to set you free?" she demanded. "I told you to tell me how I could use magic on Orion, not how Lyght or Nyght or a High Elf could!"

"But I don't know..."

"Then learn, you fool!" Provenna screamed. "Because you're not leaving this city or this palace until you tell me how!"

"But, Yar Majest..."

"Be quiet! How dare you argue with me!"

"No," Zenas moaned pitifully. "No."

Defeat

"Guards!" Provenna cried. Almost instantly the doors to the throne room were flung open and two guards ran in.

"Yes, Your Majesty?" said the first guard as he saluted.

Provenna looked down upon Zenas and spat, "Take this pig back to his chambers, and make certain he cannot leave."

"Yes, Your Majesty," said the guard as he began to walk toward Zenas. Zenas could only sit there, too overcome with anguish to say or do anything.

* * *

Abiel stood and glared at his magicians. The sun shone brightly down from overhead, and the wind rushed freely over the plateaus, but he cared nothing for that.

"Do you mean to tell me that you simply watched him as he struggled across the river, reached the other side, then turned around, and struggled back to the middle of the river so that he could help Gideone, and you shot not one arrow at him?" he demanded. "Idiots! What do you think you were doing?"

The magicians simply hung their heads and answered him not, for how could they make him understand that which they had seen and felt when they had looked into Stavros' eyes.

"Are you not warriors?" Abiel continued. "Do you not know that if Gideone came this far he came this far for a reason? Gideone may now be dead, but that doesn't mean his servant will not continue their mission-whatever it may be! Now go! Find him, and kill him!"

The magicians silently bowed then mounted their horses and rode away across the wide, open plateaus.

* * *

The banquet hall of Kozan's palace was filled with the smells and shouts and revelries of yet another feast. It seemed that all the people of Nolhol did was feast the closer the Day of Chanar drew. Mystia feared the feasts with all her heart, and her fear grew only greater with each passing one. She was terrified of Kozan and of his looks and his touches.

She screamed out silently to Joretham to rescue her or protect her or, at the least, give her the strength to endure, but he seemed so far away. Oh, how she longed for Orion to rush through the door of the banquet hall, kill Kozan, and carry her away from that dreadful place. But he was held captive far away. Perhaps he was dead; she knew not. Tears sprang to her eyes at the thought of him.

"Wench!" She started as a voice broke into her thoughts, and she turned to look upon Rolfaren.

"More wine," he ordered, not looking up at her.

She looked down at him, and, as she did so, anger and contempt filled her.

Kozan may have been someone to be feared, but Rolfaren was nothing more than a powerless worm who thought himself a mighty king because Kozan found some reason to keep him about.

When she did not immediately pour, Rolfaren looked up at her, indignation in his eyes.

"I told you to pour my wine," he said, his voice dark and menacing.

She held the pitcher of wine tightly to her breast, and looked down with flashing, defiant black eyes at him. She could feel Kozan's gaze upon her back.

"Wench!" Rolfaren cried in anger. "Pour my wine!"

With one swift movement, Mystia reached out and tipped over the pitcher, sending the ruby liquid pouring down over Rolfaren's head.

"Why you little...!" Rolfaren snarled in rage as he jumped to his feet and pulled back his hand to strike her, but, before he could, Mystia gave a scream as Kozan grabbed her and pulled her back. She fell onto his lap, and there he held her.

"Leave her alone," Kozan growled. The smell of wine was heavy on his breath.

"How dare she!" Rolfaren cried, his face red with fury. "How can you simply let her...!" He was so angry his words got choked in his mouth. "Who does she think herself to be?" Then he screamed at her, "Who are you?"

Kozan held her tighter, and Mystia sat there with her head bowed, her eyes shut, and her body tensed as she tried not to hear Rolfaren's screams or feel Kozan's touch.

Kozan laughed-a terrifying, despairing sound.

"Who are you?" he repeated Rolfaren's words in Mystia's ear. He laughed again, the bitterness in his voice unmistakable. Suddenly, he pushed her off of him, and she jumped away, but she did not run for fear of rousing his anger. She stood and with wide eyes looked down at him, as she silently cursed herself for her foolish actions.

Kozan spoke, with a low, commanding tone and a dark, bitter look in his eyes.

"Stand there in the middle of the hall," he said as he motioned with his hand.

Mystia turned her eyes to the place he motioned to, then hesitated. She suddenly realized that the hall had grown silent, and as she looked around she saw the eyes of all the guests turned toward her.

"I said stand there!" Kozan cried when she did not move.

She started and quickly ran around the long table at which Kozan feasted. The soft tapping of her feet against the hard floor was the only sound that could be heard. She took her place in the center of the banquet hall and looked at Kozan. Her breasts rose and fell with quick, frightened breaths.

"Rolfaren wishes to know," the dark king said softly, "so tell him-who are you?"

"I..." Mystia began, but faltered as she looked into Kozan's cold brown eyes, so filled with anger and bitterness and contempt.

Òeᵽcaᴛ

"Well?" demanded Kozan. "Who are you?"

"My name is Mystia," she said softly as her gaze dropped to the floor; she had not the strength to look at the dark king further. She suddenly felt sick and weak.

"And what was your country and what was your rank?" Kozan's voice was still soft, but it carried throughout the whole of the hall.

Mystia squeezed her eyes shut and struggled against the nausea taking hold of her.

"I was the princess of Nor," she whispered. There was not another sound in the room so her answer could be heard by all.

"Now what are you?"

She was so weak that her legs would no longer hold her, and she sank slowly to the floor.

"What are you?" Kozan demanded.

"Your captive," she answered before he finished speaking.

"My slave," he corrected.

"Your slave," Mystia said as a tear fell from the corner of her eye.

"And what is to become of you?"

"I am..." she began with a quivering voice, but her words were choked off with a sob, "...to be sac..." The word caught in her throat. The mere thought of being sacrificed upon Balor's bloody altar made her sick beyond measure. How could she bring herself to say the word aloud?

"You are to be sacrificed to Balor," Kozan said, when she did not continue, and at that Mystia burst into tears.

"Get up, woman," Kozan said in disgust, but the Princess had not the strength to do so. She sat there in the middle of the banquet hall in the sight of all and sobbed like a terrified child.

* * *

Orion sat chained to the wall of the dungeon. His whole body was shivering with a coldness that seemed to pierce to his very heart. He did not cry out. He did not weep. He did not beg for Mystia. He strained against his bonds, but the fury which had taken him before did not return. Fighting only made his wounds burn more. He wanted so much to stop and simply lie still, but there was something within him that would not allow freedom to escape him. So he struggled as one who had to escape and yet who knew escape was hopeless.

Suddenly, the door to his cell was thrown open. He closed his eyes and gave a groan of pain as the dark room was suddenly filled with the light of a torch.

"Leave us," he heard his mother order. He heard somebody walk from the cell, and he heard the sound of the door as it boomed shut.

Blinking against the light, he managed to open his eyes and look up at Provenna. He knew not what to feel or what to say or what to do so he simply sat and looked up at her, waiting for her to speak.

For a long moment she stood and looked coldly down upon him.

"Look at you," she suddenly spat, her lip curled up in scorn. "Here you lie beaten, broken, hopeless, doomed to die a slow, painful death unless you turn. Escape is hopeless; you know that now. You will lie chained here in the darkness until death takes you."

"You lie," Orion whispered as he pulled at his chains.

"I do not lie!" Provenna shouted as she struck him across the face. "And you know it!"

"No."

Suddenly, she grew calm. "Orion, listen to me. I do not want you to be an enemy. I want not for you to be treated as you are now treated." She looked deep into his eyes. "I want you to return to me. I want to be your mother, and I want you to be my son. I want you be a great man and be happy and at peace."

Orion gave a bitter laugh.

"Orion," she said as she knelt down before him, "I speak the truth. How could I who am your mother want anything other than your peace and happiness?"

Orion said nothing; he had not the strength to reply. He gave a shudder as the pain that held his body suddenly grew stronger. He felt as though he were being pierced by a hundred daggers.

For a long moment Provenna remained silent as she waited for him to answer, but when she saw that he would not she spoke again. "Orion, have you nothing to say? Will you return to me?"

Orion took a deep breath. Even that motion filled him with pain. He opened his mouth and with a voice so soft and hoarse that Provenna could barely understand him said, "I swore to serve Mystia."

Provenna clenched her fists and fought to keep her voice low and even as she said, "What has Mystia ever brought you?"

Orion hung his head and said nothing. The pain that filled him was unbearable.

"You see," Provenna said coldly, "you cannot answer because she has brought you nothing. Before you met her you were a free man-a prince-but now you are nothing more than her slave. Before you swore yourself to her you could have taken her as your wife, but slaves do not subject their mistresses. Before her, you were free to follow your own path, but now you, the son of Norenroth, must follow the path of Joretham, your greatest enemy."

"But..." he began. He searched for something to contradict her, but he could find nothing so he simply said again, "I swore to serve her."

"Fool!" Provenna cried as she stood up. "Look at what following her has brought you! You could have been the greatest man in the whole of Lairannare! Now what do you have? Pain, suffering, nothing!"

Orion's shoulders shook with a sob of pain and sorrow. "But Mystia..." He had not the strength to finish.

Defeat

"What is Mystia save a ring on my finger?" Provenna snarled as she held up her clenched hand.

"Mystia," Orion whispered as he looked upon the ring as it glowed faintly red, casting its soft light across his mother's hand.

Provenna stood trembling. Her face was white with fury as she searched for some way to turn Orion. Suddenly, a slight smile lit her lips.

"Do you actually think Mystia wants you to serve her?" she hissed as she let her arm drop. Her green eyes were flashing.

Orion looked up at her.

"Mystia is a child of the Shallee, and Mystia is a follower of Joretham." Provenna's voice was soft yet deadly, and it seemed to cut Orion to his heart. "You, however, are the son of Phyre--Norenroth. Do you forget what it is he did? He was the one who first turned against Mystia's God, and he was the one who almost destroyed the whole of Mystia's race. Did you ever tell her that?"

Orion gave a groan and let his head fall forward, but Provenna did not stop speaking.

"Did you ever tell her that Phyre is your father?" she continued. "And did you ever tell her that all of the evil which fills him also fills you? Deny it not, for you know it to be true."

"But..." he began, a look of utter despair upon his face, but he had nothing to say.

"You were born a creature of darkness," Provenna hissed. "Do you actually think a woman who walks in the light will want you to serve her?"

"No," Orion moaned. "No." Over and over he said it as his body shook with sobs.

"All that you suffered because of her was for naught. Mystia will not accept it, and Joretham will not accept it. No one will accept it, fool," Provenna spat. "You have suffered for nothing."

"No."

"Yes! Nothing! Your father is Norenroth! No matter what you do Mystia will not accept it because you're cursed even as Norenroth is cursed and you're evil even as he is evil!"

Orion could say nothing in reply. He could only sit there as his chest heaved with silent sobs of anguish and despair.

"Come," Provenna pleaded softly. "Return to us. We do not hate you or fear you; we love you. We will not thrust upon you ideals too high for you to ever meet; we will accept you exactly as you are. We will not demand that you serve, for you were meant to lead. You were meant to live in peace not in the torment Mystia's way has brought you. Return to us, Orion. Return."

Orion only sat there. His chains dug into his wrists and only added to the pain, which filled him. The slightest movement caused the pain to go shooting through him. He could feel his dried blood covering his back and his arms and his legs and chest. He did not know if there was one place it did not touch. He could smell the stench of the dungeon, and he shivered in the damp coldness. The terror of the dungeon and the hours and the days of torture all melted into one, and he could barely remember a time when he had been free.

He wanted to stand in an open field with the sun shining down upon him and the cool breeze upon his face. He wanted to be able to leave when he willed, and stay if he chose. He wanted to be able to lie down upon the soft grass and sleep. He wanted the pain to end. He wanted to live.

He took a deep breath and opened his mouth to speak.

Provenna looked intently down upon him.

"Yes," Orion whispered, too overcome with pain to care about anything save whether the agony would end, "I turn. Just make it stop.

Chapter 24
Two Battles

Gideone's eyes narrowed as he looked upon the blonde-haired elf.
"Sir elf," said he as he drew his sword, "you defeated me once before, but I've learned much since our last encounter, and this time you shall not be so fortunate."
The elf simply gave a sigh and drew his sword.

Orion lay in the same soft, warm bed in the same dim, silent room to which he had been taken when he had first been brought to Leilaora. His wounds were already greatly healed; the unbearable pain had subsided to a throbbing ache. He rested his hands upon his stomach and stared darkly up at the ceiling.

He had slept through the whole of the night, but, though he was still exhausted, he could sleep no more. He was filled with so many different emotions--anger, hatred, terror, bitterness, despair. They welled up within him and seemed to fill his soul until he knew not what to think or what to feel.

He could stand lying there no longer. With one swift movement, he threw the sheets off of him and sat up. He gave a groan at the sudden pain that accompanied the motion, but he forced himself to stand.

For a moment, he stood there and held himself tightly as he looked around the room. He could scarcely believe that this was not a dream and that he was indeed free. Slowly, he reached out and touched the bed. He could feel it, warm from his body and firm beneath his hand, and he could feel the carpet, soft beneath his bare feet.

Slowly, he walked across the room. His steps filled him with pain, but he forced himself to continue until he reached the door and entered into the adjoining chambers, where he stopped as his gaze fell upon a slave-girl who stood with her back to him at the table in the middle of the room. Either she had heard him approach or she had felt his gaze upon her, for she suddenly turned.

"Your Highness!" she exclaimed as she caught sight of him. Orion recognized her as Eluned, the slave-girl who had previously waited upon him.

He gave a groan of pain and held his hand to his head as he said, "Stop screaming."

Eluned was at his side in a moment.

"Forgive me, Your Highness," she said softly as she took him by the arm and began to lead him to the table. "I was told that you would heal yourself, but I did not expect you to rise so early. You were dreadfully wounded when you were brought here."

Orion said nothing; his body hurt too much for him to think of anything to say. He breathed a sigh of relief as Eluned helped him sit down and the pain once more became a dull ache. He rested his arms upon the table and let his body slump forward.

"Forgive me, Your Highness, that I have not your breakfast ready," said Eluned, "but, as I said, I expected you not to rise so early. Do you wish me to bring you something?"

"Yes," he answered softly.

Eluned curtsied and left Orion's chambers, and it was not many minutes before she returned bearing in her hands a silver platter upon which was a bowl of soup, a piece of bread, a goblet of water, and a spoon. She curtsied once again and set the platter on the table before him.

"'Tis not a large meal, Your Highness, I know, but it's not wise to suddenly eat a great deal when you have been given so little since you were brought here."

Orion said nothing but his features darkened at her words. Anger welled up within him as a thousand different images of what he had suffered since he had been brought to Leilaora rushed unbidden into his mind. Hatred filled him at the memory of what Aeneas had done to him, and Orion did not fight it.

"Prince Orion?" Eluned asked hesitantly.

"What?" he snapped as he looked up at her, his blue eyes flashing.

"Are you well?"

Orion gave a sigh and turned his eyes back to the table, and the platter resting upon it. "Yes."

Eluned was not entirely convinced, and she said, "Your Highness, when you've eaten, the healer will come and tend once more to your wounds. Perhaps you should then rest some more, for tonight you are to be presented to the people of Leilaora."

Orion looked at her in confusion, and a nameless terror rose up within him. "What?"

She gave a slightly amused smile at the look that crossed his face.

"Your Highness," said she as she sat down across from him, "for ten long years have you been gone from Jocthreal. Many have forgotten you, and many-- like myself--never knew you. 'Tis only proper then that you should be presented to us, your people, and crowned and proclaimed our prince."

"I crowned and proclaimed your prince?" whispered Orion. The mere thought filled him with fear, and his heart began to pound.

Eluned looked up at him with her large green eyes. "'Tis merely a formality, for ever have you been our prince. Queen Provenna simply wishes that fact declared to the whole of the Realm of Earth."

She paused for a moment then, when she saw the look upon his face, asked, "Does the thought of being crowned the Prince of Lairannare frighten you?"

Two Battles

"I know not," Orion answered softly as he picked up the spoon. He began to slowly stir his soup, and, as he did so, he realized his hand was shaking. He concentrated in an attempt to still it, but try as he might he could not keep it from trembling. He bit his lip in frustration as the spoon fell from his hand.

Eluned reached out and took his hand in hers, and as she looked up at him she seemed to gaze into his very soul. "There is no reason to fear. Crowns have graced far less noble brows than yours."

Orion took a deep breath, and his racing heart began to slow.

"I..." he began, but he knew not what to say.

"Lord," Eluned said softly as she held his hand to her cheek, "you have lived through so much and suffered far more than any man should suffer. You have given so much and received so little. You were born with the spirit of a king within you, and yet you were forced to be a servant. Now fate gives you a chance to grasp that which hitherto was held beyond your reach. Take that which it offers--that which you have earned--and look not with fear upon it. Become a prince, become a king, and become the heir to the throne of the Realm of Earth."

Orion was silent for a long moment as he looked down into her large green eyes.

"You speak the truth," he whispered, even as he tried to convince himself of his words. "I should not fear." He seemed no longer to look at her but through her, and his thoughts seemed far away as he continued, "In Keiliornare, I am a powerful Magic--more powerful than the arch-mages and perhaps as strong even as the Powers themselves. That strength never frightened me, and 'tis not such a great leap from there to the prince of Lairannare. No, I should not fear." But he could not convince himself it was so.

"Lord--Your Majesty--" said Eluned who still held his hand in hers, "we are your people--your humble servants--we do not want you to fear us; we want you to lead us."

Orion looked at her, and now it was he who held her hand in his, and he who gazed into her eyes and looked deep into her soul.

"My people," he said; it was both a statement and a question.

"Yes, lord."

"I am your prince and your king, and you are my servants. No longer must I hold the lives of others above my own. No longer must I live in fear that today will be my last within the Three Realms and the land of the living. No longer must I live for others, but you will live for me. And I shall not simply stand by and gaze upon the joy and peace of others, but I shall have joy, and I will be free of fear, and I shall have peace."

Eluned looked up with her soft green eyes into his spectral blue ones and held his hand tightly. "Yes, Lord."

He looked down at her. His breathing grew more steady, and he became more calm. But still there was a part within him filled with terror, and, try as he might, he could not free himself from it.

* * *

Mystia stood atop the high walls surrounding Kozan's palace and looked down upon the dark city, which lay spread out in all directions. Overhead, the sky was gray, and the wind blew strongly across the city. She held herself tightly and shivered as her dress and her veil danced around her.

Kozan, for his part, stood unmoving, with his arms crossed, his mouth firmly shut, and a dark look upon his face, as he gazed down upon his city. His face was as unmoving as stone, and what went on behind his cold, brown eyes Mystia could not tell.

The Princess turned her gaze away from the city below and looked up to the north. Somewhere, beyond the horizon--how near or how far she knew not--was Orion.

She brushed away a long strand of black hair which had escaped from beneath her veil and now blew in her face.

How he fared and whether he even lived she knew not, but something within her would not allow her to believe that he was dead. She knew he still lived, and with all her might she hoped and prayed that he would come and rescue her.

She started as she suddenly realized that Kozan was looking at her. She took a step back and held herself even tighter as she stared back at him.

He gave a sneer and said, "Tell me, why do you look with such sorrow and longing to the north?"

"I..." began Mystia, but she could think of nothing to say.

"I can tell you." Then, before she could say anything in reply, he said, "You turn your eyes to the north because to the north lies Jocthreal and Leilaora, and 'tis Leilaora which holds your love."

"And why think you that?" asked Mystia softly.

Kozan laughed--a cold mirthless sound--and answered, "One does not have three wives and a dozen concubines without learning something of women."

Mystia's eyes flashed with anger. There was still some pride within her.

"If it's through wives and concubines that you've learned of women then you are at a disadvantage," she said softly, "for I am neither."

With no warning, Kozan struck her across the face.

"Wench!" he cried. "You're less! How dare you, who are nothing more than a slave, contradict me! What do you take me for--a fool?"

Mystia's hand flew to her cheek in pain, but her face was filled with anger. She turned from him as he continued, "I know why you look there. Orion lies there, and you love him--bastard child that he is!"

Mystia looked back startled.

Kozan gave another laugh and said, "Yes, I said 'bastard', for that is what he is."

Two Battles

"And what of it?" Mystia demanded as she held her head up and looked defiantly at him. "Should I hate him or love him any less because of a sin his parents committed?"

"You can hate him because of sins he's committed, and I can tell you a great many of those," Kozan said with a sneer.

"I refuse to listen!" Mystia cried as she held her hands over her ears and turned to run away, but, before she could, Kozan reached out and grabbed her by the arm.

"A slave refuses nothing her master desires," Kozan growled as he pulled her to him. Mystia's face twisted with fury, and tears of frustration welled up in her eyes as she tried to wrench herself from his grasp, but the dark king held her closer to him and hissed in her ear, "Think you that you're the only woman who has ever loved him? Do you forget so quickly why it was that Lareina tried to rescue you? 'Twas because of Orion, whom she loved. He stole her from me, just as he stole Rhianna--my wife, my love, the only woman I ever truly cared for--and just as he stole who knows how many other women!"

"I do not believe you!" Mystia cried as she struggled against him. "Orion is a noble man!"

"Orion is a lying, thieving, ravishing murderer. No doubt a bastard father of bastard children. He cares nothing for you."

"No!" Mystia cried.

Kozan gave a wicked laugh. "His mother is Provenna."

"No!"

"And his father is Phyre--Norenroth--the King of Lairannare."

"No!" Mystia screamed as she still struggled against him. "You lie! Pig! You lie!"

Suddenly Kozan let go of her, and she went tumbling to the floor where she burst into tears.

"Little fool," spat Kozan as he looked in disgust upon her, "I don't lie!"

"You do," Mystia sobbed. "Orion could never be Norenroth's son."

"He is," Kozan said with a sneer. "Oh, he is. And he bears the curse of Phyre-- to never find Joretham's forgiveness and to enter in to Elmorran upon his death. He may act noble and pure now, but he has sinned far more than many a man, and, unlike you and-- Kozan's eyes sparkled "--unlike even me, Orion's evil soul is not one Joretham will forgive, so Orion will always be evil--that is the deepest most defining part of his nature." The dark king laughed at Mystia's tears and, spurred on by her sorrow, continued. "No matter how noble and honorable he acts--were he to appear to be the most pure man in the whole of Deithanara--his core is still evil, and one day I promise you, if he is not dead already, the mask he wears will crack and reveal that darkness within."

Mystia sat sobbing upon the ground. Kozan was lying, he had to be. She opened her mouth, but before she could speak, he said coldly, "Tell me not I am a liar, for I speak the truth as your religion declares it; you know I do."

She could say nothing in reply but simply continued to weep.

"Poor, little slave," said Kozan as he dragged her to her feet, "Not only is your love a monster, but you shall soon be sacrificed to Balor."

"No," Mystia sobbed.

"Yes," said Kozan softly as he held her close, "yes, you will be sacrificed; not even your pretty face will keep Balor from receiving his due." Then, more to himself than to Mystia, he said again, "Yes, you will be sacrificed."

* * *

The sun shone brightly down upon the open plains and plateaus and the mountains, and the wind rushed across the countryside. Abiel sat upon his horse and galloped across the plateaus. In the distance, he could hear the roar of the River of the Melted Snow as it rushed down from the mountains across the plateaus and to the plains below.

The cool wind blew against his face and body and sent his hair and cloak dancing madly to its song. Gideone was dead, and now all that remained was to kill Gideone's servant. Then would there be no one left to complete Gideone's mission--whatever it was. Victory was close--oh so close--and nothing would keep him from it.

* * *

Tnaka sat alone at a table in his dark and silent chambers. He buried his face in his hands as despair filled him. A goblet filled with wine that he had yet to touch, lay before him on the table.

With a cry he suddenly struck the goblet and sent it flying from the table, where it went clattering to the floor. All of his hopes, all of his dreams were being torn from him even as he was on the verge of realizing them. Orion had turned, and with him went all hope for peace.

Tnaka pounded his fists against the table. He wanted to scream; he wanted to cry; he wanted to run to Eagle for comfort.

He clenched his fists and forced his trembling body to be still. He could not scream; he could not cry. He was a king--a Power; it was his duty to rule. He could not show weakness. Nor could he run to Eagle, for he knew he would find no comfort from her.

He tried to calm himself. The time for Orion to be presented to the people of Leilaora drew near, and Provenna expected him to be part of the procession.

Anger and despair welled up once more within him, and again he pounded his fist against the table. How could he be calm? Orion had turned.

* * *

Orion stood with his head bowed, his hands resting upon the table and his back to the door of his chambers as he tried to calm himself. Soon it would be time for him to be presented to the people of Leilaora. He was dressed in the finest clothing to be found in the city. His trousers and his leather boots were both of the darkest black, and his tunic was a dark, royal blue. Beneath his tunic he wore a white shirt with long, loose sleeves, which covered his arms and the mass of scars upon them. His long, auburn hair was brushed and flowed freely down over his shoulders.

He tried to still his trembling hands, but the more he tried the more he trembled. The terror that welled up within him was almost unbearable.

Suddenly, he felt a hand upon his shoulder, and, turning, he found himself looking down upon Eluned. She looked up at him with her large beautiful eyes.

"Prince Orion," she said softly, "it is time."

He could think of nothing to say, and he could not make himself move so he simply stood there and continued to look down at her.

Eluned took his trembling hands in hers and said with a soft smile, "Come, Your Highness. Leilaora awaits."

He allowed her to lead him out of his chambers and through the long corridors of Provenna's palace; he could do nothing else. His head was pounding, and he felt as though he were in a dream. All was hushed and the slaves and servants looked in silent awe upon him as he walked past them.

Eluned led him through the corridors and out into the wide, open courtyard of the palace, where there stood a huge assembly of soldiers all dressed in their finest armor, which shone brightly in the light of the sun. As Orion appeared, they let out a shout of joy. He stopped in surprise and fear.

Provenna, who sat upon a brown palfrey, smiled down at him and motioned with her hand toward the large, gray charger standing beside her.

Orion could see Tnaka looking at him. The elven king's jaw was firmly set, and, though he tried to keep all expression from his face, it was impossible not to see the look of anger and despair that swirled behind his gray eyes.

Eagle stood next to Tnaka and looked silently upon her husband. What she thought and felt Orion could not tell, for she kept her face utterly expressionless.

Eluned squeezed his hand, and he looked down at her. She gave him a soft reassuring smile. He swallowed then walked to the charger and mounted.

Trumpets were sounded and the gates to the palace were slowly opened, revealing the huge crowd gathered to gaze upon their prince. Slowly, with Orion and Provenna leading, Tnaka and Eagle directly behind, the royal guards surrounding them, and the long lines of soldiers following them, the procession started forward. Drums began to roll, and trumpets began to sound, and, as Orion and Provenna stepped out of the courtyard and into the city street, the whole of the vast crowd burst into roaring cheers.

* * *

Abiel galloped across the plateaus. He was close; every fiber of his body seemed to scream out that Gideone's servant was near. The wind rushed all around him and seemed to lend him strength and fury.

Suddenly, he gave a cry, for far off at the edge of the plateau, he saw a dark figure. He turned his horse and charged off toward the plateau's edge, but he had not ridden for many paces before he gave another cry--this of disappointment. The figure he saw was nothing more than a single tree which had somehow managed to grow atop the plateaus.

He was just about to turn, when he suddenly reined in his horse and, for a long moment, simply stood and stared at the tree. At first he thought his eyes merely played tricks upon him, but the longer he looked the more certain he became that he saw another, smaller, figure standing beside the tree.

An evil grin lit the dark prince's face, and he dug his heals into his horse's side. He had found Gideone's servant.

* * *

Up they rode through the magnificent city of Leilaora, ever making their way to the great cathedral of Joretham. The bright sun shone out across the golden city, making it shine gloriously in the light.

The cheers of the people rose up and seemed to fill the whole of the city. The ground trembled beneath them, and their cries pressed in upon Orion until he felt he could stand it no longer. The setting sun shone brightly in his eyes, and he raised his hand in front of his face, but it was just as much to ward off the people as it was to shield his eyes.

Beside him, Provenna sat straight and tall as she rode her horse and smiled at the people crowding the sides of the street. Behind the Queen, Eagle rode and looked regally and yet without emotion down upon the crowd. Behind him, Orion could feel Tnaka's gaze--dark and anguished--upon his back. All around him he could hear the cries of the people and see the looks upon their faces as they reached out their hands and tried to touch him, and there was nowhere for him to run.

* * *

Fury and evil joy filled Abiel as he galloped across the plateaus toward the tree and he who stood by it. The prince was terrified that the man would run away and disappear before he could reach him. He dug his heals into his horse's sides, and his horse fairly flew across the ground. Yet Abiel had no need to worry, for his adversary stood unmoving a short distance from the tree and seemed to wait for his arrival.

As Abiel drew nearer, the figure of the man became more clear, and it seemed to Abiel that it was not the austere, unmoving form of Gideone's servant but that of another man altogether. The man was still a distance away and the setting sun cast his body into sharp shadows, which further hid his features, but Abiel's heart leapt within him at the sight.

He urged his horse on at an even faster pace, and he opened his mouth in a cry of fury. As he finally neared the man, he found himself looking down, not upon Gideone's servant, but upon the Prince himself.

Gideone stood there and looked up at Abiel. His face was deathly pale, and how he had managed to escape the river and climb to the top of the plateau Abiel could only imagine. But Gideone stood there before him, tall and proud, eyes burning with hatred.

As Abiel neared him, Gideone threw out his arms, and there suddenly erupted around him a circle of fire. The bright orange and yellow flames danced wildly around the Prince as he drew his sword. His eyes never left Abiel.

"Enter into the Ring of Fire, Abiel," he said, a look of absolute hatred upon his face, "and let us dual."

Abiel said nothing, but his face lit up with a sneer as he drew his sword and jumped from his horse. He stepped into the ring, and, as he and Gideone stood there facing each other, the fire surrounding them seemed to burn even brighter.

With a cry, Abiel fell upon Gideone.

* * *

The cathedral of Joretham rose tall and majestic before Orion--its towering spires shining golden in the light of the sun. Its massive bells chimed out in celebration, and as the procession drew near to it, the cheering of the crowed seemed to swell to a thundering climax.

Orion bowed his head and tried to make his hands stop trembling. Terror filled every fiber of his being, and as he turned and looked out over the crowed he could see in their faces only adulation. It seemed they could not even see his fear.

He looked at his mother and saw that she was smiling at him, but it seemed a cold, empty expression. She saw his fear, and she reached out and took his hand. Anger filled Orion at her touch, and, pulling his hand away, he turned his face to the crowd. He raised his hand to them and tried to smile. Out of the corner of his eye he could see Tnaka still looking darkly upon him.

Suddenly he found himself at the foot of the Cathedral of Joretham. He looked up in surprise upon it; he had not expected to reach it so quickly. Provenna, Tnaka, and Eagle all began to dismount, and after a moment Orion also did so. He did not want to; everything within him screamed out for him to turn and run away, but he was like one caught in a dream and could not control his actions.

Provenna, Orion, Tnaka, and Eagle, followed by four of the chief guards, began to walk up the long flight of steps, which led to the door of the cathedral. At the very top, there stood the Arch-Deacon, and, as they reached him, he bowed low before them and said, "Welcome, my Queen. Welcome, my Prince. May the blessings of Joretham fall upon you both."

Orion said nothing and did nothing, but Provenna smiled softly and nodded her head slightly.

The Arch-Deacon straightened, and his flowing, crimson robes swirled around him as he turned and without further words led them into the cathedral. Up, up he led them through the twisting stairways of the ancient structure, and with each passing step terror took a firmer hold upon Orion's heart. He tried to fight it, but the thundering sound of the people's cheers seemed to take away all his strength.

It seemed they rose for an eternity until, finally, they emerged on a balcony high above the cheering crowd. Orion could only looked down upon them and swallow.

* * *

Gideone gave a cry of fury, threw Abiel from him, and scrambled to his feet. He whipped his hair out of his face and raised his sword as he turned to face Abiel, but even as he did so Abiel fell once more upon him. The fire raged all about them.

Gideone gave another cry and stumbled back, and, as Abiel sent another blow crashing down upon him, the Prince tripped and fell to the ground. He rolled out of the way but did not fully escape the blow, and he gave a cry of pain as the steel of Abiel's blade cut into his arm.

He rolled to his feet, and held his arm as he looked at Abiel. His legs were weak, and his head was pounding. He struggled against the nausea which took him. His legs would no longer hold him, and, with a groan, he sank to his knees. His sword fell from his hand as he clutched at his chest in pain. He was covered with sweat, but his body was shivering with cold.

Abiel looked upon Gideone's pitiful form, and his scarred and broken features twisted into an evil sneer as he threw back his head and laughed. "Pitiful fool!" he cried. "How could you ever possibly think that you could defeat me?"

"Pig!" Gideone hissed as he struggled against the pain, "Even my sister could defeat you!"

Abiel suddenly stopped laughing, but the sneering smile did not leave his face. His green eyes gleamed as he looked down at Gideone and said, "But your sister is not here, now is she?" His leer deepened. "By now, no doubt she's far away in Nolhol enjoying the tender embraces of my father."

"Dog!" Gideone cried as he reached for his sword, but Abiel kicked it out of the way. It spun across the grass and came to rest at the edge of the circle with its blade thrust into the fire.

Abiel knelt down before Gideone.

"I can just imagine the things he's doing to her now," he hissed. "How does it feel to know that I will be the older brother of your sister's children?" With a howl Gideone lunged at Abiel, but Abiel struck him to the ground with ease, and the Prince simply lay there, clutching at his chest and fighting for breath as he looked up in fury at Abiel.

Abiel rose to his feet. The fire raged behind him as he raised his sword above his head to deal Gideone his deathblow. But suddenly he stopped and gave another laugh. "How amusing; you lost your sister to one Power and your love to the other, and the child of Tnaka hurt you almost as much as the son of Kozan is about to."

At his words, rage filled Gideone. He gave an unintelligible cry of fury as he pushed himself off the ground and sent himself crashing into Abiel. Abiel's sword flew from his hands as the two men fell to the ground.

Gideone's face was twisted into a look of absolute hatred as he drew back his fist and, with a cry, sent it slamming into Abiel's face. The dark prince cried out in pain and tried to reach for his sword, but Gideone punched him again then grabbed him by the throat. The fire in his eyes burned almost as hot as the fire that raged around him as he began to squeeze his hands around Abiel's neck.

* * *

The cheering crowd and the ringing bells and the drums and trumpets had all fallen silent, and all eyes were turned up to the balcony so high above the street. In his hands the Arch-Deacon held a crown of pure gold inlaid with sparkling sapphires. He looked down upon the people gathered and opened his mouth to speak. His voice rose into the sky and spread out to the farthest reaches of the vast crowd.

"People of Leilaora!" he cried. "We come here today to honor the greatest prince in the whole of Lairannare!"

Orion's heart was pounding, and his hands were trembling. The Arch-Deacon's voice seemed so far off, and yet they seemed to force themselves into Orion's mind and wrap around his heart.

"For ten long years has he been gone from us," continued the Arch-Deacon, "but now, by the blessing of Joretham, the son of Provenna has returned!" A huge cheer burst from the crowd, and Orion winced as if in pain. Provenna still smiled upon him, and Tnaka's face was still filled with despair.

"Kneel," said the Arch-Deacon to Orion, "and receive the symbol of your office."

Something within Orion screamed out for him to stay standing, but he felt as though another, whom he had no strength to fight, was controlling his body. Slowly, he sank to his knees.

The Arch-Deacon's voice rose above the cries of the people. "He has returned to be Provenna's son! He has returned to never leave us again! He has returned to be the Prince of the Realm of Earth!" With that, the Arch-Deacon thrust the crown above his head so that all could see. The gold shone brightly and the sapphires sparkled gloriously in the light of the setting sun as the whole of the vast crowd erupted into a thundering cry.

The Arch-Deacon turned to Orion. Slowly, he began to lower the crown. Orion's heart pounded in terror, and his whole body trembled. His mind screamed out against what was happening, but he continued to kneel, with his eyes closed, as he waited for the inevitable. The cheering of the crowd pounded against his ears, and terror clutched his heart as the crown was brought ever closer to his head.

He wanted to scream out for help or for comfort, but there was no one to cry to. In the middle of that vast city, with every eye upon him, he was completely alone. His body shuddered and he gave a groan as the crown was placed upon his head.

Slowly, he opened his eyes and looked around him. Provenna still smiled down upon him. Tnaka could not even stand to look at him any longer, and Eagle still bore no expression on her face.

He took a deep breath and forced himself to rise. His crown sparkled in the light of the sun, as he looked out over the people of Leilaora. Their cheers threatened to shake the very foundation of the city, and they were all looking up in joy and wonder upon him, the Prince of the Realm of Earth.

* * *

Gideone's hands squeezed in around Abiel's neck, choking off all air. The fire raged about them as Abiel struggled to escape the Prince's grasp, but fury lent Gideone strength. His body was trembling, and sweat was pouring down him, but he held the dark prince in a vice-like grip. Abiel grabbed hold of the Prince's wrists and struggled with all his might to escape. Finally, with a strangled cry he managed to throw Gideone from him. Gideone stumbled back even as Abiel, struggling for breath, rose to his knees.

Gideone tried to rise, but his legs would not hold him, and he sank back to the ground. He could feel the heat of the fire, so hot upon his back. He gave a cry of pain and clutched at his head as everything began to swim before his eyes.

Abiel grabbed his sword, which lay upon the ground near him, and rose to his feet. His face twisted into a sneer as he looked down upon Gideone. Gideone could only look weakly back up at him.

* * *

Orion looked down upon all the thousands of people cheering for him. They were crying out for him to lead them--for him to be their prince and one day their king. They would love him. They would serve him. They would die for him. Who in his past life would have done the same? No one, for it had been he who had loved, and he who had served, and he who had risked his life for others. And what had it brought him? Nothing! Nothing, save pain and torture and despair.

A frown darkened his face as he forced back the terror filling him. It fought to rise, but he held it down with all his might; what had he to fear? He reached out his hand across the people so far below, and his lips turned up in a small smile when he saw that his hand no longer trembled.

* * *

Abiel raised his sword. Even as he did so, Gideone looked down and found his own sword lying beside him--its blade still thrust into the raging fire. Abiel sent his sword arching down through the air toward Gideone, but as he did so, the Prince rolled out of the way and grabbed the sword from the ground. Almost immediately, he gave a cry of pain and dropped it as the heated metal burned his skin, but he had not time to stop and clutch his seared hand. Abiel ran, and swung his sword at him. Gideone jumped out of the way and fell to the ground. He whipped his hair out of his eyes and scrambled out of the way as Abiel sent his sword slicing down once more toward him. The fire burned with fury, as the Prince tried desperately to rise to his feet and escape Abiel at the same time, but the dark prince sent blow after blow relentlessly down upon him, and Gideone's feet kept slipping on the grass.

Finally, Gideone managed to rise to his feet. He stood wide-eyes with his back but a few inches from the fire and Abiel standing in front of him.

Abiel gave an evil smile, drew back his sword, and, with all his might, sent it slicing through the air toward Gideone. Gideone gave a cry and tried to jump out of the way, but his feet slipped, and he gave a scream of pain as he fell into the fire.

* * *

Tnaka looked in horror upon Orion. He could see the look upon the blue-eyed warrior's face. He could see the way he stretched his hand out over the people. He could hear the thundering cries of the people of Leilaora, and he could stand it no longer. He turned and fled into the cathedral.

* * *

Gideone scrambled out of the fire and onto the grass outside the circle. He began to roll on the ground in a desperate attempt to smother the flames, which had caught his clothing. He could hear Abiel's evil laugh as the dark prince approached him. Terror filled him. He continued to try to stop the fire burning him, but he knew he had no chance of stopping it before Abiel reached him.

Suddenly, he could hear the sound of a horse galloping toward him. Even as Abiel gave a scream of fury, the Prince looked up in surprise and found himself staring up at Stavros who was barreling toward them.

Abiel ran toward Gideone in a desperate attempt to kill him before Stavros could stop him, but Gideone managed to roll out of the way. Before Abiel could strike him again, Stavros was upon him. Abiel tried to jump out of the way, but he did not entirely escape, and his body was struck by the horse's shoulder, and he went tumbling to the ground. He gave a groan and struggled to his feet, clutching at his arm as he did so.

Gideone managed to completely smother the flames and began also to struggle to his feet, but he had not the strength. He gave a groan and clutched at his chest. His long, black hair fell down in front of his eyes, and, though he tried, he could not shake it out of the way.

Abiel started toward him, but, before he had taken two steps, Stavros had jumped from his horse and was running toward him. Abiel turned toward his attacker and gave a snarl as their swords clashed.

* * *

Tnaka ran with all his might, trying to escape what was going on around him. He ran down the twisting staircases, but the cries of the people followed him. He ran through the cathedral, but he could hear the bells ringing in glory for Orion. The despair within him grew even more, as he ran into the very sanctuary of the cathedral.

"Lord!" he heard someone cry.

He spun and found himself looking down at Eagle who had followed him.

"Look at this!" he cried in despair, with arms outspread and face turned to the heavens. The stone walls of the immense building echoed with his cry.

The sanctuary was lit by the light of hundreds of shimmering candles. The arched ceiling rose high above them, and the faint evening light shone through hundreds of beautiful stained-glass windows.

He sank to his knees, but his arms were still outspread and his face still turn to the heavens.

"This is a cathedral of Joretham!" he cried. "Is there no peace even here?"

He gave a sharp cry and covered his ears with his hands as the cries of the people filled the sanctuary.

"Fools!" he shrieked. "Fools!"

* * *

Two Battles

Stavros gave a growl as his sword clashed with Abiel's.
"Run, Gideone!" he cried. "Run!"
Gideone struggled to his feet, but the fury, which had leant him strength, had left him. He took one tottering step toward Stavros' horse, then, with a groan, fell to the ground, where he could only raise his head and look weakly upon the battle being fought before him.

* * *

"Fools!" Tnaka shrieked again as he jumped to his feet. "To blaspheme the cathedral of Joretham with praise to that unholy creature!"
"Lord..." began Eagle as she reached out to him, but Tnaka was not finished.
"How can You let them do this?" he demanded as he turned his face once more to the heavens.
"This is Your house!" he screamed as he threw his hands up above his head.
"How can You let them praise him?" He spun and motioned to where Orion stood.
He turned and cried once more to Joretham, "Fool!"
"Lord!" Eagle cried as she reached out to try to calm him.
"Kill him! Stop this!"
"Lord!"
"How can You do this to me?"
"Lord!"
Tnaka sank to his knees.
"Eagle," he whispered with a voice trembling with despair. She knelt before him and reached out to him and he to her. He held her close and began to weep, and, though he saw it not, tears fell from her eyes also. They knelt there crying as the cheers of the people filled the cathedral.

* * *

Stavros gave a howl and sent his sword slicing down toward Abiel; Abiel was barely able to block the blow. Stavros did not wait but sent another blow crashing down toward him, and another, and another. The dark prince's eyes were wide with fear as he struggled to defend himself against Stavros.
He gave a cry of pain as Stavros' sword went slicing across his side. Before he could fully recover, Stavros drew back his sword and lunged toward him. Abiel gave a cry and managed to jump out of the way. He turned and ran back toward the Ring of Fire. He leapt into the middle of the flaming circle and tried to catch his breath, but Stavros ran in after him. The dark prince gave a cry of terror and jumped back and held up his sword. His whole body was trembling.
Stavros' face darkened and his eyes flashed with fury as he lowered his sword toward Abiel and prepared to battle once again.

The fire raged all around them, and the clang of their swords echoed across the plateaus.

* * *

"When will it end?" groaned Tnaka as he rested his cheek against Eagle's soft, golden hair. "When will it end?"
"I know not," she whispered with a trembling voice.

* * *

Abiel reeled back beneath Stavros' blow. His eyes were wide, and his broken face was twisted in terror. He turned to flee, but the wall of fire raged before him. Thrice had he leapt through it, but memories of his body being consumed by fire suddenly rushed unbidden into his mind, and he dared not run through it again.

He turned back to face Stavros, and held his sword up to defend himself. Stavros' blow sent him stumbling back a step. He could feel the fire's heat upon his back. Stavros swung at him again, but fear leant the dark prince strength. With a mighty cry, he blocked Stavros' blow then lunged at him. He drove Stavros back to the center of the ring, but Stavros quickly recovered and lashed back at Abiel with even greater fury. He struck the dark prince with a terrible blow, and Abiel, with a cry, fell backward to the earth and could only look up in terror at Stavros.

Stavros, breathing heavily, held his sword to Abiel's throat and prepared to finish him, but suddenly he hesitated. He raised his sword slightly as he looked at the fire, which burned all around him. How could he, a follower of Joretham, kill a man in the Ring of Fire?

Abiel looked up at Stavros, and saw his hesitation. In the brief moment when Stavros' gaze was upon the fire surrounding him and not Abiel, the dark prince rolled out from beneath his sword. Stavros started and stepped back, as Abiel rolled up onto his knees. Stavros lunged at Abiel. With a furious cry, Abiel thrust his sword into Stavros' stomach.

Stavros did not cry out. He made no sound at all. He simply looked down in astonishment at the sword sticking out of his belly. His sword fell from his hand, and, with a slight groan, he fell forward onto his face--the bloody blade of Abiel's sword sticking up out of his back.

With a laughing cry, Abiel picked up the blade of the fallen warrior. He rose to his feet and raised the sword above his head, and with another cry he sent it slicing down through the air and into the neck of Stavros.

* * *

Two Battles

The sun had almost completely set upon the golden city of Leilaora, but the vast crowd still cheered for Prince Orion. He looked silently down upon them then suddenly turned away. Provenna stood behind him and still smiled upon him. His lips turned up in a soft smile, as empty as his mother's, and he cast one last look back at the people of Leilaora--his people--before he walked from the balcony.

* * *

Gideone struggled to his knees and looked in horror upon Stavros' dead body. "You killed him." Gideone could barely make his voice rise above a whisper such was his shock.

Abiel's evil laugh, rose into the night sky.

"You killed him," Gideone said again, scarcely believing it was true. Abiel's maniacal laughter filled the Prince's ears.

"You killed him!" Gideone screamed as he struggled to rise.

Abiel, standing in the middle of the Ring of Fire, thrust his sword over his head and continued to laugh like a madman. Suddenly, his laugh became a shriek. The sword fell from his hand, and he clutched at his chest. He looked at Gideone and laughed one more time before he fell to the ground--dead. Stavros' last sword-thrust had found its mark.

Gideone gave a cry of anger and stumbled forward. He knew not what he wanted to do, but his anger at Stavros' murder would not allow him to sit idly by. He wanted to kill Abiel again. He wanted to destroy the dark prince's lifeless body. He wanted to do anything to somehow appease the anger--the fury--and the despair, which filled him.

Suddenly, he gave a cry of surprise and scrambled back. The fire, which still raged around Stavros and Abiel, suddenly leapt up fairly fifty feet into the air. It burned so thick that it completely hid the bodies of the two men. Gideone turned his head away and covered his eyes with his arm and tried to somehow shield his body from the sudden, almost overpowering heat. From in the midst of the swirling flames, there rose the most terrible sound the Prince had ever heard; it was like a thousand different voices all screaming out in hissing cries of fear, hatred, and fury. It lasted for scarcely more than ten seconds, but it seemed like an eternity.

The fire suddenly flared up even higher and hotter. The voices rose up in screams of absolute terror. Then, almost as quickly, they were simply cut off, and the fire grew low then disappeared completely, leaving a charred circle on the grass with two figures in its center--the body of Stavros, lying just as it had been before the fire had flared up, and the bones of Abiel, completely black and without a trace of skin upon them.

Gideone looked upon them, and now it was he who laughed. His voice echoed across the plateaus and filled the night sky, until, suddenly, as quickly as he had begun, he stopped. He gave a groan and fell unconscious to the ground, overcome by fatigue and his wounds.

He lay there for almost an hour when, though he could not move and though he was still trapped more in the realm of dreams than in reality, he could hear the sound of a horse approaching. Presently, it stopped, and he could hear someone jump to the ground. The person walked to him and knelt beside him. He could feel himself being rolled over. He managed to open his eyes, and he found himself looking up into the brown eyes and homely face of Phautina.

"What?" he said weakly before his eyes closed and his head fell back, but just before he sank once more into unconsciousness he noticed the dark, gruesome scar around her neck.

Phautina walked over to Stavros horse, which stood idly by nibbling at some grass, and she quickly took off the saddle. She then returned to Gideone and with ease picked him up and slung him across the horse's back.

She mounted her own horse, and, after casting a sad look back upon the bodies of Stavros and Abiel, turned and, leading Stavros' horse after her, set off across the plateaus toward the Mountains of Scalavori.

* * *

Night had fallen many hours before. Aeneas, upon his horse, stood atop a hill and looked back through the darkness upon Leilaora. Across the distance separating him from it, he could not hear the sounds of celebration, but he knew they existed. Prince Orion had returned, and it was he--Aeneas--who had helped bring that about, and, now that he had done so, he dared not stay, for Orion would surely kill him.

The overpowering anger and hatred, which had gripped Aeneas at every thought of Orion, had melted away to be replaced with a deep shame at his actions toward his older brother. As he looked back at Leilaora, it welled up within him so strong that his body began to tremble and he felt he would throw up. It was by his own hand that he was forced to leave his mother, his home, and his kingdom. He had known very little of any of them, but he had so longed to learn more. Now he would never have the chance.

"Aeneas," he murmured, "you fool,"

He gave a sad smile then turned his horse and disappeared into the night.

* * *

Kozan and Rolfaren sat alone in the grand banquet hall. Not even Mystia was there to wait upon them, for the closer the Day of Chanar drew the more Kozan hated her presence. In anger he had sent her away.

Rolfaren stared at the great oaken doors through which Mystia, wide-eyed and terrified, had been escorted by the guards.

Two Battles

"'Tis rather a pity she must be sacrificed," Rolfaren said, breaking the silence, "for High Elves are by nature a beautiful race, and, from what little I've seen, she seems to be a beauty among beauties."

"Then what little you've seen has vastly misled you," Kozan growled darkly. "She is ugly to the point of excess."

The dark king held his goblet in hand, but he did not drink. He seemed to drift off to a place far away as he continued softly and almost longingly, "But she has eyes--so dark and beautiful--that seem to gaze into your very soul. They take you and bind you and never release you."

He tried to smile, but his face only twisted into a look of even greater despair.

"You are a captive forever," he whispered, "never to be free again."

Chapter 25
The Mountains of Scalavori

Gideone gave a groan. He found himself once more upon the Plateaus of Scalavori. He lay helpless upon the ground and watched as Stavros and Abiel battled. The Ring of Fire raged all around them, and the smoke filled Gideone's nostrils. He could see the looks of fury upon the two men's faces, and he could hear their cries as they battled and the clang of their swords as they clashed together.

He struggled to rise and run forward to help Stavros, but all strength had left him, and he could only lie upon the grass and in horror watch the battle being played out before him. He watched as Stavros threw Abiel to the ground, and, even as a cry of terror rose from the dark prince's mouth, a cry of joy escaped Gideone's lips, but, as quickly as the shout came, it died away as, in horror, Gideone saw Stavros put his sword to Abiel's throat then suddenly stop.

"Kill him!" The Prince's cry seemed to echo across the plateaus, yet Stavros seemed not to hear it. He still stood unmoving above Abiel.

"Kill him!" Gideone shouted again, but, even as he did so, Abiel rolled out from beneath Stavros' sword and with a furious cry lunged at him.

"No!" Gideone screamed as he struggled to run forward. He could see the look of complete astonishment upon Stavros' face as he looked down upon the sword protruding from his stomach.

"No!" the Prince howled again as Stavros fell to the ground--dead.

Abiel turned his face toward Gideone. The dark prince's mouth was opened wide, and his evil laughter echoed across the plateaus. Gideone gave an unintelligible cry of fury, and, as he looked upon Abiel, the dark prince suddenly disappeared, and in his place Orion stood, with his head thrown back, laughing.

"Dog!" Gideone screamed as he stretched out his hand in a futile effort to grasp the warrior and drag him to the earth. "Murdering cur!"

* * *

"Bloody coward!" the Prince murmured.

Phautina reached out to keep the unconscious prince from falling from his horse. She looked down upon him and shook her head sadly, then turned her eyes back to what lay before her.

She had already reached the Mountains of Scalavori and was now making her way along one of the few, small paths which wound through them. Her eyes moved back and forth as she looked intently around her. Tall pine trees grew along the edge of the trail, and above them there could be seen the snow-tipped mountains rising into the sky. The sound of melted snow rushing down the rocky slopes filled her ears, but there was nothing else to be heard save the sound of the horses' hooves striking the earth.

Phautina continued on, still searching the trees, for more than an hour. Nothing seemed to change. The only sights to see were still the trees and mountains, and the only sounds to be heard were the rushing water, the crunch of the ground beneath the horses' hooves, and an occasional groan from Gideone.

Suddenly, the bard thought she heard a quiet sound in the trees to the right of the trail. She continued forward, peering even harder into the foliage.

Suddenly, with a loud cry, three elves, brandishing swords, leapt out from the cover of the trees onto the path in front of her, and three more ran out behind. Both horses stopped in fear, and Phautina reached out to keep Gideone from slipping to the ground.

Even as she did so, the six elves charged and fell upon her. She did not struggle--she did not even cry out--as she and Gideone were pulled from their horse and thrown to the ground.

She tried to rise to her knees, but before she could do so one of the elves placed his foot upon her back and forced her to remain lying on her stomach.

She gave a slight gasp of pain as somebody grabbed her by the hair and pulled her head back. She found herself looking at the tip of a sword, and as her gaze traveled up it she found an elf, with long, wild hair and a sneer upon his lips, holding the blade to her throat.

"You've dared trespass upon the land of the sky elves," he growled. "What have you to say for yourself?"

Phautina struggled to take a breath, then answered, "I have come to speak to King Tmalion."

The elf gave a scornful laugh. "We throw intruders in the dungeon; we are not in the habit of giving them an audience with our king.

Phautina gave a groan as the pressure on her back began to increase. "I need to speak to the King. The man with me is Prince Gideone of Nor."

The boot on her back was suddenly removed.

"What?" the elf holding the sword cried, even as Phautina was pulled to her feet.

They looked down upon Gideone, where he lay upon the ground, and for a moment all was silent.

"I have never seen Prince Gideone," said the chief elf finally, "so I know not whether you speak the truth or lies." He hesitated then turned to her. "I will take you to King Tmalion, but if I find you have lied to me, you'll wish I had killed you now."

He turned.

"Take them," he ordered.

Phautina's hands were quickly tied behind her back. The elves, carrying Gideone, led her off the path and into the pine trees beyond. It was not many minutes before they rounded some large rocks and found themselves in an open area in which six large eagles rested.

Phautina was placed upon one of the eagles, and an elf took his seat behind her. Gideone was placed upon another, and the five remaining elves also mounted.

In a moment, the eagles spread their wings and flew up into the sky. The wind rushed over Phautina and sent her hair to dancing. Her brown eyes opened wide, and her face lit up with wonder.

The eagles soared through the mountains. Below, she could see the tall pine trees rising up toward her. The rivers of cold, fresh water rushed down from the snow-covered peaks and flowed into the valleys of the mountains or gathered together and became the River of the Melted Snow. Higher and higher they flew, until only the highest mountains still rose above them.

Phautina drew in a deep breath as she looked down. Below her, nestled in a large cleft between two peaks, lay the capitol city of Scalavori. It was a beautiful city, carved from the most pale gray stones so that it seemed to shine almost white in the light of the sun.

The eagles wheeled in the sky then dove down toward the city. They flew low over it--so low that Phautina could see the faces of the elves below turned up toward them. The wind blew hard against her face as they sped across the city.

The lead eagle gave a cry, and they wheeled once more then dove down and landed in the courtyard of what appeared to be a garrison. The elves dismounted, and Phautina was pulled down off the eagle.

"Take her and have her guarded until we learn what to do with her," ordered the chief elf.

He looked at Gideone and hesitated.

"Have a healer tend to him," he finally said.

He raised his eyes to Phautina. "Soon we shall see what will become of you." With that he turned and walked away.

* * *

Phautina was led by two guards into the throne room of King Tmalion. The guards bowed low then, with a nod from their king, turned and left.

The throne room was dim and silent. King Tmalion had sent everyone away, and now he sat alone upon his simple throne of stone. He was not old by elven standards, but he seemed worn and bent with many sorrows and troubles. His hair was blonde almost to the point of being white, and it was pulled back behind his head in a long ponytail. A plain, golden crown rested upon his brow, and his head seemed to bow beneath its weight.

He looked down upon Phautina. His face bore no expression, but his blue eyes seemed filled with despair.

"So you are the one who has brought Gideone to me," said he softly.

"I am, sir," Phautina answered.

"And 'tis you who wish me to heal him of his wound."

"What I wish," said Phautina, "is for you to do as Joretham would have you."

Tmalion gave an empty laugh. "What makes you think that I care for the will of Joretham? Do the Powers care for it? Did I not give my daughter in marriage to one of the Powers? Why then should I care for His will? By all right, I ought to kill Gideone without a thought."

"You speak as one who serves the Powers," Phautina said, "but I know you do not do so."

"And why think you that?" demanded Tmalion.

"I think that because it's true," Phautina said as she took a step toward him. Her brown eyes were flashing. "I know that, though you pretend you serve the Powers, you work ever toward their destruction. I know how you have sent your spies and your messengers across the whole of Lairannare and have gained allies and have silently undermined the authority of the Powers. I know how, after the years of patient labor, you have finally gathered together an army and even now are planning your attack against them."

As she had been speaking, Tmalion had slowly risen to his feet, and now he simply looked down in astonishment upon her.

"How do you know that?" he finally asked.

"The servants of Joretham are privy to many things," Phautina replied. The look of amazement left Tmalion's face only to be replaced with scorn. He gave a snort of derision. "So you are a servant of Joretham."

"Are you not also?" she asked.

Tmalion sat down once more and did not answer her.

"King Tmalion," said Phautina after a moment, "I have come here to ask you to take and protect Gideone and, if it is in your power, to heal him. Will you do so?"

"No," Tmalion answered simply and softly. "He is of no use to me and has done nothing to deserve my aid."

"And where is it written that one should give succor only to those who deserve it or can give payment in return?"

"I have spoken," the king growled softly, "and I will not be contradicted."

"And who are you to say that?" demanded Phautina. "You may be a king, but you are far from being a god! You're wrong, and I will contradict you!"

"Be quiet!" he thundered as he jumped to his feet. "What has Gideone ever done for me that I should help him? Has he followed after honor and duty? Has he stood strong against the Powers? Has he stood beside me as evil crushed in and tried to destroy me? No! He wandered the Realm like a common scoundrel rather than take up the duties of a prince. He took his proper place only because of my daughter, but when Tnaka came to take her away what did Gideone do? Nothing! He let that cur of a elf take my daughter, and he said not one word in protest!"

"And is that what you should do?" cried Phautina. "Repay insult for insult, evil for evil? He may have done wrong, but that doesn't mean you should also!"

Tmalion tried to answer, but his words came out as an unintelligible cry.

With a snarl, he sat down once more upon his throne. His eyes were closed, his hands clenched, and his whole body tensed as he struggled against the fury that filled him. The only sound that filled the room was his labored breathing.

"Tmalion," said Phautina quietly, "you have been wronged, but that does not mean that you should wrong others, for in so doing you become that which you hate."

Tmalion said nothing.

"You know what is good," Phautina continued. "You know what is right. All that remains is for you to follow it; save Gideone."

King Tmalion was silent for a long moment. His head was bowed, and he seemed not even to breath.

"Very well," he finally whispered. He opened his mouth to continue, but he could not bring himself to say more.

"Thank you," said Phautina. She hesitated for a moment then said, "Will you please release me now? I have other duties which I must attend to, and I cannot stay longer in Scalavori."

Tmalion took a breath then called for the guards. Almost immediately, the two guards who had first brought Phautina into the throne room walked once more in. They bowed before their king then stood at attention.

Tmalion motioned toward Phautina, "See to it that she is given whatever provisions she requires to make whatever journey she wishes to make."

"Yes, Your Majesty," the two guards answered.

"Thank you for your generosity," Phautina said, "but I require nothing." She curtsied. "Joretham be with you." And with that she turned to leave.

The two guards bowed and also turned and began to walk away.

Tmalion remained silent as he sat and watched Phautina make her exit. She was so simple and so homely, and yet there was nobility, and Tmalion could almost say a beauty, that shone far brighter within her than it did in any noble personage. How he longed to see that within another, but he had a feeling he never would so he simply gazed upon her until the doors of the throne room closed and she was lost to sight.

* * *

The room in which Gideone had been placed was quiet and almost entirely dark. He lay upon a soft, warm bed, but peace was far from him.   His body was covered with sweat, and the sheets of the bed were tangled and twisted around him because of his constant thrashing. His face was twisted in pain, and he murmured curses against Orion.

The healers had tried to cure him, but all their efforts had proved useless, and now it was left to Tmalion to tend to him.

Gideone's tunic had been taken off, and Tmalion looked down upon the web of black lines that spread out across the Prince's chest. It traveled up his neck and did not even stop at his face but continued on until the lines grew faint then disappeared completely less than an inch beneath his left eye.

Around Gideone's neck hung a golden chain. At the end of this, was a small golden amulet in the shape of a feather with a diamond embedded in it. Tmalion reached out and touched it and for a long moment simply held it and ran his thumb across it. He felt certain he had seen that amulet--or one like it--before. He struggled to recall where he had seen it, but, just when he seemed about to grasp the answer, it faded away.

He shook himself from his reverie and placed his hand upon Gideone's brow. His eyebrows shot up in surprise at how hot the Prince's skin was.

He turned his gaze from Gideone and down onto his own right hand. Upon his finger there rested a single ring. It was very plain--a soft, blue stone embedded in a band of silver. There were no markings of any kind, nor was there anything about it to set it apart as special or of particular value, but it was the symbol of power far greater than most could ever hope to possess; it was the ring of an arch-mage, and, indeed, it was the ring of he who was the most powerful of all the arch-mages.

Tmalion took a deep breath and held his hand out over Gideone.

The magic eating away at the Prince was strong, and had long been in place, and with each passing day it had been given more of a chance to take hold of him.

"Joretham, give me strength," the elven king murmured before he prepared to begin, for he knew it would take all of his power to defeat the magic within the Prince.

He closed his eyes. As he concentrated, the stone in his ring began to glow, casting a soft blue light across his hand and Gideone's face. He could feel the power of the evil magic as it spread out through the Prince's body, and he could feel the last, faint remnants of the healing balm still struggling against it. The magic was even more powerful than the king had first thought, and, taking another deep breath, he concentrated even harder.

Gideone gave a groan and clutched at his chest.

The king began to murmur words in a strange tongue. Beads of sweat appeared on his brow and began to slowly trickle down his face. His ring was glowing brightly, and magic was coursing through him, but still the evil power within Gideone held strong.

The Prince gave a feeble cry as Tmalion's chant grew louder. The king struggled with all his strength to destroy the darkness holding him, and yet his power seemed not strong enough.

His face was twisted into a grimace as he concentrated with all his might. His voice continued to rise, and, as he chanted, he was joined by Gideone, whose cries of pain grew ever louder as the moments went by.

Suddenly, Tmalion found himself shrieking out the chant. His hand no longer hovered above Gideone's chest but was pressed directly against it. The unconscious prince writhed in pain as the evil magic and the magic of Tmalion fought within him. He clawed at his chest and tried to pry Tmalion's hand from it.

The king could feel himself being overcome, but he squeezed his eyes even tighter shut and redoubled his efforts. The sound of Gideone's screams filled his ears.

Suddenly, pain far greater than anything he had ever before felt shot through the king's body, and he gave a great howl. He was thrown back across the room, and as he struck the wall and fell to the floor he gave another cry.

Then there was silence. For a moment, he simply lay there and struggled to breath.

He could hear cries in the corridor outside. The door to the chamber was thrown open, and he could hear several people rush in. They ran over to him and quickly rolled him over onto his back. He winced and gave a slight groan at their touch and for a moment silently looked up at the servants who were crowding around him.

"Your Majesty!" they were crying. "Are you all right?"

"Yes, I am all right," he finally said with a sigh as he struggled to sit up. "Help me rise."

Two of the servants took him by the arms and helped him stand, and with their help he began to walk out of the room. As he went, he cast one last look down upon Prince Gideone. It had to have been a Power who had cast that spell, thought Tmalion, for it was a stronger spell than he could ever hope to overcome.

* * *

The night had fallen and the moon and the stars shown down upon the town of Haflashon and the surrounding forest. Vayan sat alone upon a fallen log within the trees and stared sadly into the fire he had made. He had not returned to the site of Phautina's murder. He felt guilty because he knew he ought to bury her, but he could not bring himself to look again upon her dead body. However, though he could not force himself to return, he could still see her in his mind; he had relived her death a thousand times.

The anger for Gideone, which surged through him at every thought of

Phautina's murder, was unlike anything he had ever felt before. He could not count how many times--and the many different ways--he had thought of killing the Prince. He gave a groan and covered his face with his hands. The anguish that filled him was almost unbearable. For a moment, he fought the tears that welled up in his eyes, but he was the only one there; whom had he to hide his sorrow from? His body began to tremble as he stopped fighting his anguish and let the tears flow.

Suddenly, behind him, he heard someone call his name. It sounded like the voice of a woman. His heart began to pound as slowly he stood and began to turn around.

When he finished turning, he found himself looking at a woman. She stood in the shadows, and he could not see her face, but, as she stepped out into the moonlight, his heart skipped a beat, for it was Phautina who stood before him. For a moment, he could only stand there and stare in shock at her.

She gave a grin and said, "Why, Vayan, you look as though you've seen a ghost."

"But, but," he stuttered as he began to step back.

Phautina suddenly got a startled look on her face and opened her mouth to say something, but just as she did Vayan took one step back too many and stepped into the fire he had made. He gave a cry and jumped forward again and, spinning, clutched at his foot as he glanced wildly around.

"Vayan!" Phautina cried as she ran to him. "Are you all right? Here, sit down." She sat him down before he even had time to protest.

"Are you all right?" she asked again.

He could simply look at her shock.

"I thought ye were dead!" he finally cried.

She smiled. "I was."

"But...but..." he began as he continued to stare at her. "How?"

She was silent for a moment then said, "Because death does not hold those such as I."

"What?" said Vayan as he stood up and looked down at her.

Phautina was silent for another moment then said simply, "I am a Torelli."

Vayan jumped backward. "What?"

"I am one of the Unfallen."

"But...!" Vayan stopped and for a long moment simply stared at her. At first he could not bring himself to believe her, but as he looked into her eyes he knew that she had to be telling the truth. For a moment he knew not what to say, but finally he managed to ask, "Why were ye travelin' with us, and why dinna ye say who ye were?"

"I was traveling with you to help you along your journey, to protect you from Abiel, and see to it that Gideone reached the Mountains of Scalavori. I told you once before that we of the Torelli, while in the Three Realms, rarely appear in our true forms. It sets us apart and oftentimes interferes with our ability to help the people we were sent to aid."

Vayan looked silently at her for a moment as he tried to comprehend what she had just said. He thought back upon all of the days that he and she had ridden together along with his father and Prince Gideone. He could remember every cruel and insulting word Gideone had spoken and every look of hatred. He could remember when the Prince had tried to kill him, and most vividly he could remember when Gideone had struck down Phautina.

His voice was trembling as he said, "Why? Why dinna ye just heal him? Ye're a Torelli; ye must have th' power. It would have saved us all so much trouble. Why?"

"Do you not remember, shortly after we met, I told you my magic comes and goes. I am a servant of Joretham and can do only what He desires me to do. Gideone never asked Joretham to heal him; therefore, Joretham never told me to heal him."

"But..." began Vayan as he sank to the ground.

"Vayan," Phautina gently cut him off, "Joretham could have told me to heal Gideone, but what does a man's physical life matter when spiritually he's dead? During the thirty years Gideone has lived upon Lairannare, he has been given everything and has had it all taken from him. He was born the prince of a rich country and the son of a noble king, and even at such a young age he had great privilege. But did he follow after Joretham? No, he rejected the privilege, the honor, and the responsibility given to him, and instead chose to become a common man--a wandering rogue. It was a dangerous, lonely life, and yet he survived his battles, found those willing to open their homes to him, and gained wealth, great success, and at least a little renown, but did he thank Joretham? No, he did not.

"He met the woman of his dreams. He returned to his place as a prince and was met with great acclaim, for surely he who had stepped down from his position on high and taken up the cloak of a common man would make a great and noble king. All eyes were upon him as he and his love were betrothed. For a moment, he was one of the greatest men in Lairannare, but did he bless and glorify Joretham? No, he was lifted up in pride, saying it was by his hand alone that he had gained such great glory. He never gave a thought to the One who had formed him and the One who had protected him and the One who had ever been looking down and watching him.

"Eagle was taken from him and given to another, but now did Gideone, in his despair, turn to He whom he had for so long rejected? Did he even ask for help or comfort? No, he did not.

"His kingdom was destroyed and his family killed or taken captive. One of the men whom he trusted most turned and left him in his hour of need--or so Gideone believes. Now did he turn? No. Indeed, he grew angry with Joretham--He whom Gideone had never believed in, thanked, praised, or honored during times of good but now cursed in times of evil.

"Now all that is left is Gideone's life, and perhaps, when faced with the reality of his situation, he will finally realize his error and repent.

"That is why I could not save his life."

"But surely if ye had shown yerself to him and told him what ye told me, he would have turned."

"A man who desires to live in darkness will find many ways to explain away the light."

Vayan was silent for a long moment and stared at the ground. Slowly he raised his eyes to her. "Why're ye tellin' me all this?"

"Because I want you to understand Gideone and forgive him. Go to Scalavori and, while you need not swear yourself to his service as your father did, at least tell him that you forgive him."

"How can I do tha'?" Vayan demanded as he rose to his feet. The anger and despair within him seemed to rise up and fill him, "I don't think I could as much as look at him again." He turned his back to her and for a long moment was silent as he struggled to put his emotions into words.

"Ye may be alive now," he said slowly, with a trembling voice, "but tha' doesn't change the fact that he killed ye...and he was proud of it too." He turned back to her. "He killed you. He tried once t' kill me an' m' father. He gave only insults when we tried to help him, and he ever cursed Orion who you yerself as much as said did nothin' wrong.

"I know it was just because o' th' poison that he acted like tha', but I still can't help myself from feelin' this way."

"Vayan," Phautina began, "it was not because of the magic of the arrow that Prince Gideone acted the way he did."

"What?"

"Vayan, you know as well as I that magic cannot destroy a person's character and set up another in its place. No matter how strong the person casting the spell, magic cannot turn hate to love, or love to hate. It can weaken and break down defenses, and it can bring out that which was hidden, but it cannot fundamentally alter that which was there."

"And after telling me this, ye think I ough' t' go off an' tell him I forgive him?" Vayan cried.

He turned around, hiding his face from her, as he struggled to speak. "This is impious of me, I know...and I hope ye won't be too angry, but...I--" he struggled to find a proper word--"...dislike him even more now than I did a moment ago."

"Vayan," Phautina said gently as she placed a hand upon his arm, "don't hate him; pity him. He seemed such a proud, noble, joyful man, loved by many, and yet beneath that wonderful exterior what is he? Angry, suspicious, hateful, and very empty. Men such as he desperately need someone to stand at their side. Why should that someone not be you? And who knows but that you will be the one to bring him to Joretham."

"He has my father," said Vayan bitterly. "Why does he need me?"

"Vayan," Phautina began. Vayan needed only that word to know what it was she would say. He turned to her, and his eyes were filled with fear and despair.

"Your father is dead," Phautina said softly.

Vayan's face twisted into a look of anguish. His legs grew weak beneath him, and he gave groan as he sank to the ground. His whole body trembled as he covered his face with his hands and wept.

Phautina knelt beside him and put her arms around him. She said not a word but simply held him comfortingly and let him cry.

After a long while his tears stopped falling, and he simply sat there, doing nothing.

"I know it hurts." There was sorrow in Phautina's voice. "It hurts more than anything you have ever felt before, and there's nothing that can stop it, but perhaps it will help by knowing that your father is in a far better place. He sits in Lothiel with Joretham, and one day you too will be there with him, and all the time from here till then will seem as nothing."

Vayan took a deep breath but remained silent.

"Thank ye," he finally said with quiet trembling voice. "I think tha' does help a little."

For a long moment he was silent then he spoke again. "How did my father die?'

"He died protecting Gideone from Abiel," Phautina answered.

Vayan was silent for another long moment then he slowly sat up and looked at Phautina. He took another deep, trembling breath then said, "I'll think abou' what ye said." He hesitated. "If my father can--" he struggled to say the words-- "die defending Gideone, then I ought t' find it somewhere in my heart t' simply forgive him."

Phautina gave a soft smile.

"Remember," she said softly, "and take comfort--you need not forgive Gideone under your own strength; Joretham will be at your side through that and through everything that you will face."

Vayan simply nodded his head, for he could find nothing to say.

For a long moment, they both sat there in silence until, finally, Phautina stirred. She took a breath then softly said, "I know that after all you have been put through this is perhaps one of the last things you wish to hear, but still I must tell you that it is time for me to leave."

Vayan looked at her. He said nothing--he seemed not to have the strength to speak--but his face betrayed his surprise and disappointment.

Phautina rose to her feet.

"Farewell, Vayan," she said simply.

"Will I ever see ye again?" Vayan managed to ask.

"One day--if not here in the Realm of Earth than in Lothiel," she answered, "but, until that day, I bid you farewell. Joretham be with you."

She gave a small smile and inclined her head to him. He said nothing and simply looked up at her. She looked down at him, and Vayan's mouth opened as a warm, golden light suddenly surrounded her. For one moment she stood there shining as gloriously as the sun, then she disappeared from sight, leaving Vayan once more alone in the dark and silent forest.

Chapter 26
Return

King Tmalion sat beside Gideone's bed and looked silently down upon the Prince. It was by the light of but a few flickering candles that Tmalion watched Gideone as the Prince tossed and turned upon his bed and cried out in pain.

When the king had first learned that he had not the power to save Gideone, he had felt something akin to relief, for he had not wanted to heal him, but now as he looked down upon the Prince, whose face was twisted in pain and whose body was burning with fever and who was writhing and crying out in agony at the darkness which filled him, the king could feel only pity, for no man deserved to suffer as Gideone suffered.

Gideone gave another cry, one so loud and furious it made Tmalion start. It seemed to the king that, while at times Gideone was crying out in pain, at others he was crying out in fury against someone, yet who it was Tmalion could not tell.

* * *

Gideone gave a snarling cry and lunged forward. The clang of steel filled the air. All around him fire raged, and his body seemed to burn with the heat of it. He gave another cry and sent his sword arching once more through the air toward his opponent. At times he fought Orion, and, at others, he found himself battling Abiel or Tnaka, but, no matter whom he fought, his enemy always looked out at him with cold, spectral blue eyes.

Their swords clashed, and Gideone found himself gazing on the twisted face of Abiel.

"Murderer!" he snarled as he lunged toward the dark prince. They slammed into each other and were thrown back to the ground. Gideone gave a cry of pain and struggled to rise.

Abiel knelt upon the ground only a short distance from Gideone. His back was turned, and the Prince could not see his face, but he could hear the low growl of anger that escaped his enemy as slowly he began to rise.

Suddenly, the dark prince's growl turned into a snarling cry of rage as he spun to face Gideone. As Gideone looked up, he found himself gazing not upon he face of Abiel but upon the fury-filled face of Tnaka.

Gideone looked desperately around for his sword, but he had dropped it when

Return

he fell, and it was nowhere to be found. Tnaka drew his sword. His lip curled up in a cold, cruel sneer as he began to slowly walk forward. Gideone scrambled back in a desperate attempt to escape, but Tnaka continued to walk toward him.

Suddenly, Gideone found himself unable to move further. He could only look up in anger and terror as Tnaka came ever closer. The Elven king's sneer grew until suddenly he was no longer smiling but laughing wickedly.

As Gideone watched, he suddenly found himself looking up not at Tnaka but at Orion. Fury filled the Prince. Strength returned to him, and he suddenly found himself able to move again. In his hand he found his sword, and with a cry he jumped to his feet and ran forward.

"Coward!" he cried as he sent his sword slicing toward the warrior. Orion managed to block the blow and tried to strike back, but, before he could, Gideone struck him again. Orion gave a howl as he reeled beneath the force of the blow.

"Lying coward!" Gideone screamed as he struck him again. "'Tis all your fault!" He rained blow after blow down upon Orion. "If you had stayed the Sorcerer would never have defeated us! My father would never have died! My sister would not be dishonored! Abiel would never have chased us! And, Stavros would not be dead!" He sent one final blow crashing down upon Orion. The blue-eyed warrior gave a cry as his sword went flying from his hands.

Gideone's face twisted in a look of hatred as he raised his sword to deal Orion one final blow. Orion looked up at him, his cold blue eyes filled with hatred and fear.

The Prince opened his mouth in a terrifying cry of triumph and sent his sword slicing down through the air toward Orion. He could see the look of terror frozen upon Orion's face, and he could hear the thumping of Orion's heart. He could hear his own cry as it seemed to stretch on for minute upon minute, and he could see Orion's last desperate attempt to escape.

Suddenly, he heard a rich deep voice, speaking from where he knew not. It seemed to fill the air all around and echo in his mind. It said, "Why hate thee my son? And why accuse thee him? Thou knowest not why he did what he did."

Suddenly, Orion, the raging fire surrounding him, and Gideone disappeared. Instead, the Prince found himself standing in an enormous cavern. It was one of the most amazing places in the whole of Deithanara--formed entirely of the purest crystal, which glowed and pulsated with an inner fire. But Gideone did not see and did not care. He gave a cry of anger and spun around, as he desperately searched for Orion.

"Where is he?" he cried.

Behind him he heard a low, rumbling growl of anger. He spun, and suddenly found himself unable to move. He could only stand and look up in terrified amazement at the huge dragon towering over him.

"My son, whom thou wishest to kill," growled the dragon, baring his crystal teeth, "is far from here in the city of Leilaora where he lieth broken and beaten and utterly defeated." The dragon gave another low growl and turned away.

Gideone stumbled back.

"Who are you?" he finally managed to cry.

"Fool!" snarled the dragon as he turned back to Gideone. "Art thou so blind as to not know me? I who was the first of Joretham's creations? I who have existed since the beginning of time." His voice was rising. "I who was one of the three greatest creatures in the whole of Deithanara. I who was the ruler of the Realm of Magic! I who have seen every war ever waged! I who stood upon the Plains of Adalrick and saw Vallendar and Balor battle! And thou knowest me not?" His thundering voice echoed off the walls of the cavern.

Gideone hesitated for a moment, then, realizing that he had to say something, said, "From your words, Your Majesty, I must assume that you are Lyght, King of the Realm of Magic."

"My name is Lyght," answered the dragon softly, "but I am King of Keiliornare no longer."

Gideone remained silent.

"I gave up my crown and the power that went with it, so that my son might live," continued the dragon, "and now what wishest thou to do? Kill him! And take even him from me so that I have nothing left."

Gideone crossed his arms and his brow furrowed in anger.

"Orion ran like a coward and left me in my moment of trouble," he said softly, but with a deadly tone. "Had he stayed and fought the Dark Sorcerer, Nor would not have been defeated, my father would not have been murdered, I would not have been wounded or pursued by Abiel, and Stavros would not be dead."

Lyght gave a growl.

"Fool!" he hissed. "Orion was ever thy friend, since the moment he stepped foot in Nor, and how dost thou repay him? Not only dost thou accuse him of cowardice, but thou blamest him for the death of thy father, the defeat of thy country, the death of thy friend, and all of the problems thou hast faced!"

His voice was rising. "Was it Orion who did any of those things? No! 'Twas the Dark Sorcerer who killed thy father, and defeated thy country. 'Twas some nameless Delovachian who struck thee with his arrow. And 'twas Abiel who chased thee and Abiel who killed thy friend; not Orion!

"Yet dost thou blame those have wronged thee? No!" The cavern shook with his cry. "Thou hatest a poor, innocent man--a man who hast never done anything save help thee, and a man who did nothing more than run to save thy sister who was in mortal danger."

Gideone drew back in surprise as guilt suddenly swept over him.

"Yes, fool!" Lyght spat. "He risked his life- thou knowest not how great a price that is- to save thine sister from Phyre, and thou dost seek to murder him for it! Thou art no different than every other Shallean vagabond who doth roam the Three Realms--a despicable fool who hast not the courage to battle those who have wronged thee but takest thy revenge upon the innocent who cannot defend themselves."

Gideone opened his mouth to protest, but the dragon cut him off.

"Be quite, Shallean wretch!" he hissed as he turned his back to Gideone. At that, all shame left Gideone and he was once more filled with anger.

"And what does it matter if I'm a Shallean?" he demanded. "'Tis not my fault. I did not ask to be one. You, who were the King of the Realm of Magic, ought to speak with more justice than that."

The dragon gave a great roar of fury and spun to face Gideone. He crouched low to the ground and his teeth were bared in rage as his blue eyes sparked.

"Have thy wife ravished and murdered by Shallean vermin," he snarled, "and thy young son sacrificed to thy worst enemy, then speak to me of justice!"

He began to draw closer, and, as he did so, he raised a great, crystal fore claw. Gideone stood still, his jaw clenched and his face twisted in anger, as he looked up and waited for his death, but just when Lyght was about to send his claw crashing down upon the Prince, he suddenly gave a cry and spun around.

For a long moment he sat there with his great head bowed and the whole of his body trembling. He made not a sound, yet the sorrow that filled him was unmistakable. And as Gideone looked upon him, shame once more filled him. He had had no right to grow angry at the dragon, and he was just about to open his mouth to speak when Lyght gave a groan. It seemed to fill the cavern, and the sorrow and agony held within it was unlike anything Gideone had ever before beheld.

"Forgive me," the great dragon whispered. With a trembling voice he continued, "I brought thee here that I might heal thee, but instead I almost killed thee."

Gideone took a step toward Lyght. "I accept your apology, but there is no need for it; you have suffered far more than ever I have suffered."

The great dragon slowly turned. He took a deep breath and said softly, "I have not spoken of that to anyone not even Orion whom I hold most dear. 'Tis ironic then that I would first speak of it to thou who art of that people which I have hated these many centuries." He paused. "There was a time I would have killed thee upon sight but now not only have I brought thee here to heal thee, but I also tell thee my deepest secret."

Gideone was silent for a moment, but as he looked upon the crystal dragon, he finally spoke. "And why is it that you now will heal me, seeing that you've hated the Shallee for so long?"

Lyght remained quite for a moment as if lost deep in thought.

"I loved my wife and my son with all my heart," he finally said. "They were my world, my all, and when they were taken from me I had nothing left." His voice began to tremble. "I was consumed with fury and sorrow, and my hatred only grew as the many centuries passed and I found no other to love.

"But then I found Orion. He became my son, and I became his father. Many a time did he break my heart, but never did he hurt me more than when I learned he loved a Shallean maid. I was furious, but as I watched him and saw how much he loved her, I was put to shame. He served her and honored her and protected her. He had once been a wicked man, but because of her he learned to be humble and noble. He who had never lived for anyone save himself--he who is cursed to enter into Elmorran upon his death--was suddenly willing to risk his life to save hers." He struggled to convey all that he felt and thought. "If he can love a Shallean maid that much, can I not at least leave behind my hatred and my anger?" He took a deep breath. "That is why I save thee--because of thy sister and the love my son doth hold for her."

Gideone could say nothing. He simply bowed his head and stared at the floor as shame rose even stronger within him. He could feel Lyght's unwavering gaze upon him. He heard the dragon give a sigh, and he could sense a large, crystal claw above him.

Suddenly he could feel a great warmth rising up within his chest. It grew greater and greater until it no longer remain in his chest but spread out through the whole of his body. He felt a strength and a life that he had not felt for many a day. He took a slow deep breath. All pain had left him.

Slowly he raised his head and looked up at Lyght. The dragon's head was cocked to one side as he regarded Gideone closely.

"Thy wounds are healed," Lyght said with his rich, low voice, "but there shall be scars; let them serve a purpose, to remind thee of that which hath taken place here this day, and that which thou hast learned."

"Thank you," said Gideone. "I will never forget what you have done for me." He hesitated for a moment. "And I pray that you can forgive me for the hatred I bore Orion. I am truly sorry."

"I accept thine apology, and forgive thee I do," answered Lyght as bowed his head. "And I pray that one day my son and thee shall meet again and that thou shalt be able to receive also his forgiveness."

"As do I," replied Gideone.

The dragon was silent for a moment then said, "Now 'tis time for thee to awaken and return to the Realm of Earth."

Gideone bowed low before the great, crystal dragon. "Thank you, sir, for all you have done."

* * *

Tmalion leaned back in his chair and let his eyes close. He had sat there for he knew not how long, and he was ready to fall asleep. Slowly, his breathing began to match the slow, steady breathing of the Prince who lay before him.

Suddenly, the King awoke and sat quickly up. He shook his head then looked down intently upon Gideone, for it seemed the Prince was beginning to stir.

For a moment Tmalion knew not what to do. True he had not wanted Gideone to die, but he balked at the thought of having to speak face to face with the man who had forsaken Eagle, and had not even dared oppose the Powers until Nor was threatened.

He rose to his feet and, wavering, looked down upon the face of the slowly awakening prince. Suddenly he turned and strode out of the room. In the adjoining room there were several servants standing ready to wait upon King Tmalion.

"Call a healer," Tmalion ordered. "The Prince is awakening."

Then, without even waiting for them to reply, he passed out of Gideone's chambers and into the corridor beyond.

* * *

Gideone stood alone in his chambers and quickly pulled on a blue tunic. He turned and looked at his reflection in a nearby mirror. The web of black lines had faded slightly, but they still reached all the way up to the left side of his neck, and a few lone lines managed to stretch all the way to his cheek. Those marks would most likely remain with him for the rest of his life.

"Your Highness?" he heard a voice behind him say.

He started then turned to see whom it was who had spoken. It was a servant-boy.

"King Tmalion wishes to speak with you," the boy said.

"Very well," answered Gideone, suddenly growing nervous. "Just a moment."

Quickly, he pulled his hair back and fastened it tightly behind his head. Then he turned to go with the servant.

* * *

King Tmalion sat upon his throne as he waited for Gideone to arrive. The throne room was empty for he had sent everyone away, and all was silent. Suddenly, the doors were opened, and a servant walked in.

"Prince Gideone of Nor," he announced then stepped aside to allow Gideone to pass through the door. Once the Prince had entered, the servant left, and the doors were once more closed.

Slowly, Gideone began to walk across the long, empty throne room to King Tmalion. His footsteps echoed loudly off the hard, stone floor.

Tmalion looked down upon the Prince. It had been three years since he had last seen Gideone. Gideone had grown a beard, but little else had changed. As far as Tmalion could see, Gideone was still nothing more than the carefree rogue he had been before.

Gideone finished the long walk from the door to the foot of the throne and stood before Tmalion. For a moment he simply looked up at the king, then bowed low before him and said, "Your Majesty."

Tmalion rose stiffly and said, "Welcome, Gideone. Tell me, what brings you to Scalavori?"

Gideone looked up at him and after a pause answered, "I came here to seek your help. As you no doubt know by now, I was wounded by an arrow of the Dark Sorcerer, and I came in hopes that you would be able to heal me."

"And why sought you succor of me?"

"Because you are the most powerful of the arch-mages, and because you seemed the one least likely to give me over to the Powers."

Tmalion crossed his arms, and there was anger in his voice as he spoke. "And why thought you that I would not turn you over to the Powers?" His eyes narrowed. "Is not my daughter the wife of a Power?"

Gideone's whole body tensed, and for a moment he could simply stare up at Tmalion. He tried to hide his sudden fear, but Tmalion could see it in his eyes.

The Prince licked his lips, took a deep breath, and finally spoke. "I came here because you were the only hope I could see. I knew that there was a great chance you would hand me over to the Powers, but I hoped otherwise. If I am wrong, then there's nothing I can do." He bowed his head. "Do with me as you will."

Tmalion's features darkened as he took a step toward Gideone, drew back his fist and sent it slamming into the Prince's jaw. Gideone gave a slight cry of surprise as he stumbled back and fell to the floor. His dark eyes flashed as he began to rise, and his hands tightened into fists, but suddenly he caught himself and stood still, looking at the King.

"Fool!" Tmalion cried. "What makes you think that I would ever help you? Have you ever done anything for me? You claimed to love my daughter; you sought her hand in marriage! But when Tnaka came to take her away what did you do? Nothing!"

"But..." Gideone began.

"But nothing!" Tnaka cried. "You did not a single thing! Without a word, you abandoned my daughter, and you abandoned me, and you ran back to your country and the safety of your high walls! And, now that the Powers have destroyed your country and you have nowhere else to turn, you run to me-- whom you forsook-- and seek my help!"

"But I didn't intentionally abandon you!" Gideone cried.

"Then why did you not fight for my daughter?" Tmalion demanded. "You who have boasted countless times that you've never been defeated in a duel--why did you let Tnaka have her?"

Gideone was silent for a moment as he struggled to find words to answer Tmalion--words that expressed all the emotions which welled up within him-- but they fled from him, and he was left standing silent with his head bowed in shame and despair.

Tmalion looked down upon Gideone. He saw the pain and the sorrow and the remorse. He saw the Prince's struggle to convey all that was within him, and he saw him give up in despair. And, as he looked upon Gideone and watched all of that take place before him, the anger and the bitterness filling him began to melt away.

He took a step toward Gideone and placed his hand upon the Prince's shoulder. "Forgive me," he said softly. "Now is not the time to speak of this. I see now that you did not want or mean to abandon Eagle. One day, no matter how painful it is for you, I want to know why you did what you did, but today is not that day."

Gideone looked up at him. His dark eyes were filled with sorrow. "I love your daughter. I truly do."

"I know," Tmalion answered. Then, with a stronger voice, he said, "And perhaps there is yet hope for you and her."

Gideone looked at him in confusion.

The King smiled weakly and said, "If there is any good that has come from that which has happened, it is that I have been able to give the semblance of being completely aligned with the Powers. But, even as outwardly I have followed, silently I have worked toward their destruction.

"There are few in Lairannare who love them, but, because of the Powers' great strength, there are also few who are willing to rise up against them. But I have finally managed to raise an army that I believe is strong enough to destroy the Powers." It was impossible not to see the excitement that filled his eyes.

"I believe now is the perfect time to strike," he continued. "My spies tell me the Powers are hopelessly divided. Kozan is positioning himself to take Provenna's place and is becoming more insolent by the day. Provenna seems to have no idea how to deal with him, and Tnaka is so weary of the wars waged by Provenna that he is pushing desperately for peace.

"On top of that, Provenna's long lost son has suddenly reappeared. She is going to--or perhaps already has--declared him the Prince of Lairannare and the heir to her crown, which has further separated her from Kozan, who wanted to kill her son, and it has even managed to drive a wedge between herself and Tnaka, who was completely set against her declaring him the Prince and heir.

"In addition to that, some of my spies even think that the Dark Sorcerer holds his allegiance more to Provenna than to Kozan.

"If we strike now, we can surprise them while they are still divided and before any one of them triumphs."

He paused for a moment then spoke again. "When you were first brought here I did not intend to tell you what I have now told you. I thought you to be a coward and a man not to be trusted. But now I believe I was wrong, and I wish to ask you to join me in the coming battle."

"I would count it a great honor," Gideone answered.

Tmalion smiled. "Thank you."

Gideone suddenly got a thoughtful look upon his face.

"Your Majesty," he said, after a moment, "a moment ago you said that I was brought here."

Tmalion looked at him and waited.

"Who brought me here?"

"You know not?" the King asked in surprise. "It was a young woman; her name was Phautina. I was under the impression that you and she had been riding together."

"We were," Gideone said, a confused look upon his face. He shook his head and banished all thoughts on the subject. "Never mind."

He looked back at Tmalion. "I suppose you ought to tell me your battle plans in full."

"Yes," Tmalion agreed. "Come with me."

With that, they walked from the throne room.

The next several hours were spent in deep discussion as Tmalion outlined his plans to Gideone. Even though the Powers were divided, still did their strength and their armies far outstrip that of those they ruled. If they were even given the chance to recover and attack, all hope would be lost. The only chance to defeat them was to surprise and destroy them in one, great battle.

Tmalion's army was huge--so huge that it filled Gideone with amazement. It was composed of nearly every race, from humans to elves to dwarves. Even the goblins and the orcs had joined.

To make certain that the Powers would not be able to send aid to one another Tmalion was forced to divide his army and send one part against Nolhol and the other again Leilaora, for were the three Powers ever to come together and fight as one, there would be no hope of defeating them.

Many painstaking months had been spent in trying to transport troops quietly into the countries of Delovachia and Jocthreal. Almost every way imaginable had been used from the long, dark underground passages of the kingdoms of the goblins and the subterranean elves to a great and powerful noble of Jocthreal calling for a huge tournament to be held.

Most of the two armies were ready, but there was still a good portion of men who had yet to enter Jochthreal or Delovachia. Thankfully, many of them were sky elves who could ride quickly upon their eagles to where it was they were supposed to be.

There was little that could be changed or added; the plans were set, but there were some things that could be, and, with Gideone's many questions and suggestions, the two men stayed up very late going over the plans.

Suddenly, in the midst of their discussion, they were interrupted by a servant, who informed them that a woman named Constantia, claiming to have been sent by Queen Eagle, desired to speak with Tmalion.

Immediately he and Gideone left and went to the throne room. Tmalion took his place upon his throne, and Gideone stood behind and to the right of the King.

Return

Not five seconds after they had taken their places, the doors to the throne room were opened and a servant announced, "The arch-sorceress Constantia." Immediately following, a woman, who looked to be in her mid-thirties, strode purposefully into the room. She was tall and very beautiful, but there was a hardness about her that would have made many a man stop and think before speaking to her. She was dressed plainly in the clothing of a man--leather boots, black trousers, and a leather jerkin with a brown shirt underneath. At her side hung a sword. Her long brown hair was pulled back tightly behind her head. Several strands had come loose and now hung down in front of her eyes, one of which was covered by a large, black patch.

She reached the bottom of the dais and bowed low before Tmalion.

"You are an arch-sorceress?" Tmalion question.

She straightened and looked up at him with her one good eye; it was a cold brown color.

"Aye, Your Majesty, that I am," she answered with an obvious Delovachian accent. "In fact, I'm th' last o' the arch-sorcerers; the other eleven havin' been killed by the Dark Sorcerer."

"Why come you here?"

"I have come because Queen Eagle, th' Princess o' Scalavori, sent me. She was asked by a man named Orion t' give aid t' the country of Nor."

Gideone felt a twinge of shame when he heard this.

"I came too late t' be of any help," Constantia continued, "but I did larn tha' Prince Gideone--" she looked at him--"had managed to escape, and I, with m' five fellow sorcerers, set out after him in order tha' we might help him. We were unable to catch up with him until now, so here we are; I stand here talkin' t' ye, and my five men wait outside." She motioned toward the doors of the throne room.

"And how am I to know that you were sent by my daughter?"

"The sign o' those who serve th' Queen is of an eagle, carryin' in its claws a Lumellia, silhouetted by a silver moon."

"Very well," Tmalion said. "I must admit I knew not that any of the arch-sorcerers still lived, and I certainly expected not to find one serving my daughter. I welcome you."

Constantia bowed again. "Thank ye, Majesty."

She straightened again and there was a sudden softness to her as she looked once more up at Tmalion and Gideone and spoke. "There were three other people travelin' with th' Prince. From th' descriptions I was given, th' two men appeared t' be Stavros an' Vayan. Where are they? May I see them?"

Gideone hesitated for a moment then answered her, saying softly, "You were right in believing they were Stavros and Vayan, but you can't see them for they are no longer here. Vayan ran away, and Stavros--" He took a breath--"Stavros is dead."

She turned around suddenly but not before Tmalion and Gideone saw the look of complete anguish which filled her face.

Almost instantly, Tmalion was at her side.

"Stavros is dead?" she repeated.

"Yes."

She took a trembling breath and slowly sank to her knees. One hand covered her face, and the other was pressed against the floor.

Tmalion knelt down beside her and put his hand on her shoulder.

"What is wrong?" he asked gently.

"He was my husband," she managed to whisper.

"Servants!" Tmalion called.

Gideone could only look at Constantia in disbelief.

Two servants entered and bowed low. "Yes, Your Majesty?"

"Escort this woman to a private chamber and see that she is not troubled."

He helped Constantia rise, and without a word, with scarcely even a sound, she went with the two servants, but Tmalion could see that her whole body trembled.

When the doors to the throne room had closed, Gideone turned to Tmalion. The Prince's dark eyes were clouded as he said, "Stavros did not have a wife."

"What?"

* * *

Tmalion knocked upon the door of the room Constantia had been taken to. He waited for a moment, but when he received no answer he quietly pushed it open and entered.

The room was dark, and it took a moment for his eyes to adjust. He could hear Constantia's soft sobs. Slowly, he looked around, and finally found her curled up in the darkest corner of the room.

He approached her slowly and knelt down beside her, and for a moment he did nothing save look at her. How could she not be Stavros' wife?

"My lady," he finally said very softly, "Gideone says that Stavros had no wife."

"That was what we wanted everyone to think," she said between her sobs, "Or, at least, what we wanted the Royal Family and everyone else in Zaren to think."

She struggled against the sobs which shook her body, but when she found she could not stop she simply continued. "My father is Kozan. My real name is Deifilia. I was once the High Priestess of Ashti." With a supreme effort she managed to stop crying, though her body shook with a lone sob every now and then.

"As ye can image, I was not a particularly popular person. We were terrified of wha' would happen if anyone found out," she whispered. "The kindest people can become monsters when faced with secrets like tha'." She took a deep breath. "We used t' see each other all th' time, but then he was called t' Zaren, and it became more and more dangerous t' see each other." She began to sob. "It was six months! Do ye know how long tha' is?" She covered her face with her hands, and her whole body shook with anguish. "I thought I would die, and now I'll never see him again." She began to weep again.

Tmalion could only look down in sympathy upon her, for he knew not what to do.

A long, long moment passed, during which only Constantia's sobs could be heard.

"How did he die?" she finally managed to ask.

"Gideone said that he was killed by Abiel," Tmalion answered quietly.

Suddenly--so suddenly that Tmalion fairly jumped--her tears stopped. She struggled to her feet, and stood with her head bowed and her back to him.

"Killed," she whispered, "by my own brother." The rage and the hatred which filled her voice, fairly cut through the King.

For a long moment she stood there with her head bowed, her hands pressed against the wall, and her whole body trembling.

"Tell me," she said; her voice was a low, soft growl, "are th' rumors I've heard true? Will ye soon be going t' war?"

"They are true," he answered her, "and I am going very soon."

"Then I shall weep later." Her voice was filled with deadly rage. "I want t' fight Delovachia."

"Gideone says Abiel was killed by Stavros."

"So?" she cried. "I can still kill Kozan! I can still kill Abiel's mother! I can still kill every bleedin' monster in tha' whole dark city!" She struck the wall hard with her fist.

Her one brown eye flashed as she looked at him. "I am an arch-sorceress! I am the last of the arch-sorcerers! I am a warrior who can fight as well as any man! Let me help you defeat th' Powers."

Tmalion simply looked at her for a moment. Her breast rose and fell with great breaths, and her whole face was twisted in a look of anguish.

"Very well," he said. "You will fight against Delovachia."

Chapter 27
The Rising Storm

Gideone stood in the middle of a forest. The leaves of the trees were turned all shades of red and yellow, and the warm sun shone down through the colorful canopy. A soft breeze caressed his face, and nearby a small stream wound its way through the forest.

But Gideone cared nothing for the beauty surrounding him. He stood and looked in hatred upon the blonde-haired elf who stood before him. With cold, gray eyes, Tnaka looked back in contempt.

Slowly, Gideone drew his sword; the sound of the blade scraping against the sheath filled the quiet forest.

"Twice you have defeated me," he growled, as he held up his sword, "but this time you will not."

Tnaka answered with a sneer, as he also drew his sword.

With a cry, they fell upon each other. The clang of their swords echoed throughout the still and silent forest. Over and over they flew at each other only to reel backward beneath the force of the other's blow. Over and over they drove the other back only to, in turn, be driven back also. For hours, it seemed, they battled, neither overcoming the other, until, with a great cry, Gideone dealt his opponent a bone-shattering blow. The elf staggered and fell to the ground.

With another howl, Gideone rushed at him and raised his sword to deal the final blow, but, even as he did so, Tnaka managed to summon the strength to scramble out of the way.

He rolled to his feet and faced the Prince. His gray eyes burned with rage, and from deep within him there emerged the soft, low growl of a deadly beast.

Gideone's lip curled up with fury as he and the elven king slowly circled each other.

Suddenly, with a cry, they both flew once more together. The ground fairly shook beneath their impact. Over and over their swords clanged together, sending sparks showering down upon them.

With a cry of fury, Tnaka struck Gideone with all his might. The Prince staggered beneath the force of the blow and sank to his knees. His sword fell from his hands.

Tnaka drew back his sword to deal Gideone a final blow. Gideone, struggling to breath, scrambled back as quickly as his strength would allow, but he was not quick enough. A strangled cry of pain escaped his lips as the steel blade of

Tnaka dug deep into his leg. With a snarling cry, the elven king sent his sword crashing down again and again. The Prince scrambled back over the fallen leaves and the dried sticks of the forest underbrush, leaving a trail of blood behind him, until finally he found himself scrambling across the stream of water. His hand slipped on a rock, and he fell backward. The water rushed over his body and was turned red with his blood. He tried with all his might to move, but he could do nothing save look up in terror at the elf who towered over him. Tnaka's cold gray eyes sparkled evilly and a terrible, cackling laugh escaped him as he raised his sword to deal the final blow.

Gideone sat up with a start. His body was covered with sweat, and his heart was racing as it had never done before. For a moment, he could only sit there, trying to catch his breath. Slowly, he began to look around him. It was night, and he was in a tent. He could hear the chirping of crickets and the soft murmur of a brook outside. He began to breath easier as he remembered where he was and what was happening. He was in Tmalion's camp just outside the country of Jocthreal. He gave a groan and lay back down. His wound was healed; why did he continue to dream?

* * *

Provenna stood in the palace armory and looked over the many weapons assembled there--swords, spears, axes, flails, and many other weapons, as well as all types of armor. At her side stood the High General of her army. Slowly, she walked through the armory, inspecting each of the weapons. As she did so, she spoke. "Lately, there have been rumors of rebellion and reports of armies being mobilized. What think you of this?" She reached out and ran her hand along the shaft of a spear. "Empires such as yours have always been plagued by rebels," answered the General. "Few were the rebellions that were successful, and 'tis my belief that the rumors you hear will remain simply that--rumors. However, I would not be worthy of the rank of general if I allowed my men to grow lazy. They are in constant readiness, and, since the rumors began, they have been even more diligent in their duties." "Excellent." She picked up a mace and looked at it. "I trust that your weapons are all in good repair." "Of course, Your Majesty," answered the General, who then launched into a long speech on what had been done to maintain the weapons. While he was speaking, Provenna set the mace back down and reached out to touch a sword. The General suddenly stopped speaking and reached out to stop her, but before he could Provenna had run her thumb along the blade. She lifted up her hand

and regarded the wound she had given herself. Blood welled up from it and began to flow down her hand.

"'Tis a sharp blade," she said then turned her head to the General. "The blade is poisoned is it not?"

"Yes, Your Majesty."

Provenna waved her other hand over the wound, and instantly the cut and the blood disappeared.

"'Tis a good strong poison--one that would weaken even an arch-mage. I trust all of the swords have been so treated."

"Yes, Your Majesty--as have the arrows and the spears."

"Good."

She looked directly at him and continued, "I want everything to be kept constantly ready. Something tells me that these rumors are not simply rumors. There is a storm rising, and, whether it be great or small, I intend to weather it."

With that she turned and walked from the armory.

* * *

Aeneas peered out from the thick foliage of the forest along the road. More than a dozen of Provenna's soldiers galloped along it. He held his breath as they ran past him, and he held tightly to the reins of his horse, hoping against hope that she would not neigh or make any other sudden noises.

It took but a few moments for the soldiers to pass, but, to Aeneas, it seemed to be hours, and it was not until they were almost out of sight that he began to breath easier.

"Does my mother not know that she would only bring me back to my death?" he murmured as he gazed at where the soldiers had disappeared.

Since almost the moment it had been discovered that he was missing, soldiers had been scouring the countryside for the young prince. It had gotten so that he dared not even walk upon the road but instead made his way through the forest that ran alongside it.

Slowly, he turned and began once more to walk. But, suddenly, he stopped, for, somewhere within the surrounding trees, he could hear the rustling of leaves. He drew his sword and slowly began to walk toward where it was the sound was coming from.

Suddenly, through the trees, he caught sight of a creature unlike anything he had ever seen before. It stood as tall as a horse and had a huge pair of wings spreading out from its shoulders. Its lissome, black body was like that of a large cat, but its head was like that of a bird of prey. It took but one look for Aeneas to realize that it was a griffin.

The young prince, too stunned to say or do anything, stood staring dumbly at the creature. For a moment, the griffin simply stared back. He cocked his head, blinked his large white eyes several times, and, after evidently deciding that

Aeneas was to be trusted, spoke. "Put away thy sword, for I mean thee no harm." Aeneas, still in shock, continued to stare, until suddenly, realizing what the griffin had said, he snapped back into reality. He shook his head and sheathed his sword and, as he looked at the griffin, breathed in awe, "Who are you?"

"Men call me Nightfall," the griffin answered with a bow of his head, then, after pausing, continued, saying, "Thou art pursued by Provenna's soldiers so methinks thou art one to be trusted. Tell me, know thee anything of a man whom the Dark Sorcerer brought to Leilaora? His name is Orion."

Aeneas started. "You know Orion?"

"Yea, I know him," the griffin answered. "He once did save my life, and for that have I faithfully followed him and stayed by his side." There was pleading in his voice as he continued, "I see by thy reaction that thou knowest him also. Please, tell me what hath happened to him."

Aeneas was silent for a moment. He hung his head and answered quietly, "'Tis because of him that I flee from Leilaora." He paused again. "He is my brother and the Prince of all Lairannare."

"What?" the griffin exclaimed.

Aeneas proceeded to tell Nightfall all that had happened and everything he knew about his brother. The griffin listened carefully to every word and, when Aeneas had finished speaking, remained silent and thoughtful.

"Tell me," said Nightfall after a moment, "thou art remorseful for what thou hast done?"

"Yes," Aeneas fairly cried. "You know not how much I wish that I had never heard the name Orion, much less ever done to him what I did! If there were any way to undo the past, I would gladly do it, no matter how great the peril."

"The past is the past and cannot be changed," said the griffin slowly, "but there may be a way to undo the damage which thou hast caused."

Aeneas leaned forward. "How?"

Nightfall hesitated. "Now, I am a griffin," he said, "young in years and unknowledgeable of man and his ways, but there is a certain woman whom Orion hath sworn to serve and who, methinks, doth hold certain sway over his heart. Were we to bring her to him, he would, perchance, remember his former self and turn from the path he doth now trod."

"Where is this woman?" Aeneas demanded.

"Therein doth lie the problem," answered the griffin, "for she is held captive by Kozan. She is Princess Mystia of Nor, and 'twas because of her that Orion was captured in the first place. As near as I can see, she is still locked away in Kozan's dark palace, if she hath not been killed already."

"Can you take me to Nolhol?" Aeneas asked. "My life is in dreadful danger, and I fairly destroyed my brother through my hatred and stupidity. If I must brave my father's palace to bring about restitution, then I will do so."

Nightfall cocked his head and blinked his eyes. "Thy father's palace?"

"Uh...I..." Aeneas' voice trailed off, and his face flushed.

Nightfall simply gave a shake of the head and said, "Ye humans truly are a mystery.

"But now for the task at hand." He looked at Aeneas' horse. "Take the saddle from thy horse and come with me."

Aeneas took the saddle as he was told and began to follow the griffin through the forest trees. They walked for but a short distance when Nightfall paused. He then walked behind a fallen tree and quickly returned, carrying in his beak a large saddlebag, which someone had carefully packed. Out of it, Aeneas could see the end of a sword, too long to fit entirely in the pack.

The griffin dropped it to the ground. "Take this."

Slowly, the young prince bent and picked it up and opened it.

"What is it?" he asked quietly.

"'Tis Orion's armor. Methinks it shall fit thee."

Aeneas gazed upon the red, dragon-scale armor. "But I can't wear this--not after what I did to him."

"Take it; thou hast no other armor, and who knows if in the days to come thou shalt be in need of some. Wear it; if thou art successful in thy mission and bring Mystia to him, he shall readily forgive thee for any insult, and, if he doth not turn, then, by thine own words, he shall kill thee, so wearing his armor will matter little."

"True," said Aeneas after a moment's thought and began to put the armor on. He was by no means weak, but he had yet to gain his brother's hardened, muscular body, and the armor had to be tightened as much as it could be for it to fit him.

He took a breath and picked up Orion's sword; it was heavy in his hand. He unsheathed it partly and looked in wonder upon the crystal blade.

"This is his sword?" he breathed in awe.

"Yea, it is. Ronahrrah is its name, and with it Orion has killed many an enemy. A better blade thou shalt never find."

Aeneas pushed it back into its sheath and with a deep breath buckled it around his waist.

"Now," said the griffin, "take thy horse's saddle and place it upon my back, for we have far to fly."

* * *

Tnaka's chambers were dim and silent. Night had fallen, and the elven king stood by a window and stared out into the dark palace garden below. His hands were pressed against the cool glass of the window, and his chest rose and fell with labored breathing. His face was twisted in a look of anguish, and the bitterness and anger and sorrow, which welled up within him, threatened to choke off all breath.

For a long moment he stood there, barely moving, barely making a sound. All of his hopes for the future, for Eagle, for his child, had been broken--all because of Orion.

Suddenly, he gave a cry and sent his fist smashing against the window. A pane of glass shattered beneath the blow, and the shards went falling to the ground. Tnaka drew back his hand--it was covered with blood--and sent it smashing once more against the window.

He turned and, with one swift motion, picked up a chair standing behind him. He spun around and sent it flying toward the glass. The whole of the window shattered. Glass flew in all directions, covering the floor of his chambers and falling outside to the ground far below.

For a moment, the king, wild-eyed and breathing deeply, stood and stared at what he had done. Then he turned and ran from the room. There was still time: if only he could make Orion turn. Like a madman, he ran through the corridors. He saw not the slaves who started in horror and fear as he ran past. He felt not the pain in his hand, nor saw the blood that poured from it. He knew only that he had to speak to Orion.

Suddenly, he found himself before the warrior's door.

"Orion!" he fairly screamed as he pounded against it, leaving a bloody mark upon the wood.

Over and over he pounded against the door and over and over he screamed out Orion's name, until suddenly the door was thrown open and he stumbled in.

The door was slammed behind him, and Tnaka spun to find himself looking up at Orion. The prince's spectral blue eyes flashed with fury, his long auburn hair fell down wildly around him, and his bare chest rose and fell with heavy breathing.

"What do you want?" he demanded softly.

For a moment Tnaka could not answer; he simply stood staring at Orion.

Suddenly, he heard a soft noise, and, looking behind the prince, he caught sight of a woman standing in the darkness of a doorway. She held her hands to her breasts, keeping her dress from falling down. Her long, blonde hair tumbled over her and partially covered her shoulders left bare when the sleeves of her dress had slipped off.

Anger filled Tnaka.

"Look at you!" He screamed. "Have you forgotten everything you learned? What are you doing?" He tried to strike Orion across the face, but Orion grabbed his hand and held it in an iron grip. His blue eyes flashed as he looked deep into Tnaka's.

"What does it look like I'm doing?" he growled softly.

"But what of Mystia?" Tnaka demanded.

With a cry, Orion threw Tnaka to the floor.

"Never say that woman's name!" he snarled.

"But...!" Tnaka began.

"I said never say it!" He spun around. "What was she but an ideal I could never reach? She was so beautiful and innocent and pure--" he turned back to face Tnaka; his face was filled with bitterness-- "and what am I but an unchaste, murdering monster? She was a daughter of the race most loved by Joretham, but what am I?" His face was twisted in anger as tears welled up in his eyes. "I am the son of Phyre." He turned away again. His whole body shook as he struggled against the fury and sorrow that filled him.

Tnaka picked himself up off the floor.

"Orion," he said as he placed his good hand upon the warrior's trembling shoulder, "you are worthy of her; you are more than worthy of her. That Phyre is your father means nothing; you couldn't help it, and simply because he is evil does not mean you are."

"Fool!" Orion screamed as he threw Tnaka's hand from him and turned once more to face him. "Do you not understand? I am cursed, even as Phyre is cursed! Had I lived a perfect life--had I never sinned--perhaps it would not matter. But I did sin--freely and of my own accord I did things that rival even Kozan's actions--but, unlike others, I cannot find forgiveness because I bear my father's curse!"

He turned away and continued softly, "She was perfect--so beautiful and so innocent--and I thought that if I simply served her, with my whole heart and with my whole will and strength, I would find favor in Joretham's eyes." His voice rose with anger. "I was a fool! I told myself that my love for her was pure--that it was far greater than mere physical desire--but in my heart of hearts I wanted her just as I have wanted every other woman!"

"Orion," Tnaka began, but the Prince cut him off.

"Speak not to me!" he snarled as he turned once more to face the elven king. His blue eyes were fill with anger and hatred. "You come here to try to turn me back to what I was." His voice grew soft, but deadly. "If you dare ever try to do so again, I'll kill you; I swear it."

"But, Orion..."

"Who are you to tell me to be noble?" Orion demanded. "When have you ever been noble? Are you not a Power?" His voice was filled with spite. "Tell me not the Powers are noble. You've filled the Realm with more blood and destruction than any other could, yet you dare tell me to be noble? You've waged wars and conquered so that the whole of Lairannare is under your power, yet you want me not to conquer and wage war?" He glanced at Eluned, and with even more anger continued. "You grow angry when you see me with a woman, but I am not taking her against her will. I am not stealing her from the man she loves--the man she was promised to! I am not condemning her to life of bitterness and loneliness in a country far from her own with a man she despises!"

Tnaka wanted to contest Orion's words. He wanted to cry out with all his might that Orion lied, but when he opened his mouth no words would come.

Orion paid no heed but continued, crying, "Fool! Why should I be noble or chivalrous? I have lived among the righteous, and I have seen their lot--

oppressed and hated, with all their hope held up in the life hereafter.
"But I have not their hope. Why should I live as one oppressed? Why should
I give, when, upon my death, everything will be taken from me?
"No! I will not be a fool! I will conquer, and I will rule, and I will grow great,
and I will find what little pleasure I can now."
For a moment Tnaka could only stare up at Orion. He struggled to find
something--anything--to say, but as he looked up into the prince's eyes, so filled
with fury and bitterness, he knew there was nothing.
"No," he groaned. "No." With that he turned and stumbled from the room.

* * *

Orion watched Tnaka leave, and, when the door had been shut, he took a few
stumbling steps to a table which stood nearby and steadied himself against it.
He could hear the quiet tread of Eluned as she approached behind him, and he
could feel her soft touch upon his skin.
"Orion," she whispered as she rested her cheek upon his shoulder and put her
arms around him. For a long moment they stood there like that, neither moving,
neither speaking. Orion's whole body trembled with the anguish that filled him.
"Orion, Orion," Eluned whispered--so soothing.
He turned and held her in his arms and buried his face in her soft, golden hair.
"Eluned."
Suddenly, he pulled her tightly to him. He kissed her forehead and her brow
and her lips. She wrapped her arms around his neck and kissed him in return.
He could feel her body pressed against his, and he could taste her sweetness on
his lips. She was not Mystia, but what did it matter? Her long, golden hair
cascaded down over her shoulders and back and over Orion's arms. He could
feel her hands against his shoulders and his back.
He pulled her tighter to him and tried to force all thoughts of Mystia from his
mind. What was Mystia to him? She had never loved him.
He began to undo the clasps of her dress, but, even as he did so, he could still
see Mystia. He could see her standing outside the house of Zenas, with the
setting sun shining upon her. He could see her--so frail and sick--resting her
head upon his shoulder in the dungeon of Kozan's palace, and he could see the
tears she shed for him, when she saw him beaten and broken from Kozan's
torture.
He could still feel Eluned's lips pressed to his. He started and turned his face
from her as he pushed her roughly from him. She gave a gasp as she stumbled
back and fell to the floor.
"Orion," she began.
"Stay away from me!" he snarled.
He ran into his bedchambers and picked his tunic up from where it lay upon
the floor. With one swift motion he pulled it on then turned. Eluned stood in

the door, blocking his way.

"Orion, please," she said as she reached her hand out to him, "let me help."

"Stay away," he growled.

She took a step toward him. With no warning, he leapt forward and grabbed her by the throat. Her eyes grew wide with terror.

"I said stay away!" he cried. His voice lowered to a hiss. "Worthless harlot." His hands tightened around her neck. Tears streamed down her cheeks as her fingers clutched at his hands. He threw her from him, and she fell gasping to the floor, as he dashed from the room. Out from his chambers he charged, through the long, empty corridors of the palace, and out into the moonlit courtyard. Across the courtyard he ran to the stables, where he saddled up his large gray charger and galloped out--out of the palace, and out into the dark streets of Leilaora.

They were cold; they were empty; they were silent, and they held no comfort within them, yet, still through them, he rode, seeking peace, or at the least, seeking solitude. But he found neither, for his emotions welled up within him and threatened to overpower him, and the large silver moon shone down upon him--his constant companion for the whole of the night.

* * *

Eagle stood alone in her chambers. A fire burned low in the fireplace and lit the whole room with flickering orange light. Outside, the silver moon shone through the window and fell upon the floor until it disappeared into the light of the fire.

Near to the window there sat a round, wooden table, upon which rested a goblet and a carafe of wine. She began to walk across the room to it--the thick red carpet was soft beneath her feet--but, as she did so, she caught sight of herself in a large mirror, which hung upon the wall.

She stopped and looked at it and after a long moment walked closer and stared at her reflection. Her long, blonde hair was loosely braided, and several strands had escape and now fell down around her face. She was dressed in a simple, light blue nightgown with long sleeves and a skirt that fell all the way to the floor.

She pressed her hands to her belly--right hand over left--and held them there for a long moment. A soft smile lit her face. As she held her hands there, she could feel the ring upon her left hand. She held it up and looked at it. It was a beautiful ring--a gold band with a diamond surrounded by five sapphires--her wedding ring. She held it out and watched it sparkle in the light of the fire.

Suddenly, there came a soft knock at her door. She started from her reverie then turned to face it. Another knock came, and she quickly walked across the room and opened the door.

When she saw whom it was standing there, she stepped back in surprise, for she found herself gazing upon Tnaka. He looked exhausted. His hair and clothing were disheveled, and upon his face there was a look of despair that she had never seen before.

"What is it?" she asked in alarm.

"Forgive me," he cried with a trembling voice as he took her hand in his. She started back in surprise. Then looked down in shock at his bloody hand. "I am a fool," he continued, his face twisted in anguish, "a selfish fool. I should never have taken you from Gideone.

"I hoped that, perhaps, one day, I could win your love and make you happy as he made you happy, but there's no hope. There's no hope; there's no future; there is nothing! Nothing save more war and more death and more destruction."

He turned away from her and whispered, "Forgive me." Then he began to walk away.

Eagle reached out to touch him, but he pulled away and began to run from the room.

"No, wait!" she cried, but he continued running.

Out of the room and down the corridor he charged. Eagle ran to the door after him, but she knew she had no hope of catching him.

"Tnaka," she pleaded as she watched him go, "come back." But he did not hear her.

* * *

Kozan stood alone in the great sanctuary of the Temple of Balor. He stood before the altar at the very top of the large pyramid of steps. The only light came from four flaming torches, one at each corner of the top step.

His face was twisted in a look of pain, and his hands were raised to the heavens as he cried out, "Great Balor, give me strength!" He struggled to say more and yet, though his mouth moved, no words came.

He fell to his knees. His shoulders were hunched over, and he covered his face with his hands.

"Help me," he begged. "Tomorrow I am to kill her. Give me the strength to do your will." His voice sank to a whisper. "When I look into her eyes--so black and beautiful--let me see darkness; let me see hatred; let me see filth and blasphemy." He took a trembling breath. "But let me not see what I see now.

"Oh, Balor, give me strength."

Chapter 28
The Battle

Provenna's face was almost expressionless, but her green eyes flashed and her voice was filled with anger. "My father hated me. Aiden left me. Kozan used me. And the whole of the Realm despises me. Soon they shall learn to fear me; now I will be the one who hates and uses and despises."

The sky was black as Tmalion stood in the middle of a dense forest. All around him were soldiers busily preparing for battle, but, though the camp was in a flurry of excitement, scarcely a sound could be heard, for, though hidden from view by the trees, just outside the forest there lay the city of Leilaora; the soldiers dared not make any noise that would betray their presence.

The elven king's heart was racing with anticipation. All of his hopes and dreams of freedom, all of his plots and carefully executed plans had culminated in this day. He and his army would either triumph or be destroyed. There was a part of him that felt completely giddy and sick, but there was also a part that was calm and collected, waiting patiently for the time to attack, and it was that part which was seen by men.

All was in readiness. The eagles stood nearby ready to fly at a moment's notice. The elven warriors also stood ready to storm the city. Beneath Leilaora, in the dark tunnels of the goblin kingdom, thousands of goblins and elves stood ready to blast through the ground and charge out into the city.

Tmalion knew that, far away, at the city of Nolhol similar preparations were being made for a battle that, like the one he would soon wage, would mean either complete victory or complete defeat.

He looked up into the sky. Soon the sun would rise, and with it the battle would begin.

He took a deep breath and slowly sank to his knees. His eyes were closed, his head was bowed, and there upon the hard, uneven forest ground he prayed, "Joretham, give us strength, and, if it is something that can be given in the midst of war, give us protection." He was silent for a moment. "Oh Joretham, let us be victorious."

* * *

The Battle

Mystia sat alone in Kozan's chambers. She was dressed in a long, flowing robe of white samite. Before Kozan had left for the Temple, he had ordered her to put it on. When she had asked him why, he struck her hard across the face then coldly, scornfully, told her that since she was to be sacrificed upon the morrow he wanted her to look her best. With that he had turned and stormed from the room.

She had seen no one else save the slave-girl who had brought her dinner. The food, long cold, still rested upon the table before her, for she had not the stomach to eat.

She had long ago flung her veil aside. Her long, black hair tumbled freely over her shoulders and down her back. Her head was bent and her hands covered her face. Her whole body shook as she wept tears of anguish and terror.

"Joretham," she sobbed; it was a strangled cry. She tried to say more, but the words were choked back by her tears. She closed her eyes and tried to fight the terror which threatened to overwhelm her, but, as she did, a thousands different images rushed unbidden into her mind--images of Kozan, filled with anger, striking his wife, images of Lareina lying dead upon the floor. She could feel Kozan's hand against her own cheek. She could see him, in the Temple of Balor, towering over the Shallean who was to be sacrificed, and she could see him plunge the dagger into the man's heart. She gave a choked cry and clutched at her own heart.

For a long moment she simply sat there, not crying, scarcely making a sound. Her whole body trembled as she held herself tightly.

Slowly she began to regain her composure, and after a moment she sat up straight and touched her hand to her face. Her skin was wet with tears and sweat, and she tried to dry her face with her hand. She took slow, deep breaths and held herself tightly once again. She began to shiver; she felt colder than when she had been in Kozan's dungeon.

At that thought, tears sprang once more to her eyes, for she could picture Orion, beaten and broken, lying chained to the dungeon walls. She had never before seen such pain and terror as she saw written upon his face. Her own features twisted into a look of agony as she remembered all of the things Kozan had told her about Orion. Suddenly, all of her pain and suffering seemed like nothing.

"Joretham," she whispered with a pleading, trembling voice, "if You can hear me, help Orion. What happens to me matters not, but please help Orion. Kozan says he is the son of Norenroth, and, though Kozan is an evil man, I find myself believing him." Her hands were folded tightly and her eyes, so hopeful and innocent and yet so filled with sorrow, were turned up to the heavens. "I know not if there is any way to free him of the curse which binds him, but I know if there is any way 'tis through You. Please help him. I fear death, but if it meant that he would live I would gladly give my life up."

She was silent for a long moment, and when she spoke again her voice was so soft it could barely be heard. "I love him. Without him I know not what I would do."

Then even softer she pleaded, "Please save him."

* * *

The first faint hints of sunlight were showing in the sky, as Orion stopped his riding--his wandering--and stood still. He found himself in an open place, surrounded on all sides by cold, gray buildings. Before him stood a fountain, tall and made of stone, with the water quietly bubbling out of the top and falling down into the large circular basin. His horse occasionally shook its head and struck its hoof against the cobblestone, but yet the place seemed so still and silent with the darkness of the morning and the fountain standing there all alone. A cool breeze blew softly across his face.

Orion sat there upon his horse for a long a moment and looked at the fountain. All of his hatred and anger seemed to disappear at the sight of that solitary object, and he felt only loneliness and sorrow.

He dismounted his charger, and, taking the reigns in his hand, slowly walked to the fountain. He reached it, and, as he looked down into the water, he saw a single leaf, which had flown from he knew not where, resting upon the clear, liquid surface. He reached out and brushed his fingers through the water.

His gaze fell upon the rim of the basin. It was wide so that a person might sit upon it. He touched his hand against the hard, cold stone seat, and as he did so a hundred different memories rushed unbidden into his mind of that night--it seemed so long ago--when he and Mystia had sat at the edge of a similar fountain and conversed. He could see her eyes, so black and beautiful, looking up at him as she fairly begged him to leave while he still could.

Suddenly anguish filled him such as it had never done before. It was like a sickness spreading out from his belly, clutching at his chest so that he could not breath. His legs grew weak and slowly he sank to his knees.

He gazed into the water and gave a soft sob.

"Mystia," he whispered as he covered his face with his hands. "Mystia. Would that I had done as you desired; would that I had fled Zaren and never looked back." He took a trembling breath. "You were so kind and gentle. I remember not anyone who treated me as you have." His voice filled with bitterness. "But how did I repay you?" His voice grew soft--so soft that even he could barely hear it. "I fell in love with you." His voice rose again. "I, the most cursed, wretched, evil man in the whole of Deithanara, fell in love with you, the most perfect, beautiful--" he struggled to find words to describe all which he saw in and felt for her, but they would not come--"woman who has ever lived and ever will live."

He reached for the ring which she had given him, but, when his hand pressed against his chest, he did not find it. The ring, the ring Mystia had told him never to lose, was gone. Fear filled him, and for a moment he simply held his hand to his chest as if he hoped that the precious object would suddenly miraculously appear beneath his palm.

Suddenly he gave a cry of fury and leapt to his feet. He remembered what had happened to it. He spun to face the palace of his mother. He could barely see it over the roofs of the buildings, but his eyes burned with rage at the sight of it.

He turned to his horse and with a growl began to mount, but, even as he did so, he drew short, with one foot in the stirrup, and listened, for suddenly, through the early morning stillness there could be heard a low rumbling. It was like far off thunder, but, though it could barely be heard, the ground trembled beneath it.

* * *

Mystia sat, unmoving, upon the chair. Her arms rested upon the table, and her head was cradled in her arms. She could not sleep, but all of the emotions she had gone through during the night had left her exhausted. She could hear nothing, save the sound of her own soft breathing.

Through the stillness, the low, mournful sound of Balor's horn suddenly broke. She started at the noise and looked wildly around as she sat up straight. She realized what it was and, pressing her hands to her breast, began to take slow, deep breaths to slow her racing heart.

The sound of the horn died away, and the Princess was left once more in silence. But as she sat there, she suddenly thought she heard something like far distant, rolling thunder. She sat, her head tilted slightly, her breath held, and listened.

* * *

Orion looked up. The morning had just broken. Its pink rays spread across the sky. There was not a cloud in sight, yet still it thundered. His horse gave a nervous shake of its head as the thunder began to grow. Orion stumbled back and looked around in confusion as the ground began to shake more violently.

The thunder rose and rose until it swelled into a deafening roar, and, as it did so, the ground continued to shake until it seemed a great earthquake had taken the city. The warrior gave a cry as he was thrown to the ground. His hand and his arm scraped against the uneven cobblestones, leaving a long, burning cut on his skin. He began to scramble to his feet, but, even as he did so, there suddenly came, from somewhere within the city, a blinding flash of light, and, as it spread across the sky, the city was shaken with a dreadful crashing roar.

He gave a groan as he was thrown back once more. As he struggled to his feet, he looked up, and his mouth fell open in surprise. Above the city there flew more than a hundred eagles. Their voices were lifted up in croaking shrieks of war as they sent balls of fire raining down upon the city. Already flames were spreading throughout the buildings and rising to the sky.

* * *

Mystia gave a gasp and ran to the window. She pressed her hands against the glass as she tried to see what was happening. She could see nothing, but she could hear the savage cries of men, and she could feel the city shake with the pounding of hundreds upon hundreds of feet. Her heart was pounding in her chest, and her whole body was trembling. She barely dared hope that an army truly was attacking Nolhol.

Her legs grew weak, and, slowly, she sank to the floor. She rested her brow against the cool glass, which trembled with the commotion outside.

"Joretham," she whispered, "let it be."

* * *

Leilaora fairly shook with the savage war cries of thousands of men. Orion snarled and spun around. He could feel the pounding of men's feet as they ran through the streets and spread throughout Leilaora.

From his boot, he pulled a long dagger. He could hear the men as they came closer. He looked wildly around for his horse, but it had fled in terror. For a moment he simply stood, body tensed, knife held ready, uncertain whether to flee or face the enemy.

Suddenly, out from behind one of the nearby houses, soldiers began to pour into the place which had but recently been so still and silent. Orion saw only a flash of armor, for even as they began to appear, he turned and ran. He could hear cries behind him and the footsteps of men chasing after him, but he did not look back. He ran through narrow, twisting streets until he found himself in a long, dark alley. He sped down the street until his path was blocked by a high wall.

With a snarling roar, he spun around to face his pursuers. His face was twisted into a look both of hate and pleasure. The long blade of his dagger seemed to gleam with the same light with which his spectral eyes sparked.

The human and the goblin who had been pursuing him stopped short as they found themselves looking into his face. Orion took advantage of their momentary surprise and, with another terrifying cry, lunged toward them. The human tried to raise his sword, but, before he could, Orion fell upon him. He plunged his knife through the small space where the armor met the belt and into the soft flesh beneath. The man gave a cry of pain, but, even as he did so, Orion, with one swift motion grabbed the man's head in his hands and twisted sharply. The soldier gave a slight gurgle and fell dead to the ground.

With a snarl, the warrior, not bothering to retrieve his knife, charged the goblin. The goblin bore a huge battle axe, but he could not swing it in the narrow alley. He dropped it, and, as it clattered to the ground, he gave a low growl and met Orion. The ground fairly shook with their impact. The two went flying to the ground. With another howl, Orion scrambled madly onto the goblin's stomach and grabbed his neck with his hands. The goblin gave a grunt and reached up to tear the warrior's arms away, but he could barely make Orion's arms move.

The goblin's eyes grew wide with terror. In a desperate attempt to save his life, he reached up and grabbed hold of Orion's neck. Orion's mouth simply twisted into a mocking grin as slowly his grip began to tighten. The goblin gave a choked grunt as he struggled desperately, but it was no use. Slowly, Orion's grip tightened until, finally, there could be heard the sickening sound of bones crunching. The goblin's arms grew limp and fell from Orion's neck.

"Fool!" the warrior cried then gave a spiteful, desperate, bitter laugh--the laugh of a man half mad. "Did you think you could defeat a half dragon?" He began tearing at the goblin's armor. "Did you truly think you had any hope of defeating me?" There came another sickening crack as Orion yanked the helmet off. "I, who am the son of Norenroth?"

He said not another word as he finished stripping the goblin of his armor and putting it on himself. The fit was decent, though not nearly as good as Orion would have liked, but it fit far better than the armor of the human would have-- Orion cast a look of contempt back upon the human who lay dead but a short distance away.

With one swift movement, he picked up the huge battleaxe that the goblin had dropped and turned to leave. He could hear the battle raging so very near. He looked scornfully down upon the face of the dead goblin and, spitting upon it, walked away.

* * *

Aeneas held tightly to the saddle as Nightfall cut his way swiftly through the low hanging clouds. The young prince shivered; he may have been wearing a cloak, but it offered little in the way of warmth. It seemed the closer they got to Nolhol the colder and bleaker it became. He could still not forget the forest he and Nightfall had stopped and slept in during the night; it had seemed so empty and dead. It was gray and bleak, and barely a sound could be heard within it. He had known he needed to sleep, but sleep was difficult to find in a place such as that. However, though he had slept little, he was awake and alert; he was not about to let himself fail his mission.

It seemed the closer they drew to Nolhol, the more attentive he became. His heart was pounding and his face was alive with anticipation. Nightfall continued on, calm and steady, with large, slow beats of his wings, but inside he too burned with anticipation, for every flap of his wings brought him closer to what he hoped would save Orion.

Presently, through the stillness and the fog, they heard a sound. It was very faint--nothing more than a soft murmur--but it did not die away. In fact, as they continued flying it seemed to grow louder. It sounded like a huge waterfall far off in the distance.

"What...?" began Aeneas, but he did not finish, for, even as he spoke, Nightfall flew out of the clouds and the young prince could see the surrounding countryside. It was all gray and empty and barren; not a thing of green could be seen.

As he looked ahead of him, he saw Nolhol, standing on the horizon, its black towers and palaces rising into the gray and empty sky. His mouth fell open, for, though the city was yet far away, he could tell the very moment he looked upon it that it was under attack.

"Come on, Nightfall!" he cried. "We have to hurry!"

* * *

Vayan gave a cry as he was thrown to the ground. He scrambled backward and to his feet in a mad attempt not only to escape being struck but also to avoid being trampled. Gripping his sword tightly, he whipped his matted, sweat-soaked hair out of his eyes and faced his opponent.

His enemy was a hulking, giant of a man. One direct blow from his sword would finish Vayan, but Vayan had speed and agility on his side. He took a deep breath, then, with a howl, charged. The man swung with a wide, sweeping blow. Vayan jumped out of the way but was not quick enough to escape unwounded, and the man's sword left a long gash in his arm.

He gave a groan of pain but did not allow himself even a moment of rest. With a growl he lunged once more at his enemy. Their swords clashed together, and Vayan's whole body shook at the impact. He swung once more, only to be blocked again.

The man swung at him, but Vayan leapt back and escaped harm. The man gave a cry of fury and drew back his sword to strike again. With a howl, Vayan drew back his own sword. He could see the man with his teeth bared and his hair flying wildly all around. He could see the sword slicing through the air toward him. With his own teeth bared, he began to spin out of the way. He could still feel the sword slicing toward him. He ducked and continued to turn, holding out his sword to strike. He could feel the sword of the giant man pass over his head, cutting some of his hair. Even as it did so, Vayan's sword connected with the man's leg and dug deep into the skin.

The man gave a cry and sank to the ground. Vayan pulled back his sword and, before the man could move, sent it slamming through his head.

He straightened and looked wildly around. The city was filled with raging fire, and men were battling everywhere. The smell of blood, death, and smoke filled his nostrils. He gasped for breath and his whole body trembled with fatigue.

Suddenly, through the smoke and the crowd of men battling around him, he caught sight of a man with long, wild, auburn hair. For a moment he could simply stare, until he caught a glimpse of spectral blue eyes.

"Orion!" he cried, but his voice was drowned out by the cries of a hundred other men. Orion did not see or hear him and instead disappeared behind a building.

Vayan began to run, as fast as he could, through the battling men toward where he thought Orion disappeared.

"Orion!" he cried again.

* * *

Provenna stood upon an open terrace at the top of a tall tower of her palace. Her green eyes flashed with fury as she looked down upon her golden city filled with fire and bloodshed.

She could feel the strength of hundreds of Magics pressing down upon her-- struggling to hold back the whole might that she, as a Power, wielded, but though they could hold her back a little they could never completely overcome her.

Above her she could see scores of eagles flying over the city, raining arrows down upon her men. She drew back her hand and with a cry flung it upward. She could hear the shrieks of agony and terror as the two nearest eagles were engulfed in flames. Even before they had fallen to the earth another eagle burst into flames, then another, and another.

One by one they fell to the earth, and as each fell Provenna's fury grew. There was no escape. Her wrath was certain. How dare they come and attack her and destroy her beautiful city! Her long, flaming hair danced madly around her as the wind rushed over her. Was she not a Power? Did they not owe her allegiance? She looked down and saw a group of horsemen. She had never wanted to be a Power. She flung her hand out and the horsemen were engulfed in flames. Yet they hated her for something that was beyond her control.

Her face was twisted into a look of utter bitterness. Another eagle fell from the sky. She could hate too.

* * *

Orion swung his huge axe wildly as he struggled desperately to make his way through the sea of men. He was covered with sweat and blood, and his body was filled with pain. He had been battling for hours, yet he could still barely see the palace, and the crowd of battling men grew only thicker with every step he took.

As he struggled to make his way through the streets of Leilaora, he could sometimes see, over the roofs of the buildings, his mother standing atop a palace tower, raining death down upon her enemy. It was as if she stood there taunting him, as he was repeatedly pushed back away from the palace. With each glimpse his anger grew until, finally, when he reached a place where it seemed impossible for him to move forward, he caught sight of her once again, and his anger boiled over.

He gave a howl of fury and frustration and began to swing his axe madly at all who stood in his way. His spectral eyes were wide and filled with the inhuman look of a monster. Like a wild beast he struck at everyone, whether of Provenna's army or Tmalion's.

He gave a cry of pain as the steel blade of a sword bit into his shoulder. He stumbled forward slightly then caught himself. With a growl he turned around and sent his axe slicing down through the head of the nearest soldier. Blood splattered up and struck Orion's already bloody and grime-covered face.

The pain that filled his arm was excruciating. It shot out all the way to his fingertips, and his whole arm throbbed with it. But it only leant him more fury. His face was twisted in a look of both agony and anger as he once more resumed the battle. Provenna would not escape.

* * *

Tnaka stood alone by a window in an empty room of the palace. It was a room high up within a tall tower, and from there none of the death and destruction which took the city was lost to him. All day had he stood there and simply watched as the hours passed and death took firm hold of Leilaora. Fires raged throughout the city, consuming all within their paths, and eagles flew back and forth through the smoke-filled sky. The palace shook with the sound of thousands of men crying out with savage war cries, and far below him he could see the streets filled with blood and battling men.

If Tnaka looked up he could see the tower upon which Provenna stood. It was very near, and it would take him little more than a minute to run there, but he did not do so. He could see the Queen standing there, her hair and dress blowing madly in the wind, and he could picture the look of hatred upon her face as, with hands outstretched, she lashed out in fury at her enemies.

He gave a groan--a sound of agony rising up from the depths of his soul. The cries of the battling men filled his ears, and he shuddered beneath it. He swayed slightly and leaned against the wall for support. He squeezed his eyes shut, but he could still see the fire and smoke rising into the sky and the blood-filled streets.

His legs grew weak beneath him, and he clutched at his chest. With another groan he sank to his knees.

When would it end?

The Battle

* * *

Constantia rode upon a huge eagle over the city of Nolhol. Black smoke rose from the dark city into the gray sky. The streets were filled with battling soldiers, and the city shook with the cries of men and the clash of arms. The tall dark buildings and towers of Nolhol rose into the sky. The sorceress could see her father's palace, and she could see the Temple of Balor standing against the sky with the raging, gray sea behind it.

The cold wind bit at her face and sent loose strands of hair flying around her. She had long ago thrown her cloak away and was now left with her simple traveling garb. Her sword was buckled at her side, and in her hands she held her staff--the staff of an arch-sorcerer. The dark red ruby in its head glowed brightly as she held it out over the city.

She swooped down and flew low over the streets and buildings, until she caught sight of a large pack of Delovachians driving back those of Tmalion's army. With a cry she held her staff out toward them. There was a blinding flash of light, and the Delovachians fell with groans and screams to the ground, some never to rise again.

She turned her eagle and continued to swoop over the city, searching for more prey.

* * *

Mystia nervously paced back and forth in Kozan's chambers, her long black hair tumbling down over her flowing white dress. She could hear the sounds of battle, so very loud and terrifying, right outside the window. Freedom seemed so very near, but she could not leave the room. When the battle had first begun she had tried to escape, but the door was locked. She had used all of the magic she knew, but Kozan had evidently protected his chambers from the magic of others. Now she was left there, fearing that at any moment Kozan or the Dark Sorcerer would walk through the door and, while freedom was almost within reach, do she dared not think what to her.

All day had she been there as the minutes slowly turned into hours. She had jumped in terror when, through the roar of the battle, there broke the sound of Balor's horn, signifying the midday sacrifice. She had clutched at her stomach and weakly sat down. The sickness, which filled her at that sound, was unlike anything she had ever before felt. Even in the midst of pitched battle, sacrifices were being offered to Balor.

It had been a long time before she had been able to rise and resume her pacing. Occasionally she would cast a quick glance toward the window, but she did not go near and look out for, though she could see very little through it, what she could see filled her with sickness and horror.

She held her hands to her face and gave an involuntary gasp of pain as she pressed against the bruises Kozan had left her with.

She laughed, but there was fear within it.

"Silly fool," she told herself. She had been so sad and frightened that she had forgotten she could heal herself. She held her hand to the bruises and whispered a few foreign words, and almost instantly the bruises were gone.

She continued pacing back and forth across the whole of that dark and dismal room. She had reached the door and had turned around and was almost half way across the room when she suddenly heard a key being placed in the lock of the door. She gave a gasp and spun around. Her black eyes were wide and her heart was racing with terror. She could hear the key turning in the lock. She ran to the table and, grabbing hold of it, continued to look in terror at the door.

A small cry escaped her lips as it was thrown open, and her heart began to beat even quicker as the Dark Sorcerer strode in. He stopped inside the door, looked at her, and said, "Come with me."

Mystia held even tighter to the table and, looking up at him, said nothing.

He began to walk toward her and, holding his hand out to her, again said, "Come with me."

"No," she said with a quivering voice. Her face was white and her whole body was trembling, but there was something in the way she stood that told the Sorcerer he would have to drag her out.

He stopped short in surprise, and, for a moment, simply looked at her in confusion. Suddenly a look of realization crossed his face and said, "You misunderstand me, Princess, I've come to rescue you."

"Get away from me," she said, her voice soft and menacing.

"Mystia," he said, his own voice growing dangerous as he took another step closer, "if you want to live you will come with me now."

"I said get away from me!" she cried as she positioned herself behind the table away from him.

He took another slow step toward her, his arm still held out. "I am not here to take you to Kozan, nor am I here to take you for myself. I have a love, and I am no servant of Kozan's."

"Stay away from me!" Mystia growled her eyes burning with fury.

The Dark Sorcerer's face filled with anger.

"I left Leilaora for you!" he cried. "I put off, once again, my only hope for happiness just to come and rescue you! Now come with me!"

Mystia gave a scream as, with a lightning fast move, he sprang around the table and grabbed her by the arm.

"Let go of me!" she shrieked as she struck him hard across the face with her free hand. Her nails dug into his skin and dragged across his face. The Sorcerer gave a cry of pain, and, even as he did so, Mystia herself cried out in disgust and horror as she felt one of her fingers dig into his eye. He flung her from him, and she gave another scream as she fell hard to the floor.

The Sorcerer swore and turned away from her. His shoulders rose and fell with painful, labored breathing. After a long moment, he turned back to her. He was covering his eye with his hand, but Mystia could see blood running down his check.

He took a deep breath and then began to breathe more evenly. After another moment he took his hand from his eye. He had cast some sort of spell for his eye appeared relatively intact, but it was very red, and the Sorcerer was looking at her so strangely that Mystia wondered whether he could see out of it.

He took another breath, and his anger seemed to leave him.

"Get up," he said, "I want to help you escape."

Slowly the Princess rose, making sure to keep some distance between him and her.

"I am not here to hurt you," he said.

She looked distrustfully at him for a moment before she finally said, "I am not willingly going anywhere with you until you tell me why you want to help me escape."

The Dark Sorcerer was silent for a moment as he considered what he should do.

Finally, he said, "Very well, I see we shall go nowhere unless I tell you." He took another breath. "I am Darus, enemy of Kozan and son of the last true king of Delovachia."

Mystia could only look at him in shock.

* * *

The battle raged all around Gideone. He coughed as smoke filled his nostrils. He was covered with dirt, and sweat and blood streamed down his body. Strands of hair stuck to his face and hung down in front of his eyes. He gasped for breath.

His whole body screamed for rest. All day had he battled. He had not caten since early morning, and he had had but little to drink during the day. He felt as though he would drop from fatigue, but he pressed on, knowing that if he fell he would surely be killed.

Slowly, Tmalion's army was closing in upon Provenna's palace, but the closer they came the greater the opposition grew, until they were barely able to move forward at all.

Gideone saw a man charging at him. With a grunt he raised his sword to defend himself. They crashed together, and the Prince reeled beneath the impact. He shook his head and with a growl ran forward and sent his sword slicing through the air toward his attacker. The man jumped out of the way but was not quick enough to escape unscathed, and he gave a cry as Gideone's sword sliced deep into his arm.

With a growl Gideone sent his sword smashing down once more upon the man. His attacker staggered back and almost fell to the ground, but he caught himself and, raising his sword, ran toward him.

The Prince, his face twisted in anger, drew back his sword. The man was almost upon him. Gideone gave a cry and sent his sword slicing down through the air toward the man's legs. The man tried to parry the blow, but he had not expected Gideone to strike low. He gave a scream as the blade sliced deep into his leg, and he fell to the ground.

Gideone drew back his sword. The man held up his hand to try to ward off the blow. With a cry, the Prince sent the blade arching down through the air. The man screamed in pain as it sliced through his outstretched arm, but his cry was abruptly silenced as the sword sliced through his neck. His head rolled from his body and blood began to pour out onto the ground.

Gideone did not even look at it. He simply stood, bent over slightly, as he struggled desperately to catch his breath. His face was twisted into a look of pain as he fought against the fatigue overtaking him.

He looked up expecting any moment for another soldier to come charging at him, but all of the men who fought around him seemed as weary as he.

Suddenly, he caught sight of a man, very nearby struggling desperately to make his way through the mass of battling soldiers. He wielded a huge axe, and, as Gideone caught sight of his face, his eyes grew wide with surprise, for it was Orion. He tried to cry out, but his mouth was so dry he could not speak, nor would it have mattered, for the thundering cries of men would have drowned out his voice.

All fatigue left him, as he began to run toward the warrior, but, even as he did so, Orion managed to force his way into an open place. He did not stop but instantly began to run as fast as he could, until he disappeared into one of the small, winding side streets.

Gideone shook his hair out of his eyes and started after him, but he was blocked by a whole crowd of men. With a cry, he charged and began to battle his way through.

He would find Orion.

* * *

Nightfall made his way as quickly as he could down the long, twisting stairs that led to the dungeon of Kozan's palace. It had taken fairly half the day for him and Aeneas to be able to enter the palace. When they finally had, they had split up and were now searching desperately for the Princess.

The griffin shook his head and gave a soft hiss of annoyance; his large body could barely fit in the small space between the two walls. His muscles were tensed as he tried to make himself fit in such a small space. Still, he continued downward. Step upon step, turn upon turn, deeper and deeper he went, the smell of blood and death growing stronger the further he went.

The Battle

Suddenly, he found himself at the end, and he walked out into a small, but more open room. Looking around only enough to notice the door leading to the long hallway of cells, he spread out his wings and stretched out the whole of his body.

Even as he did so, he heard a man cry out. His head shot up, and he looked around to find the source of the noise. He gave a hissing croak as he felt the sting of a whip upon his back.

With a snarl, he spun around and found a man, lash in hand, standing behind him. With his body low to the ground, the griffin narrowed his eyes and opened his beak in a snarl. The man's eyes filled with fear and he turned to run, but, even as he did so, Nightfall leapt toward him. The man gave a cry as he was thrown to the ground and crushed beneath the griffin. With one swift swipe of his forepaw, Nightfall finished him.

He could hear the cries of other men, and, spinning around, he could see them running through the corridor of cells. With a hiss he charged toward them.

They screamed out in terror as he barreled down upon them. With a shriek, he crashed into them. He crushed one man beneath him, and opening his mouth he snapped at another. The corridor was narrow, however, and he could move but little. He gave a cry of pain as he felt the blade of a sword dig into his shoulder.

With a hiss he sent his paw smashing into the head of the man who had pierced him. He could feel the bones crack beneath him.

The cries of the prisoners filled his ears as he struggled forward.

The guards ran before him, and he managed to push his way out of the small hallway into the room beyond. He gave a hissing cry of anger and disgust as he found himself in Kozan's large torture chambers.

There were only two guards left. With a snarl, Nightfall charged them. They cried out in terror and ran before him. He fell upon one and broke his back.

With a hiss he spun and walked menacingly toward the one remaining guard. The man stood, pressed against the cold, dark wall and stared in terror at the huge, black griffin. Nightfall's eyes narrowed as he growled, "Release the prisoners."

For a moment, the man could only stand there, still petrified.

"I said release them!" Nightfall snarled.

The man started and ran forward. He quickly found the body of the dead chief jailer, and, taking the keys from him, began to do as the griffin had ordered. Nightfall watched him closely as first the prisoners chained in the torture room were freed, then one by one the cells were opened.

He watched expectantly, each moment hoping to see the Princess emerge from one of them. When she did not, he gave a hiss, shook his head, and began to make his way once more through the cell-lined corridor, out in the room beyond, and up the long, winding stairs into the palace above.

* * *

The sky above Nolhol was filled with eagles and harpies that darted madly back and forth through the smoke rising from the city. Constantia looked wildly around her. She was covered with dirt, sweat, and blood. Her dirty, disheveled hair stuck out madly in all directions.

Her one good eye, opened wide as she saw at least five harpies flying straight toward her. Early in the battle, the Delovachians had realized how great a Magic she was and had been trying desperately ever since to kill her. With a snarling cry of fury she held her staff out toward them. Almost instantly, they were engulfed in flames. She would not let them kill her. She had to find Nirreloyn; Abiel's mother would pay for Stavros' death.

* * *

Aeneas pounded his fist against the wall in fury and frustration. He stood in one of the corridors of Kozan's palace. He had searched every room he came across for Mystia, but he had yet to find her.

He gave a growl of anger and struck the wall once more before turning and beginning the search again. He felt certain that if he found the harem he would find Mystia, but he had never before so much as laid eyes upon his father's palace much less entered it and become acquainted with its halls and rooms.

He opened a door and looked it. It was nothing more than a servant's chambers. He gave a growl of disgust and slammed the door.

"Mystia!" he shouted. "Where are you?"

* * *

"Sit down and let me tell the tale," the Dark Sorcerer said. He could hear the battle raging all around. The glass of the window shivered beneath it.

Slowly, Mystia did as he said. She looked up at him with her black eyes. Her distrust was still evident, but she waited silently for him to begin. The Sorcerer gave a sigh of disgust, for, as he looked upon her, he realized he would have to tell the tale in its entirety for her to believe he was who he claimed.

"I was born in a country far away across the sea," he began. "I have no recollection of my true mother or father. My oldest memory is of the streets and the darkness they held.

"I had no friend, and I had not a penny to my name." He paused. "Fate, however, sometimes smiles on even the most unfortunate people, and, when I was scarcely more than a babe, it became apparent that I held great magic power; 'twas at least as powerful as that of an arch-sorcerer if not more so.

"I knew nothing of how to properly wield it, so I remained simply a child on the streets, unable to raise myself up out of that position.

"When I was nine or ten--I know not exactly how old--my father, Constans,

The Battle

the King of Delovachia, came and waged war against my country. His soldiers swept over the whole land, leaving only blood and death behind them. My country was completely overcome; the king was killed as were most of the nobles, and the few lords who yet lived were forced to pledge themselves to my father.

"He then left, taking with him hundreds of people whom he had captured and made slaves. I was one of those." He was silent for a moment, and then continued. "We traveled across the sea to Delovachia where I was made to serve in the palace. I served well, and I soon became one of my father's most trusted slaves.

"He had no wife and no children. He was distant from almost all, and most considered him proud and selfish. But he was a good and honorable man who ruled firmly but justly, and I would have given my life for him.

"He had many enemies, and, during an assassination attempt, I saved his life. It was more accident than intention, for it was by my magic that I saved him. As a result my father learned of the great power I held. He made me his son and heir and had the greatest teachers of magic come and instruct me in the use of my power." He paused again, as a look of quiet sadness filled his face. "I became great; I was so young and yet my magic was so strong. With such strength, I could bring greatness to Delovachia such as it had never before possessed." A look of pain filled his face. "But, it was not meant to be. When I was twelve or thirteen it was all taken from me. How I know not. I was taken with a fever and almost died. When I finally grew well, all of my power was gone." He struggled to speak. "It seems impossible; there is not one record of anything like that happening ever before, but it happened to me. My magic left me, and I was left weaker than even the weakest warlock."

* * *

Kozan rode upon a huge, black charger, and looked down in anger and spite upon those who battled around him. Soldiers lashed out at him, trying to cut him down, but how could they kill him--a Power? He struck them down with his magic before they even touched him.

All around him the city burned, and, above it, the sky was filled with dark, foreboding clouds. Occasionally, he could hear the soft rumbling of thunder-- sign that a storm would break. What did he care? Let it burn; let it storm. His army was slowly emerging triumphant. At the end of the day, Nolhol would still stand, and his enemies would be destroyed.

The evening approached quickly and with it the time for the evening sacrifice. The dark king made his way through the streets of Nolhol toward his dark, towering palace. All day had he waited, but he could wait no longer. Balor's altar screamed for blood, and Balor's Law demanded the death of all High Elves. Mystia would be sacrificed.

* * *

Mystia looked up at the Dark Sorcerer as he continued his tale.

"My father loved me, and he did not throw me out because I no longer possessed magic strength," the Sorcerer said. "I redoubled my studies in the subjects other than magic, but, when I came of age, I left Nolhol and, with my father's blessing, went out into Lairannare in search of some way to regain my lost power.

"For six years I searched, but I found no answers. I had traveled the length and breath of Lairannare and finally concluded that there was no hope. I was making my way back to Delovachia when I met a people. They were a race I had never seen before--a race that existed only as villains in all the stories and all the histories stretching down from the beginning of time: the Shallee.

"They took me into their midst. They showed me things I had never dreamed existed and taught me how to use magic again. For one year I resided among them, my magic growing ever stronger. I had yet to grow as powerful as I once had been, but I hoped that in time I would reach that point."

His eyes had been sparkling, but suddenly his whole face filled with anger and his voice began to quiver. "I left them and returned to Delovachia, but when I did I found my country subjected and my father murdered by Kozan." He covered his face with his hand and tried to speak, but the words would not come.

"I joined his army," he continued quickly, trying to force from his head all that Kozan had done. "I hoped that I would be able to destroy him from the inside. I was a good soldier and an able leader, and I rose quickly through the ranks.

"I was made the High General of all his army, and I worked even harder toward increasing my magic power and my standing with the people so that when the time was right I would be able to kill him and take his place with as little rebellion as possible."

He paused for a moment then said, "So, you see? I am no friend of Kozan, and I wish to help you because you are of the Shallee, the people who helped me regain my magic. Now, will you please come with me?"

Mystia's black eyes were filled with tears as she looked at him.

"You killed my father and destroyed my country," she said, her voice quivering.

She gave a deep sigh and, with a look of resignation, said softly, "But you are the only one here who can help me, so I suppose I must go with you."

She rose and, with her face turned to the floor said, "I hope you will not grow angry with me if I am unable to thank you for what you do."

"No, Your Highness," the Sorcerer said gently. He reached out and touched her arm. "Now, please, let's leave."

She gave a nod of her head, and they walked from the room.

The Battle

* * *

Provenna gave a snarling cry and sent yet another blast of fire down upon her enemies. For a moment afterwards, she simply stood there gasping for breath. Her hair fell disheveled around her, her body was covered with sweat, and her face was filled with pain and fatigue. Her head throbbed with pain as hundreds of Magics pressed down upon her with their power.

She saw an eagle flying toward her. With her face twisted into a look of anger and agony, she drew back her hand and unleashed another fiery blast of magic. She looked wildly all around her. Where was Tnaka?

"Tnaka!" she cried with all her might. "Tnaka!" But there was no answer. With a growl she continued battling.

* * *

Gideone gave a grunt and hauled himself up to the top of a wall at the end of an alley and for a moment simply lay on his stomach. With a sigh he rolled over it and landed upon his feet on the other side. He took a deep breath then started jogging slowly down the alley on the other side. He could not see Orion but he knew that he had disappeared around the next corner.

He could still hear the cries of battle, very close, but Orion had led him into the dark, twisting alleys and back streets of Leilaora--streets that were too narrow for fighting. But, though Gideone no longer had to battle, he was still exhausted and out of breath. Leilaora's back streets were so very twisting and maze-like, what with being filled with walls and a score of wrong-turns, that Orion had led him on a very merry chase indeed. More than a couple of times Gideone had lost track of the blue-eyed warrior, and it was only through luck that he found him again.

Orion was slowly making his way to the palace. The streets led him on a very roundabout path, but even going indirectly it was quicker than trying to battle through soldiers.

The buildings around Gideone were too high for him to see anything save a small bit of sky right above him, but he knew that the palace was very close. Perhaps soon he would be able to catch up to Orion.

* * *

The Dark Sorcerer walked so quickly through the corridors of the palace that Mystia was fairly out of breath just trying to keep up with him. The halls were almost completely empty, though occasionally they would pass a terrified slave. The sounds of war were muffled by the many rooms and thick stone walls which separated the Sorcerer and the Princess from the outside of the palace, but they could still be heard, and they seemed to lend speed to the steps of the two.

The Sorcerer led Mystia through a door, and they found themselves on the balcony, which overlooked the banquet hall. Quickly they walked along its length to the stone steps leading down to the hall. The only sound in that large empty room was that of their feet striking the floor.

They quickly reached the bottom and began to make their way through the tables to the main doors of the hall. Mystia gave a gasp as she suddenly noticed King Rolfaren lying unconscious at one of the tables--a pitcher of wine beside him and an overturned goblet before him. The Sorcerer seemed not to even notice, but stalked past him to the doors. He threw them open and disappeared behind them. Mystia cast one last look back at Rolfaren before she also walked through the doors.

* * *

Constantia gave a cry and ducked as a harpy sped over her head. Some of her hair was caught in the harpy's fingers, and she gave another cry as it was torn from her head.

The harpy gave a shriek and, turning around, sped back toward her. With a growl, Constantia sent her staff smashing, like a club, into the face of the harpy. The harpy gave a scream as lightning suddenly encircled her body.

Constantia pulled back her staff and the harpy began to fall to the ground. She tried desperately to catch herself, but the lightning had so stunned her that she was unable to. With a shriek she continued to plummet to the ground until she smashed into the top of a tall, black building. Her arm was crushed beneath her body, and her scream was suddenly cut short as her head smashed into the ground, sending blood and bits of bone splattering everywhere.

With a growl, the sorceress turned once more to the sky around her. She could see two more harpies flying toward her. With a cry she flung her staff out, sending a huge ball of fire speeding toward them.

Even as she did so, she heard a shriek of rage behind her. The wind rushed over her as her eagle sped through the air. She turned her body to look behind her, and her eyes widened as she saw another harpy speeding after her.

Her huge black wings beat with steady strokes, bringing her slowly closer to Constantia. Her long dark hair streamed out behind her, and her face was twisted into a look of utter rage. It was Nirrelyon.

With a cry, Constantia turned her eagle and sped toward her. And with a snarl, she sent a bolt of fire hurtling toward the queen. The harpy dodged it and continued speeding forward.

With a terrible cry she crashed into Constantia. The sorceress gave a cry as her staff flew from her hand and she was almost thrown from her eagle. Nirrelyon held onto Constantia, and the two of them clawed and struck each other atop the eagle.

The eagle gave a croaking cry as he struggled to fly properly, but with the two

The Battle

women battling on his back he was unable to. Slowly, he began spinning downward. Constantia's face twisted in pain as Nirrelyon dug her claws into her back. With a growl, she grabbed the harpy's neck and sent magic coursing into her. Nirrelyon gave a scream of pain, and Constantia was able to push her away.

The eagle managed to regain his flight. He was flying low over the buildings, and the air was filled with smoke and fire. Arrows filled the sky, and the cries of the soldiers shook the ground. Kozan's palace loomed dark and terrible before the eagle, and the closer he neared it the more furious the battled seemed to be.

Constantia threw out her hand and hurled a fireball at Nirrelyon. The harpy screamed as it struck her in the stomach, but instead of bursting into flames she simply tumbled backward through the sky.

They were almost directly over the palace now. With a snarl Nirrelyon righted herself and sped once more toward Constantia. Constantia howled as the force of the impact sent her flying from her eagle. Clawing at the air in a desperate attempt to stop her fall, she went plummeting toward the palace below. Nirrelyon sped after her and, with a clawed hand, struck her hard across the face. Constantia gave a groan, which suddenly turned into a cry as her body smashed into the stone roof of Kozan's palace. Her arm was crushed beneath her chest, and she felt as if every bone in her body was broken.

She gave a strangled cry as Nirrelyon kicked her hard in the side. Grimacing, he tried to strike the harpy with magic, but before she could Nirrelyon struck her again.

"Monster!" Constantia managed to growl before the harpy kicked her once again.

"Fool!" Nirrelyon spat, a sneer upon her face.

* * *

Kozan ran through the halls of his palace. His clothes were torn and dirty and his face was covered with dirt and blood. His hair fell in a disheveled mess around his face, and, with a growl of anger, he brushed it away, only for it to fall once more before his eyes.

The cries of war filled his ears but he paid them no head. He had to get Mystia.

* * *

"Where is she?" Aeneas cried as he struck the wall in frustration. He had found the harem, only to then remember that Mystia was a High Elf and would therefore never be loved by his father. He had checked to make sure, and, just as he had expected, she was not there.

With a growl of anger he turned and began to run back to the main entrance of the palace where he and Nightfall had agreed to meet. Hopefully, the griffin had been more successful then had he.

* * *

Constantia struggled to her knees, and looked up at Nirrelyon. Her face was filled with anger as, fighting against her pain and weakness, she struck the harpy with all the magic she could muster. For a moment Nirrelyon's eyes grew wide, and she clutched at her chest as she leaned forward in pain. But, after a moment, she shook her head and stood straight, a look of scorn upon her face. "You always were a weak, pitiful little fool, Deifilia," she spat. With one quick motion she drew back her hand and struck Constantia hard across the face. She gave a groan and fell back to the ground. Nirrelyon kicked her, and Constantia gave a gasp of surprise and fear as she rolled over and found herself looking down over the edge of the roof at the palace courtyard far below.

* * *

The Dark Sorcerer and Mystia walked quickly down a long hallway open on one side. The roof overhead was supported by a stone colonnade which ran the length of the hallway and was built atop the low, wide balustrade which kept people from falling into the courtyard far below.

Mystia started, as there came a crash of thunder. The clouds, which all day had threatened to storm, had finally broken and had begun to send rain down upon the city. It was not a heavy rain, however, and did little to interfere with the battle. The cries of war and the screams of pain, now not blocked by the walls of the palace, filled Mystia's ears.

* * *

With a snarl, Constantia rolled away from the edge of the roof. Nirrelyon kicked her again, trying to force her back, but Constantia did not move. "I'm no' that easy t' kill," she growled. Then, with a furious cry, she hurled a huge blast of magic at Nirrelyon.

* * *

Mystia paused for a second to try to catch her breath then quickly ran after the Sorcerer. They had almost reached the other side of the arcade. She shivered as the rain fell and struck her.

Suddenly above the sounds of battle, a scream of pain and fury broke. Both Mystia and the Sorcerer stopped and looked around, startled, for the cry had been very close.

"There!" Mystia pointed as, looking out, she saw two figures lying upon the roof before and adjacent to them. One of the figures struggled to her feet; it was a harpy, and as the Sorcerer and Mystia looked closer, they could see it was Queen Nirrelyon. With a snarl she whipped her hair out of her face and turned to the woman who still lay upon the ground. She ran forward and kicked the fallen woman hard in the side, sending her rolling dangerously close to the edge of the roof. With a cry, the woman flung out her arm and with a huge blast of magic fire sent Nirrelyon flying back.

For one moment the fallen woman's face was turned to Mystia and the Sorcerer as she looked down at the courtyard far below her, but it took only that one moment for the Sorcerer's eyes to grow wide with recognition.

Casting a quick glance at Mystia, he said, "I'll be back." Then he ran forward to the end of the arcade, jumped up onto the balustrade, and started to struggle up to where the two women battled.

* * *

"Your son murdered my husband!" Constantia cried as she sent another blast of fire at Nirrelyon. The harpy staggered back then caught herself and lunged forward.

"You slaughtered my harpy kindred!" she screamed sending her own blast of magic toward Constantia.

The sorceress screamed in pain as she was struck, but, twisting her face into a grimace of determination, she lashed out once more with magic at Nirrelyon.

Pain shot through her body and threatened to overcome her, but she fought it and struggled with all her might to rise to her knees. The rain fell down upon her, and she could see her blood flowing all around her. Her hair, wet with the rain, hung down in front of her eyes, and she was too weak to brush it away.

Looking up, she could see Nirrelyon charging toward her.

"Stavros!" she screamed as she struck the harpy with every last bit of magic within her. Nirrelyon gave a scream of pain and went flying backward. She struck the roof and lay still. Constantia weakly looked at her, a look upon her face that was both a wince of pain and smile of victory.

Suddenly, Nirrelyon began to stir. She struggled to her knees and, with a look of utter hatred upon her face, began to crawl toward Constantia.

Constantia could do nothing. She gave a soft laugh and murmured, "I almost won," then fell forward, unconscious.

For a moment, Nirrelyon continued to struggle forward, her right wing dragging broken and useless behind her, but even as she reached out to strike Constantia, her pain overcame her, and she also fell forward unconscious.

* * *

Mystia stood at the edge of the arcade and stared up as the Dark Sorcerer made his way across the roof to the two fallen women.

"Hurry," she murmured as she cast a quick glance around her.

The Sorcerer looked down upon Nirrelyon's unconscious form. She lay very near Constantia and only a little way from the edge of the roof. With one swift motion he picked her up and threw her down to the courtyard below.

He made his way over to where Constantia lay upon her stomach. One arm was broken and twisted in the most gruesome of manners, and he knew not how many other bones were broken. She was sorely wounded, and it would take several minutes to heal her.

As he touched her she gave a soft groan and stirred.

"Deifilia?" he said softly.

She turned her head and looked up at him. She could barely see him because of the patch over her eye, but still she recognized him.

"Darus?" she murmured.

"Yes, Stantia," he said. "Just lie still. I need to heal you."

* * *

Mystia looked up at the Sorcerer as he knelt beside the fallen woman. He was evidently healing her. She bit her lip and tried to calm her racing heart.

"Please, hurry," she pleaded softly.

Suddenly, she heard footsteps pounding against the stone floor of the arcade, and, looking up, she saw Kozan running toward her. Her face turned completely white and for a moment she could do nothing save stand there and look in terror at him as he drew near.

"How did you get here?" he demanded as he grabbed her by the arm.

"Let go of me!" she screamed as she tried to run away.

With a growl he pulled her tighter and began to drag her after him.

"Let go of me!" she shrieked. His fingers dug into her skin, and he held her close against his body. She struggled against him with all her might, and, giving a huge cry, managed to wrench one of her arms free. With a snarl she sent her fingernails slashing against his face. He gave a cry of pain and let go of her. She twisted away from him and began to run as fast as she could down the arcade.

"Sorcerer!" she screamed.

Kozan gave a snarl of fury, as he spun toward her. She screamed in pain and fell to the ground as she was struck with a blast of magic. She struggled to rise, but she could barely move her head.

She heard Kozan run toward her.

"Let go of me," she sobbed, as, with a growl, he picked her up. Ignoring her, he flung her over his shoulder and began to walk from the arcade.

The Battle

* * *

Sweat poured down Gideone's body as he ran down a long, narrow street. He cursed silently. He had lost sight of Orion and had not been able to find him again. He had continued on in the direction of the palace, but that would do little good if he were unable to find Orion.

His lungs screamed for air, but he continued on through the twisting streets of Leilaora, barely noticing where he was, simply running in the direction of the palace. He knew he was close, but he knew not how close until, all of a sudden, he burst from out of the streets and nearly ran into a tall, white stone wall. He gave a cry of surprise and jumped back. Looking up, he realized that it was the wall of the palace.

He paused for a moment as he leaned against it and tried to catch his breath. As he did so, he looked around, trying to figure out exactly where he was. He was somewhere behind the palace, obviously at a place that was very difficult to get to. There was only the narrowest of passages between the palace wall and the surrounding buildings.

Taking one last deep breath he began to make his way along the outside of the wall. It was not a straight wall but filled with curves and angles, for, over the hundreds of years in which the city had existed, many of the rulers had increased the palace grounds, forcing them outward into whatever space was available.

Gideone was careful as he made his way along the twists and turns, but even he was not prepared when suddenly he stepped out into a small but open courtyard. In the wall there was a small iron gate, in front of which two guards stood.

They gave a cry and ran toward him, but even as they did so Gideone drew his sword and stepped back into a fighting stance. The guards drew up short and for a moment simply stood there, swords drawn, regarding the Prince. All three of them stood still, each staring at the other, none wishing to be the first to strike.

Suddenly, a huge cry broke the silence. The guards started, and Gideone, taking that moment, lunged. The guard he struck at managed to raise his sword and ward off the blow, but he was off balance and stumbled backward. Gideone raised his sword to deal the final blow, but, before he could, the second guard struck him. The Prince reeled back, but, with a cry, caught himself and charged forward. He crashed into the guard sending him sprawling to the ground, then, with another howl, sent his sword slicing through his head.

He spun to face the other guard, but when he did so he saw that he already lay dead. Looking up, he saw Vayan, gasping for breath, standing there with a bloody sword in hand.

"What are you doing here?" Gideone cried in surprise.

"Lookin' f'r Orion," Vayan answered between breaths.

"So am I," said Gideone, but even as he spoke Vayan was running toward the gate, saying as he did so, "I think he went in here."

Gideone quickly looked down at the belts of the two guards. "They don't have any keys."

"And the gate's sealed with magic," Vayan said after a moment.

"Then we'll have to climb it," Gideone said as he ran over to it. He grabbed hold of the metal bars and began to struggle to the top of the gate.

Vayan paused for a minute as he looked up a Gideone. His face clouded, and he bit his lower lip. Then, shaking his head, he gave a small rather sad smile and, grabbing hold of the bars said, "Aye, we'll have t' climb it."

* * *

Tmalion leaned low in the saddle as he sped through the air on his eagle. The wind rushed over him, and the cries of the battling men filled his ears, lending him strength and fury. The setting sun shone out across the whole of Leilaora, bathing the city in golden light.

Tmalion could see Provenna standing atop the tall palace tower. Her hands were lifted above her head, and her hair and her dress blew madly in the wind. Her face was twisted in a look of hatred and her mouth was open in a cry of fury as she rained death and destruction down upon Tmalion's men.

Tmalion's eyes narrowed as he looked upon her. Throughout the whole of the day not one person had been able to get near her, but he would; he had too. If the battle was to be won, Provenna had to die.

With a growl, he spurred his eagle on. He raced over the golden buildings of Leilaora. The cries and screams of battle were lost in the rushing of the wind.

Suddenly, Provenna's head turned and her gaze fell upon him. She opened her mouth in a cry of fury and stretched her hand out toward him.

Tmalion gave a gasp of pain, and he suddenly felt as though his whole chest were on fire. He squeezed his eyes shut, and his face twisted in agony as he clutched at his chest and struggled against the spell Provenna had cast. He could feel the fire spreading out from his chest to the rest of his body, and with a growl he struggled even harder.

He opened his eyes enough to see that he was quickly approaching Provenna.

Sweat was pouring down his face, and his whole body was trembling. Slowly, he began forcing back the fire in his chest.

He was drawing even closer to Provenna. Soon he would have to jump. His fingers dug into his chest, and he gave a huge cry as he struggled with all his might against Provenna's spell. Suddenly, it weakened then caved beneath him.

Tmalion gasped for breath, but he had no time to regain his strength. He was almost upon Provenna. He slowed his eagle, and, standing up as much as he dared, prepared to jump. The tower was just a little in front of him. With a huge cry he leapt into the air. Still howling, he sailed forward and landed hard on the top of the tower. His cry was cut short as the wind was knocked out of him, and he went rolling across the stone floor.

Struggling to breath, he scrambled to his feet. Pain shot through his leg as he did so, but he forced himself to rise. He drew his sword and faced Provenna. She stood a short distance away and for a moment regarded him silently, a mixture of fear and hatred on her face.

The king took a faltering step toward her, his sword shining in the light of the sun. Provenna gave a cry of fury and, with magic, knocked him to his knees.

* * *

Tnaka knelt beside the window in the same empty room he had been in all day. His head was bowed and his face was twisted in a look of anguish. He knew not what to do or what to think. He simply knelt there, unmoving.

With a sad smile, he turned his gaze once more to what lay beyond the window. The battle still continued and the blood still flowed through the streets. His gaze traveled slowly upward until it came to rest upon where Provenna battled.

When it did, Tnaka started and jumped to his feet. Provenna stood upon the tower, but another figure was also there. It was a soldier, with long, almost white hair whipping in the wind. He knelt before Provenna, but, as Tnaka watched, the soldier slowly struggled to his feet. He took a few steps toward Provenna until he was knocked once more to his knees. He struggled to rise and, his sword held up, continued toward the Queen.

Tnaka stood silent, not knowing what to do. He hated the war and the evil Provenna had brought about, but she was the Greater Power; he could not simply let her die. For one moment more he stood looking at the soldier and the Queen, then he turned and ran from the room.

* * *

Tmalion struggled forward and, with a cry, struck Provenna with his magic. She reeled back and for a moment could only stare at him in shock and fury.

"How dare you!" she snarled as she struck him with a huge blast of magic. He gave a grimace of pain and fell to his knees, only to struggle once more to his feet and continue toward her.

"I will kill you!" he cried. "I swear it!"

Provenna gave a scream of fury and threw her hands out toward him. He gave a cry of pain as he went flying backward and struck the ground hard. His head hit the hard stone of the tower and for a moment he lay there stunned.

He gave a cry of pain as Provenna struck him again. Fighting against the agony, he struggled to his feet and looked at her. His face was twisted into a look of pain and determination. With a growl, he took a slow step forward, then another one, and another. He felt Provenna's magic weaken, and he continued forward.

Provenna's face was filled with fear, but still she battled.

Tmalion continued slowly forward. Provenna struck him with all the magic she could muster, but he forced himself to go on. He could feel her weakening even more. He raised his sword and took another step. He felt her falter, then suddenly she lost her hold on him. He gave a howl and rushed forward. Provenna screamed and raised her arm in a desperate attempt to ward off his blow.

Tmalion began to send his sword crashing down on her, but, even as he did so, he was suddenly struck with a huge blast of magic. He flew backward and smashed into the stone barrier at the edge of the tower. He fell to the ground and lay still.

Giving a groan of pain, he looked weakly up and saw Tnaka standing beside Provenna. Suddenly, anger filled him such as he had never felt before. With a growl, he struggled to his feet. Pain shot through his leg, but he forced it back.

"Hello, son," he spat as he raised his sword and prepared to battle.

* * *

Eagle ran into the palace armory. The battle was drawing near and soon, she feared, the soldiers would storm the palace. There were few weapons left, but, when she reached the place where the swords were supposed to be, she found one remaining. She paused for a moment, breathing quickly with excitement, then reached out and grasped the hilt.

She held the sword up and looked at it for a moment. Its steel blade shone in the orange light of the torches lighting the armory. The sword was obviously too small and light for any soldier to use, but it was almost perfect for her. She took a few simple practice swings, then her confidence growing, flipped it around expertly and pretended she was battling an opponent.

Suddenly, she heard footsteps echoing in the corridor outside the armory. She turned and ran to the door and, looking out, caught sight of the powerful form and wild, auburn hair of Orion. He ran down the corridor and disappeared around a corner.

For a moment Eagle stood and stared after him. Then, taking a breath, she set off down the corridor after him.

* * *

"Kill him," growled Provenna who then turned and walked from the top of the tower.

Tnaka stood, sword in hand, and stared at Tmalion.

"You heard the woman," Tmalion sneered. "Kill me!" With that, he gave a howl and charged at Tnaka. Tnaka raised his sword to defend himself as

The Battle

Tmalion crashed into him. The elven Power stepped back then struck Tmalion hard. Tmalion reeled back, stumbled, and gave a sharp cry of pain. It was obvious that his leg was severely wounded.

"Tmalion, stop this," Tnaka cried. "I don't want to hurt you!"

"No," Tmalion spat, "you only want to subject my kingdom and ravish my daughter!" He lunged forward, and Tnaka stepped out of the way. Tmalion fell to the ground, clutching at his leg.

Tnaka opened his mouth to say something, but his words caught in his throat. There was nothing he could say save hypocritical words of apology or excuse. So, with his sword arm hanging at his side, he simply stood and looked down at Tmalion.

With a growl, Tmalion rose to his feet, and, with a speed that caught Tnaka off-guard, lunged forward once again. Tnaka tried to jump out of the way, but he was not quick enough, and Tmalion's blade went slicing across his check.

Tnaka held up his sword as Tmalion sent his blade crashing down on him again and again. The elven Power struggled to defend himself, not wanting to run, yet unwilling to strike. Tmalion gave a huge howl and struck such a blow that Tnaka went reeling back. He fell to the ground and for a moment could only look in surprise up at Tmalion.

With a scornful laugh, Tmalion charged toward him.

* * *

Provenna stood in the corridor outside the tower. Her whole body trembled with rage. How dare Tmalion try to kill her! He and his whole army would pay for what they had done; she swore it! She leaned against the wall and closed her eyes. Her body screamed for rest.

Suddenly, she heard the sound of feet pounding against the stone floor. She looked up and saw Orion running toward her.

"Orion!" she cried, "Where have you..." but her voice trailed off as he drew close and she saw the look in his eyes--a look of absolute hatred. Her face grew completely white, and her mouth fell open. A cry escaped her lips. Then, turning, she ran as quickly as she could down the corridor.

* * *

Tnaka rolled out of the way of Tmalion's sword and scrambled to his feet. He faced the enraged king and did nothing.

Tmalion gave a groan and fell to his knees, clutching at his leg.

"I will kill you!" he cried. Tnaka still did nothing.

Tmalion struggled once again to his feet.

"Please, listen to me," Tnaka pleaded. "I never wanted to do you any harm. I never meant to do Eagle any harm. I never wanted to do any harm to anyone."

"'Tis too late for apologies," Tmalion growled as he took a painful step forward. "The time for vengeance is here!"

Tnaka started as a scream suddenly rang out from nearby within the palace. He cast a quick glance at where Provenna had disappeared; it must have been her.

He looked back at Tmalion. The king was still struggling forward.

"Please stop," Tnaka pleaded.

Tmalion gave another growl and continued walking forward.

Tnaka cast another quick glance at the door of the tower. He knew not what was happening, but he knew Provenna was in danger.

"I have no time for this," he said.

"Then make time." Tmalion said, his face twisted in pain and fury, as he continued forward.

The elven Power suddenly stretched out his hand and struck Tmalion with a blast of magic. Tmalion gave a cry then fell unconscious to the ground.

Tnaka turned and ran from the tower. He flew down the twisting stairs, until he reached the first door. He ran out into the corridor beyond and looked wildly around for Provenna. She was nowhere to be seen, but he could hear the sound of feet striking the floor, and as he looked down the corridor he could see Orion disappearing around a corner.

He gave a cry as he realized what was happening.

The elf took off with all his might down the corridor after him. Orion had to be stopped; he had to be killed. If he killed Provenna the whole of Lairannare would hail him as a great hero. They would set him up as a king, and he would end up bringing war and death ten time worse than that which Provenna brought.

Tnaka skidded around the corner and continued running as fast as he could. He could see Orion before him.

"Orion!" he cried, in a desperate attempt to stop the blue-eyed warrior, but Orion continued on as if he had not heard.

"Orion!" Tnaka cried again.

Holding his sword in one hand, he continued running as fast as his legs would carry him. He began to gasp for breath, and sweat started forming on his brow.

Suddenly, a figure stepped out from one of the side passages and barred his path. Tnaka skidded to a halt and looked at who blocked his way. It was Eagle. She stood, sword in hand and jaw set firm.

"Get out of the way!" he cried desperately as he saw Orion disappear around another corner.

Her voice was steady and her face was filled with determination as she said, "Tnaka, leave him alone."

* * *

Aeneas paced back and forth near the main entrance of the palace. Every so often, he would cast a quick glance up in hopes of catching sight of Nightfall. The sounds of battle rang in his ears. They were so loud it seemed the battle was being raged right outside the doors.

Aeneas reached one end of the huge, intricately carved set of doors then spun around and walked back the other way.

"Where is he?" he muttered.

He reached the other end of the doors and immediately turned and started back. He had almost reached the other side when, behind him, he heard a soft thumping. He spun around and found himself looking at Nightfall who was galloping up the corridor toward him.

"Did you find her?" the young prince cried, but, even as he did so, he saw that Mystia was not with the griffin.

Nightfall screeched to a halt, and for a moment the two simply looked at each other.

"Now what do we do?" Aeneas finally demanded.

"Calm thyself," the griffin said. He cocked his head to one side. "We have to think. She is not in the dungeon..."

"Or the harem..."

"Or anywhere in between, as near as we can tell. So, she is either dead or held somewhere that we have yet to find."

"This is hopeless," Aeneas moaned, slumping against the wall.

"Nay, 'tis not hopeless. We simply have to think harder."

"And what good will thinking do?" Aeneas demanded. "You yourself said she's not in the dungeon. She has to be dead then; where else would my father keep a High Elf?" He stopped suddenly, and he and Nightfall looked at each other.

"The Temple!" they cried together.

* * *

Mystia struggled against Kozan as he dragged her through the dark corridors of Balor's Temple. Tears were streaming down her face, and her whole body was trembling. With a cry, she managed to yank one of her arms free. Kozan gave a growl and grasped for it. His fingers got entangled in her long, black hair, and she gave a sharp cry as he pulled her head back.

"Let go of me," she sobbed.

He said not a word, but continued to drag her through the twisting hallways. The sounds of the battle filled the place, echoing off the cold, stone walls. Their way was lit with the evil, orange glow of torches lining the passageways.

Mystia gave a choked sob of fear as, suddenly, they emerged from a corridor into the vast sanctuary of the Temple. The huge pyramid of steps towered over her. A strangled cry escaped her lips as Kozan began to drag her up toward the altar.

"Let go of me!" she screamed as she fought against him. His fingers dug into her flesh as he pulled her roughly after him. Her legs scraped against the stone steps as she struggled with all her might to twist away. With a cry, she pulled as hard as she could. Kozan gave a cry as he tottered back. His grip loosened, and Mystia screamed as, no longer held up by him, she tumbled to the ground and began to roll down the steps.

She managed to catch herself and scrambled to her feet. Out of the corner of her eye she saw Kozan struggling to rise. Gasping in fear she began to run down the steps.

With a snarl, Kozan sprang toward her. The Princess screamed as he suddenly caught her wrist. She lost her footing and fell forward. For a moment, it seemed she would drag Kozan with her, but, with a cry, he yanked her to him with all his might. Clutching her tightly he sprang up the steps. Mystia sobbed in terror and tried to grab onto the steps in a desperate attempt to hold herself back.

In a moment they reached the top. With a growl, Kozan threw her onto the altar. King Ibrahim's staff was knocked from the foot of the altar and went tumbling to the ground. Mystia screamed and tried to scramble away, but Kozan held her fast. He chained one hand, then the other. She kicked at him as he tried to chain her legs. He grabbed her bare ankle, and she gave a cry of pain as he twisted her leg hard and chained it also. She kicked at him one last desperate time with her free leg, but that too he took and chained.

For a moment, he stood, breathing heavily, looking down upon her. She looked up at him with tears streaming down her face and her black eyes filled with fear.

"Kozan, please," she sobbed, "stop. Let me go."

She pulled against the chains. Her whole body was shaking, and her breasts rose and fell with great, sobbing breaths. Her long, raven locks fell all around her, and a sleeve of her white dress had fallen off her shoulder. Her dress, torn and disheveled from her struggles, was twisted up around her knees, revealing her long, shapely, legs.

"Please," she begged, "let me go."

"No," he murmured as he looked down upon her.

He shut his eyes and turned away. His voice rose. "No, you must be sacrificed."

* * *

"What are you doing?" Tnaka cried in horror as he looked down upon his wife.

"Defending Orion," she answered, her gray eyes flashing.

Tnaka tried to step past her, but she held her sword up and blocked his path. "If you want to kill Orion, you have to kill me first."

He stepped back and looked at her. "Eagle, please..." There was desperation in his voice.

"Leave him alone."

He stepped forward and struck her sword hard with his own, trying to knock it from her hands. She blocked him and held fast.

"I do not want to fight you," she said, her voice trembling, "but if I have to I will."

He struck her sword again. "You know not what you're doing."

"I know exactly what I do!" she cried as she lunged at him, forcing him to jump back. "You yourself said he's the son of Phyre! How can you even think of killing him when you know what death will do to him?"

Tnaka struck at her. "If he kills Provenna, Lairannare is doomed!"

"And I suppose the good of the many outweighs the good of the one? The one who only lives because of Provenna." She swung at him, forcing him further back. "The one who Provenna chased after when he ran from evil. The one Provenna turned back from the righteous path he chose." She struck at him again. Her eyes were filled with tears. "Now you want to kill him?! 'Twas Provenna who made him what he is! Kill her, and perhaps you can turn him back."

"No!" Tnaka cried as he lunged toward her. "His father is Phyre. Back to what? He's evil!"

He tried to run forward, but as he did so Eagle sent her sword slicing through the air toward him. He gave a cry of surprise as he was struck across the chin. He jumped back and for a moment could only stare at her in horror as he held his hand to his chin. He could feel the blood pouring from it, and he could feel poison entering his body. The poison he banished with a wordless, motionless spell, but his horror remained.

Eagle's voice trembled, but her face was filled with determination. "I said leave him alone."

* * *

Provenna ran through the corridors of the palace, her slippered feet making but a faint tapping sound against the stone floor. Her breath came in short, quick gasps, and she cast terrified glances behind her. She had managed to evade Orion, but with every step she expected him to suddenly leap out from behind a corner and slay her.

She rounded a corner and found herself in the corridor that ran before the throne room. She leapt toward the great oaken doors. Her whole body was trembling as she opened them. She ran through, then turned around and pulled them shut as softly as possible. She winced when she was not able to entirely keep them from booming shut.

For a moment, she stood there, gasping for breath, her back pressed against the doors. She was trembling, and her brow was covered with sweat.

For a full minute she simply stood like that, but, finally, taking a deep breath she looked around. The room was entirely empty, save for her. The smooth stones of the floor spread out unbroken until they met the walls. The stained-glass warriors and kings looked down from where they hung upon the walls.

The beating of her heart began to slow, and she began to breath more easily. Was this not her palace and her throne room? Was she not a Power? What had she to fear? She walked across the floor and made her way toward her crystal throne.

She was just mounting the dais when she suddenly heard something pound against the great doors behind her. She spun around. Even as she did so, the doors were thrown open, and a sharp cry escaped her lips as Orion ran into the room. His clothes were torn, and his body was covered with dirt and blood-- both his and that of others. In his hands he bore a huge battle-axe. His auburn hair fell wildly around his face, and he looked up at her with cold, blue eyes filled with murder.

His lips turned up in a sneer as he took a step toward her.

* * *

Aeneas crouched low upon Nightfall's back as they sped across the city. The rain had stopped, and now the sky was simply filled with mist. Every now and then a low rumble of distant thunder would pierce the cries of war.

Before him, Aeneas could see the huge Temple of Balor rising ominously into the gray sky. With each beat of Nightfall's wings they drew closer, but they flew not fast enough for Aeneas. They sped low over the buildings, the wind rushing over them. The young prince's face was wet with sweat and mist.

"Hurry," he whispered. "Hurry."

Suddenly, the Temple of Balor was below them. Nightfall lifted up his voice in a shrieking cry and began to descend. The top of the temple was composed of many levels and balconies, and it was difficult to find any doors leading to the interior.

The griffin landed at the topmost level of the Temple roof, for it was the widest and most open.

Aeneas slid off and the griffin spoke. "If we split up we shall have a better chance of finding her."

Aeneas nodded. "All right." Before he could say another word, the griffin leapt into the air and sped off toward the main entrance of the Temple.

Aeneas turned and began to search for a way into the Temple.

* * *

Mystia looked up in terror at Kozan as he stood over her. His jaw was clenched tightly shut, and he looked down at her with cold brown eyes that seemed to pierce her to her very soul.

"Let the ceremony begin," he murmured.

Mystia gave a soft sob and pulled against the chains, which held her. There was a spell to break bonds, but terror had driven it from her mind. What was it? Kozan opened his mouth and began. "Powerful is Balor and mightily he conquers." Mystia turned her head away as he stretched his hands out over her. "Feel the fire of his power."

Suddenly, her body was filled with pain--searing pain that spread out from her chest to the very tips of her hands and feet. She felt as if her heart was on fire. She screamed, as her whole body convulsed. She pulled against the chains with all her might, and the iron dug deep into her skin.

"Joretham!" she shrieked over and over. "Stop it!" But the pain only grew. There was no way for her to fight or make it stop. It would not throw her into unconsciousness, so she was forced to endure. She writhed and twisted beneath it, screaming in agony, begging for mercy. "Stop it, Kozan! Please, stop it!"

Suddenly, she felt his hand upon her cheek--it felt so cool against her burning skin--and slowly the pain began to die away. She lay there, trembling in terror, sobbing softly. She looked up at him with her tearful black eyes, so beautiful and innocent, filled with terror and agony.

"Please let me go," she pleaded softly.

He gave a scornful, bitter laugh and pulled his hand from her cheek. "The pain you feel is not that great." After a moment, he added softly and angrily, "Not as great as what I feel."

She burst into tears and strained against her chains. What was the spell?

Kozan bent over and picked up a jar of oil, which lay on the ground beside the altar. With trembling hands he opened it and dipped the fingers of his right hand into it. Mystia stared up in terror as he reached his hand out to her. She shuddered slightly as he ran his fingers across her forehead.

"Clean of mind," he murmured.

For a moment afterwards he hesitated, then he reached and touched her lips. "Free of blasphemies." His fingers lingered for a moment longer before he finally drew them back and reached for the dagger on his belt. He drew it and held it up. Mystia nearly choked when she saw it.

"No," she groaned. "No!" She pulled against her chains--if only she could remember the spell.

He reached out with his left hand--it was trembling--and forced her to turn her head so her right cheek was exposed. She struggled against him, but he held her firm.

"Great Balor," he said softly, "we give you the blood of your enemy."

"No," she sobbed as out of the corner of her eye she saw him bring the knife to her cheek. She felt its blade against her skin, and she suddenly screamed as he pierced her with it. He dragged it across her skin carving the symbol of Balor into her cheek. She reached for him, trying desperately to pull him away, but her hands were held back by her chains.

Finally, he let go of her, and, sobbing, she turned her face from him. Pain shot through her head, and she could feel the blood pouring down her cheek. She yanked against the chains; Joretham, what was the spell?

Suddenly, her eyes grew wide, as she saw Kozan raise the knife above her. For a moment she could do nothing save stare at him. Then she began screaming in terror, crying out unintelligible words in a desperate attempt to remember the spell.

"No!" she shrieked as she saw him bring the knife closer to her. His hand was trembling, and, though he opened his mouth, no words would come.

She turned her face from him and struggled against her chains with all her might. What was the spell?

Suddenly, instead of the cold, blade of the dagger digging into her chest, she felt Kozan's lips upon her neck. She gave a howl of anger and terror. She could feel his hands upon her breast and his tongue upon her skin. What was the spell? He held her tightly, half lying upon her, pressing her against the altar, covering her with his saliva. She could feel his hands running across her body, touching her breasts and her hips and traveling down her legs. He grasped the bottom of her dress and began to lift her skirt. She could feel his hands upon her thighs.

"Joretham!" she shrieked. "Help me!"

As if in answer to her cries, she suddenly remembered the words to the spell. With all her might she screamed them out over and over again. Her shackles flew apart, and with a huge cry she pushed Kozan from her with all her strength. As she sprang from the altar Kozan reached out in a desperate attempt to pull her back. He grabbed hold of the sleeve of her dress, and she could hear the collar tear slightly as she yanked her arm free.

Kozan snarled in fury and scrambled after her. Running from him, the Princess looked wildly around for some way to escape. Her gaze fell upon her father's staff, which lay upon the floor. With a cry she leapt toward it. She could feel Kozan's fingers brush against her arm. She leaned over and reached toward the staff. Her feet suddenly slipped out from beneath her, and she fell forward. She grabbed the staff and rolled to her knees.

Scrambling to her feet, she spun to face Kozan. He was almost upon her. She screamed in terror and struck him with the staff. There was a blinding flash of light, and the king gave a great howl as he went flying backwards. He landed at the edge of the topmost step and went rolling down several steps before he caught himself.

He scrambled to his feet and walked back up to the top. Mystia stood ready, her father's staff in hand. She gripped it like a bow-staff, and the diamond in its head shone bright with magic light. Her flowing white dress was torn, and one sleeve had fallen from her shoulder. Her body trembled, but her black eyes flashed with fury and determination.

Kozan's lips curled in a sneer. "So, the little wench can use magic."

"I am no wench," Mystia said, her hands tightening around the staff, "and I am not your slave. I am the Princess of Nor, and if you dare come near me I swear I'll kill you."

* * *

Nightfall swooped down and landed upon the steps of the Temple of Balor. Men were battling in the street below, but they paid no heed to the griffin. He turned toward the main entrance of the Temple and began to walk up the steps. As he drew closer, he noticed the two statues of the Baltuil standing guard. They stood even taller than he. Their granite faces were twisted in hideous grins, and they stared out with unblinking, ruby eyes that glowed red with evil.

His steps grew smaller and smaller the closer he drew to them until he stopped all together and simply stared up at them. To enter he would have to pass beneath their evil gaze. The thought terrified him, for they seemed so lifelike, as if they were ready to spring upon him the moment they saw him. He shook his head and tried to banish the thought. What a foolish idea. They were only statues; of course, they could not hurt him.

With a flick of his tail and his head held high he walked forward. He could feel their gaze upon him, and it made his fur stand on end. Quickly he passed from under them and for a moment paused and let out a long breath before continuing forward.

He had gone not three steps when he suddenly heard a noise behind him. He stopped short and for a moment could only stand there not daring to move. He heard a great cracking and creaking behind him, followed by the sound of stone scraping against stone. Slowly, he turned his head. His eyes grew wide and a slight squeak escaped him as he saw the Baltuil--alive--standing behind him. They crouched low to the ground, their granite lips curled back to reveal granite teeth, their glowing red eyes narrowed and fixed upon him.

With snapping snarls they sprang toward him. He cried out in terror as he jumped away and turned to flee into the Temple. One of the Baltuil growled and lunged toward him. Nightfall gave a shriek of pain as he was struck hard to the ground. He could see the monster raise a giant stone paw above his head. He cried out in terror and rolled out of the way. A croaking cry of pain escaped him as his wing was crushed beneath the Baltuil's paw.

The griffin tried to scramble to his feet, but his wing was held by the stone monster. He lay upon his back, his eyes wide with terror, and with all his might he clawed at the Baltuil. His claws scraped against the stone not even leaving a scratch.

The second Baltuil slowly approached. His hideous stone face was twisted into an evil grin of delight as he drew back a paw and struck Nightfall hard across the head. The griffin gave a cry and clawed once more at the Baltuil who was holding him before he fell limp.

He looked weakly up at his attackers. He could see the second one raise its paw to deal him the final blow. He tried with all his might to lash out and defend himself, but he could barely move. He could only look up in terror as the paw came crashing down through the air toward him.

Suddenly, a shrieking cry filled his ears. He could see something red streak through the air toward the Baltuil. With a loud snarl it rammed into the second Baltuil and knocked it to the ground, barely saving Nightfall from being struck.

The first Baltuil turned in surprise toward the attacker and let go of Nightfall. The griffin struggled painfully to his feet and looked to see who had saved him.

Before him he could see Glorious Dawn crouching, her black eyes narrowed as she looked up at the two Baltuil, a low growl coming from her throat. With a snarl, the two monsters charged toward her. She gave a shrieking cry and leapt toward them.

"Dawn!" Nightfall cried as he ran to help her, his wing dragging useless behind him.

Glorious Dawn leapt into the air even as the Baltuil lashed out at her. She gave a hiss as she saw Nightfall leap toward the stone creatures.

"Fool!" she cried. "Run!" But even as she did so, the Baltuil turned and lunged toward him. Dawn gave a snarling hiss and struck one of them hard across the face. It turned and lashed out toward her. She landed and bounded quickly out of the Temple and onto the open steps leading to the entrance. The Baltuil, his teeth bared, chased after her.

Nightfall gave a cry as he was struck to the ground by the other Baltuil. He scrambled to his feet, trying desperately not to be struck again. He turned and fled from the Temple, the Baltuil close on his heels.

Dawn leapt up high into the air. With a shriek, she turned and sped down toward the monster chasing Nightfall. With a hiss, it turned toward her. She crashed into it sending them both sprawling to the ground. As she scrambled to her feet she could see Nightfall running back to help.

"Run!" she cried. For a moment he hesitated.

"Run!" she shrieked as she leapt once more into the air. The Baltuil leapt toward her. She gave a hiss as his claws dug into her. With a snarling roar it pulled her back to the ground. The other Baltuil was charging toward her.

Suddenly, she could hear Nightfall give a terrifying shriek of fury as he rammed into the Baltuil holding her. The stone monster went tumbling forward, and Dawn leapt to her feet.

"Nightfall, come!" she screamed. She turned and began to make her way down the steps toward the street, stopping every moment to look back and see if Nightfall would follow.

The black griffin jumped to his feet and turned to chase after Glorious Dawn. The fallen Baltuil gave a snapping snarl and, twisting, clawed at him, barely missing his hind leg. The standing Baltuil charged after him, but Nightfall paid no heed. He ran after Dawn with all his might, and together they galloped down the remaining steps and charged into the crowd of battling men. The Baltuil sped after them, sending soldiers fleeing in terror.

"Dawn!" Nightfall huffed as he ran. "Thou art well?" He could scarcely believe it was truly she who was beside him.

"Aye," she answered with a laugh, "I needed nothing save a healer. 'Tis as though Phyre never touched my leg."

Nightfall cast a quick glance behind him. The Baltuil were still chasing after them. "Why art thou here?"

"To help thee of course."

Glorious Dawn's eyes sparkled as she continued. "Lyght hath turned. Even now he is racing here to save Princess Mystia."

"What?"

She laughed as she continued charging forward. "Is it not wonderful?"

* * *

Kozan stood and for a long moment simply looked at Mystia. His face betrayed no emotion. Suddenly, with one quick motion he drew his sword. His lips curled up in a sneer as he said, "If the little wench wishes to battle far be it from me to interfere."

Mystia's face paled, but she held her staff ready, and the look of fury never left her eyes.

Kozan did not even bother to raise his sword but simply began to walk toward her. Mystia, trying to keep calm, slowly backed away. Her feet were bare and she could feel every chink and crack in the cold hard stones beneath her.

Suddenly, Kozan laughed and said, "You'll have to fight better than that." Even as he said that Mystia gave a gasp as she stepped back but found no stone beneath her. Her foot fell back to the step beneath her, but her balance was lost. Even as she struggled to regain it, Kozan gave a cry and struck her with a huge blast of magic. She screamed as she was thrown backward.

She struck the ground hard and began to roll down the stairs. She struggled to stop herself even as she continued to hold onto her staff. She could see Kozan leaping down the steps after her. With a growl she scrambled to her feet and spun to face him. He was almost upon her.

With a cry, she sent her staff smashing into him. He gave a howl of pain and fury as he was thrown back. The Princess gave him no chance to rise but charged after him and sent her staff crashing against his head. He gave another cry of pain and held his hand up to shield himself.

Mystia tried to strike him again, but, even as she did so, he reached out and grabbed her ankle. She started and jumped away but not before pain shot through her leg. She gave a cry as she stumbled and began to sink to the ground. She clutched at her ankle and looked up in anger and fear as Kozan rose.

"We," he spat as he reached out and grabbed her by the arm, "have unfinished business."

He started to drag her up the steps, and her staff went tumbling from her hands and clattering down the steps to the ground far below. With a cry she wrenched herself from his grasp. Kozan gave a snarl and lunged after her. Mystia ran down the steps, crying out a healing spell as she did so. When she reached the bottom the pain in her leg was entirely gone.

She leapt toward her staff and grabbed it from where it lay. She spun and faced Kozan. His face was twisted in a snarling cry of fury as, with his sword raised, he rushed toward her. She raised her staff and, with a cry, lunged toward him. In a blinding flash of magic, they crashed together.

* * *

Provenna gripped the back of her crystal throne tightly and looked in terror at Orion as he walked across the wide, empty floor toward the dais. He held his huge battle-axe ready. His hair, matted and wet with blood and sweat, hung wildly around his shoulders. His clothes were torn, and he was covered with wounds, dirt, and blood. His face was twisted into a look of absolute hatred.

"Orion, what are you doing?" Provenna asked with a trembling voice.

"What I should have done a long time ago," Orion hissed. "I'm going to kill Kozan, Tnaka, Aeneas, and Phyre, but first--" his blue eyes flashed--"I'm going to kill you."

Her grip on the throne tightened.

"But, Orion," she pleaded, trying to force back tears of terror, "I am your mother."

Orion's eyes narrowed. "Tell that to the scars on my back, or tell that to Mystia whose soul you wear upon your finger."

"But Orion..." She stopped short at she realized what he had said.

"I never..." she began as she looked down at her hand, and, as her gaze fell upon the ring, she suddenly realized what it was.

She looked up, her green eyes wide, at Orion as he continued toward her. Then she looked back down at the ring. She could hear Zenas' voice echoing in her mind, telling her that perhaps a High Elf could use magic upon Orion.

Her son was almost upon her. With a cry, she threw her hand out toward him and channeled all her magic strength through the ring. A huge blast of fiery blue-white light shot through the air and struck Orion in the chest. He gave a howl as he was thrown back across the throne room. His axe went flying from him. He struck the doors of the room and fell to the floor.

For a moment he could only lie there, clutching at his chest, as he stared in amazement at her. Slowly, he struggled to his feet and reached for his axe, which lay on the ground nearby.

"I know not how you did that," he said softly, still struggling to breath, "but if you think that is going to stop me, then you are mistaken."

He gave a growl and started to run forward, only to give a cry of pain as he was struck once more to the ground.

"You little fool!" Provenna cried as she walked to him. "Did you actually think you could kill me?" She struck him again with her magic. "Did you actually try to murder me--I who am the ruler of the whole Realm of Earth?"

Orion gave a snarl and lashed out at her only to suddenly convulse and cry out in pain as he was struck once again. He struggled to rise but could not. Provenna's magic filled his body, sending pain shooting through him. He clawed at his chest in a desperate attempt to somehow battle the magic with held him. His skin scraped against the stone of the floor as he struggled to rise, but Provenna's magic held him fast. There was nothing he could do but lie upon the floor and howl in agony as magic took hold of him.

* * *

Mystia gave a sudden scream of pain. Her staff fell from her hands as she clutched at her chest. Pain filled her body. It shot out from deep within her into every part of her body, until it threatened to overcome her. She sank to her knees, her eyes wide with pain.

Kozan looked scornfully down at her and kicked her hard, sending her sprawling. She lay upon her stomach, her whole body trembling.

"No," she murmured. "Stop."

Her body began to shake with sobs.

"Stop," she groaned again, but it seemed not to be to Kozan she pleaded with.

The dark king looked down upon her and held his sword above her head, but he knew not what to do. He looked up at the altar high above him then back down at the Princess who lay at his feet. She seemed not to see him, but lay there sobbing, clutching at her breast. Her long, black hair fell all around her, and dark red blood flowed from her wounds. Her flowing white dress was slipping off both her shoulders now.

He could feel the sacrificial dagger where he had shoved it in his belt. He clutched the hilt with his left hand and slowly drew it. He looked at the blade shining orange in the light of the torches. Then he looked down at Mystia. His face hardened in a look of anger. Had not Orion stolen his wives from him? Was it not then right for him to take Orion's woman?

He dropped the dagger and fell to his knees.

"No," Mystia groaned as he pulled her to him, but she had not the strength to struggle; the pain which held her threatened to sink her into unconsciousness.

"Joretham," she murmured as she felt his hands upon her.

"Kozan!" She suddenly heard a huge cry ring throughout the sanctuary and echo off the walls.

She opened her eyes and looked up to see the Dark Sorcerer running down the steps toward her. His sword was drawn and a look of fury was upon his face.

Kozan threw Mystia from him, and she gave a cry as she struck the ground hard. She rolled onto her stomach and for a moment simply lay there. Finally, with her palms pressed to the floor, she rose to her knees.

She heard a terrifying crash as Kozan and the Sorcerer smashed together. She looked over and saw them both fly backwards and go tumbling to the floor.

"Run, Mystia!" the Sorcerer cried.

His words seemed to fill her with new strength. She staggered to her feet and began to run. She heard Kozan cry out. She screamed as pain suddenly shot through her leg. She stumbled and fell. She looked down at her leg and gave a sharp cry as she saw the hilt of Kozan's dagger sticking from it. Gasping in terror and pain she grabbed it and pulled the blade from her leg. The pain mixed with that which already filled her so much that she fell completely to the floor and for a moment could not move.

She could hear the clang of steel upon steel as Kozan and the Sorcerer battled.

She forced herself to sit up. Blood was pouring from the wound. She held her hand over it and cried out the words of the healing spell. Over and over she cried them, but the wound would not close all the way.

"Run!" the Sorcerer cried again.

Sobbing, she struggled to her feet and began to limp away as quickly as she could.

She cast a quick glance back. She could see Kozan staring in fury after her, and she could hear his cry of despair as she fled. He lunged after her, but the Dark Sorcerer barred his path. The dark king howled out in fury as he struck the Sorcerer with all his might.

Mystia turned her head and ran as fast as she could. She limped and stumbled across the floor of the sanctuary until she reached the wall. A cry of relief escaped her lips as, in the shadows, she caught sight of a door. She ran through it into the dark corridors beyond.

Behind her she could still heard Kozan and the Sorcerer battling. Their cries and the clanging of their swords filled her ears. With all her might she ran forward in a desperate attempt to outrun the sounds of their battle. Before her, she could hear the cries of the battle raging outside, but what did she care? She continued forward, stumbling through the corridors and up flights of stairs. She could no longer hear Kozan or the Sorcerer but still she ran. Her breath came in short, terrified gasps. Blood poured from her wounds, and she could feel the sting of sweat entering them. Her long, black hair fell down in front of her eyes, and she tried to brush it away only to have her fingers get tangled in it. She tripped upon the long white skirt of her dress, but she caught herself and continued forward. The cries of the battle outside were very near now, but she noticed not.

The Battle

Suddenly, she plunged through a door and found herself standing not in the darkness of the Temple but in the cold, gray light of outside. She looked wildly around her. The cries of men filled her ears. Smoke filled the sky, and all around her she could see eagles and harpies speeding through the sky. The cold wind rushed over her, blowing her dress and her hair wildly around her. She stopped running and simply looked around, not knowing what to do. She looked up. The rest of the Temple rose high above her. She could see no way to get down, other than going back the way she came. She held herself tightly as she began to shiver with cold.

Suddenly, she heard a huge cry of fear and surprise rise from the lips of hundreds of men. She started and looked wildly around. Her eyes grew wide and her mouth fell open in terror and shock as she suddenly saw a huge dragon rise up into the sky from somewhere behind the Temple. His innards swirled with billowing smoke and raging orange and red flames.

For a moment she could only look silently up at the huge, terrifying dragon, then she fell to the ground and burst into tears.

* * *

All movement left Aeneas, and for a moment he could do nothing save look up in amazement at the huge fiery dragon in the sky above. He had never seen anything like it in his whole life. The dragon spread his wings out to their full extent and, with a terrifying roar, began speeding across the city toward the Temple.

With a cry, Aeneas turned and fled. He had managed to make his way off of the roof and down a level. Now he ran down a long open balcony and searched desperately for a door leading into the Temple.

There was no wall or barrier of any kind to keep people from falling off of the balcony, and Aeneas gave a cry as he reached the corner, tried to turn, but almost went charging over the edge instead. He screeched to a halt and went tumbling to the ground and rolling over the floor until finally he stopped with his chest pressed against the floor and his shoulders and head hanging out over empty space.

He gave a gasp and for a moment dared not move. He could feel himself growing dizzy. He took a deep breath and slowly began to inch his way back. As he did so, he looked down at the lower levels of the Temple and suddenly caught sight of a person far below on the lowest roof of the Temple. She was far away, and he could discern little detail, but he could see she was a woman, for she wore a long, white dress that whipped madly about her in the wind.

He leaned forward to get a better look, and almost succeeded in sending himself tumbling off the balcony. He scrambled back and to his feet, and cast one last look down at the woman below her. She had to be Mystia. He could see none of her features save her long black hair, but he knew it had to be her.

He turned and looked wildly around for a way to get down to her. Overhead he could see the dragon nearing the Temple.

Nearby he caught sight of a door leading into the Temple. He leapt toward it and disappeared into the darkness beyond.

* * *

Mystia hugged herself tightly as she sat upon the ground and leaned against the wall of the Temple. Her whole body shook with great sobs of terror and anguish. Above her she could see Phyre circling the Temple. She wanted to run, but she dared not enter the Temple again so she pressed herself even closer against the wall and hoped against hope that he would not see her.

She gave a soft groan. The pain had not abated; if anything, it had grown.

"Orion," she sobbed as she clutched at her breast. At times, if she closed her eyes, she could see him, lying upon the ground, convulsing in pain. She could hear his cries of agony; they seemed to pierce her to her very soul. She covered her ears with her hands, but still she could hear them.

"No," she sobbed. "Stop it." But still they continued.

She looked up again, and shuddered at the sight of Phyre still circling the Temple. He was searching for her--she new it--but there was nowhere for her to hide.

Suddenly, she heard the sound of feet pounding against the stones of the floor. She gasped and turned. Her eyes grew wide and her mouth fell open as she saw, running toward her, a man dressed in armor made of red dragon scales.

"Orion?" she cried, but, even as she did so, she looked upon his face and saw he could not possibly be Orion. She scrambled to her feet and stared in terror at him.

"Mystia!" he yelled as he ran to her.

She pressed herself tightly against the wall. "Who are you?"

Gasping for breath, he stopped before her. "I'm Aeneas, Orion's brother. I'm here to rescue you."

She looked at him in confusion. "What?"

He reached out and took her by the arm. "Just come." He turned and began to run across the wide stone balcony. The Princess allowed herself to be pulled after him, but when she saw he was running toward the door of the Temple she stopped short in terror.

He turned and looked at her in surprise. "Come!"

Her whole body was trembling and she was too terrified to speak as, shaking her head, she began to slowly back away.

"Mystia!" Aeneas cried and began to jump after her, but he suddenly stopped short and looked up at the sky in a mixture of surprise and fear.

Mystia spun around, and her eyes grew wide as she found Phyre towering above her, gazing down upon her with glowing red eyes filled with evil. He gave a terrifying roar that shook the Temple to its very foundation and began to dive down through the air toward her. She screamed and turned to run. Aeneas grabbed her arm and pulled her quickly toward him. He pushed her behind him and, drawing his sword, faced the fiery dragon.

Phyre took one look at him and gave a great hissing roar of fury. He turned his eyes from Mystia and instead dove toward the young prince. Mystia fled. For a moment, Aeneas could simply stand there, petrified with fear. As the dragon drew nearer, strength returned to him, and he turned to run after Mystia. He gave a cry of anger when he saw that, instead of running back into the Temple, she had turned and run down the balcony. He charged after her.

He heard a terrifying crash behind him, and he was thrown to the floor as the whole Temple was shaken. He threw his arms over his head to protect himself as rocks fell through the air. He looked back to find a huge portion of the wall and balcony destroyed, but it was still possible to get back to the door. If he could only get Mystia, he could still bring her to safety.

He scrambled to his feet, as, with a roar, Phyre sprang up from the rubble of the building. He stood there, breathing heavily, not knowing what he should do. He watched as Phyre sped up through the sky and prepared to dive back down again.

Suddenly, through the cries and screams of battle there broke a huge roar. It was a deep, growling sound that seemed to spread across the whole of the city. Aeneas started and looked wildly around, for it had not been Phyre who roared. His mouth fell open and a slight cry of surprise escaped him as in the sky he saw a second dragon. The creature was huge, with a body made entirely of the clearest crystal. His blue eyes flashed with fury and his lips were curled back as he growled.

Phyre gave a hissing snarl and plunged down through the air toward this new opponent. With another roar the crystal dragon sped toward him. They crashed together and went tumbling down through the sky into the city below.

* * *

Kozan gave a cry and sent his sword smashing down upon the Dark Sorcerer. The clang of steel against steel rang through the sanctuary. Slowly, they circled each other, their eyes burning with anger and their swords pressed together. The Sorcerer gave a grunt as he suddenly picked up his foot and sent it slamming into Kozan's knee. The king gave a howl of pain and stumbled back.

The Sorcerer cried out and sent his sword slicing through the air toward Kozan, but, even as he did so, Kozan held up his hand. There was a blinding flash of light, and the Sorcerer was thrown backward. He struck the ground with a hard thud, and his sword went sliding across the floor.

Shaking his head, he struggled to his feet. Kozan was charging toward him. The Sorcerer looked wildly around for his sword. Only a few feet away he found King Ibrahim's staff. He lunged toward it. Kozan was almost upon him. The Sorcerer grabbed the staff and, holding it like a club, spun around and sent it falling through the air toward the king. Kozan raised his sword to ward off the blow but was only partially successful. He reeled but did not fall.

The Sorcerer struck him again, and Kozan's sword went flying from his hands. With a cry, the dark king lunged forward and grabbed the end of the staff. His face twisted in a look of fury as he sent his magic coursing through the staff and into the Dark Sorcerer.

The Sorcerer's eyes widened with pain, and he slowly sank to his knees, letting go of the staff as he did so. Kozan took the staff in both hands and, with all his might, struck the Sorcerer across the head with it.

The Sorcerer gave a groan and fell to the ground. He struggled to rise, but Kozan kicked him hard in the side and sent him back to the floor. He rolled over and found his sword lying by his hand. He grabbed it and, with a grunt, scrambled to his feet.

He held his sword up and faced Kozan. Blood was trickling from the side of his mouth, but he seemed not to notice. His eyes flashed with fury as he growled, "It will take more than that to kill me."

* * *

Tnaka gasped for breath and stared at Eagle who still blocked his path. She also gasped for breath, but she gave no other sign of tiring. Her long blonde bangs hung down in front of her face, and, from beneath them, she looked up with gray eyes that still flashed with determination. She held her sword up, ready for when Tnaka would spring again.

There were several wounds on his body--proof that Eagle was firm in her opposition. He knew not what to do. He wanted not to hurt her, yet he needed to pass. So he fought her, though he used neither magic nor all the skill he possessed with the sword, but Eagle was such a skilled fighter that with neither of those two assets he was unable to defeat her.

"Eagle," he begged, "let me through."

Her eyes narrowed. "Over my dead body."

"But Eagle..."

"Fool!" she cried, her face twisting in anger and her eyes filling with tears. "Stop this! Think of our child!"

Tnaka ran forward and their swords clashed together. "I do think of him! Why do you think I do what I do?"

"I know not why you do it!" she spat. "But I know you do it neither for me nor for him!"

She swung at him, and her blade just nicked his shoulder. He could feel poison enter his body, and he pushed it back with his magic.

A look of pain crossed his face. "But I do it for you! Don't you see? If Orion

The Battle

lives Lairannare will be destroyed!"

"Provenna and Kozan have ravaged Lairannare and you never did anything to stop them."

She paused and for a moment simply looked at him. Tears were streaming down her cheeks.

"Tnaka, please," she begged, "I know you have at least some honor left. Leave Orion alone. If you kill anyone kill Provenna, but leave Orion alone."

Tnaka swung at her. "Let me through!"

* * *

Mystia looked dazedly around. Phyre and Lyght battled above the city. They slashed and clawed at each other and sank their teeth deep into the other. Fire poured down from Phyre's wounds onto the streets of the city. The bloodthirsty roars of the two dragons shook the Temple.

Mystia gave a groan and held her hands over her ears but still she could hear their terrible cries. Phyre's voice rose high above the cries of the soldiers and the shrieking of the wind as he sped toward Lyght. Mystia seemed to reel beneath it.

She turned to try to walk away and found herself standing at the edge of the balcony. There was a low stone wall to keep people from falling off the edge and behind that was empty space and the sea far below. The choppy gray waves were tipped with white, and foam was sent flying through the air as the waves crashed together.

Mystia leaned against the stone wall and stared down at the water; her pain and exhaustion were such that she could do nothing else. She pressed one hand against her breast.

"Orion," she murmured.

She could hear the sound of someone approaching, and she could feel somebody's hand upon her arm. The person pulled her gently away from the edge of the balcony, and, as she turned, she could see it was Aeneas.

"Come, Your Highness," he said. "We have to get away from here."

She looked at him in confusion. She could barely hear what he said. He bothered not to repeat himself but held her hand and began to lead her along the balcony back to the door of the Temple. She limped after him; the pain in her leg was almost unbearable. With a soft groan she stumbled and fell to the ground. Aeneas turned and knelt by her side. He reached out to help her rise, but she pushed him away.

"Leave me alone," she moaned.

"But, Your High..."

She curled up into a ball and with a choked sob murmured, "Just leave me alone." Then even softer she said, "I want Orion."

* * *

Orion knelt upon the ground with his palms pressed against the floor. His long, auburn hair fell down over his face. He struggled to rise, but, no sooner did he do so, then he was thrown once more to the ground by Provenna's magic. He rolled onto his back and gasped for breath. His blue eyes were wide with pain and his face was filled with agony. His body was covered with wounds and soaked with sweat and crystal blood.

"Mystia," he groaned.

His mother laughed a cold, bitter, spiteful laugh.

"You fool," she sneered, "you have your little mistress to thank for this."

Orion gave a strangled cry; he felt as if every bone in his body was broken.

"You could have returned to me," Provenna spat. "You could have been my son again. You could have been the Prince of the whole Realm of Earth! You could have had any other woman you wanted, but, no! You had to have her!" She struck him again and her lips curled up in a sneer. "Who would have thought 'twould be through her you died?"

Orion's spectral eyes flashed with fury as he looked up at her. With a growl he began to rise. She lashed out at him with all the magic she possessed, but he managed to struggle to his knees. His face was twisted in pain, and his eyes burned with inhuman rage. Against the pain he struggled forward toward Provenna. She was toying with him--torturing him--but she would regret not killing him; he swore it.

* * *

The Dark Sorcerer snarled and lunged toward Kozan. Their swords crashed together. They circled each other, sweat pouring from their brows as they stared into each other's eyes. Kozan's lips curled up in a sneer.

"You love her," he laughed.

With a cry, the Dark Sorcerer threw Kozan back. The king stumbled, fell to the ground, then quickly rolled to his feet and faced the Sorcerer.

"Do you think love is the only reason I would fight you?" the Sorcerer demanded as he ran toward him. Their swords clashed together. "What about revenge? Revenge for the murder of my father and the oppression of my country!" His face twisted in even greater fury as he sent his magic rushing into Kozan. "Revenge for the plunder of my kingdom and my position!"

Kozan gave a low growl as he struggled against the Sorcerer's spell.

"Do you think I care?" he hissed.

The Sorcerer struck him hard. "You will when I finish with you!" Kozan reeled beneath the blow. "I am Darus; Delovachia is my kingdom, and I swear you'll pay for what you've done to it!"

Kozan regained his balance and rushed toward the Dark Sorcerer, and they

The Battle

both went tumbling to the floor.

"Another day perhaps," Kozan growled as he struck the Sorcerer with a huge blast of magic. Dark Sorcerer gave a cry of pain and struggled against the magic holding him. Kozan rose to his feet and raised his sword. With a cry he sent it slicing down toward Dark Sorcerer. The Sorcerer barely managed to roll out of the way. He sent his foot slamming into Kozan's knee. Crying out in pain, Kozan stumbled back. Dark Sorcerer scrambled to his feet and rushed toward the king, but even, as he did so, Kozan opened his mouth in a howl of fury and threw his hand out toward him.

The Sorcerer gave a cry of pain. His sword slipped from his hands and went clattering to the floor, and, clutching at his chest, he stumbled and fell to his knees. He felt as if a hand was clutching his heart and slowly tightening its grip. He gave a slight choking sound and fell completely to the ground. His whole body was trembling with agony, and blood and sweat poured from him.

He struggled desperately against the spell that held him. He could see Kozan approaching him, and with a growl, he forced himself to rise to his knees. He reached weakly for his sword, but, as he did so, he fell once more to the ground. He rolled onto his back. Kozan stood above him, his sword raised. With a cry, the king sent it slicing down toward the Sorcerer. Dark Sorcerer raised his arm. He gave a strangled cry of pain as Kozan's blade sliced through it just below his elbow. The severed part fell to the ground where it lay, the fingers twitching.

Kozan raised his sword again and with another cry stabbed into the Sorcerer's stomach. The Sorcerer's mouth opened but no sound came as the dark king twisted the blade hard then withdrew it.

"Die slowly," he growled as he stepped over him and walked toward the door through which Mystia had run.

* * *

With one arm Aeneas held Mystia tightly around the waist and half carried her as he made his way slowly across the roof of the Temple toward the door. With his other hand he held Orion's sword. He looked nervously up at the two dragons as they battled in the sky. Phyre's mouth opened in a terrible roar as, with claws outstretched, he sped through the air toward Aeneas and Mystia. The prince's eyes grew wide, and his hand tightened around his sword.

With a roar, Lyght lunged after Phyre and dug his claws deep into the fiery dragon's back. Phyre gave a hissing snarl of pain and struggled to turn upon Lyght.

Aeneas turned and continued to make his way toward the door. Mystia gave a soft groan and whispered Orion's name. Aeneas looked down in concern at her. She shivered as the wind rushed over her. Her torn, bloodstained dress had slipped once more from her shoulders and barely covered her breasts. Her body was covered with bruises and streaked with dirt, blood, and sweat. Her mouth was open slightly as she took shallow breaths, and blood trickled from the side of it. Her eyes were closed, and Aeneas doubted she was even aware of what was happening around her.

Another terrifying roar broke from the mouth of Phyre, and Aeneas turned and once more up at the sky.

"Orion?"

Aeneas started as a voice filled with surprise and fear suddenly broke through the cries of battle and the sound of the wind. He turned and found himself staring at his father who stood in the doorway but a few feet away.

Mystia opened her eyes, and when her gaze fell upon Kozan she could do nothing save stare at him, a look of confusion and despair upon her face.

When Kozan saw it was Aeneas who stood there and not Orion, all fear left his face and his lips turned up in a false smile.

"Aeneas," he said, "so, you've come to help your father, have you?" He held out his hand. "Let me have her."

Aeneas let go of Mystia and pushed her behind him. He held up his sword and looked steadily at Kozan. "I came to help my brother."

All hints of a smile left Kozan's face as his features twisted into a look of absolute anger.

"If that is how you want it!" he growled. With a cry, he threw his hand out. Aeneas gave a cry as he was thrown backward to the ground. His sword flew from his hands.

Mystia gave a sob and began to limp away.

Kozan rushed forward, and Aeneas could only look up in terror at him. Kozan's sword was raised above his head. Aeneas squeezed his eyes shut, but, before Kozan could deal his son a deathblow, Phyre let out a huge roar. The whole Temple shook beneath it, and, for the first time, Kozan noticed the two dragons battling above his city. For a moment, he could only stare in surprise.

Phyre saw the Power-king standing on the roof of the Temple. With a shriek he sent himself slamming into Lyght. He dug his claws deep into the crystal dragon and together they went tumbling down through the sky into the city below. Whole buildings were crushed beneath their huge bodies as they went crashing to the ground.

Lyght gave a snarl of pain and fury and struck Phyre with all his might, but Phyre seemed not to feel it. He sent his clawed forefoot smashing into Lyght's face. The dragon gave a thundering roar of pain and fury. Even as he did so, Phyre dug his claws deep into the crystal dragon's stomach. Lyght tried to strike him, but Phyre pushed off of him and leapt into the air. The crystal dragon struggled to rise, but scarcely had he risen into the air when he fell back down into the city.

Phyre sped through the sky toward the Temple.

"Unholy demon!" he shrieked. His red eyes burned with blood lust, and his great foreclaws were stretched out toward Kozan. Kozan looked up at the fiery monster, and his face filled with fury. He gathered all of his magic and, with a huge cry, struck Phyre with the whole force of his power. The dragon went tumbling backward to the ground. With a growl he scrambled to his feet and faced Kozan.

"How dare you come here!" the Power snarled.

"Thou hast dared love a High Elven woman yet thou darest ask me why I come here?" the fiery dragon shrieked. "Thou hast denied me my sacrifice, and thou must pay!"

Kozan's eyes flashed with rage. "I worship Balor not you! I owe you no sacrifice."

Phyre suddenly opened his mouth in a terrifying, evil laugh. "Know thee not who it was who heard thy prayers to Balor and accepted thy sacrifices to Balor and who received thy praises to Balor?" His hissing voice rose in an even greater, twisted laugh. "'Twas I! 'Twas I Phyre--Norenroth--who gave Balor his power, and 'twas I, Norenroth, who gave thee thy power, and 'tis I, Norenroth, who take thy power once more from thee and return it to he who did first possess it."

Kozan cried out in both fear and anger, and his voice was joined by Phyre's as the dragon lifted up his voice in a huge shriek. He screamed out strange words, and Kozan gave a cry and clutched at his chest.

Aeneas scrambled to his feet and stared at his father.

Kozan's face was twisted in a look of absolute agony. He fell to his knees.

"No!" he screamed as he reached out his hand and tried to strike the fiery dragon down with magic, but nothing happened.

"No," he groaned as he sank completely to the ground.

* * *

The Dark Sorcerer lay upon the floor of the vast sanctuary of Balor's Temple. He stared weakly up at the ceiling as he struggled to overcome the spell, which held him, and heal the wounds that covered him. He took a deep breath and his eyes seemed to brighten as, lying there almost dead, he felt magic fill his body-- magic from a long time ago, magic that he had thought he would never feel again. It entered his chest and filled his body with warmth as it spread throughout his body to the very tips of his hands and feet.

"The Power," he whispered, "the Power." Then, with a sigh, he gave up his life.

* * *

Orion lay curled up in a ball. The stones of the floor were wet with his blood, and his voice was hoarse from screaming in pain. His axe lay only a few feet away, but he had not the strength to reach for it. He could only lie, twisting and writing in agony.

Suddenly, Provenna gave a shriek and stopped her torment. For a moment, the warrior lay there gasping for breath. Then he turned his head and looked weakly up at her. She stood bent over, clutching at her breast.

She looked at Orion, her eyes wide with fear. With a groan, he forced himself to his knees and reached for his axe. Provenna held out her hand and tried to strike him down with her magic, but nothing happened.

With a growl, Orion grabbed his axe and forced himself to his feet. He turned and looked at Provenna, and there was murder in his eyes.

* * *

Tnaka gave a cry and stumbled forward, Eagle's sword grazing his side as he did so. His sword fell from his hands, and he tumbled to the floor.

"Tnaka!" Eagle shrieked as she threw her sword away and fell to her knees beside her husband.

He gave a slight groan as she helped him roll over onto his back.

"Are you all right?" she cried.

He gave a slight grin, which turned into a grimace of pain, and he clutched at his wounded side.

"What happened?" Eagle demanded, her voice trembling with fear.

He answered not but gazed up at her, a look of confusion upon his face.

"Tnaka, answer me!"

* * *

Aeneas picked up his sword and cast a quick glance behind him. Mystia had fallen to the ground a short distance away and now held herself tightly and looked tearfully around.

Phyre gave a huge roar and lunged toward her. With a wordless cry, Aeneas spun around and began to run toward her in a desperate attempt to somehow protect her. Even as he did so, Lyght shot up from the ground and sped toward Phyre. With a terrifying snarl he dug his claws deep into the fiery dragon's back, making him tumble backward away from the Temple.

Aeneas reached Mystia and started to take her by the arm when he saw her eyes widen as her gaze fixed upon something behind him. Letting go of her, he spun around and found his father bearing down upon him. With a cry, he raised his sword and barely managed to deflect Kozan's blow.

There was a terrified look of madness in Kozan's eyes. Aeneas stumbled back as the dark king struck at him with all his might.

"Give her to me!" Kozan cried. "I need to kill her!"

Aeneas rushed forward and sent his sword slicing toward Kozan.

"I need my Power; I need to kill her!"

Aeneas was thrown back again, but he did not fall. He regained his balance and held firm.

Mystia, in a daze, began to crawl away. Kozan was behind her and Phyre above her. She struggled to her feet and continued to limp down the long balcony. The cries of battle surrounded her, and the wind howled around her. Before her she could see the sea--gray and stormy. There was nowhere for her to run or hide, but she continued on, knowing only that she had to escape.

* * *

Orion took a halting step toward his mother. She looked in terror at him then turned and fled.

His body was filled with pain, but he pushed it away and, with a growl, forced himself to stumble after her.

* * *

With a huge cry, Kozan threw Aeneas to the ground. He leapt forward and charged after Mystia. The young prince jumped to his feet and dashed after him, but he would not reach him in time. With a cry, he threw his sword with all his might. It spun, end over end, through the air toward Kozan.

Kozan gave a cry and stumbled forward as the sword flew past him, cutting into his leg. He fell to the ground, and Aeneas raced past him. He grabbed the crystal sword from where it had fallen and spun back to face his father. Kozan scrambled to his feet.

Aeneas lunged forward and sent his blade arching down through the air toward Kozan. Kozan blocked the blow and staggered back, then, with a cry, pushed himself forward and slammed into him.

* * *

Eagle looked down in horror upon her husband.

"Are you all right?"

His face was filled with pain, and he shook his head slightly. "Your blade was tipped with poison."

"But surely you can heal yourself!" she cried, half hysterical.

He gave a sad smile. "My power is gone."

For a moment she stared at him in disbelief.

"What? No!" She burst into tears.

* * *

Phyre slashed at Lyght's face and tried desperately to fly

toward Mystia. Lyght dug his claws into his back and forced him to the ground. Fire poured from his wounds.

With a huge hiss he opened his mouth and sank his teeth deep into Lyght's neck. Lyght went tumbling backward as he struggled desperately to free himself. He sent his left hindclaw scraping along Phyre's stomach. The fiery dragon gave a shriek of pain and let go of Lyght's neck. With a roar, the crystal dragon lunged forward and slammed into Phyre.

* * *

Aeneas fell to the ground, but as his father tried to run past him he reach up and grabbed his leg. Kozan tumbled to the ground, and Aeneas scrambled to get on top of him. He sent his fist slamming into his father's face. Blood splattered everywhere, and Kozan gave a cry of pain. He reached up and grabbed Aeneas by the neck. With a growl, he pulled the prince's head to his chest and rolled over.

Aeneas gave a muffled cry as he was crushed beneath his father. His face was pressed against Kozan's chest and he could barely breath. He gasped for breath as Kozan sat up then gave a strangled gasp as Kozan punched him in the face.

With a growl, the dark king stood and pulled Aeneas up with him. With a grunt, he tried to throw the young prince over the edge of the balcony but had not the strength to do so. Aeneas managed to turn and face Kozan, but his father held him tightly and pressed his back against the wall of the balcony.

"Die," Kozan hissed as he held Aeneas by the neck and began forcing him to bend over backward.

* * *

Mystia reached the end of the balcony. Stumbling forward and falling against the wall, she found herself looking down at the raging sea beneath her.

She looked up to see the two dragons battling above her, and groaned as their roars filled her ears.

Behind her, she could see Kozan and Aeneas battling. She gave a soft sob and turned her face away.

* * *

Aeneas struggled to breath as Kozan tightened his grip around his neck. He held onto his father's arms and tried desperately to pull them apart. His eyes were squeezed shut and his face was twisted in pain.

With a grunt he raised his left foot and smashed it into Kozan's leg. Kozan lost his footing, and Aeneas pushed him away. He fell to his knees and, holding his hands to his throat, gasped for breath.

The Battle

With a snarl Kozan rose to his feet.

* * *

Mystia slowly pulled herself up onto the rail of the balcony. She swayed slightly in the wind, but she did not fall. She looked down upon the sea far below. The raging gray waters swirled madly and the waves crashed together, sending foam spewing high into the air.

Her face was filled with pain, but there was a slight smile upon her lips as she looked upon that sight.

She could here Phyre's roar, so loud and terrible.

Slowly, she raised her arms.

* * *

Aeneas and Kozan crashed together tumbling to the ground, grabbing at each other's throats, and went as they did so. They kicked and clawed, trying desperately to squeeze the life from the other.

Kozan grabbed a great fistful of his son's hair and yanked so hard that Aeneas felt sure his neck would break, but even as he did so, Kozan looked up and his eyes grew wide with horror. He let go of Aeneas and scrambled to his feet.

"No!" he cried as he began to run forward.

The prince rolled onto his stomach and looked at what Kozan had seen. His eyes grew wide and his mouth fell open.

"Mystia!" he shouted.

She stood on the rail at the edge of the balcony and looked as though she were going to jump.

A huge, snarling cry shook the Temple. Aeneas looked over to see Phyre send his claws smashing into Lyght with all his might. The crystal dragon tumbled backward into the city. He tried to rise, but Phyre, with a huge roar, sped through the sky and smashed into him. He went crashing back into the city and did not rise. Phyre leapt up, and, with a shriek, turned and sped toward the Princess.

* * *

Mystia stood with her eyes closed.

"Joretham avenge me," she whispered. For one moment after that she stood with face held up and arms outstretched. The wind rushed over her, making her flowing white dress and her long black hair dance madly to its song. Then she bent her legs slightly and pushed with all her might. She flew forward, the wind seeming to push her along. Then she began to fall, down, down, to the sea far below her.

* * *

"No!" Kozan and Aeneas both cried.

Phyre sped after her.

"I will have my sacrifice!" he snarled as he plunged down toward the sea after her.

There was a huge crash as he struck the water. He gave a shriek as water began to enter his wounds. It poured into his body, extinguishing his fire. He struggled desperately to rise, but the water filled him, holding him back. For one moment, he did escape the grip of the waves. He tried to fly up to the city, but he had not the strength. He tottered then, with one final shriek went falling back into the sea, where he disappeared beneath the waves.

* * *

With a cry, Aeneas ran to Kozan. The king spun around, his eyes wide with disbelief. He gave a scream of fear as he saw Aeneas charging toward him. He turned to run, but Aeneas caught him. The prince dragged him over to the edge of the balcony and, with all the strength fury had to give, threw him over the edge. Kozan plunged down toward the streets of the city, and his scream of terror was lost in the howling of the wind.

Aeneas ran to where Mystia had stood and looked down into the sea.

"No!" he cried, then even louder, "No!"

* * *

With a growl of pain, Lyght rolled onto his stomach then leapt up into the air. He flew out over the sea and circled the water, searching for any sign of life.

After a minute, he gave a growl and turned to the north. With his wings beating slow and steady, he began to speed toward Leilaora.

* * *

Orion groaned as he chased after Provenna. Pain filled his body, and his axe was heavy in his hands. He stumbled but caught himself and continued on.

Provenna gasped for breath and looked wildly around, desperately searching for some means of escape. Orion was close on her heals. His spectral eyes flashed with fury as he ran after her. She gave a sob, which turned into a cry as she tripped and went tumbling to the floor. With a strangled scream, she scrambled to her feet. Even as she did so, Orion gave a snarl and raised his axe. As Provenna ran forward, his sent it smashing into her back. She could not scream but only gasped in surprise and pain as the force of the blow threw her to the floor. Blood splattered everywhere as the blade lodged in her body, and there was a loud crack as her face smashed into the floor. Her hand twitched, then she moved no more.

Orion looked down upon his dead mother and swayed slightly. He took an unsteady step toward her. Even the slightest movement sent pain shooting through his body. He could see Mystia's ring upon Provenna's finger. The red glow within the stone had almost completely died. Painfully, he reached out for it, but, as he bent forward, his legs would not support him, and, with a groan, he fell to the ground. He lay unmoving upon the ground, with one hand stretched out toward the ring.

"Mystia," he whispered. "Mystia."

* * *

Eagle cradled her husband's head in her arms and struggled with all her might to overcome the poison in him. Her face was twisted in a look pain and anguish. Sweat poured from her brow, but the poison was too powerful.

"No!" she cried. "No!" Tears began to flow from her eyes.

Tnaka looked up in confusion at her as he saw the sorrow and desperation within her. In a halting voice he said, "You love me?"

"Oh yes," she sobbed, "yes. A hundred times over."

"But I thought you loved Gideone."

Her whole body shook as she wept. "I did once, but not anymore. You're my husband; I love you." She burst into uncontrollable tears.

"Eagle," Tnaka murmured as he reached up and held his hand to her tear-stained cheek.

"If I had only told you sooner, but I was too proud." She held onto his hand as the tears flowed down her cheeks. "I didn't want to love you--you were a Power. If only I had told you sooner none of this would have happened."

"Hush, love, hush," he breathed. His face was filled with pain. "Blame not yourself. 'Twas my own fault. You did what you thought was right, and you are an honorable woman for it."

His arm had grown weak, and his hand fell away from her face. He gave a slight groan, and his face twisted in pain. He touched his hand to Eagle's belly and looked weakly up at her.

There was a look of pleading upon his face. "Tell our child about me."

Eagle choked back a sob. "Of course I will."

He gave another groan and clutched at his side.

"Tnaka," Eagle said through her tears.

He looked up at her. His skin was deathly pale and his face was filled with pain, but in his eyes there was a look--a look too difficult to describe, one of both joy and despair, defeat and yet hope all at the same time.

Eagle, her gray eyes filled with agony, stared down at him.

Suddenly he reached up and, encircling her neck with his arms, pulled her down to him and pressed his lips to hers. For one moment they lay upon the ground, body to body as he held her tightly to him. The cries and screams of battle echoed all around, but they heard them not. For one moment, they were together, their spirits as one, desperately in love and yet bidding farewell. Then he let go of her and whispered, "Goodbye, my love."

Eagle opened her mouth but no words would come.

Tnaka smiled at her. He gave a sigh as his head fell back, and he gave up his life.

Eagle looked down in horror and despair upon her husband.

"Tnaka!" she cried and, throwing herself over him, burst into tears.

* * *

Lyght flew through the sky toward Leilaora. His huge, powerful wings brought him toward it far faster than any other creature could travel. Already he could see the smoke of battle upon the horizon.

Mystia had perished, but perhaps there was yet time to help his son.

* * *

Gideone and Vayan ran through the halls of the palace. They had lost sight of Orion and were now desperately trying to find him again.

Gideone swore under his breath.

"This is hopeless," he growled. He threw open a nearby door and stepped inside, Vayan right behind him. He stopped short, and his eyes grew wide. For a moment, both men stared in surprise and horror.

From a rope tied to a beam in the ceiling, there hung an old man. His skin was covered with wrinkles. He was dressed in a plain gray robe, and his silver beard fell to his waist. His neck was broken by the noose, and his head was bent to the side. His mouth was open slightly and a small trickle of blood had dried at the corner of it. Zenas had sought peace, but even in death, there was a look of absolute despair about him.

Slowly Gideone and Vayan backed out of the room. They looked at each other, then the Prince quietly shut the door.

* * *

Lyght alighted within the gardens of the palace. In a swirl of magic dust, his great dragon body disappeared to be replaced with a human one. He was beaten, broken, and covered with wounds, but it mattered not.

The palace was nearby, and he forced himself to run toward it. He had to find his son.

* * *

Aeneas looked in confusion around him. The howling of the wind and the cries of battle filled his ears. What was he to do? Mystia was dead. He stumbled back, away from the edge of the balcony.

He shivered as the wind struck him in the face. He struggled forward, trying to make his way to the door. He tripped and fell to the ground. He gave a groan. His whole body was filled with pain.

He forced himself to rise and struggle forward once again. He was almost halfway back when he stumbled and fell once again. For a moment, he lay upon the ground, as he tried to gather his strength. Then, with a growl he struggled to rise. He managed to get to his feet, and when he did, he fell against the wall and gasped for breath.

He stood there for a moment, his chest and face pressed against the stones of the wall. He turned his face to the sea, and, as he did so, he suddenly caught sight of something. He stood up and leaned forward, trying to get a better look. It was something upon the horizon, but he could not tell what it was.

He squinted and took a step closer and suddenly stopped. All blood drained from his face, and his heart began to pound as he realized what he saw. It was a huge wave, rising out of the sea making its way toward Nolhol.

He took a step back, and his mouth fell open in voiceless terror. The wave was rising up higher and higher until it towered over the city.

"Joretham avenge me." Mystia's words seemed to echo on the wind.

Aeneas turned and fled, knowing he could not escape yet trying to anyway. He charged down the balcony, not daring to look behind him.

Suddenly, from out of the sky, a great red creature flew down in front of him. He cried out and fell backwards and looked up in terror at that which was before him. It was a griffin, smaller than Nightfall, and entirely red.

"Aeneas!" she cried as she rushed toward him. "Nightfall said I would find thee here. Get on my back!"

The prince needed no urging. He leapt to his feet and lunged toward the griffin.

The huge tidal wave was almost upon Nolhol.

He grabbed tightly to the griffin's neck as she shot into the air. She flew up into the sky as fast as she could go.

Aeneas, his heart pounding, looked back upon the city. The tidal wave seemed to hover for one moment over it. Then, with a huge roaring sound it went crashing down upon it. As it did so Aeneas thought he heard the sound of Balor's horn, low and mournful, spreading across the city; it was time for the evening sacrifice.

* * *

Lyght ran through the corridors of the palace. He knew Orion was near; he could almost sense him.

"Orion!" he cried. "Orion!" But there was no answer.

He rounded a corner and found himself in the hallway that ran before the throne room. As he neared the doors to the throne room, he saw that they were open. He peered inside and stopped short. A gasp of horror escaped his lips. In the middle of the room, near the wall, Provenna lay upon her face with her hands spread out and a huge axe buried in her back.

A few feet from her, Orion also lay, one hand stretched out toward her. His matted, auburn hair fell down around him. His body was covered with wounds, and his crystal blood was pouring from them.

"Orion!" Lyght cried as he rushed forward. He fell to his knees beside his son and, reaching out, gently rolled him onto his back. Orion's eyes were closed and he made no sound, but, as Lyght looked down upon him, he saw his face twitch slightly in pain.

After a long moment, the warrior slowly opened his eyes and stared up at Lyght.

"Father?" he whispered so softly he could barely be heard.

"Yes, Orion." He reached out and touched his face and chest; he needed to heal him.

"The ring," Orion murmured. "Give me the ring."

Lyght looked around. "What ring?"

"Mystia's ring." Orion's eyes closed with exhaustion, and he said very softly. "On Mother's finger."

Lyght looked over at Provenna's body and saw on her outstretched hand the ring Orion spoke of. Rising, he quickly made his way over to her and pulled the ring from her finger. He recognized it as the ring bearing Mystia's soul stone. The red glow in the crystal was almost completely gone.

Lyght returned and knelt once more beside Orion.

"Here, Orion," he said, trying to keep his voice steady, as he held out the stone. Orion's lips turned up in a very small, sad smile as he looked upon it. He tried to reach up and take it, but he had not the strength, and his hand fell back to the ground almost before he had raised it. Lyght took his son's hand in his and pressed the ring again his palm.

Orion's face twisted in pain, and he gave a slight groan.

Lyght reached out and touched his hands to Orion's face. His own body was covered with wounds, but he tried to push his pain away. He needed all of his energy to heal Orion. He took a deep breath and closed his eyes, then, with all his might, concentrated.

His breath suddenly caught in his throat. Provenna was dead, but the magic she had cast remained. It was a magic such as he had rarely encountered before-

-the magic of a Shallean, and a powerful Shallean. It spread throughout Orion's body, slowly eating away at him from the inside. Normal magic Lyght could have overcome no matter how wounded and wearied he was, but this he knew not if he could. He gave a low growl.

Orion looked up at him. His face paled as he saw the look upon his father's face.

"Can you heal me?" he asked, his eyes filled with fear.

"I..." began Lyght. He tried desperately to think of an answer that would give comfort, but he could not. "...know not."

Every last bit of color drained from Orion's face, and his whole body began to tremble.

"I don't want to die," he said, his voice filled with terror. "I don't want to die."

Lyght gave a grunt and squeezed his eyes even tighter shut. Sweat was pouring from his body.

Orion's heart began to pound, and his whole body began to shake. His mind filled with images of torture--torture far greater than anything he had ever suffered; there was no escape, there was no peace, there was no rest; it stretched on and on for eternity.

"No!" he cried. Mystia's ring fell from his hand as he reached up and grasped Lyght by the collar of his tunic, pulling himself close to him. His eyes were wide with terror. "Father, save me!"

"I am trying. I am trying," Lyght said as he struggled desperately against the magic that held his son.

Orion fell back to the floor, his body shaking with great sobs. He gave a groan and convulsed slightly. The pain was almost unbearable.

Lyght gasped for breath as he held his hands even tighter to Orion's head.

"Joretham, help me," he pleaded. His face twisted in pain, and he struggled to keep the agony of his body from overcoming him.

He cast a quick glance down at his son. The brief moment of strength fear had leant the warrior had disappeared, and now Orion simply lay trembling upon the floor. His eyes were closed tightly, and his face was twisted in pain and terror.

"Mystia," he murmured weakly over and over again. He convulsed and gave a violent cough, spitting up small drops of blood. He gave a groan and twisted in pain.

"Hold still!" Lyght ordered, his voice sharp with fear. He could feel Orion slipping away beneath him.

"I don't want to die," Orion whispered.

"I will save thee!" Lyght cried. "So help me I will!"

Orion gave a soft, bitter laugh, which was at the same time a sob of agony. He stared up at his father, but he seemed not to see Lyght--rather to look through him. He gave a soft sigh, and his eyes began to close. Another tear rolled down his already tear-stained cheek.

Lyght looked down at him and saw that he was drifting away.

"No!" he sobbed. "Orion, wake up!" But Orion simply lay there.

Lyght began to weep as he gathered his son in his arms and held him close. "Wake up," he pleaded. "I can heal thee."

He could feel Orion move slightly.

"Father," he whispered, then, his whole body trembling, he buried his face in Lyght's chest.

Lyght held him close and did not let go. Orion's eyes were closed, and his breath came short and shallow. His body trembled slightly, but other than that, he did not move. Slowly, moment by moment, he was drifting further and further away. His breath became more shallow and irregular until, suddenly, it seemed to stop all together.

"No!" Lyght cried. "No!"

There was a long moment of silence, then Orion stirred once more. He opened up his mouth and spoke. He was so weak he could barely be heard, but in his voice there could be heard all of his terror and pain, all of his bitterness and sadness, all of his hope and desire for life.

"Joretham," he whispered--pleaded--"save me." Then his head fell back and he moved no more.

Lyght gave a groan of agony. "No. No."

Tears were streaming down his face as he held Orion to him for a moment longer then slowly, gently laid him down upon the floor. As he did so, his gaze fell upon Mystia's soul stone. It lay upon the ground near Orion's head. The faint red glow within it had completely died out.

As Lyght looked upon it, his brow suddenly furrowed and he leaned forward, for it seemed to him that something rose up from within the stone. It was like mist or water or fire; he knew not what. It glowed with a soft, warm red light and swirled about as it rose up from the stone upon the floor.

A slight gasp escaped Lyght's lips and his eyes grew wide as, looking up, he caught sight of a man--or, rather, a shadow, a hint of a man--standing before him. His hair was long and white and fell down over his shoulders. His face was young yet seemed as old as time itself, and his piercing green eyes were hard and yet filled with love. Lyght knew that face, for it was the first thing he had ever seen. It was the face of Lyght's Maker, the face of the Creator of the whole of Deithanara, the face of Joretham.

Joretham reached out his hand and the rising mist flew toward Him and encircled His hand.

He turned and looked down upon Orion. There was a soft smile upon His lips. He knelt down beside the fallen warrior and held His hand above his chest. The mist swirled around His hand for a moment longer before it slowly pulled away and entered into Orion's chest. A soft sigh escaped Orion's lips as it did so.

Joretham looked upon Orion's face and touched His hand to his forehead.

"I give you a gift," he said. "'Tis the soul of Mystia, your love. Use it well."

Then, with that, he rose to his feet and disappeared.

The Battle

The warrior took a deep breath and slowly opened his eyes. Lyght knelt above him. Orion said not a word but simply looked up at his father for a long moment. The look upon his face was one of wonder and yet that also of a man who did not fully understand all which had happened to him, though he knew it was amazing. Slowly he smiled, a soft expression for he was still very weak, but it was the smile of a man who had finally found peace.

* * *

Gideone and Vayan nearly tumbled over each other as they ran through the doors of the throne room. Before them, they could see Orion lying upon the floor and an old man kneeling at his side.

"Orion!" they both cried.

The old man looked up in surprise at them. He cast a look back down at Orion then disappeared in a swirl of blue and gold dust. Both Gideone and Vayan stopped short in surprise.

Slowly Orion sat up. His body was covered with wounds, but his face seemed fairly to shine with joy.

"Your Highness, Vayan," he greeted them. The two men ran to him.

"How are you?" Vayan cried even as Gideone asked, "Who was that man?"

"He is my father," Orion answered, his smile never leaving him.

Vayan's eyes grew wide as he saw how many wounds covered Orion. "What happened to ye?"

"'Tis a long story."

"Are you all right?" Gideone asked.

Orion laughed. "Yes. I am."

Chapter 29
Farewell

It was mid-morning on the second day following the battle. The sky was clear and the sun shone brightly down upon the city of Leilaora. For all of the violence done within its streets, the city itself had suffered surprisingly little damage. Many houses and palaces had been burned by the fires, which had raged during the battle, but few had actually been destroyed. Very little looting had taken place; Tmalion had made certain of that.

The war was over, and the Powers had been destroyed, but there was little rejoicing. Though the city itself had suffered little damage, the streets were strewn with the bodies of thousands upon thousands of dead men. It was left to those who had survived to take the bodies outside the walls of the city and destroy them. Great fires burned, spewing smoke and ash into the air. Thankfully, there was a southern wind, which blew most of the stench of the burning bodies away from the city.

Aeneas stood in the middle of Tmalion's camp and looked about. Nightfall stood beside him and also quietly surveyed that which was around him. Leilaora presented a far different sight from Nolhol. Kozan's city had been completely swept away; not one stone had been left. There had been very few survivors-- only harpies and eagle riders. Both sides, after witnessing the complete destruction of their fellow countrymen, had been ready to take their anger and despair out upon the other, but, thankfully, a woman named Constantia had stepped forward and managed to keep both sides from destroying each other.

Aeneas had left shortly afterwards, and now he stood and looked rather nervously around him.

"How am I supposed to do this?" he moaned.

"Find thee someone in authority and ask them if they knoweth where Orion is," the griffin answered.

Aeneas crossed his arms and glared at Nightfall. "Are you intentionally being difficult?"

Nightfall simply cocked his head and blinked at him.

Aeneas threw his arms up in the air. "You are! How can you be like that? I have to find my brother, who never liked me to begin with and certainly likes me far less now, considering I tortured him and probably was not particularly silent it my desire to simply kill him outright, and I have to tell him that the woman he loves was beaten by my father, perhaps even raped, and eventually committed suicide, and I did nothing to stop it. And all you can do is stand there and be difficult." He crossed his arms again and turned away from the griffin.

There was a moment of silence.

"Forgive me," Nightfall finally said.

Aeneas gave a sigh and turned back.

"I meant not to be troublesome or flippant," the griffin continued. "What I said was true. If Orion doth still live, thou shalt have to tell him eventually. Is it not better to do it now rather than later?"

"Why do I have to tell him?" grumbled Aeneas. "Why do you not?"

Nightfall cocked his head slightly. "I suppose I could, but I am not the one seeking forgiveness."

"Oh, all right!" Aeneas growled. "I'll tell him."

He looked down and realized he was still wearing Orion's armor. "I suppose I ought to take this off before I do."

He began to unbuckle the sword, and, as he did so, he started to look around again. "Nightfall, who do you think will know where..." But, even as he spoke, his eye grew wide as he suddenly saw Orion making his way through the tents and men within Tmalion's camp.

"I take it all back," he said. "You tell him." With that, he stepped behind the large, black griffin in an attempt to hide himself from Orion's view.

"Nightfall!" he suddenly heard Orion cry.

"No," he groaned.

Nightfall looked at him. "'Tis generally unwise to hide behind the best friend of the one whom thou art trying to hide from."

At that moment, Orion walked up to them and for the first time noticed Aeneas.

Aeneas' face turned completely pale, but he forced a weak smile. "Oh, uh, Orion, uh, fancy meeting you here." He took a step backward. "About the armor, I was just, well, I was, uh, that is to say," he fumbled with the belt buckle, "I needed some armor, and, well, yours just happened to be there, and I just sort of, um, sort of, uh, that is..."

He took another step back and tripped on a rock. With a sharp cry, he went tumbling to the ground. He had just managed to unbuckle the sword, and it went falling to the ground with him. With a sharp intake of breath, he grabbed the sword from where it had fallen and held it up to Orion. "Here, take it. I didn't know it was yours."

Orion tried to fight the grin he felt forming as he looked down upon his brother. He looked him over closely then said softly, "The armor fits you well. Keep it."

Aeneas' mouth fell open and for a moment he could only stare up in surprise at Orion.

"You're not going to kill me?" he finally managed to say weakly.

Orion held his hand out. "No."

Aeneas stared at his brother's hand for a long moment, then finally took it and let Orion help him to his feet.

Aeneas continued to stare at him. "You are not angry at me for what I did?" Orion smiled slightly. "I have done things far, far worse than what you did, yet I was forgiven. It would be wrong then for me not to forgive you."

There was an awkward silence as neither knew what to say, but Aeneas finally held up Orion's sword. "You will, at least, want your sword back."

The warrior looked silently at it for a moment then said, "The sword is named Ronahrrah. It means 'remembrance'. My father gave it to me so that I would remember him and, hopefully, remember to follow after Joretham and not darkness." He took a breath. "I have something else--something far more precious--to remind me of that now, and I would like you to have the sword. We knew each other for only a short time, but in that short time I managed to treat you poorly enough to make you want to kill me."

"Are you sure you want it not?"

"Yes, I am." He grinned. "Besides that, though it be the less practical of the two weapons, I am rather partial to the axe."

There was another moment of silence, which was broken by Nightfall.

"I apologize for interrupting," he said, "but there is something you need to know."

Aeneas looked at the griffin then, taking a deep breath, looked back at Orion. "Princess Mystia is..."

The look of pain that filled Orion's face was so great that Aeneas could not go on.

"Dead," Orion finished for him.

Aeneas took a step toward him. "We tried to save her, but..."

Orion turned away and held his hand to his mouth.

"I had thought as much," he said with a weak voice, "but I had hoped..." He could not continue.

"Excuse me," he whispered then walked quickly away, leaving Aeneas and Nightfall to look sadly after him.

* * *

Eagle sat upon a marble bench in the gardens of the palace. It was the same bench she had sat upon almost every day since she had first come to Leilaora. It was the bench she had sat on the night Provenna had celebrated Orion's return. She remembered that night as though it had been yesterday. It was the night Tnaka had come and spoken to her. She remembered how he had fairly begged her to call him by his name and not by his titles and how he had given her the Lumellia. She remembered how he had said he feared he had neglected her but would try to never do so again.

She gave a groan as tears welled up in her eyes. "Tnaka, 'twas not you who neglected me, but I you."

She sat there for a long moment, with her hands pressed against her belly, as she struggled against the tears threatening to fall. Her whole body seemed to ache along with her spirit. Her long, blonde hair fell down and partially covered her face, but anyone who looked upon her would have been able to see the anguish that filled her.

Finally, she brushed the tears from her eyes and, with a sigh, rose to her feet. Slowly, she began to make her way back to the palace. The flowers had all begun to bloom, and the garden looked beautiful that warm, spring day, but the young queen saw it not. She stared at the ground as she made her way along the winding path leading back to the palace.

As she walked, she became aware of someone walking down the path in her direction. With another sigh, she raised her head and suddenly stopped when she saw who was before her. It was Gideone.

He walked forward and stopped but a few feet from her where he stood and looked silently at her. He wore a blue tunic over a loose-fitting white shirt. His long, black hair was pulled behind his head. From beneath his collar, Eagle could see a thin web of black lines, like some sort of tattoo, rising up the left side of his neck onto his face where it terminated near his cheekbone.

He took a deep breath then began to walk the final steps to her. "Hello, Eagle."

Her heart began to pound.

"What are you doing here?" she asked weakly.

"I wanted to see you."

She turned quickly away from him as tears began to well up in her eyes. She held her hand to her mouth. "Why?"

His brow furrowed. "Why would I not? We were once to be married, after all."

She remained silent, for she could think of nothing to say.

There was sadness in Gideone's voice as he spoke. "I must admit I thought you would be happier to see me."

"Happier," Eagle repeated with a dull laugh. She turned and looked up at him. "We were once to be married, but Tnaka came and took me from you. You said not one word in protest but stood idly by while I was forced to marry him, and now, after three years of being his wife, you think I will still love you and be happy to see you?"

A look of pain crossed his face as he said weakly, "You do not love me then?"

A sob escaped her lips as she turned. "No."

She began to walk away, and, as Gideone watched her, his eyes suddenly grew wide as realization struck him.

"You love Tnaka!" he cried.

Eagle spun around. Her gray eyes were stormy. "And what of it? You act as though 'tis some sort of sin for me to love my husband."

"But, Eagle, how could you?" he demanded as he ran to her. "Tnaka was a Power--everything you stood against."

She slapped him across the face, and, for a moment, he looked down at her in shock, one hand held to his cheek.

"Speak not of Tnaka in that manner," Eagle said softly, her eyes still filled with anger. "You know nothing. Tnaka was a good man, forced to play the villain because he had not the strength to oppose Provenna and Kozan." A tear fell from her eye and she turned away. Her voice trembled as she continued. "He was made to be the ruler of one country, not the whole Realm of Earth. He hated war; all he wanted was peace, and so he stood by and watched Provenna and Kozan destroy the Realm, with each conquest hoping that their lust for power would be satisfied." She gave a sob. "He was surrounded by people who followed loyally after Provenna and Kozan. If he had had but one person who would have stood beside him he might have had the strength to stand for what he believed, but I, that one person, said nothing.

"When I first met him, I hated him. I thought he was like Provenna and Kozan. I should have known right from the start that a man like that would never have wanted to marry me." As she had spoken, her voice had grown softer and softer until now it was almost a whisper. "As I look back, I think he married me because he wanted me to oppose him. He wanted me to give the extra strength he needed to do what he knew was right." Her voice grew bitter. "But what did I do? In the guise of being a humble wife, I said nothing and let him continue down the path he was on. Even after I finally saw him for what he was, even after I fell in love with him, I said nothing; I was too proud. I told myself that he was still a Power and that I ought to hate him." She gave a groan. "I was such a fool." With another sob, she began to walk away.

"No, wait," Gideone cried, despair in his voice. "Eagle come back." She did not even pause, but continued to walk slowly away.

"Honoria," he pleaded. At that word, she stopped and slowly turned around.

"Call me not 'Honoria'," she said softly, "for one more noble than you has deigned call me 'honorable woman'."

"Eagle, please," he begged, as he ran to her, "give me another chance. I love you, and, though you want not to marry me now, perhaps a year from now 'twill be different. I know I can prove myself to you. I do love you."

She regarded him silently for a moment, then said softly, "Why did you not do anything when Tnaka took me from you?"

Gideone looked down at the ground and for a long moment was silent. Finally, he took a breath and began to speak. "Many years ago, as you know, I ran away from home. I was searching for adventure. I wanted to win honor and glory for myself, as the knights of old had done."

He paused then continued. "I had learned the art of battle from some of the greatest teachers, and, though I was yet young, I was able to defeat all whom I faught. However, about a year into my travels I came upon an elf. He looked to be some sort of noble and I hoped that he would be able to provide me with some actual sport." A pained look crossed his face. "I challenged him to a duel, and he defeated me.

"He could have killed me, but instead he let me go. I was shaken, to say the least, but I was not about to give up. I went and sought out the greatest swordsmen I could and fought them in an effort to hone and increase my skill.

"Several years later, shortly before I traveled to Sha-Lalana and met you, I returned to the place where I had battled the elf. I met him again and challenged him to another duel." He shook his head in disbelief. "He defeated me again.

"Once again, he could have killed me, but just as before, he did not. This time, however, he said that were I to challenge him a third time he would not be so lenient. The first time he had spared me because I had been scarcely more than a boy. This time he had spared me because he understood why I would have wanted to challenge him a second time. But now I ought to have been completely convinced that he was the better swordsman and if I ever bothered him again he would kill me, for he misliked having strange men whom he had never met before come up to him in the middle of the forest while he was minding his own business and try to hack him to pieces for the sole purpose of proving their skill with the sword."

He was silent for a moment, then said quietly. "As you have probably guessed, he was Tnaka. When he came to take you, I was at a loss for what to do. If I had defied him openly he would have probably simply killed me, for he had said as much when we last met. He would not have been lenient with me as he would perchance have been had I been any other man." His face filled with agony. "I sought desperately--you know not how much I searched--for some way to keep him from having you, but I could think of nothing. Almost before I knew it, the wedding day had come, and it was too late."

He took her hands in his and gazed deep into her eyes. "I love you. I never meant to let you go, but there was nothing I could do."

Eagle looked sadly up at him and slowly pulled her hands from his.

"'Tis a reasonable explanation," she said softly, "but not one which will make me fall into your arms." She stepped back, and a tear trickled down her cheek. "Too much has changed, and I cannot love you as I once did." Her voice dropped to a whisper. "Goodbye, Gideone."

She turned and began to slowly walk away. The Prince watched in despair as she went.

"Eagle," he groaned, but she disappeared around a bend in the path and was lost to sight.

* * *

Nightfall lay stretched out upon the grass a short ways from Tmalion's camp.

There was nothing he could do to help around the camp or with the cleaning up of the bodies. He had had his first full meal in more days that he cared to count, and now was feeling rather sleepy. He did not, however, want to fall asleep; it made him feel rather guilty, considering just earlier that day Orion had learned of Mystia's death.

He gave a glum sigh and rested his head upon his crossed forelegs. He wished there were some words of comfort he could give his friend, but he could think of nothing.

He had lain there for a long time wrapped up in his own, sad thoughts when he heard someone approaching from behind. He sat up and, looking back, saw Orion. The warrior's face was pale and drawn. He seemed completely drained of energy, and his eyes were filled with anguish.

He came and sat down beside the griffin and, giving a sad smile, said, "Hello, Nightfall."

"Hello, Orion," answered the griffin, not knowing what else to say.

Orion did not speak again, and Nightfall looked him over in concern.

"Orion, art thou well?" he finally asked.

The warrior gave another wan smile and, nodding his head slightly, said, "I will be fine."

He was silent for a moment then said, "'Tis probably better that she died, for now she is in Lothiel. I doubt I would have made a good husband anyway; she deserved a far better man than I. And, on top of that, she probably didn't love me."

"Orion, say not that," the griffin said. "I admit I am rather lost when it comes to love among ye humans, but the more I think of it the more I am convinced that she did indeed love thee." He told Orion of the exchange he had with her on their journey to Zenas' house. When he had finished the warrior remained silent for a moment as he thought.

"I know not whether that makes her death harder or easier to bear," he finally said.

"Orion, forgive me. I meant not to cause thee more pain."

Orion reached out and put his arm around Nightfall's neck. "Pay no heed to me. It was good for you to tell me."

For a long moment they sat silently side by side and stared out at the countryside before them. Finally, Orion broke the silence.

"I came not here to force you to share in my misery," he said. He paused slightly then continued. "We have reached a turning point in our lives, and I was wondering what you will do."

"Stay with thee, of course," the griffin answered, with a tone that seemed to say he was surprised Orion would even think of asking such a question.

"Nightfall," Orion said as he turned his face to him, "I once saved your life, and for that you've stood by my side and risked your life a hundred times over. You have more than paid the small debt you owed."

"But without me whom wilt thou have?"

"By your question, you imply that if you follow me not wherever I go we will no longer be friends."

Nightfall thought for a moment. "I suppose what thou sayest is true, but still it seemeth not right to leave thee when Mystia hath just died."

"Nightfall, just because I have been unlucky in love does not mean you should willingly forsake it."

The griffin cocked his head to the side and stared at him.

"You speak as though you have nothing to lose, as if there is nothing you leave behind if you come with me," Orion continued, "but I would be willing to wager that is not truly the case. You may be blind when it comes to humans being in love, but I do not think I suffer in kind. There is a certain red griffin with whom I think you are dreadfully smitten."

"Orion!" If Nightfall could have blushed he would have.

For the first time since they had begun speaking Orion smiled a real smile. "I knew it." He paused for the briefest of moments then continued. "Nightfall, I will be fine on my own. You have a whole life to live; let it not slip away on my account."

Nightfall was silent for a moment.

"Thou art certain we shall remain friends?"

"Of course. If you wish, I will come and visit you as often as I can."

"And for my part, if thou art ever in need of aid, thou hast but to ask and I shall willingly give it."

"'Tis settled then. We shall go our separate ways but cross paths often."

Nightfall nodded his head.

The warm spring breeze blew across their faces, and for a long time after that, the two friends sat silently side-by-side and stared out at that which was before them.

* * *

Gideone sat alone within the giant throne room of Provenna's palace. He dared not sit upon the crystal throne itself, so instead he sat upon the steps leading up to the dais and looked glumly up at the stained-glass pictures circling the hall. He could still scarcely believe that Eagle had truly left him. He swore under his breath and stood up.

Suddenly, the doors creaked slightly. The Prince turned his gaze to them and began to walk across the floor toward them. As he did so, the doors were pushed open, and Orion walked through. He shut them behind him then turned and walked to Gideone.

He bowed low. "You called for me, Your Highness--or should I say 'Your Majesty'?"

"No, no," Gideone answered, "'Your Highness' is fine. I have yet to be crowned, after all." He hesitated. "Truth to tell, I would not mind if you called me simply 'Gideone'."

A slight look of surprise crossed Orion's face, and he gazed at Gideone, waiting for him to speak further.

"I called you here because I have a bit of a confession to make." Gideone took a breath. "During the battle for Zaren, I saw you and Nightfall fly away. I thought that you had fled the battle, and, because of that, I took you to be one of the greatest cowards I had ever known. Now that I think of it, it seems utterly foolish that I would have thought that, but I did. I know now that you did not flee but instead went to rescue Mystia, and I would like to apologize for misjudging you so badly."

"I forgive you, Your Highness, though there is little if nothing to forgive; 'tis quite understandable why you would have thought what you thought."

"Thank you," the Prince said.

He paused for a moment then spoke again. "There is another reason why I called you here....You once swore to serve the Royal Family of Nor." A look of pain filled his face. "Now I am the only one left, but I know 'twas not because of me you swore thus. I know you loved my sister." He face was filled with sadness, as he paused for a moment. "I am sorry that she died; I think you would have made a good brother." He took a breath. "Now that she is dead, your reason for serving the Royal Family is gone. I release you from your oath."

Orion bowed his head. "Thank you, Your Highness."

"Please," the Prince said, "call me 'Gideone'. If we cannot be brothers through blood, we can still be brothers in spirit."

Orion nodded his head slightly. "Very well, Gideone."

He turned to leave, but he had not gone many steps when he hesitated then turned back. There was a questioning look upon his face. "Before I leave, I would like to know something."

"Yes?"

"The night before Zaren was defeated, you told me that you cared nothing for Joretham. You wished to have what you could see and touch and not intangible spirits. After all you have been through since that night, do you still think that now?"

Gideone was silent for a moment, and his brow furrowed in anger.

"I have lost my father, my mother, my sister, one of my greatest friends, and my love," he answered bitterly. "Speak not to me of Joretham."

Orion opened his mouth to say something, but Gideone cut him off. "Please--" his face was now filled with pleading--"say nothing more. I wish to part as friends and not in anger."

Orion hesitated for a moment then, bowing his head, said softly, "As you wish." Then he turned and walked away.

* * *

Lyght stood in the wide, open glade; the meeting place of the Council of the Three Realms. Surrounding him were all manner of creatures from the Realms of Magic and the Heavens. Lyght stood beside the large, circular pool of water in the center of the glade. His great, crystal body was covered with wounds. He was hunched over with exhaustion. His head was bowed, and he could see the stars reflected in the water of the pool.

Nyght, the dark Queen of Bellunare, was speaking.

"So," she hissed, "thou dost admit to battling Phyre in an attempt to keep him from killing a Shallean?"

"Yes, I admit it," Lyght answered softly.

A murmur rose from the lips of those who were present.

"Then there is but one thing to be done," Nyght declared. "Thou didst interfere with another creature's lawful right to kill a Shallean, and in so doing thou didst cause his death. For this thou, like Phyre before thee, shalt have thy magic weakened so that thou art less than a Power."

Lyght gave a low growl. "Do it quickly."

Nyght gave a slight, scornful laugh. "As thou wishest." She threw back her head and gave a terrifying roar. Then, returning her gaze to Lyght, she narrowed her eyes and began to growl foreign words.

Lyght swayed beneath her magic, and after a moment gave a slight groan. Nyght continued spitting out her words, until the crystal dragon gave a slight growl and fell forward, clutching at his heart. The creatures gathered there watched in horror as the great dragon began writhing beneath Nyght's onslaught, but he made scarcely a sound.

Finally, Nyght stopped. For a moment, Lyght simply lay, gasping for breath, upon the ground. With a low growl, he finally forced himself to rise, and he stood there, looking at Nyght.

"Thou didst thy duty well," he said with a bitter laugh. With that, he disappeared in a swirl of blue and gold dust.

For a moment, the creatures stared at the place where he had stood then, one by one, they too began to disappear, until finally, only Nyght was left. She looked upon the empty glade and gave a scornful laugh.

From somewhere behind her, there flew a raven with one red eye. It was the very same raven who, so many nights before, had told Abiel that Gideone hid within the Forest of Raia-Torell.

"Redeye," she laughed, "this is truly a great day. Phyre is dead, Lyght hath been defeated, the Powers of Lairannare have been destroyed, and Gideone, who could have been a great enemy, hath rejected Joretham. All is falling into place, and, where Phyre failed, I shall succeed. I swear I shall rule the Three Realms."

Chapter 30
Far Distant Suns

Even in the dark of night, the stars still shine, and what are stars but far distant suns?

--Vallendar

The war was over and the Powers defeated, but peace still remained a distant dream. Nyght, true to her word, continued to seek silently after power. Darkness and turmoil still filled the Realm of Earth, as indeed it did the whole of Deithanara. Some did not notice but went about their lives locked up in their own small worlds. Others shrugged and said Deithanara was supposed to be dark. Others continued on, fighting for what they believed in, delighting in present moments of happiness, and hoping for the day when peace would be a reality.

Gideone was crowned the King of Nor. A large portion of Delovachia as well as much gold and other riches of Jocthreal were given to Nor, and Gideone began the process of rebuilding his county.

Eagle returned with her father to Scalavori. She did not stay until she had her child, but left after only a month. Where she went who can say? But the people of Scalavori claim that she returns every year in the middle of the winter when the Lumellia are in full bloom, and they say that she brings with her a small blonde-haired child. What his name is they know not, for none, not even Tmalion, have spoken with Eagle. She stands far off and gazes down from some rocky place upon the flowers and the city that she holds so dear, but, if anyone tries to approach her, she disappears without a trace.

Nightfall left Orion and had several adventures before he finally married Glorious Dawn.

And, as for Orion, he traveled for a time across Lairannare, going wherever it was he felt led. He mourned Mystia's death, yet, at the same time, he was at peace for he knew that she was in Lothiel. He still wore, on a chain around his neck, the ring the Princess had given him. Her soul stone no longer glowed for it was empty, but that also gave him comfort for he knew her soul was within him.

He was by no means perfect, but he served Joretham faithfully. For a time, he traveled throughout the land, defending small villages from the forces that preyed upon them. And for a time, he became a seaman and saw more of the

Realm of Earth than he had ever dreamed of. After that, he and Aeneas joined together and bought their own ships. They became merchant sea captains who, in addition to trading, tried to keep the trade routes free of pirates. His thoughts turned often to Mystia, but he was by no means unhappy. He loved his life. He loved the sea. He loved Joretham. He loved being free.

* * *

Orion stood upon a tall grassy hill and looked down upon his ship in the harbor beneath him. He and his men had been returning home after a long and successful voyage when they had been caught in a storm. They had despaired of escaping, but instead of sinking, they had been driven to an island.

It was a small but beautiful island--very lush with tall, stately pines and strong, solid oaks as well as other tree varieties. It was early autumn, and the leaves had turned many different bright and beautiful colors. The temperature had yet to grow cold, and one could comfortably walk outside without a cloak.

Much to Orion's surprise, the island was inhabited. The people were fishers mainly, though some were farmers. From time to time, they had seen ships pass far away upon the horizon, but Orion's ship was the first to land upon their shores.

He grinned as he recalled how they had all rushed out to gape at the ship and crowd around the sailors who came ashore. They were not in the least bit wary and when Orion explained the situation they willingly offered all the help they could.

Surprisingly little of the cargo had been lost, but the ship itself was in need of repair. Orion and his men had, at least temporarily, fixed the most urgent of the problems, but it would take a little more than a week for the ship to be seaworthy again. Orion had decided that before they began the repairs they would rest for a day; he knew everyone needed it.

He sat down upon the grass and continued to look down upon his ship. A slight breeze blew across him, but he was not cold. He wore a simple, black jerkin over a white shirt with flowing sleeves. His boots were scuffed, and his black trousers were slightly threadbare around the knees, but his clothes were all clean. His auburn hair was shorter than it had been. It fell only slightly below his shoulders, and it was pulled tightly behind his head save for the few strands that had come loose and now blew softly in the breeze. The early afternoon sun shone across the island. He looked around at the trees and the ocean then lay back and turned his clear, spectral eyes to the sky and the clouds above.

It had been almost five years since the war had ended. Mystia would have been twenty-two years old. Orion sat up. Or would she have been twenty-three? He did not know her birthday. He grinned and shook his head. Even if he had known it, he would not have been at all certain of his answer. He had always hated arithmetic, and dates had never failed to cause him trouble.

As he sat there, puzzling over Mystia's age, a voice suddenly broke into his thoughts. It was the small, almost frightened, voice of a village girl, saying, "She's a fine ship, sir. Does she have a name?"

He started slightly then began to turn around, speaking as he did so. "Yes, 'tis the..." But, as his gaze fell upon she who spoke, his words died in his throat. His mouth fell open, and for a moment he could simply stare. Before him stood Mystia. She wore no veil, and she was dressed in a simple brown dress, which ended midway down her calf. Her long, black hair tumbled down over her shoulders and to her waist. Her skin was tanned, but her face was incredibly pale, and she leaned against a tree for support.

"Orion?" she said a nervous, hopeful look upon her face.

His arm, which he was holding himself up with, suddenly grew too weak to hold him. He fell back to the ground.

Mystia gave a gasp and ran to him.

"Orion!" she cried as she knelt down beside him.

He struggled to sit up. He could feel her hands upon him. He reached out and touched her arm.

He stared in shock at her and finally managed to say weakly, "I thought you were dead."

She gave a soft smile. "I was."

"But how...?"

Even as he spoke, she suddenly threw her arms around his neck and held him tightly. "I missed you so much."

His whole body stiffened, but he put his arms around her waist, and for a long moment the two sat there, silently, as he held her close. His heart was pounding in his chest; he could scarcely believe Mystia truly was alive, but he could feel her body against his chest, and he could feel her silky hair against his cheek.

Slowly, he let go of her, fearing that at any moment she would disappear and prove herself to be only a dream.

"What happened?" he asked, his voice unsteady. "How did you survive?"

She straightened and looked at him, a small smile upon her lips. For the first time, Orion noticed a scar upon her right cheek--so pale against her otherwise tan skin.

Mystia noticed where he looked and, giving a sad smile, held her hand to her cheek and said, "The sign of Balor--given to all who are to be sacrificed." She saw the look of horror that crossed his face and nodded. "Yes, Kozan tried to sacrifice me. I managed to escape and tried to defend myself against him, but I was easily defeated." A sad look crossed her face. "The Dark Sorcerer came to defend me."

"What?"

"Yes." She looked up at him. "He really was not so very evil, and I find myself rather sad at his death. Under other circumstances I think he would have been a great man." She gave a sigh. "But, what is done is done. He held Kozan off long enough for me to escape to the roof of the Temple." A look of confusion crossed her face. "After that I am not certain what happened. I saw Phyre above the Temple, and I began to cry. After that everything is a blur. I remember somebody tried to rescue me. He wore your armor, but he was not you."

"Aeneas," Orion said.

"Who?"

"My brother. He tried to rescue you."

She leaned forward, and her eyes lit up. "You have a brother?"

He nodded.

"Is he all right? He didn't die did he? I need to thank him."

"No, he is quite alive. In fact, he and I are partners. We own two ships, and he's the captain of the other."

"Really? Orion, you must tell me everything that's happened to you." She started to stand up. "And I want to see your ship, too."

"But wait!" He reached up and took her arm. "You have to finish telling me your story."

She waved her hand. "Oh, I know not what happened. Kozan came, and Phyre was battling another dragon in the sky. I was terrified, and I must have jumped into the water." She suddenly grew thoughtful. "I know not how I survived the fall. I remember striking the water. It felt as if every bone in my body had been broken." She sank back down beside Orion. "I was knocked unconscious, but I must have remained alive because I remember the water swirling around me. I would get pulled beneath the waves, and my whole body would scream for air, but just before I completely ran out of breath I would be thrown once more to the surface where I could catch a quick breath. But there was once, when I was pulled beneath and did not rise. I had nothing to breath. Pain filled my body, and suddenly, it was as if I awoke from a dream, and I found myself in Lothiel." A far off look filled her eyes, and her whole face lighted with a beautiful smile. She tried to speak, but she could find no words to describe that which she had seen and felt.

She shook her head and continued. "Joretham was there, and he told me that my time had not yet come. He told me I would have to return to Lairannare. He sent me from Lothiel and back to the Realm of Earth where I was rescued from the ocean by one of the fishermen from this island."

She suddenly laughed and rose to her feet. "Now I want to see your ship and hear all about what happened to you." She turned and began to disappear into the trees.

"But wait!" Orion cried as he scrambled to his feet. "Is there nothing more to the story? Aren't you going to tell me what Lothiel is like?" He plunged into the trees after her. "Your Highness!"

He had thought it strange that, to get to the ship she had turned around and walked into the forest rather than simply walking down the side of the hill nearest the harbor, but as they walked he realized that she had a considerable limp and probably could not easily descend the other side of the hill, which was steep.

"Your Highness, what happened to your leg?" he cried.

She slowed her pace and a look of pain crossed her face as she said, "Not all scars heal. Kozan gave it to me."

A look of anger crossed Orion's face.

Mystia gave a slight smile. "Now, now, there's no reason to grow angry at those who are dead."

"But how did he do that? Is there not a Magic to heal it?"

Mystia shook her head. "There is no Magic on this island who can heal it. We have a sorcerer here, but he has not the strength."

"Why not?"

She was silent for a moment. "The wound was made by the knife used to kill the sacrifices to Balor. There surely must be very strong magic within such a tool as that, and I doubt that anyone will be able to heal me."

"It seems hardly fair," Orion said softly.

She looked up at him and smiled. "Fair enough, considering that, out of all the dreadful things which could have happened to me at the hand of Kozan, that was all which did."

They emerged from the trees and onto the green grass beyond.

"When said like that I suppose not," Orion said, "but it wasn't fair for you to ever have been captured by Kozan in the first place. You should never have had to suffer like that."

Mystia grew silent as they continued walking toward the beach. The wind caressed her face, making her hair dance softly beneath it.

"I once shared your thoughts," she said quietly. "I was terrified of Kozan and what he could do. I prayed to Joretham, yet it seemed he did nothing. I wanted so desperately to be free and to simply have everything return to how it had been, but," she turned her dark eyes to him, "if I had not been captured by Kozan, I would never have died, and the part of my soul within the soul stone would never have been freed to be given to you."

"I suppose," Orion began. "I never thought of it that way before."

Mystia laughed. "Look not so surprised, for oft does Joretham work thus."

Orion said nothing, but Mystia could see the questioning look in his eyes. She forgot about seeing his ship, as, with a quiet smile, she began to explain further.

For the rest of the afternoon, they walked back and forth along the beach and talked of Joretham. The wind blew across their faces, and the waves fell quietly upon the sand. The warm autumn sun shone across the island, making the leaves of the trees seem even more beautiful.

Orion asked questions and occasionally made observations of his own, but it was Mystia who did most of the talking. She held onto his arm as she did so, looking up at him or turning her gaze to the trees or out across the ocean. There seemed to be such a light within her eyes.

As the hours wore on and Orion listened to her and looked upon her, there slowly grew a sinking feeling within him. She was so wise and so innocent. He deserved not a woman like her. How could he have ever thought of marrying her?

He turned his eyes from her. The sun had sunk behind the island. A few rays of light still lit the western sky, but, for the most part, the sky had turned purple with the night. The lapping of the waves--now also dark--upon the beach filled his ears. He could feel Mystia so very close to him, her arm still wrapped around his, but he did not turn his gaze to her.

"Orion?" he heard her say. "Are you listening?"

He looked back down at her. "Yes."

Then, turning his gaze once more to the sky, he said, "'Tis late. I should walk you to your home, Your Highness."

"Orion," Mystia began then stopped.

He turned his gaze to her. "Yes?"

There was a sad tinge to her voice. "Why do you still call me 'Your Highness'?"

He stepped away from her. "What else should I call you?"

"You once asked to call me 'Mystia'."

He remained silent. She looked up at him, her black eyes so filled with hope and pleading and love that he could not stand to look upon her. He turned away suddenly and gazed out across the ocean.

"Orion, what is it?" she asked, worried, as she took a step toward him.

"Look not upon me like that," he pleaded, "for I deserve no such looks."

"Orion..." she began, but he cut her off.

"You are so noble and innocent and good," he said, as he turned and walked a few steps away. Bitterness filled his voice. "But what am I? An unchaste, cruel, murdering, ravishing..." He could not go on.

He turned his eyes to the sand. "You deserve a far better man than I."

For a moment there was silence, then Mystia spoke.

"Orion," she said, her voice filled with pleading, "I know that was how you once were, but I also know 'tis no longer what you are." She paused then continued. "When you were Norenroth's son, when you had his soul, 'twas only normal that you would act as you did; it was your nature. But now, you have been given a new soul, and you are no longer Norenroth's son. Let go of your past."

Orion said nothing, but he began to slowly turn to her.

"Orion, I was sent back to Lairannare for a reason. What it is I know not, but perhaps it was to be with you." She turned her eyes to the ocean. "Look around you. Phyre may be dead, but darkness still remains. Even on this small, solitary island we can feel it. It frightens me. I know not what the future holds, but I know I want not to face it alone."

Orion was silent for a moment, and, when he did speak, his voice was soft.

"You are certain then that you do not hate me or despise me for what I did and was?"

Mystia smiled and, cocking her head to one side, said, "You speak of impossibilities."

"You forgive me?"

"If Joretham has, how can I not?"

"And it would not pain you to be my wife?"

Her voice trembled as she said, "It would please me more than anything else in the whole of Deithanara."

He ran and took her in his arms.

"Mystia," he whispered.

She held him around his neck and buried her face in his shoulder. Her whole body trembled as she wept. He held her close and rested his cheek against her head. For a long, long moment, they stood like that.

He kissed her hair, and as she looked up he pressed his lips to hers. As he did so, all of the pain which both of them had suffered seemed to melt away as they were lost in each other's arms.

The End

About the Author

Joshua J Marsh

There's not much interesting to say about Joshua.
She was born up Nort' in Wisconsin. Her second earliest memory is of
watching The Empire Strikes Back, which has warped her brain (You
can tell her brain is warped because
(1) She's a writer and (2) She's a fantasy writer.
She's also a college drop-out whose main goal is to be a bum her whole
life.
(and own a cute little cat :)